D0850031

IN CONCERT

THE COLLECTED SPECULATIVE FICTION OF

STEVE RASNIC TEM
AND MELANIE TEM

This is a Centipede Press Book
Published by Centipede Press
2565 Teller Court, Lakewood, Colorado 80214

Story acknowledgements appear on page 365,
which constitutes an extension of this copyright page.

Cover image: Salvador Dalí
Daddy Longlegs of the Evening – Hope!, 1940
Oil on canvas, 25 × 51 cm
© Salvador Dalí. Fundación Gala-Salvador Dalí, (Artist Rights Society), 2010.
Collection of the Salvador Dalí Museum, Inc., St. Petersburg, FL, 2010. © 2010
Salvador Dali Museum, Inc.

Front endpaper image: Max Ernst
The Eye of Silence (*L'œil du silence*), 1943/44
Oil on canvas, 108 × 141 cm
Washington University Gallery of Art.

Rear endpaper image: Max Ernst
Somnambulistic Divers (*Les scaphandriers somnambules*), 1936
Oil on paper laid on card, 24 × 33 cm
Private collection.

ISBN 978-1-933618-56-2 (hc.: alk. paper)

September 2010
www.centipedepress.com
Printed in China.

CONTENTS

PROSTHESIS

CANDELARIA GASPED. Only with deliberate effort did she manage to hold her ground. The little alien thrust itself at her again in a broadly suggestive way, touched and then massaged her sides with the broad blue flats of its hands.

It was squealing excitedly in rapid-fire and heavily-accented English. She could catch some of the words. "Hello, lady! Hello, pretty lady! Welcome to my world! You are new here, are you? Oh, you are new! Will you talk to me? May I show you around? Buy you a drink? Can we—"

She shook her head and pushed the alien away. It stayed close, all but touching her, still talking. Another hustle, she thought wearily. She ran into this on practically every assignment, and by now could recognize a come-on even through the most confusing cultural overlay. Irritating as the routine was, her impulse this time was to laugh. The alien was clumsy, the line a conceit, a parody, and outdated at that.

"Alien" was not, of course, the right word. Candelaria was the outsider, the visitor, and in fact she felt very out of place. But this creature surely couldn't be called "native," either, even if it had been born here. It looked made up, artificial in a hodgepodge way; she stared at one part of it after another, cataloguing. She should have been prepared for this, by her own research, her journalistic training, and the briefing—such as it was—that she'd received from the main office for this particular assignment. But the longer and more closely she looked at the creature who had accosted her, the more amazed she was.

The alien was short; it came barely to her shoulder. On its head was a blonde beehive wig through which she could see down to the pinkish rubber scalp among the remaining follicles of old-style nylon hair. It wore a bulbous fake nose, an enormous glue-on moustache, two artificial legs and three arms of various skin tones affixed at distorted angles to its body like the fins of an impressionistic pinwheel. The makeup on its face and neck had not been blended into its blue-gray skin, and had turned dark and crusty where the edges overlapped. A female breast replacement with a flushed areola and raised nipple jutted outside the tattered jacket, which looked as if it had probably come from one of the NASA Surplus Stores that languished elsewhere but reportedly flourished here, with sales volumes out of all proportion to the size and real income of the population.

"Bizarre," she observed into the tiny microphone that hung like an appendage around her neck. "Clownlike. Childlike." But none of the adjectives seemed quite right.

The alien was rubbing itself against her like a hungry cat, squealing and hissing in a frenzy. It crossed her mind to step back, but she didn't. The alien reached up and patted her cheeks. Its hands were cold, metallic; she couldn't tell if they were real or not. "What's your name, lady? What's your name?"

She hesitated, but could think of no graceful way to withhold the information and no good reason for doing so. "Celia Candelaria," she said, and instantly, for no good reason, regretted it.

The alien seized her name, wrapped its garishly-painted mouth around it, drew frames for it in the air with both real and artificial limbs. "Celia Candelaria Celia Candelaria Celia Celia Celia Candelaria Celia." It repeated her name so quickly and so many times that the name lost its meaning in her own ears. She was distinctly uneasy, as though she'd provided the creature with some intimate part of herself, something that could be fashioned and used against her, like the lock of hair in the guts of an ancient voodoo doll.

To stop the alien's chanting of her name, she asked sharply, "Is this Simms' Emporium?"

"Right!" The alien grinned and showed capped teeth. Candelaria could see that its teeth were naturally broader at the base than those of humans, so that the inexpert dental work had resulted in cracked enamel and torn gums.

"Masochistic," she said into her machine. "A perverse kind of vanity." That had a nice ring to it and so she might use it, but she knew it wasn't quite right either.

"Simms! Simms!" The alien was hissing frenetically. "What you want from Simms, pretty lady? Oh, he got everything!" It had reached up high to stroke the sides of her head; fortunately her hair was too short and straight for it to tangle its fingers. "What you looking for, pretty lady?"

"I'm looking for Mr Simms himself."

The alien made a series of short noises that was unmistakably laughter. "That be hard."

"Why?"

"I take you in. I introduce you. I—"

"No," she said stiffly. "I prefer to speak with him alone."

The creature stepped back as though she'd slapped it, and Candelaria found herself feeling guilty. Peculiar reactions; she made a mental note of them. She also noted that she felt both relieved and abandoned now that the little creature was abruptly no longer touching her, now that she no longer had any physical contact with it. That was peculiar, too.

Then the alien writhed its head in a gesture she could not interpret, making the fluffy blonde wig slip backward so that a shiny expanse of its blue forehead was suddenly exposed. Shocked, Candelaria averted her eyes. The creature laughed again and scuttled away.

Candelaria took a deep breath and pushed open the lightweight metal door to Simms1 Emporium. Inside it was dusty and dim; her nose began to itch almost immediately, and her eyes to widen reflexively. She stood still for a few moments in an attempt to get her bearings, then proceeded with caution.

The place looked like a warehouse. Obviously there had been little attempt to set up an attractive sales floor. Boxes were stacked everywhere; some hung open, others were sealed shut, while others still bore shipping tags. Candelaria had to squint and peer to read the labels: "Hands." "Noses." "Feet." "Ears." Here and there an item of merchandise protruded, a hand or a foot gleaming pink or yellow or brown or black in the half-light. Though she was moving slowly and carefully, Candelaria tripped over something—a leg, its synthe-flesh ripped in places to reveal the wires and hydraulics underneath. She stifled a twinge of irrational horror.

She laid the leg down and resisted the impulse to wipe her hands on her pants. She advanced slowly, her reporter's senses askew. She was so disoriented that she was experiencing some actual vertigo and was afraid to brace herself against the towers of boxes for fear they'd tumble down and scatter fake human body parts across the floor. The image made her laugh, made her stomach lurch. Rocket lag certainly, and the effects of unfamiliar food no matter how terrestrialized it was claimed to be, and the emotional aftermath of that oddly intense encounter with the alien outside the Emporium.

But there was also something intrinsically disorienting about this place itself. Candelaria made a whispered impressionistic note about her responses for later refinement, not wanting to disturb the eerie silence by speaking aloud. There were state-of-the-art recorders that could pick up subvocalizing; of course, *Infonet* wouldn't spring for such a thing. Candelaria frowned irritably.

Suddenly she stopped short, face-to-face with what was apparently the Emporium's only display. It was crude, but—she told herself wryly—effective: her heart was pounding. A shabby antique mannequin had been set up near the center of the cluttered floor. Thick blue-gray paint layered its egg-shaped face. It wore synthetic ears, two left hydroarms, four breast replacements with the straps and connectors dangling. Enormous and very white false teeth jutted from the gaping mouth cavity. A fake nose was attached to the dummy's abdomen where the navel should have been; one nostril ring glinted silver. Candelaria's gaze traveled on downward and she laughed aloud; a giant dildo had been fastened in an erect position between mismatched hydrolegs.

"May I help you?"

Candelaria started, then turned to peer along a corridor formed by two high walls of boxes all labeled, with racist imprecision, "Face Paint Flesh Tone." A figure stood in this irregular canyon, one arm extended as if gesturing toward her. The figure was distinctly human, but for an instant she thought there was something subtly wrong with it—a shoulder out of line, perhaps, or a hip turned at an unnatural angle, or the torso bent impossibly. Like a body viewed through running water, she thought, or like an ancient human being's fantasy of what an alien would look like.

The figure came toward her and the distortion was gone. Candelaria couldn't imagine what she'd seen that had confused her, and that confused her even more. This person seemed normal enough, although at first she couldn't decide the gender.

"May I help you?" the milky voice repeated. "Looking for something special? A memento for the kids? A novelty gift for the lover?"

Annoyed to be taken so lightly, Candelaria said firmly into the slightly-echoing space between them, "I'm not shopping. My name is Celia Candelaria, and I'm a reporter for Infonet." She offered him her card. It seemed to take a long time before the card was out of her hand and into his. "Mr Simms, I presume."

He bowed. "At your service."

"You're the manager of—all this?"

"Manager, owner, proprietor, founder, monopolist. If I do say so myself. To what do I owe the honor of your visit, Ms. Candelaria?"

"There's been a great deal of interest at home lately in colony businesses. And yours is rather well-known, Mr Simms."

"Gordon," he said, taking charge, and stepped toward her with both hands extended. He came so close so quickly that she would have stepped away if her back had not already been pressed against the wall of boxes. As it was, she took advantage of his proximity to take stock of his appearance for use in a future report. Her first impression was that he was a remarkably unhandsome man. He was tall, probably in his late thirties, dark-haired, somehow awkwardly built. Candelaria found herself more interested in him than she'd expected to be. She also noticed that he held her hand in both of his slightly longer than necessary.

"I thought you'd be much older," she told him. "According to my research, you were one of the first merchants here."

He nodded. "Been here a long time."

He sat down on a box marked "Breasts" and casually crossed his legs. In this context, the commonplace gesture seemed almost obscene. She leaned gingerly against a stack of makeup boxes and switched on the mike, reflecting on the strange and inconvenient places she'd conducted interviews since her assignment to the colonies. She was tired of it, tired of the travelling and the perpetual

sense of rawness, of the feeling that everything was just now form-
ing rules and patterns everywhere she went.

But it was a living, and anyway she'd found no place worth staying, no place from which she really regretted moving on. And at
the moment here she was, starting an interview with what appeared
to be a willing subject, and a story with a readymade angle. Things
could be worse. She sighed.

"Spent some time in the service here," Gordon Simms was saying.
"Bought my early discharge in order to stay on. I know an opportunity when I see one. Developed my contacts, did a little start-up
promotion, and that was all it took. My wares sell themselves. All I
have to worry about is keeping up the inventory."

Candelaria moved away from him among the dusty boxes, turning up the mike as she went. "I notice that not much of your over-
head goes to—appearances."

He chuckled. "Ah, but Celia, that's what my business is all about.
Appearances."

"You know what I mean." She waved her hand testily, rapped her
knuckles against the side of a box so that dust flew. "This place is a
mess. A lot of your merchandise is dirty and damaged."

"I used to worry about that," he agreed. "Professional pride or
something. Business ethics. But my customers don't care what shape
the stuff is in, and I certainly don't need to lure them with clever
displays. Usually they know what they want when they come in, and
they find me by word of mouth. And actually they'll pay more for
damaged goods. They like to think of it as being more used, more
authentic, more *personal*. You ought to hear some of the conversations about who might have used this or that and for what purpose."

"Like slavefans," she said, both to him and into the microphone.
"Tearing off a piece of the holo-star's shirt so they can feel close to
their idol."

"I'd thought about worshippers," he said, "and their religious rel-
ics that for some reason make it easier for them to pray."

Candelaria shook her head and laughed. She was fascinated, almost despite herself. She was interested in Gordon Simms. She *liked* him, wanted to know him better than would be necessary in order to produce the slightly-better-than-puff piece her editor was expecting. Such feelings were unwise. They would get in the way, and deadline was fast approaching.

Frowning, she picked up a bent and dusty left arm from the floor and turned it over in her hands, getting used to the cold-flesh feel of it as she said to him, "Some people think your little enterprise here is immoral, Mr Gordon Simms."

"Immoral?" He raised his eyebrows.

"Pandering to some grotesque need of these poor people. Creatures. Whatever. Exploiting a cultural neurosis. Demeaning the human body."

He shrugged, and for some reason she thought it a clumsy motion. "I don't think much about human morality anymore. It doesn't seem to have much point in an alien culture. But now that you mention it, I guess I'd be more likely to say there's something morally *right* about what I do. I think I'm performing a service. Facilitating communication. Making it possible for there to be meaningful contact between species." He chuckled and waved his hand in a gesture of dismissal. "Not that that's why I do it, of course."

"Why *do* you do it?" Candelaria demanded, though she would have thought the answer would be obvious.

"To make money," he said. "I know an opportunity when I see one."

Candelaria nodded. Carefully she laid the arm back into its box. Its fingers grazed her own, and both real and artificial digits moved slightly in response to the unexpected contact between them.

Simms stood up. "I was just going to close up and go to dinner when you came. Would you care to join me? I know a little place that specializes in old-fashioned Terra food, cheeseburgers and eggrolls, that sort of thing. It's kind of a nice change."

She looked at his hands, outstretched toward her again, and for a moment the skin looked mottled, as if it had been bruised or inexpertly painted on. She avoided his touch, but said, "Sounds good. I am tired of space food," and preceded him to the door.

"Wait!" he called.

She stopped and turned, her hand on the door swinging it partway open. The motion of the door sent a swatch of bright light back and forth across the interior of the Emporium, so that boxes and appendages and mannequins and Gordon Simms himself were alternately lit and shadowed.

"Wait," said Simms again, and came toward her smiling. "Wear this. In honor of your visit, a gift from the Emporium."

He handed her a pair of cat's-eye sunglasses with iridescent sparkles in their pale-lavender frames. She stared at them, then shook her head and held them out to him. "I don't accept gifts from subjects. Corrupts professional objectivity. Makes me beholden."

"Please." She could see that he was still smiling, but the smile had gone out of his voice. "A bit of local color, then. For verisimilitude."

"I hardly think they're my style."

"Please," he said again. "They'll look lovely on you."

When she still hesitated, he took the sunglasses from her and settled them firmly on the bridge of her nose, reaching under her hair to hook the earpieces in place. For some reason, though they dimmed her vision considerably, Candelaria left them on.

The neighborhood around the Emporium was poor and rundown and colorful, with crowded open markets and a cacophony of voices. There'd been at least one spot like that on every planet she'd visited. The streets were teeming, practically impassable in places. Aliens were everywhere, bits of their blue skin shining through bizarre disguises. Huge glasses over their tiny semi-circular pink eyes. Massive thighs squeezed into "suntan" pantyhose riddled with runs and tears. A stout female sporting several wigs of different colors, a handlebar moustache, and a goatee. At the mouth of an alley, a spirited wrestling match over a mechanical knee joint between a short middle-aged female and a very old male who wore four multicolored brassieres and a glass eye dangling from one earlobe.

Simms and Candelaria walked through the alley, something she would not have done by herself, for unfamiliar alleys anywhere seemed dangerous whether they actually were or not. At the other end of this one was a vendor's stand with a gay striped canopy. Simms slowed as they approached it, and Candelaria saw that the counter was crowded with artificial eyes. The vendor—who wore at least four whining and crackling hearing aids on a string around his neck—touched the eyes one after another with a long, thin, pointed instrument, causing them to blink crazily; Candelaria guessed that he was applying minuscule electric shocks, and she was impressed by the ingenuity of the system as well as by its oddity. The crowd murmured and cheered.

Watching a child pop a handful of artificial eyes into its pocket like marbles, Candelaria found herself leaning against Simms, his hand lightly at her waist. She straightened and adjusted the sunglasses. "What's it about, do you think? Why this fascination with human body parts?"

"I think it has something to do with an obsessive need to make contact. Ever since the first explorers dropped out of the sky with their sleek ships and wealth, the natives have been fascinated by humans, and they seem to have both a terrible need and a terrible fear of being in intimate contact with us."

"But they're not 'in intimate contact.' All those prosthetic devices make any contact phony."

"Exactly. And that makes it safer. They can pretend that they're really communicating while they make sure they really don't. They can have it both ways." She was struck, touched, by how much thought he'd obviously given this puzzle.

A labor robot stopped beside them; as they passed it, the head unit stayed rigid, but the strip holding the visual sensors rotated slightly to keep Simms and Candelaria in view. She imagined trying to make intimate contact with a thing like that, and shuddered. But in a way it would be easier, she thought, because you'd know from the beginning what you were dealing with.

Simms glanced at her, glanced away. "In all the years I've been here," he said, "I've never once seen a native without a human prosthesis of some kind attached to its body. Never once."

The meal was surprisingly good, the restaurant charming with its thoroughly anachronistic eclecticism. It was altogether a pleasant hour, and Candelaria hated to spoil the mood by asking questions. She sipped the pale heady wine and almost reflexively checked the mike with a quick touch to the front of her shirt, reminding herself sternly that she was here on business and, after all, an expense account.

But she could think of nothing sensible to ask. Her prepared questions now seemed totally irrelevant. She smiled a little sheepishly at Simms and with disproportionate pleasure concentrated on finishing her pepperoni pizza.

They walked together back to her hostel. Not knowing the customs, she had left the sunglasses on in the restaurant, and she didn't remove them now either though the streets were nearly dark. At first the few passersby didn't look to her to be disguised at all, and that was a little unnerving. She wondered why, and decided to wonder about it later, when she was alone.

She took off the glasses to see better and, feeling oddly exposed, rubbed her eyes. Then she began to see that every native they passed was indeed wearing all sorts of prosthetic devices—wigs, teeth, bands, hips, feet. But these appendages had been constructed and attached far more skillfully than any she'd seen before. Maybe nighttime fashion standards were more sophisticated.

She slipped the glasses back on and edged a little closer to Simms. Welcomingly, he put his arm around her. The stars were a hazy cloud of milk drops, the buildings a moody jumble across the deep blue of the sky. Everything was unfamiliar. Arousing. She stopped, turned, looked up into Simms' shadowed face. She could hardly make out his features, and she wanted to see him, so she took off the glasses again. Then she put her hands on his shoulders, stood on tiptoe, and kissed him.

He stiffened, did not return the kiss or the embrace. Shocked, she stepped back. "I—I'm sorry," he said hastily. "I guess I'm just not used to being so close to a pretty woman any more." She regarded him carefully. She couldn't read his expression. He looked to her like no man she'd ever known.

During the next weeks, Candelaria found herself seeing more and more of the little creatures who inhabited the planet—and more and more of Gordon Simms. In the daytime she walked the streets by herself, filling the storage area of her recorder with notes and observations. The natives stared at her, especially the children. Some of the bolder ones reached out and fingered her hair, stroked the exposed skin on her arms and neck.

Once a group of them trapped her in an alley; both exits were blocked by their squat little bodies, and at her back was a wall. For awhile she was frightened, and to calm herself she kept talking into the microphone. "One of them is wearing an Afro wig that's half as big as she is. One of them has long fake nails on every finger and toe. I suppose they could be used as weapons, although they're so long they'd probably bend and break. One of them has braces that are too big for him on both legs, and a gigantic neck brace that keeps his head from moving. One of them—"

She was still talking when the squealing, tittering crowd disgorged one of its smallest members toward her. This child came racing and leaped into her arms; she was so startled that she nearly dropped him and had to lean against the wall for support. She gazed into the blue face of the little creature, which was unadorned except for sequined false eyelashes glued all around his semi-circular pink eyes, extending almost to the tip of his wide flat nose.

"Hello there," Candelaria said softly. "What do you want from me, little one?"

Chittering under his breath, the child reached up, took off her glasses, and dropped them onto the ground. Then he placed his palms on her cheeks and spread his long flat fingers. She closed her eyes and held her breath. The child moved his fingers over every part of her face, lightly probing her eye sockets, her mouth, the soft spots behind her ears. Then he pulled her close and briefly laid his own cheek against hers. His skin was soft and cool. Candelaria was moved to the brink of tears, though she had no idea what any of this meant or what she was expected to do in return. Apparently finished or filled, the child wriggled free of her and scampered back to his peers, who had been quiet and who now exploded into shrieks of laughter and scattered out of the alley, letting her go.

Her deadline came and went. She sent a message explaining that the assignment had turned out to be more complex than they'd thought and requesting an extension; by the time the grudging approval made its way back, nearly half the approved extension period was already gone. "My editor won't know what to do with all this stuff," she told Simms, laughing, showing him the bulging stack of notes edited from the tape by the portable processor set up in her rooms. "*Infonet* isn't exactly known for its in-depth features."

He was lying on the bed in her hostel room. She was sitting cross-legged on the floor not far from him. They passed back and forth a pipe of some sweet-smelling native vegetation, and quiet music from home played in the background. The scene had all the makings of intimacy, but Candelaria knew better than that by now. This man was not easy to get close to, physically or otherwise.

Especially physically, she reflected ruefully. He would take her hand to guide her when they walked the dark night streets, or put an arm protectively on her shoulder, and once or twice when they'd parted for the night he'd touched his lips to the top of her head. That was all. Candelaria had been confused, frustrated, hurt. Now she was acutely curious, a a woman attracted to an enigmatic man, a reporter on the trail of the angle to her story.

"Why don't you give your editor what she's used to?" he asked now, eyes closed above the pipe. "A little sensationalism? A little—'yellow journalism,' I believe it's called?"

She laughed, almost startled. "I haven't heard anyone use that since my History of Journalism professor."

Gordon was silent. Candelaria was thinking how oddly humorless the man was, when he spoke up again, "I was only suggesting that perhaps you could give your editor what she wants, and satisfy your own boundless curiosity at the same time."

She waited, holding her breath, longing to switch on the mike under her shirt but afraid he'd notice. Instead, she adjusted the shoulder pads he'd found for her in a shipment last week; she wasn't used to wearing them, and they itched and chafed, but she liked the square angles they gave to her silhouette.

When Simms said nothing, she asked carefully, "What is it you're offering?"

"I'm not sure." He stood up abruptly, swayed a little, caught himself. "But come to the shop tonight after dark. Maybe we can wrap this thing up."

Wordlessly, Candelaria watched him go. Conscious of being hurt and angered by his apparent eagerness to have her done with the assignment and out of his life, she wondered again if she'd completely misread him. That was a fruitless line of thought, of course, because she had no clear reading of him at all and no way of checking out her constantly shifting perceptions.

With a sigh she turned off the music, turned up the lights, extinguished the pipe. Then she seated herself at the cramped little desk to begin the laborious process of pulling notes together into a coherent form.

It was barely dusk when she approached the Emporium, but she was too eager to wait any longer. The shop's shabby grotesquerie was almost welcoming. She stepped inside and closed the rattling door behind her. It swung a few times and then was still. From out of the shadows Gordon Simms came toward her. She knew it was Simms because she didn't think it could be anyone else, and because something about his walk was familiar, but otherwise she would not have recognized a single thing about him. She gasped, stared, and was chilled.

He was much shorter than she knew him to be, coming barely to her shoulder; looking down at his bare feet, she guessed he'd always before worn platform shoes. He was almost completely bald, and the skin of his head where it had been sheltered so long by the wig was a much paler blue than that of his face and neck. His gums were bleeding and be had no teeth; his mouth cavity had collapsed inward so that his chin jutted forward, and his flat wide nose had spread halfway across his face. She saw that both his hands were gone, one above the elbow and one just below, and that his squat body was twisted so that not all of it seemed to be facing her at once.

"Celia?" he said, and she would not have known his voice. She tried to see the place in his smooth blue neck where a voice synthesizer had been inserted and recently removed, but the light was too dim.

"Gordon?" she asked shakily.

He came closer, nodding erratically. "This is who I am. Without prostheses. Without the disguise. Without anything between us. This is who I really am." He held out his arms.

He was offering her something that terrified her. She was breathless with the enormity of what he was offering, the bareness. She was horrified by the naked alien sight of him, when she'd thought he was one of her own kind.

Abruptly Candelaria turned away from him. Though she couldn't move very fast in the clutter of the Emporium, she felt as though she were running. Boxes and crates closed in around her. Dust filled her eyes and nose, coated and numbed her skin. Human body parts were everywhere. Frantically she told herself that they were fake, and then touched her own arms and lips and breasts to make sure they were still there.

A swarm of glass eyes tilted toward her out of the dimness. Watching her. Winking in a sordid way. She swung the flat of her hand against the corner of the crate, and the eyes spilled out in a deluge, each for a split-second glinting like a hard round tear, clattering and rolling away from her feet. Countless hands reached out to caress her, to hold her, to keep her from moving past; she could shake them off, but they fell with a disgusting rubbery sound, bouncing a little against her ankles.

She could hear breathing hard behind her; the alien Simms was following her. Her flight took her deeper and deeper into the Emporium, which was much larger than she had thought, much more labyrinthine. She could hardly breathe. Everything she saw and heard was distorted. Once she cried out, and was frightened by the sound of her own voice.

"Celia!" called Simms. He was very close. "Wait!"

Candelaria turned a corner to hide herself from him. She didn't have much time. A box on the floor in front of her overflowed with fur; she pulled out a handful, pulled the things apart, found a red wig and a full gray beard and put them on.

"Celia!"

He sounded slightly farther away now, as if he'd taken a wrong turn. In this part of the Emporium—its heart, she imagined—there was almost no light. She crept sideways, like some scuttling kind of creature. Her hands found a tall crate, eased the lid open, pulled out appendages that felt more like flesh than her own flesh, attached them at random places on her body with the straps and hooks only approximately fastened. Some part of her body bumped against a box and she heard bottles clinking together; she pulled out a large one, unstoppered it, and doused herself with scent like nameless flowers and musk.

"Celia." He was not inches away from her. She could feel his body beat, smell him, hear her name as be whispered it again and again. "Celia."

Stumbling over her own unfamiliar arms and legs and breasts, she turned toward him. Her chest ached; she felt on the verge of tears. But her hodgepodge disguise was strangely calming. She imagined herself embracing the twisted little creature. She imagined touching him, her fingertips resting on alien skin, and found she could retain the image a few seconds before having to turn away. She gathered her cloak of prostheses closer to her own flesh, and the feel of plastics and fiber was oddly warming.

From inside her shirt she pulled the microphone and extended it toward him like a hand, both welcoming and distancing. She wanted to ask him something, but she was still too panicky to frame the question. She wanted to ask him. She turned up the volume. She fought for control. She wanted to ask him. Her voice was muffled by the heavy beard in a comforting way. He stared at her with what might have been apprehension. "Tell me," she said, her voice beginning to break. She moved the microphone closer, a reaching or a threatening. "I need you to tell me about it. Please. Gordon, I need you to tell me how it is."

THE SING

LAST NIGHT I WOKE UP from a nearly formless dream, shaking with the realization that Rae and I had never Sung together. It was hard to comprehend, so much a part of my life now are Sings and so integral to every Sing are my memories of Rae. She is dead. We'll never Sing together. It was a new grief; it kept me awake the rest of the night, and today it will send me to the Cleer.

Forever alien, I'll stand among the Cleer in the rough-hewn amphitheater, my mouth open like theirs even though it can't tremble in the same way. I'll make my sound, which will never be quite the sound the Cleer make but is close enough. Rae will swell my voice. My mind will be flooded with images: oval faces, vague stick figures dancing, the seasons changing with the Song. Images from human myths, from old Earth songs, maybe from Cleer things that I couldn't name. Images of Rae. I have no way of knowing what the Cleer see when they Sing; we can't talk that precisely or poetically to each other, after all this time, and when they touch me I don't know for sure what it means. But I have come to recognize their tears, and I think they recognize mine.

Then — if I'm lucky, if it's a good Sing for me, if it works — the sound will pull greedily at my throat and my thoughts, the dark stones and the gentle disfigured Cleer and the grim Matchhead sky and even my precious thoughts of Rae will recede into nothing, and for awhile all of my attention will be needed for the Song.

For now, though, I sit alone at my tiny dusty window with my morning cup and watch the Matchhead sun come up over the flat Matchhead horizon. The stark landscape, the dreary vista of featureless stone and night-colored clay, echoes what I'm feeling, verifies it, makes it resonate. A retired mining engineer I used to know — I wonder whatever became of him; he was old and weary when I knew him — told me this was called "pathetic fallacy," and he said that was one reason why people came to Matchhead. More and more, I think he was right. Earth has lost its capacity for pathetic fallacy. It doesn't respond so intimately to its inhabitants anymore. There's no room there for feelings outside the self.

I think I glimpse a Cleer go by. It enters and leaves the area I can see out my window before I can really tell who or what it is. Up early, I think, and then realize how little I know about these creatures who have come to mean so much to me, how seldom I've tried to learn anything about their customs or habits, how few words I understand of their musical language, how unreliable is my ability to distinguish one of them from another. I remember hearing a good deal about them before I first came to Matchhead. Back then, I dismissed most of it as exaggeration, tall tales; now, I can't tell how much of it was true, or in what way.

"Voices like birds they have, birds you never heard nor heard of. Why, I hear they *sing* the precious ore out of the ground!"

"I saw a Cleer once. Yes, indeed. Opened its mouth to a friend o' mine and my friend near died o' joy. That's a fact."

The planet Matchhead itself has acquired legendary qualities. It draws people like a frontier, like a new world or a promised land. In ancient times there was the French Foreign Legion; now, Matchhead attracts disappointed lovers, misguided romantics, dreamers in search of a dream. Because the corporations that run the place will hire with few questions asked, debt-dodgers come, criminals and ex-criminals and those on the brink. Matchhead pay is good and there aren't many taxes, so we have men and women who know no better way of supporting families on Earth; they always plan to stay only as long as it takes to accumulate a nest egg, and usually only their paychecks ever see home again.

Myself, I don't remember why I first came here. Maybe my reasons were clearer to me then, or maybe I never had real reasons; it was a long time ago, and I was a very different man. Probably there was some element of adventurousness to it, although I don't remember. I was alone, but I'd always been alone and I didn't think of myself as lonely; certainly I wouldn't have known what it meant to be heart-broken. I wasn't escaping anyone or anything; nobody ever got close enough for me to need escape, and I didn't take many chances.

It couldn't have been because of Rae, although there are times now when it seems that everything is or was because of her. I didn't know Rae then. I didn't imagine that she existed. If anyone had asked —if I'd known to ask myself —I'd have said I wasn't looking, for her or for anything in particular.

Matchhead from a distance looks just as its name implies: small and bright red from all the iron ore, with white polar caps, the larger on the north end. Not that you see matches anymore, except in museums; those first engineer/explorers must have been quite the romantics themselves.

I am not a romantic. Not anymore. I'm a realist. For the first time in my life, I know what I need. Even when I had Rae, I didn't know I needed her. It was only after she died —long after she died —that I understood what I had lost. The Cleer showed me that. I'm neither grateful to them nor bitter.

I check the time, get up stiffly from my seat at the window, fix breakfast. Soon I can go to the Sing.

Matchhead was Inter-Ore's biggest find; it virtually made the company, and nothing has equaled it since. When Inter-Ore got to Matchhead, the Cleer had already been here for a very long time. A routine had been established so long that it must have seemed like a cultural tradition indigenous to Matchhead: Every once in awhile a huge Cleer ship arrives —presumably from their home planet, wherever that may be —to pick up ore and Cleer and to deposit more Cleer. The rest of the ore —mined, ready for transport and processing —is simply left behind. Inter-Ore considers it a bonanza, and it may be some kind of payoff or kickback or bribe, but more likely it's just more than the Cleer can use, and so they pay it no attention.

The Cleer are expert miners; they seem born to it. They're geologically and mechanically knowledgeable, efficient, persistent. But there is no greed in them, hardly any of what we'd even call a work ethic. When they're not mining they're staring silently off into space, and one activity doesn't seem to interfere with the other. If you're working near a Cleer encampment, you're not surprised when one of them appears to help repair broken-down equipment or dredge a stubborn vein. It's not unheard-of for Inter-Ore prospectors to come upon a particularly rich lode that the Cleer are already working; politely, quietly, the Cleer just move on.

I met Rae after I'd been out awhile. I'd been doing scheduling at a temporary outpost on one of Matchhead's gigantic, country-sized mesas, and had made a little error, putting one driller operator in for a double shift. When a tall figure strode into the office, dust hood making it look like some sort of enormous desert insect, I prepared to take cover.

"So you're the bastard —" she began.

The female voice surprised me enough to delay my answer a few beats. Women on Matchhead tended to hold upper-echelon jobs, engineers and surveyors and the like; I'd never encountered a woman on a crew.

She took off her hood and impatiently shook her head. Her sandy hair was stringy and matted with grime against her skull, but she had astonishing green eyes, and she was beautiful.

Finally I said, "I'm the bastard," and she chuckled.

It's dangerous to be remembering all this in such detail when I'm by myself, when I'm not at a Sing. I switch on the morning news for distraction, but nothing much has happened during the night and it doesn't help. I can't stop thinking about Rae, and she's been dead now for nearly half my life.

Love in all its variations is free and easy on a mining outpost. There's not much talk about commitment, but it's not cold, either, as a lot of people think. It's friendly. At first I didn't take love with Rae very seriously; I was used to going through friends and lovers without giving any of them much thought.

But before I knew it, things were different with Rae. I liked talking to her. I liked touching her. I liked looking at her. We talked a lot about Earth, how neither of us had been able to find what we wanted or needed there. Of course, we admitted, we couldn't find what we wanted or needed on Matchhead either, but here we could justify putting the search on hold.

We spent nearly all our time together. We arranged with the dispatchers — it wasn't hard; nobody much cared — to be sent on the same sequence of jobs at roughly the same time. We worked well together. We talked well together. We slept and lived well together, and we made marvelous love. Looking back on it, I think I accepted her as if she'd always been part of me and always would be. There are ways in which that is true.

Rae and I never Sang together, and I regret that enormously; it's an irretrievable loss. But once we sat on a hot sandy hillside and watched and listened to the Cleer at a Sing.

Probably everything about the Cleer is more interesting than their physical appearance. Their bodies are practically featureless, except for a few strategic orifices; their skin is translucent, almost transparent, and the body-workings you can see through the skin look amazingly uncomplicated. "Cleer" is apparently a variant of "Clear"; those first engineers weren't all that imaginative, and they obviously took note, as we are trained to do in this profession, of surface details.

But Rae noticed something else that day on that dusty hill, before we were both caught up speechless in the beauty and pain of the Song itself. "Look," she said suddenly, and leaned forward, tightening her grip on my hand. "They're hurt. Maimed. Every one of them."

I looked. I wasn't as sure as she was — Rae had an exquisite eye for detail — but at last I thought I saw what she meant. Every one of the Cleer in the crowded amphitheater below us seemed to have something wrong with its body. Some hole, some misalignment, some painful awkwardness.

Physical disfigurement among humans isn't uncommon on Matchhead; mining is hard and dangerous work, and the sophisticated technology has been applied less to ensuring miners' safety than to getting the ore out. The bars in Pull Out, Oretown, Packett are full of miners retired with plastic arms, legs, feet. I was used to that. So it shouldn't have shocked me to make the same discovery about the Cleer. But I remember shivering a little as Rae said, "Come to think of it, they don't fix the damage to their bodies the way we do. Obviously they could. They have the technology. It's as if the hurt were some kind of badge."

"They seem so *peaceful*." I said.

"I know. More peaceful than you or me." She squeezed my hand.

I was suddenly full of curiosity. "I wonder what they do on their own planet. I wonder how long any one individual stays on Matchhead — and, for that matter, why they come here. I wonder what their lives are like."

30

Then the Song reached us. A deep sound, liquid, translucent, like a collective recollection of which Rae and I shared only a tiny piece. Like a soft breathing animal. Like the sand that blows all the time on Matchhead, billowing and searing. Like the vast sky, somehow, though in truth I've never seen such a sky here or anywhere. The Song filled us. We were filled with all we had felt and had not said. The Song pushed out of us, gently drew us with it, until we were free of our bodies and the whole world was Singing and Rae and I were huddled in each other's arms.

The morning light comes through my slit of a window now like a weapon. I get up to dress, and I'm so weak I can hardly move. Already I'm exhausted, and ahead of me is another long day at a developing site in the stage of chaos and clamor and productivity that demands full attention and energy. I'm foreman now; it's my responsibility. I don't have time to go to a Sing this morning. But I will go. I have to go. Half-naked and chilled, I stand still in the middle of my room and can't stop myself from thinking about Rae and about the Cleer.

My first field assignment for Inter-Ore was to prepare an inventory of equipment abandoned on company properties. I was to match serial numbers from historical documents and set aside, for cataloguing into a planned Matchhead History Museum, any equipment used in the original exploration. It was slow, dirty, boring work, but I finished it, finally; the museum has yet to be built.

One day I was working in the southern hemisphere — broad red and gray plains, mostly gravel, hard flat rock, stiff clay. The colors are dark and muted until sunlight touches them; then there are brilliant highlights. Vegetation is sparser here than in the north, a few brush strokes of black and silver, narrow cracks of life in the barren landscape. Although I didn't see any fauna at all on that first desolate assignment, I know now that there are some: rodents, tiny flying snakes, a few brown insects. The one outstanding feature on the southern half of the planet is a broad steep-sided mesa, against which much of the equipment was piled.

I was crouching on a rock ledge that jutted out from the side of the mesa, trying to make out the serial number stamped on an ancient earth mover. It looked to be a historical piece, and I remember actually being excited by the find, which shows just how dull the job had become. I remember also that I was trying not to think about the four miners who'd died just east of the mesa a few days earlier when their ground-effect vehicles were caught in a furious, blinding dust storm. The ledge shifted. I tried to scramble off. It collapsed, and I fell.

I lay there a long time with my leg twisted back under me. I knew I wasn't in any real danger; I'd triggered a beacon immediately, I had plenty of supplies, and I'd never heard of any life forms on Matchhead that would pose a threat. But I was scared. I felt like a child. My leg hurt. Nobody would worry about me. Maybe Rae would worry a little; we'd just met. The desperation with which I hoped she'd worry about me made me feel frightened and foolish, and I was crying.

Then I saw a dark form silhouetted against the bright brown starlit sand, coming swiftly toward me. I sobbed and waited, foolishly, for the end.

The Cleer stood over me, two of them, their strange expressionless eyes fixed on my face. One stooped and touched my leg. I pulled away in revulsion, and pain catapulted through me. Its oral cavity gaped, and I could hear a slight continuous hiss. When it stood up again it turned to its companion. They didn't speak, but in concert they picked me up and carried me out of the rocks and into the open night.

I was so frightened, so overwhelmed by strangeness and pain and by alien will, that I didn't pay attention to where they were taking me. Suddenly I was aware of being on a broad rock plain, out of the edge of which had been gouged a depression like an amphitheater. Sound drifted toward me, music, beautiful and agonizing. They had brought me to a Sing.

I was surrounded by Cleer, and my fear dissolved. The Song was a living thing. I wanted to be part of it; I didn't want just to sit there with my mouth closed. But something held me back. I looked around at the others in embarrassment.

They lulled me to sleep with their Song. When I awoke they were all gone, and one of our rescue copters was setting down nearby. I was taken to a hospital post where the leg was set and cast, and before long it was as good as new. But I always knew, even before I understood it, that the real healing had come from the Sing.

I have managed to dress, all but my boots, which I can't find. I'm sitting on the floor now, cross-legged like a child, supposedly looking for my boots. But my hands are limp in my lap and tears are streaming down my cheeks. The Cleer have taught me to mourn. It's not as good alone, away from a Sing; in fact, it's dangerous. But it's better than nothing.

Rae died toward the end of our first tour of duty on Matchhead. Sometimes I've wondered if we would have re-upped, or if we'd have gone home to Earth together. It doesn't matter, of course, because suddenly it was all over.

I didn't see it happen, but I heard it. I was talking to one of the other drivers when somebody shouted, "Slide!" Part of the rim was giving way. I ran with the others away from the site until I remembered that Rae was operating an augur out near the edge. By the time I had turned around, there was a tremendous roar and red swirling dust had climbed into an impenetrable wall. It was a long time before I could get any closer, and we never did find her body. Matchhead had swallowed her.

I think I hear snatches of Song now and, though that's unlikely —our huts are soundproof, dustproof, encapsulated —the illusion makes me hurry. My boots are by the door where I left them. I shove my feet into them, clamp the fastenings shut. My need for the Sing makes my stomach roil, my head swim. The Sing will remind me of all I haven't admitted, and there is still much. It will fill me, fill the empty spaces where pain lies in wait.

I've been Singing ever since Rae left me, and that was a long time ago. The first time, when I thought I'd go crazy and thought maybe I wanted to and thought I'd stumbled into the Sing by accident, the Cleer welcomed me — not with words, of course, but they made room. I understand now that I'd been expected. And when the time came to open my mouth and let the sound come, I didn't hesitate. I'm not a good Singer, even yet, but it's impossible to Sing badly. The collective music pulled my own weak voice along, rounded and amplified it, until I couldn't believe the beauty of my own voice and then, at last, I stopped searching for the sound of my own voice and lost myself in the Song.

Walking out into the blinding Matchhead morning, raising a hand in greeting to a fellow miner whose face I can't see for the sunshine, I reflect that I've become a little like the Cleer, or like what I imagine the Cleer to be. I don't talk much these days. I think a great deal, though not often in words or sentences. I remember a great deal. I Sing as often as I can. I don't really know what happens when I Sing, but I know that I'm part of — something. And it's better then.

I've done well on Matchhead. There's a lot of money in my account. I'm a better foreman than miner, actually; my workers seem to like me and they listen to what I have to say, although I have no friends among them and I know they think I'm odd. I can tell when the newcomers have heard stories about me: they begin to look at me as if they can see through my skin to the workings of my mind and body and still find me baffling. That's all right. My loneliness is as flat and barren as the Matchhead landscape, as rich in potential for pathetic fallacy, and I know how to live in it now.

The ships still come; some Cleer leave and others are left behind.

34

Now I can see their hurts, their losses, their deformities, and I've wondered if somewhere an endless battle is being waged, and the injured come here to recuperate. And to grieve.

I suspect we are the lucky ones, these Cleer and I.

I still don't know why the Cleer mine. I don't know why I do, either. But I remember that mining is not the important thing.

This is a place to Sing. A spiritual place.

I walk to the amphitheater through the bright morning dust. As I step down into the midst of the Cleer, relief and sorrow bring tears to my eyes and the Song trembling into my throat. I look around once, before I close my eyes and open my mouth to Sing. Their heads are thrown back, their mouths open, filling me, lifting me, so that I too can Sing, my face, their faces, streaming with tears, demanding my attention, a presence, oval faces, stick figures writhing and dancing, Rae coming to me, I'm making the same sound, my Song, a living creature, a shared recollection, combined memories, my sorrow, my injuries, their injuries on display, I feel one with them, unreal, out of my body and a part of them, this Song…

RESETTLING

W HEN HANNAH FOUND HERSELF KNEELING
on the bed screaming hateful things at Perry and
punching at his stomach through the tangled bed-
clothes, it didn't occur to her at first that the
house had anything to do with it. Perry, who was her life, whom
she'd waited for all her life and lived in fear of losing. Later
they made frantic love with all the lights out; it was very late at
night, and it was then that Hannah first felt without question the
absorbing presence of the house.

She had lived in the neighborhood for nearly ten years, before
and since Perry and Ashley. She'd looked at the house for all those
ten years and wanted it for most of that time. At first, she remembered, it had seemed overwhelming. It sat on a hill in the middle of
a crowded residential block. Not a very high hill, not much higher
than the lots of its neighbors, but it seemed to tower over them.
Dark red brick with black trim, ivy encrusting all the south wall,
high, narrow windows that seemed to reflect any kind of light. Just
around the corner Hannah had been amazed to discover a twin, a
house clearly built at the same period and from the same design,

probably by the same builder, but, for reasons she could never quite determine, a friendlier house, lighter, more open, with white trim and a wide, sunny porch and half a dozen tall bright trees. A far less interesting house. Hannah found herself drawn to the house on the hill.

Routes to the bus stop, to the grocery store, to the cleaner's could, if she went just a little out of her way, take her right past it, and those soon became her regular pathways. She saw the house then in all kinds of weather, at all times of the day and night. In snow it hulked like a Minotaur guarding its treasure. In morning sunshine it seemed cool and impenetrable, and it cast a tall triangular shadow all the way across the street. At night black clouds scudded breathtakingly behind its peaks.

"I hate you!" she heard herself shouting at Perry, the man she loved more than anyone else in the world. "You're not the man I married! I am not going to live like this!"

Perry was crying. She'd seen him cry before, in fact, his emotional openness was one of the things that endeared him to her. But now, for an awful moment, she was repulsed, as if he had turned into a monster. "So leave!" he shouted, and pushed his fist against her chest so that she sprawled back across the bed. "We'd all be better off without you!"

And then they'd stared at each other in horror while the house surrounded them like a palpable spell, and they'd fallen into each other's arms.

Hannah was determined she would keep her daughter from knowing that anything was wrong, as if she could protect her from being poisoned, too. Ashley was so precious, so fragile, and she always knew when things weren't right, often before Hannah did. Hannah's worry that she couldn't adequately take care of Ashley was long-standing and persistent. And it was getting worse. She heard herself speaking more sharply to Ashley than she would have thought possible, and resolutely turning away from the small, distressed face. It seemed to Hannah that she damaged the child in small ways a dozen times a day, and that she couldn't help it.

As her arguments with Perry became more frequent, Hannah became obsessed by memories of her life before Ashley was born. She and Perry had been alone in their first, much smaller house. Those had been their best years, with nothing but time for each other. But she had wanted children; she'd had no idea what that might be like; she just knew she wanted them. They had tried to have a child for almost ten years, mostly at her insistence; Perry adored his daughter but could, she knew, have been quite content living all his life with just her.

Childlessness for her was, truly, barrenness, and, after a time, conceiving became the most important thing in her life. They'd made love regularly for so long that she'd almost forgotten that sex could be anything but dutiful and charted. They'd undergone every imaginable fertility test, and the doctors could find nothing wrong with either of them. She'd taken a variety of fertility drugs, which created a variety of bizarre side effects. And every month she'd had her period, regular and painful and bloody, making her feel as if she were being emptied out.

Perry had wanted to stop. "It's not worth it," he'd say, or "We can always adopt." Intellectually she'd understood him; she'd even agreed with him. It made no difference: She had to keep on trying.

And one day she was pregnant, and nine frantic months later Ashley Anne was born. The perfect baby, the answer to every dream, and not for one moment what Hannah had thought she would be.

Ashley, whose every smile was a miracle, whose every act was a discovery and a terror. Ashley, the repository of the family's moods. When Perry and Hannah fought—even if it was in the middle of the night, quietly, with the door of their room shut tight—the next day Ashley would silently take their hands and draw them together. When one of them had had a bad day at work, Ashley would cry and try very hard to be good. When they were more worried than usual about money—even if they'd been meticulous about not letting her know—she'd bring her piggy bank and empty it on their bed.

Ashley hadn't wanted to move. She didn't like change. It frightened her. She said something awful was going to happen. But now that they were here she seemed the member of the family most taken by the house. On bright days, when sunshine streamed through the leaded-glass windows, Ashley sparkled and danced. At night she, like the house, closed in on herself.

Ashley was truly happy here. Hannah wouldn't spoil that. Hush! Ashley will hear! It had become a kind of chant, or prayer, and served only to make both her and Perry more incensed.

In the years before the house was hers, Hannah had never seen people living there, although there had been signs of habitation—lights on at night, the lawn mowed, for a while a fierce black Doberman leaping at the wrought-iron fence. Then the house was empty for a long time, and a "For Sale" sign sat at the bottom of the hill, well away from the house itself.

When Perry sold a series of paintings for more money than they'd ever imagined, they bought the house on the hill. Just like that. It took less than a month from Hannah's first incredulous call to the Realtor until closing. Everything progressed with an almost eerie ease: They sold their squat, *cozy* little house to the first couple who looked at it; their loan application was processed faster than the agent had ever seen; they toured the house on the hill one time and everyone in the family—even Ashley—felt at once that it was theirs. It was as if the house, with its elegance, its concentrated energy, had reached out and claimed them, like a new mother counting her infant's fingers and toes. After that tour Hannah found she couldn't remember details—exactly how the rooms converged, what color the wallpaper was—but she remembered the feel of the place, the atmosphere, the sense that she had no choice but to accept the claim of that house.

"Why has it been on the market for so long?" Perry had thought to ask, adding lamely, "It's a wonderful house."

The Realtor, a cool young woman with long eyelashes and expensive clothes, had smiled. "Who knows? Maybe it was just waiting for you."

Indeed, there was such a sense of relief and completeness about the house now that Hannah felt as if she were part of an organic process. Sternly she told herself that this was foolish anthropomorphizing, to which she was prone anyway; when they'd moved out of their old house she'd stood in the empty living room after all the others had left and aloud she had said "Good-bye," and "Thank you."

But the sensation was inescapable. Struggling with the sticky front gate after a long day at work while she balanced her heavy briefcase in the other hand, reading the Sunday paper in the quiet parlor while elsewhere in the house Ashley and Perry watched "Doctor Who"; eating breakfast at the sunny kitchen table (she'd always wanted a kitchen with a breakfast nook, but it had seemed such a silly criterion for house-buying that she hadn't mentioned it to anyone; now here it was)—in a dozen intimate little ways every day Hannah felt the house growing around her, into her, like an oyster with a grain of sand, she and the house taking on aspects of each other and becoming something new.

Now, scarcely a month after moving into the house, Hannah heard herself shrieking outrageous and cruel things at Perry that she didn't think she meant, and then frantically studying his reaction for something familiar. As she whispered, "I love you," and took him inside her, her mind ejected another phrase like a many-layered pearl for her to see: "He's not the man I married." She didn't know what it meant.

Hannah was a social worker, and she was very tired. After ten conscientious years, it was now abruptly clear to her that she didn't understand human nature, that no one did, that human nature was not accessible to human understanding. That troubled her like a betrayal. She remembered as if it were a youthful foible, slightly embarrassing and endearing at the same time, how much she'd wanted to be a social worker, how she'd never even considered another profession. Things weren't fair and she was going to change them. But once she'd entered the field, it was not what she had expected. It was almost as if by wanting it so much, pursuing it so single-mindedly, she'd changed it. The longer she worked the more keenly she saw the occupational hazards: hypocrisy, arrogance, disrespect, confusion. Coming home at night, especially to the house on the hill with its darkness enveloping the lights inside, was an intense relief, even though almost every night she bruised her hand on the front gate latch.

Hannah was clinical director for a program serving the noninstitutionalized chronically mentally ill. Over the years she'd worked with other groups—elderly in nursing homes, battered women, alcoholics, families of delinquent teenagers. Every time she'd changed specialties she'd been excited at first, eager to learn and to see what difference she could make. Every time the boredom, the sense of deja vu returned sooner than before.

She saw now that the characteristic common to all these people was disappointment: Having gotten exactly what they'd wanted, it was not what they wanted anymore. The old man near the end of his life, the wife beaten by a man she could not leave, the drinker in search of the perfect high, the parents whose children were not what they intended them to be—all of them disappointed. As in all the cruel old fairy tales about the dangers of wishing, the thing had changed to become something evil and monstrously familiar.

The schizophrenics were the most unsettling, because much of the time you couldn't tell the patients from the staff. Their psychosis was only an elaboration of the way everyone else lived, yet they seemed unable to perform even the simplest daily tasks without running full tilt into the truth that, more and more, seemed to Hannah the central fact of human existence: Things are not what they seem.

Sometimes when she came home at night she'd see the patients staring at her out of the shadows that clung to the odd corners of the house, stubborn shadows that would not leave even when she replaced all the light bulbs with ones of higher wattage. Their eyes and voices, the way they held their hands, seemed haunted, possessed. She was seeing that same look now in her husband. The look of those who cannot believe their eyes.

Many of the patients could feel it coming on. "I'm going to be crazy," they'd say, and then the staff would alter medications or set up more structure, or just watch, helpless to provide more than the most minimal protection against the outside world. "Out of touch with reality," it said on the charts. Lately Hannah sometimes found herself all but incapacitated by confusion over who was out of touch with what.

"I'm going to be crazy." Hannah sat in the claw foot bathtub late at night and said it aloud to see how the syllables would feel in her mouth. She found them almost comforting.

"Mom," said Ashley seriously one day when she came home from school. "Are there ghosts in our house?"

Ashley was eight. In the last month or so she'd undergone one of those growth spurts that so disorient parents. There were moments when Hannah barely recognized her.

"Why do you ask? Have you seen something?"

"All my friends say this is a haunted house. It *looks* like a haunted house."

Ashley was a poetic child, aware at a distressingly early age that frequently things are not what they seem. Knowing she wouldn't be reassured by a mother's simplistic protest that ghosts aren't real, Hannah explained matter-of-factly: "If a house is haunted, Ashley, it's only by the spirits of people who've lived there. Other people who've loved our house the way we do There's nothing to be afraid of in that."

Ashley's blue eyes widened with interest. "Oh, Mom, then do our spirits haunt this house, too?"

"I think so," Hannah told her. "In a way." Hannah suddenly felt distressed, wondering what it was she was teaching her child.

Perry was the only one of the family who hadn't immediately felt at home in the new house, who didn't seem to have a natural place here. Wonderful as the house was, there were a number of things to be done to it, and Hannah understood that most of that responsibility fell to Perry: He was the handyman. What she did not understand was his need to get everything done so quickly, even at the expense of his painting. Nearly every waking moment he was doing something to the house. Often he didn't come when she called him for meals, and she was afraid to call him twice, though having the family scattered at mealtime felt to her like a potentially fatal flaw.

"I don't know what it is," he told her, "but I just can't do the work until things feel right around here, and they don't feel right just yet."

Hannah worried. Always before, he'd been able to paint even at the most awkward times. When they went on vacation, even on overnight trips, Perry took an easel and paints along and worked, sometimes until dawn if he felt particularly inspired. Hannah had not been jealous; to deny the need to paint would be to deny Perry himself. Now it was as if something had altered Perry's personality, and she was afraid she didn't know him anymore.

He erected all the bookcases, replaced the broken windows, reattached separating wallpaper. She appreciated all that. His artist's hands also were remarkably skilled at manual labor. But then he started making "improvements." He decided to finish their enormous attic. "For guest rooms," he explained, "and you may want your own office someday." He repainted both stairwells. Suddenly one day he decided to add a redwood deck on the south side of the house.

"See how much better the house looks," he said. "It'll be happier this way."

44

"It?"

"Sure. The house needs things." She desperately wished he would smile. He used to give her a playful smile when he talked like this. "Just as you and I need things."

"But what do you need right *now*, Perry? Your painting . . ."

He cut her off with a wave of his hand. "I'm doing fine. Just let me finish a few more things around here."

One day when Hannah came home from work she found him up on a ladder repainting the eaves a glossy black.

"Why are you doing that now? Can't it wait till summer?"

"It has to be done sometime," he said between clenched teeth. Hannah realized she was afraid to talk to him; he'd seemed to be angry with her all the time lately. But she wanted to make him stop; she wanted him to be happy.

"I really don't mind if you'd like to do that later, Perry. I don't think it's a high priority."

He jerked his head around so suddenly she was terrified he'd fall. The ladder rocked, and he grabbed at the soffit. She saw that his feet were on the step above the little sign that said: DANGER: DO NOT STAND ABOVE THIS STEP. She wanted to make him stop, but he was glaring at her, and she backed off.

Perry had always been terrified of heights. She didn't understand.

Every time they had an argument Hannah waited for Perry to say, "I don't love you," or "I'm leaving." He never did. He said he never would.

She woke up in the middle of the night. She felt around the edges of their bed in the darkness. Alone. She got up quickly and almost stumbled out the door. "Perry," she whispered. She could hear Ashley snoring lightly from across the hall. It was pitch-dark in the hallway; there wasn't a light fixture there, and Hannah was afraid that Ashley would tumble down the stairs. But she was more afraid of asking Perry to do something else to the house.

45

The odd narrowness of the second-floor windows and the thick, lens-like ornamental panes did strange things to the light from the streetlamps. The shadow of her flowing gown rippled the flocked wallpaper, as if she were passing through a distortion in the architecture of the house. "Perry." The whisper would not carry.

Every old house has noises—in their previous home they could hear almost everything that happened anywhere in the house—but this one seemed to have far fewer than most. There was a hush in this house. There was the sound of the huge gas-forced-air furnace coming on, and the pipes creaking as the dust inside them slowly heated up. But nothing else. She couldn't even hear her own footsteps because of the thick carpeting in the hallway. Sound did not carry in the house, and she had liked that. Even the real estate agent had commented on it.

But now that feature disturbed her. As if the house were suppressing even the smallest of disturbances. Hannah didn't think she liked that very much, the house holding things down, muffling her family. She wanted to know where Perry was right now. And this house wouldn't let her hear him.

When she reached the end of the hall, she saw the sliver of light under Perry's studio door. He hadn't been in there since they'd moved. He hadn't even made the improvements he needed in order to paint. The light was inadequate, there was only one outlet, and he hadn't yet built the cabinet for storing his paints. When she'd told him she thought he should make the studio his first priority, he'd just shrugged it off. "I'll get to it," he said. They'd been using it as a storage room; boxes were stacked shoulder-high.

When she opened the door he was sitting before his easel, jammed between walls of boxes. She felt a momentary elation, until she noticed that he was cutting long slits in the canvas with a utility knife.

"Perry?"

He stared at the canvas, jabbing at it playfully with the knife.

46

She came to his side. From what she could see between the numerous vertical tears and holes he had made, it was a dark, smudged canvas, with a streak of red near the middle. Incredibly amateurish; Hannah had never known him to paint so badly.

"Perry, what are you doing?"

He looked at her. She was sure he hadn't had those lines in his face before. "Playing. Just playing." He looked at the knife. "You know ... I want to paint, Hannah. I *need* to paint."

"I know." She touched his shoulders. They were trembling.

"But I can't. Something's not right, and I don't know what it is. I do everything I can think of, but I can't seem to make it right. *I can't paint*, Hannah."

"It's just a bad spell. It'll get better. You'll see. You paint very well, you *know* that."

"It's never been this bad." He looked back up at her. "Sometimes you want something so bad you poison it. It's like you haunt it, drive it crazy, make it something cheap and negative, and it's never the same again. I'm . . ." He looked down at his hands, the hands that Hannah so dearly loved. He was holding the knife. For a moment she was afraid he might cut those, too. "I'm not making any sense."

Hannah looked around at the shabby room, dim and filled with boxes, and tried to imagine the rest of the house beyond it, her wonderful dream house. No clear images came. She rubbed Perry's shoulders. "No, you make perfect sense," she finally said. And wondered wearily what they were talking about.

Every night Hannah came home from work exhausted from the senseless task of trying to make sense out of things. The house welcomed her, and her relief at coming home to it approached a lover's passion. The longer she lived there the better she came to understand its little idiosyncrasies: The front gate opened easily now to let her in, but stuck the other way as if reluctant to let her out. She didn't dare mention it to Perry. He would fix it, and she didn't want him to. She was beginning to think they shouldn't be imposing their will on this house.

Ashley had become an obsessive housekeeper. She was forever polishing the wooden floors, vacuuming the red-carpeted stairs, scurrying to pick up the smallest bit of litter in the yard. They'd figured out that her room, fittingly—the small back bedroom at the top of the narrow winding stairs that the Realtor had called "the servants' stairway"—had probably been the maid's room.

When Hannah caught her in the midst of a flurry of housekeeping and pulled her into her lap, Ashley wouldn't look at her. She fidgeted, played with her hair, even struggled to get down. That wasn't like her. It worried Hannah, made her angry, and she pressed. "Ashley, what's all this about? You've been acting strange since we moved. Don't you like our new house?"

Ashley's eyes widened in surprise. Seen from the side, they seemed to bulge a little. "I *love* our house!" she protested. "I love it just the way it is!"

"Then what's going on?"

"Nothing."

"Ashley." Hannah felt a sudden flash of anger, almost rage. Her hands tightened around the child's upper arms until she was sure it hurt, but Ashley didn't flinch, and she, to her own dismay, didn't loosen her grip. Instead she shook the girl, until Ashley's small head lolled. *"Tell me what's wrong."*

Abruptly Ashley turned to her and cried, "Mommy, our house is haunted and I can't find the ghosts!"

Hannah caught her breath. In that split second of laxness her daughter slid out of her lap and ran hysterically up the steps, slamming the door to her room. It was a very muffled sound, without echoes.

"I'll bet there's a secret passageway somewhere in this house," the Realtor had told them. At the time, knowing it was part of the sales pitch and completely unnecessary, Hannah hadn't taken it seri-

48

ously. But there were signs. The house had been remodeled many times—Perry discovered the evidence everywhere. Too many times to suit Hannah.

Beside the basement stairs was a cubbyhole that extended three feet back under the foundation for no apparent reason and then just stopped. In a dark recessed corner of the laundry room Perry had come upon a thin false wall with a tall, empty space behind it.

Under the flowered rug in Ashley's room was a sealed trap-door. Its edges were so neatly nailed and painted that it was almost indiscernible, but Ashley had discovered it and hadn't told anybody until Hannah noticed the uneven way she'd replaced the rug. Even then she'd lied, insisting fearfully that she knew nothing about it. Finally Hannah—who abhorred physical violence and had never used it with her child—spanked her, and then Ashley confessed. "I was looking for the ghosts!" she sobbed. "I thought maybe the ghosts lived down there!"

Frustrated, guilt-ridden, Hannah had shouted at her: "Now you listen to me! There's no such thing as ghosts!" But Ashley, of course, did not believe her, and would not take comfort in her arms.

She'd hardly seen Perry for several days. He was up before she was, off somewhere making God knew what alterations to their house. And he was up long after her, working at this or that. She never could figure out exactly what, and was afraid to ask. He made almost no noise, no more than the noises the house might normally make by itself: the creakings, the tiny scrapes, the soft and distant thuds, the resettlings. She sat up in bed sometimes, late into the night, listening for him, trying to distinguish his sounds from the house sounds. Sometimes she'd wake up suddenly in the middle of the night, as if something had awakened her, and find him missing from the bed. Then she'd try to hear the sound that had awakened her from sleep, the sound that might have been him working in the house somewhere, changing their house, altering it until it no longer resembled the house she had coveted so long, her dream house. But that telling sound was no longer present. It had disappeared, just as Perry had seemed to disappear, somewhere into the too-vast shadowed corners of the house.

When Perry did come down for meals, he came reluctantly, obviously displeased by the interruption. He'd serve himself in silence and then stare glumly at his food. His agent had called three times asking about commissioned works. Hannah had taken the calls because she couldn't find Perry in the house. The first time, she spoke to him about it, but he yelled at her to mind her own business, and after that she left him notes, which he did not acknowledge.

Now she could hear Perry coming down the main staircase for dinner, almost half an hour after everyone else had sat down. The third message from his agent was by the telephone in the hall. She glanced at Ashley, who looked tense and drawn, jabbing at her food with a fork that trembled visibly. The child knew everything. Hannah's heart went out to her. It was all too much. This life wasn't safe enough for her little girl, and she couldn't make it better.

Something slammed into the wall out in the hall. Ashley jumped as if struck, crying. A face so pale Hannah barely recognized it appeared at the dining room door. The eyes were pinkish, the hair dark and flat against the skull-darker than it should have been, as if filthy with the dust of ages.

"I can't eat today, Hannah," Perry said.

"Don't worry about your agent," Hannah began. "I'll—"

"You won't do anything," he said coldly. "I just can't eat today!"

There was almost a growl in his voice. Hannah looked immediately at Ashley, who was sobbing now. And suddenly Hannah felt an uncontrollable anger as well. "Don't do it, Perry. Not *now!*"

"I've got work!"

"You have to eat! *Look at you!*"

Hannah saw Perry draw back his fist and thought he was going to strike her for the first time. He was going to beat her, maybe go on beating her until he had killed her. Perry, who had been visibly shaken when Ashley had had a mere touch of fever.

But the fist struck the dining room wall instead, several times, sending plaster and torn wallpaper cascading to the floor. Hannah thought the fist seemed to float in the air by itself, as if it had nothing to do with Perry. She felt drunk or drugged. She wondered if she might be hallucinating.

Ashley was on her feet, screaming. If it had not taken Hannah a few moments to grasp what was happening, she might have taken her beautiful little girl, her dream child, into her arms right then, comforted her, calmed her down, made her safe again. Stopped the worst from happening.

Ashley was hysterical. "You've hurt the house! First you changed it so it's not the same anymore! Now you've *hurt* it!"

"Ashley, honey . . ." Hannah felt herself pull out of the chair.

"You've done it, too! You've *poisoned* things, Mommy!"

Hannah stopped, rigid. Her hand was out to her daughter, but Ashley was already running toward the stairs. Hannah glanced at Perry—something had broken in his face, and he was looking at her, and she knew that her husband was back with them for a time.

But what about Ashley?

"Ashley! Darling, it's all right now!"

But Ashley didn't answer. Perry looked panic-stricken. "Listen!" he said.

Door after door closed upstairs, one after another as if following the progression of Ashley's flight, her escape into the safety of the house. Finally the slamming stopped, but not before Hannah realized that there had been far more slams than there were doors in the house.

She couldn't find Ashley. She wandered through the house day after day, like a wraith herself, looking in all the hidden places she knew, trying to imagine if there were more. Perry was desperate, and blaming himself the way the old Perry would have, tearing out all his improvements, trying to find the extra doors they had both heard that day. He was convinced he had accidentally covered some of them up in his remodeling, and yet Ashley had still found a way through to the original house.

Hannah lifted the rug in the child's room and dug at the edges of the old trapdoor with a putty knife and a screwdriver, but it was still wedged tight. She went outside, into the gray night air of the city that was never still, and called her daughter's name. Her voice echoed against the walls of the house and stopped.

Sometimes at night Hannah would awaken, and again Perry would be gone from their bed. But now she knew he was busy searching, and she felt guilty because she had taken a rest. She could hear him walking through the rooms, pounding on the walls, looking for hollow places, whispering his daughter's name. She could hear everything now.

"Give my baby back to me," she whispered, but the house refused to answer.

Perry thought the mirror on the bathroom wall might hide a passageway, so together they spent hours trying to remove it. The house gripped it tightly as if it were part of its own skin. At last they collapsed into each other's arms, crying softly, staring into the mirror from the floor. Hannah thought their images in the mirror were too faded and pale to be real. Two malevolent spirits haunting this wonderful old house, haunting the little girl who lived here.

The sounds rose and fell outside the bathroom door. Hannah could not distinguish individual strains in the tide. She listened for a very long time.

"I'm going to be crazy now," she whispered to the house. And whispered it through the rooms for years.

But sometimes it grew quiet and there were other sounds, soft footsteps and a child's laughter, the sound of someone happy in her house of dreams.

52

KITE

"IMAGINE," said Stuart's new friend again.

But Stuart didn't have to imagine. He was sure the dragon was real now. It sliced through the air, leaving a shimmer of brown and gray in the bright blue sky. Its tail of torn black diamonds sailed high above his head, then dipped playfully until it almost touched his hair. It was a terrible, wonderful thing. The dragon flew as if he wasn't even holding onto its string.

"*Imagine*, Stuart. Show me what you can do." His friend wasn't watching the dragonkite. He was watching Stuart. He'd been watching Stuart ever since they'd met a few weeks ago, in the woods nobody had told Stuart existed, right at the boundary of the compound, farther away from home than he or any of the other children was ever allowed to go.

"You have everything you need right here," the grownups told them. Or, sometimes, "We need you to stay close to home." Stuart didn't understand. It often seemed to him that grownups were not the same species as children. He'd never, of course, seen a child grow up into an adult; now that they were all eleven, he still couldn't imagine it.

The dragon unfolded its black wings to hug and trap the wind. Stuart didn't think he'd made it do that. Its long tail swayed elegantly back and forth, stroking the wind, turning the wind cold and almost visible.

Stuart thought nervously of his mother. Her songs to him were about rainbows and flowers and fuzzy little creatures who would do anything for you—be your pet, mascot, protector, friend—as long as you thought well of them. His mother wouldn't like the dragonkite.

She wouldn't like this new friend of his, either. "What's your name?" Stuart had asked after they'd walked a short distance into the woods. "My name's Stuart. What do I call you?"

The small, thin man—not much bigger than the children but considerably older, although younger than any of the parents—had smiled, showing teeth of many colors; some of the front pointy ones were black, making Stuart look away. He'd said a word that Stuart had never heard before. Stuart had frowned, asked him to say it again.

"Eliahedron," he'd said, or something like that.

Stuart found he couldn't hold a picture of the name in his mind, and when he was away from Eliahedron he wasn't even really sure what the man looked like or why he was his friend. It was the first time in his life he could remember that happening; everything else was much more real in his mind than anywhere else.

The dragon puffed and spun and turned itself inside out. It became some other thing then, but was still a dragon, too, and still a kite. Stuart held on tight to the string because that's what you were supposed to do with kites, but he wasn't entirely sure that the string cutting across his palms had anything to do with the giant creature soaring and gnashing its teeth.

"That's good," Eliahedron said, watching him. "You're good at this, Stuart. The best I've seen." Stuart smiled.

He'd have to go home soon; it was getting late. His mother would

54

already be worried, and he'd be in trouble if he wasn't inside by the time his father got home from work. Children were allowed a few minutes of twilight sometimes, but none of them had ever seen real night. The evening routine was much the same when Stuart spent the night at a friend's house as at his own. Before sundown they were fed dinner, and then the parents talked to them quietly about the day, while outside the kitchen window the sky took on more and more of the dusty opaque color of smoke.

Some parents, Stuart had observed, were better at this part than at others. His mother was very good. She talked to him soothingly about how to think about what had happened today and how to imagine what was going to happen tomorrow. Then she popped his pill into his mouth—cherry, raspberry, apple—and, while it was taking effect, sang to him. Not all parents sang. His mother's songs were about light and color and uncomplicated love.

It never took very long for him to fall asleep, and when he awoke it was always morning. Even lately, when he'd been dreaming about dark flying things with teeth and tails, he never said so in the face of the bright morning sunshine and his mother's bright morning songs.

His father wasn't home very much these days, but if he was Stuart wouldn't even get the singing and the gentle talking after dinner. He'd taste the pill in his milk—as if his father thought he might not take it otherwise—and he wouldn't even get to see the sky turn gray, let alone black. He'd have to dream it, or imagine it for himself.

Just as, he allowed himself to admit for the first time, he had started to imagine the night. And other bad things without names. And dragons.

Stuart sighed, and must have tugged at the kite string, for the dragon swooped invitingly down at him. Its fanged mouth—a red-lined slit in the long thin black muzzle—was open and curved up as if it were hideously grinning. He reached with his free hand for one of its wings, but it bobbed and backed away out of his reach.

The wind swelled to fill the kite, opening it farther and farther. The kite changed shapes like the clouds in the sky, but these shapes, he knew, were dark, evil. Guiltily, he knew many of their names, although he'd never seen any of them outside the books he kept hidden from his parents. Long shiny black sides, scaled like a snake's. Wings like a huge bat's; he'd read that bats were blind but could always find you, that their wings were pronged and sticky and got tangled in your hair. Many legs like a spider's, spinning a mysterious web of poison.

It occurred to Stuart that Eliahedron would know about snakes and bats and spiders, that probably he'd seen the real things, that maybe he'd know names for other creatures the kite was turning into. He glanced over at his new friend, and realized with a start how low the sun was, how gray and thick the sky. He had to be getting home. The dragon—snake, bat, spider, nameless creature with teeth and claws and spinning dark thoughts—rose through the evening sky, and Stuart recklessly tried to imagine himself flying with it, filling with wind and excitement, soaring, becoming more than he'd ever been before.

"Stuart!"

His mother's voice on the belt unit was soft, but insistent. The sky above the dragon was turning dark and smoky in earnest now. If he waited much longer, his mother and maybe his father would come looking for him, and then they'd see the dragon, and then they'd *know*. "I gotta go," he said to Eliahedron.

His new friend nodded. When he moved his head like that, colors rippled and black sparks flew. Stuart stared, then turned his gaze back to the dragonkite. Reluctantly, but with concentrated effort, he imagined it back into the kite his parents had given him, Snake scales elongated, softened, became yellow and pink feathers. The head grew rounder; the jagged snout became a bright blue beak. The wings fluttered, turned fluffy and rainbow-hued. The wind stilled, and the bright bird-of-paradise drifted to settle companionably at Stuart's feet.

Eliahedron clapped his hands and said softly, "Bravo!"

"I gotta go." Stuart gathered up the pretty kite, folded it into its carrying pouch, and turned to leave.

"I'll walk you home," Eliahedron said, catching up to him.

Stuart didn't know what to say, and he didn't have time to think about it. He raised a hand in hasty acquiescence, and together they headed across the brilliant green park—between the rose garden and the lilac bushes, both in full bloom—toward Stuart's home.

In the rose-colored house where Stuart lived, his mother waited anxiously at the wide picture window in the kitchen, adjusting the range controls to keep her son in focus as he hurried down the long hill toward home. Someone else was with him, a small thin figure she didn't recognize at this distance, and she didn't like that. But the impossible green of the grass, the very bright hues of the flowers calmed her somewhat, and thinking how Stuart would picture the house in his mind before he got here: white Colonial columns accenting the wraparound porch, lacy Victorian gingerbread at the peaks and eaves, delicately curved polycomposites outlining doors and windows. It was easily the nicest house in the compound, the most finely imagined. She was very proud of her son.

The sky was in her viewer, too, lowering and darkening alarmingly. Stuart had gone farther than he was supposed to and was later getting home. Night would fall very soon; they'd have to eat dinner the minute Stuart walked in the door, and there'd be precious little time for talking and singing. Fortunately, she and some of the other parents had been discussing just the other day that the children didn't seem to need so much of that now that they were older, more independent, surer of themselves and their abilities.

Across the street, kitchen lights in the long, low, crystal-white Sanchez house and in the Bartholomews' peach-colored dome had been on for some time, and she'd seen Abby Sanchez and Michael Bartholomew come home almost an hour ago. The huge yellow flowers on Abby's mother's apron and the red ones on the one Michael's father wore had glowed cheerfully in the sun, which had still been high and bright. The flowers on Stuart's mother's apron were shades of purple, his gift to her because, when the aprons suddenly became so popular, she'd mentioned to him that her great-grandmother used to wear one like them, made, however, of polyester and cotton.

All over the compound, good parents in bright flowered aprons had already gathered their children inside, safely beating the darkness. Stuart's mother bit her lip. She shouldn't have let him stay out so long, wander so far; she should have made him come home. He loved the park, would play there all day every day if she'd let him; whenever she watched him race up over the brow of the hill and disappear out of her sight, she was profoundly uneasy, for the park was a place utterly beyond her imagination.

Hearing the heavy basement door slide open, she knew that her husband was home. She sighed in relief—he was later than usual, too—and consternation—he'd be angry to discover that Stuart wasn't home yet and, if he'd been just a few minutes later himself, he'd never have known.

She stood with her fists in the apron pockets, debating. She should go downstairs to welcome her husband home, to help him change, but if they were both in the basement when Stuart came home he'd want to come down, too, and they couldn't, of course, have that. So she contented herself with listening to her husband's movements, cataloguing them to herself.

Now he was taking off his weapons, armor, mask; she heard the storage compartment behind the basement door whisper open and then shut again, heard the tiny pop as it sealed. Now he'd be unfastening his uniform and stepping out of it; uncounted times she'd watched it pool around his bare ankles like melted skin, watched him scoop it up distastefully and deposit it into the chute that led somewhere deeper than their basement—neither of them had any idea where. Now the shower came on; she could hear the hum. Although he was disinfected before he left work, he always stayed in the shower longer than he needed to, far longer than was recommended, letting the rays and the vibrations massage his skin until it felt loose on the bone, before finally getting into the soft, loose clothing she had ready for him on the bench.

As he came up the stairs now, she heard him sniffing. She frowned; it was an irritating, unsettling habit, this constant sniffing for the odor that he said would not go away.

She turned back to the window as he came into the room. The more distant window of the sky was filled with thick gray-black, like the smoke she knew he'd been in all day. "He's not home yet?" She clearly heard the criticism in his voice.

She didn't turn around. "Almost. He's just across the street. He took his kite to the park again."

"His kite? I didn't think he much liked it when we gave it to him."

"I know, but lately he's been taking it out almost every day. He comes home for lunch and then goes right back out again."

"What about the other children?" She heard him rubbing his palms up and down the soft fabric of his pants, as if trying to get something off his hands. Another habit he'd developed lately.

"He doesn't play with the other children anymore."

"Not at all?"

"Very little."

He leaned past her. "Who's that with him?"

"I don't know. I can't quite tell. One of the children from the other side of the compound. Maybe he's just developed new friendships."

"Dressed in *black*?"

She waved at the window as if at the coming night. "Hush now. Here he comes. We don't want him to hear." She turned and looked at him, put her hands on his shoulders, lightly kissed him. "Stop imagining things. You might imagine the worst."

He leaned his forehead against her. He was always very tired when he got home from work, and tonight he seemed on the edge of exhaustion. "He imagines better than the rest of us. Better even than the other children."

"Well, of course. We've always known that. What are you trying to say?"

He shrugged and pulled away from her as Stuart came in the front door. The window had faded completely to a dull gray that would very soon be black. "Let's just eat and get him to bed. As soon as we can."

Stuart dreamed, as he'd done every night of his life. He always remembered his dreams, of course, and deliberately replayed them in his mind, as he'd been taught, while he awoke into the sunny mornings. All the children did that, some better than others.

Their dreams were of the same piece, the same every night and the same as each others'. First there was always the sky, the hard line of it, the bubble that contained everything they knew and loved, the bell whose model sat at the front of every classroom and whose likeness hung on the wall of every kitchen so that parents and teachers could emphasize a hundred times a day in a hundred ways how vital a shape it was to them all. Every morning all the children, in concert and in their own minds, re-created the sky, refined and strengthened it, and then the world inside it. Every morning when they awoke it was all really there, and they all lay until their breakfasts were ready, imagining it all wakefully, fixing it in place.

Stuart and the others knew some of the story; the older they got, the more they were taught, in careful increments, at home and at school. The children were capable of imagining things that their parents couldn't, because of something that had been done to them before they were born—before they were conceived, Stuart guessed, although it embarrassed him to think about that. "A great experiment," some grownups called it; "the two years of hope."

Stuart's father sometimes referred to it simply as "the salvation." For a long time Stuart hadn't known what that meant, but he was beginning to understand it now and it made him nervous, thinking about his part in it.

Stuart listened sleepily to his father getting ready for work, as he did every morning, and incorporated the familiar sounds into his imaginings. His father leaving for work was part of the pleasant order of his life and the life of the compound.

Soon it would be time for him to get up, dress in his soft, bright, very clean clothes, and have breakfast with his mother, who would sing and touch his hair. Then he would go to the park. He thought of the kite, red and blue and feathery in its pouch on the shelves across the room, and did not think beyond that. He thought of the brilliant green of the park, the smell of the sunshine, the feel of the ground springy under his feet, and did not think of Eliahedron except to put him out of his mind.

"I'm a soldier." His father was talking to his mother, who must already know that. Stuart hadn't known that. He listened. "I imagine war. That's my job and I'm good at it. I imagine faces exploding, cities collapsing, skin burning blue-hot, trees charring from the inside out."

"Oh, honey." If she was trying to make him feel better, Stuart wondered, why didn't she just sing? Somewhat petulantly, he started to imagine it, but stopped when she went on. "You are good at your work, and it's nothing to be ashamed of. You keep the war away from us, you keep it outside the bell. If the soldiers did less, then what would happen to us? That's important work."

"It's primitive work. It's pushing away, and shouting away, and thrusting and striking and gnashing and killing—it's what I think about each day, what I fill those waking dreams I have at the control center with. Dreams human beings have been having since the apes, no better."

"It's what you have to do. You have no choice, if we're to live as we do."

"There's more to it than that. The truth is, I—enjoy isn't the right word. I need it. I'm addicted to it. The energy of it, the color. The battles take me out of myself somehow, elevate me to a higher plane. They excite me."

Hearing that, Stuart found himself imagining the dragonkite, huge and black because he imagined it that way, cutting frighteningly through the sky because he imagined it that way, threatening either to pull the kite string out of his hands or to yank him up into the sky himself.

"But," his father went on, "I never can imagine the compound. The living trees, those enormous bright flowers the kids like so much, this house. No matter how hard I try, I can't imagine *this place*. So every time I come home, it's a revelation to me."

Now his mother sounded impatient. She didn't talk like this very often, and he listened carefully. "But you know that. We've all always known that. That's what the compound is all about, have you forgotten? That's why Stuart is who he is."

Killing. Fire. Smoke. *Dragons*. If Stuart's parents found out that now he had those bad images in his mind, too, they'd try to take them away from him.

Dutifully, he lay in bed a while longer and imagined, as all the other children all around the compound were doing. The pretty houses, the loving families, the aprons with flowers, the smooth blue sky. But he was bored. It all seemed so *ordinary*, so easy and plain. His thoughts kept sneaking off to his father's war, and to the dragonkite,

62

and to his new friend Eliahedron who might already be waiting for him in the park.

"Did you know," Eliahedron asked him, "that dreams sometimes used to upset their dreamers? That dreams used to sometimes be about bizarre things that people were afraid to think about while they were awake?"

Stuart kept his attention on the dragonkite, black and scary and beautiful against the still blue sky. The kite was flying so high and fast now that he thought it might be bumping against the bell, scratching it, tearing holes with the sharp tips of its wings. He didn't reel it in, although he was confident that he could if he wanted to.

He wouldn't answer Eliahedron, either. Everybody knew that it was dangerous to talk about, or, worse, to think about anything bad.

"What kind of things?"

At first, Stuart thought that Eliahedron was talking to himself, had asked himself the question. Then he had to admit that his own mouth had moved, that the voice asking the question—asking it again—was his.

"What things?"

"War," came the prompt reply.

At first Stuart thought that he himself had somehow given the answer, that now he was talking to himself. In fact, he did seem to feel the vibrations of the forbidden words in his own throat as Eliahedron uttered them.

"Violence. Cruelty. Death."

"If they dreamed things like that," he demanded, not sure he should believe any of this, "then how did they make the world?"

"The world had bad things in it. As worlds must."

"And if they dreamed things like that, what did they imagine?"

"All sorts of things. Evil things. Boring things. A few were able to imagine peace. And love. And beauty. Other choices, to go beyond the bad. But that's always been hard, and in order to do it they had to use everything."

"Everything?" Stuart repeated in a small voice.

"Imagine, Stuart," Eliahedron urged softly.

Suddenly the dragonkite leaped. The string stretched taut and cut into Stuart's hands. Then it relaxed, and the kite floated rapidly downward. Stuart rewound the string frantically, afraid it would tangle, and at the same time found the exact spot in the sky where the kite had been. There was a slit, a tiny break in the sky. Already, gray-black smoke was seeping in.

"Stuart," Eliahedron murmured again from somewhere behind him. "Imagine."

"I can't!"

"You're talented. You're the best I've ever seen. You can."

"Leave me alone!" Stuart whirled to face this strange man and found that he had turned into other, terrible and enchanting things. A demon with a bloody mouth. A devil with horns.

"A demon is a god unrecognized," Eliahedron whispered. "War is peace unimagined."

Stuart wrenched his frightened gaze away from the leering, muttering Eliahedron in his many guises, but couldn't get the creature completely out of his line of vision. Everywhere he looked, a piece of Eliahedron was there, both obscuring Stuart's world and highlighting it.

Terrified, he looked for the kite. He couldn't find it; he thought he'd lost it. The smoke drifting across the sky disoriented him as he squinted, tipped his head, turned from side to side. Eliahedron, some part or version of Eliahedron, was always there in his peripheral vision, confusing him. He heard distant sounds that he'd never heard before but recognized at once—sobbing, shrieking, Eliahedron's imprecations which Stuart could have been making himself. A coppery odor filled his nostrils, and then his mouth was coated with it. He found it oddly stirring.

64

The smoke made huge talons and crooked fingers across the sky. Or holes, he thought dazedly; maybe they were holes. He glimpsed twisted spires of blue metal from exploded machinery, flying pieces of pavement, balls and bubbles and bells of fire.

He looked away, looked back. The sky was flying apart before his eyes.

Finally he found the kite, draped over a silver maple tree as if a piece of the sky had, indeed, charred and fallen. Afraid to move, he stood where he was and tugged gingerly on the string, but the kite was stuck, tangled among the leaves and branches of the pretty little tree.

Stuart took a step forward and jerked on the kite string. The kite just settled more securely over the tree, wings covering it nearly to the roots, snout gaping as if hungry for more.

He ran to the tree and thrust his hands up and under the dragon. Finding its wing slimy, warm, and moving as if with breath, he snatched his hands back, repulsed by its touch, even though he knew it was part of himself.

Then Eliahedron's gravelly voice sounded in his ear. No, he realized. It was in his head, his throat, his heart. "Imagine, Stuart! Don't stop now!"

The dragonkite lifted its wing and pulled Stuart under it. He gasped and cried out. The ragged wing of his dragon tented over him like another sky; from so close under it he could see that all the colors it had drawn into itself to make black were still distinguishable, scarlet and cerulean and royal purple and silver, pulsing at his fingertips and behind his eyes.

Eliahedron's voice skittered around inside this new bell, now close on his left, now more distant on his right, now seeping like smoke through rents in the kitewing, now coursing like blood just under the surface of his skin.

Stuart threw his arms around the vibrating trunk of the tree. He shut his eyes tight and imagined.

Almost at once, the dragon-wing sky over him softened and

shrank. Colors faded, became ordinary: red, yellow, blue feathers tousled his hair, brushed away his tears. For a fleeting moment his world looked familiar and lovely again from under the wing of the bird-of-paradise, but the wings kept retracting until they had folded themselves neatly and Stuart could lift the pretty little kite up out of the tree. The tree was dead.

Tucking his toy under his arm, Stuart started for home. He thought Eliahedron was with him, but when he looked he was alone. He thought Eliahedron was chasing him, but when he risked glancing over his shoulder he saw only Abby Sanchez, yelling his name in a loud scared voice, and Michael Bartholomew, crying. There were dark circles under their eyes, and their hands were over their ears, their mouths; as Stuart hurried past them, he thought they looked more than just scared. They looked ashamed. They were hurrying, too, trying to keep up with him, and all along the path bushes exploded into flames and dark strange shapes flew.

Stuart ran faster, as fast as he could. As he raced down the last hill toward his home, he stumbled over something in the grass.

It was a body. An old man, or maybe an old woman. Somebody Stuart had never seen before.

He stopped, crouched, peered at the body, poked it with one forefinger. The mouth was open and empty of teeth. The eyes were closed. Confusedly, Stuart wondered how anybody could sleep through all this noise.

Then he saw the smoke stains, and the slits in the old man's or old woman's body. They looked like the rips his dragonkite had made in the surface of the sky. Soft things peeked out of the slits. Suddenly Stuart simply could not imagine it, and he pulled away, stood up, started again toward home.

All around him, bodies were raining from the smoky holes in the sky, drumming against the grassy slope, crashing onto the trees, breaking through the pastel roofs of the houses. He could hardly

66

see. He barely avoided the falling bodies. The sky was darkening now, as if for night, and Stuart had to get home.

Stuart's parents were waiting for him in the front yard. He could tell by their faces, by the way they waved their arms, by the terrible sound of their voices crying his name that he had done something wrong. That the coming-apart of his world and their world was his fault. He was sorry. He was scared. But he was also more excited than he'd ever been in his life.

His father grabbed him and half-pushed, half-carried him into the house. "What were you doing?" his father was yelling, holding him close and then pushing him away hard. "You'll let everything in!"

"Why didn't you tell us?" Stuart yelled back.

His mother was singing to him, reaching under his father's arms to stroke his hair. Her own sad face was wet with tears.

His father thrust him into his mother's arms. He was too big for her and by now he was struggling, but she was strong and she held on. "Get him to bed!" his father shouted, turning to punch at the control pad. The door locked just as a rain of heavy blows pummeled the outer shell of the house. Stuart was worried; the shell had been designed to be attractive, but he had no idea whether it was strong. Through the screens, through his mother's hair falling across his face, he saw dark shadows, like pieces of a phantasmagoric kite tail, contorting, writhing, tearing apart.

Quickly, Stuart got ready for bed. He didn't entirely want to, but he didn't know what else to do. His mother sang to him the whole time, her voice straining, trying too hard, the cheerful songs nonsensical and off-key. She kept crying. Finally she gave him his pills—three of them this time—and almost with the same motion reached to tuck him in. He stowed the pills under his tongue. She didn't check. He pulled the covers up under his chin, smiled up at her, closed his eyes. When she kissed him, he felt the tears on his eyelids.

Outside he heard thunder and other bright noises. Deep inside his head he heard Eliahedron calling his name. Without opening his eyes, he set about imagining Eliahedron's face—multicolored, angled and planed in wondrous ways—into the darkness of his world, his house, his room, his mind.

"It's wonderful!" Eliahedron cried, and Stuart understood that it was. "Bravo, Stuart!"

Stuart shook his head furiously and imagined Eliahedron away. Then he got out of bed. Shakily he stood up and stared at his wall, thinking suddenly that he'd really been hearing Eliahedron's voice inside his head all his life. Until Eliahedron had taken form and become his friend, it had been a secret, dangerous voice telling him about all the things he wasn't supposed to know, reminding him every time he tried so hard to forget. The voice of a demon, he'd secretly thought, since he wasn't supposed to know anything about demons. The voice of a god, equally out of reach. One of his own many voices.

It took a very long time, but eventually Stuart imagined a tunnel through his wall, through the outer shell, into the dark and multicolored outside. The tunnel had demons and gods in it, but he knew they didn't mean him any harm. Their hands were all Eliahedron's hands as they reached out to help him, and he recognized all their voices as beacons telling him the way.

They should have told us, Stuart kept thinking as he made his way through the compound that was unraveling into the night.

He'd thought, when he'd dared to think about it at all, that night would be one blackness, one continuous absence of light and color. But this night land had shades and textures, places where the darkness seemed thicker and deeper than others, stretches that felt more dangerous and more alluring than the rest.

And it wasn't still. It moaned and sighed and cried out—in pain, Stuart understood, and in ecstasy. He wasn't supposed to know either of those words, but he did, and he understood the ideas behind them, too. The night land shuddered and swayed with the passage of many feet, many wings.

Thousands of dragons filled the jagged sky; thousands more were plummeting in through the flaws in the heavens, which Stuart now couldn't see because of the dragons' wings and tails. Crimson dragon-mouths spat smoke and fire. Long crooked tails dragged the ground, making fissures across the once-perfect surfaces. Everywhere people ducked and screamed and rolled on the ground, but they couldn't get out of the dragons' path and so were torn apart.

"You didn't tell us!" Stuart wailed, desperately wondering if anyone was left to hear.

He knew dragons better than anybody; he knew that, once you'd seen a dragon and it had seen you, you couldn't escape. So he stood, finally, in one place, not knowing where he was because the whole compound was in rubble and the bell was torn away, and let the dragons come. Some of them were kites, and some were machines and not-machines, great strange objects that he had no names for. They swooped at him, threatening to lift him out of himself. They roared and sang.

Abby Sanchez came up beside him with her mouth wide open, keening or singing back to the sky full of dragons. Michael Bartholomew danced in an elaborate, exquisite, grotesque rhythm across the park, which had thrown itself up, turned itself inside out. Another boy whose face Stuart couldn't quite see came at them with a huge shiny gun, laughing and howling as if he didn't know who he was. Other children wandered out of their tidy little houses. They walked the broken paths of the compound with hungry eyes stretched open, as if filling them for the first time.

"You can imagine a kite as easily as a gun," Eliahedron said softly. "With all this, you can imagine peace as well as war. Not everybody can, Stuart, but you can. You're good. You're the best I've ever seen. Don't stop now."

Stuart was moving now, stumbling through the dreams of his elders: Pineapple beetles crawled over tortured bodies, splitting their shells and spilling out floods of rich yellow soup that absorbed the bodies a limb at a time. The many beaks of great green birds tore open the backs of the dead and extracted the spines, for use as combs to clean the blood out of their dazzling feathers. Hundreds of tiny rats' heads were tethered to luminous cords that guided them to anything still warm and breathing. Broad fishtails, equipped with insect eyes like sequins among the scales, swept and scraped the ground a layer at a time, exposing the newly-dead for quill-headed dogs to devour. Blind cats' skulls trotted the broken paths, now and then stopping to taste delicately of the smoked flesh before padding on.

These were his parents' dreams. They didn't have to be his. Stuart stopped and stood still again.

One by one, the other children joined him. Abby, still singing. Michael, still dancing. The boy with the enormous gun. A girl with a knife as big as she was, mirroring her and the others in its variegated blade. The children made a tight circle and held each other to watch the fecundity of their parents' imaginations play out around them.

Stuart spoke first. "Beautiful!"

"Wonderful," someone else said.

"But they stopped. They didn't go far enough," Stuart said, and his friends nodded, and they opened up their circle.

For a very long time the children of the compound walked the ravaged earth. They talked their parents' nightmares out of the smoky sky, out of dark feeding holes and armored nests. They laid their hands on hideous forms and made them their own.

"Wonderful, but wrong," they said.

By morning, a flock of new kites soared lazily through the opened and many-hued sky.

THE TENTH SCHOLAR

H E ANSWERED THE DOOR HIMSELF. I was disappointed that it wasn't his aide-de-camp; the term had always made me think of tents and marshmallows and songs around a fire and two weeks in the country, where I'd never been. "A woman," he said.

"Yeah," I said. "So?"

We looked at each other. I knew I couldn't let him stare me down; I had experience on the streets, and I'd thought about this a lot before I'd come here, practiced looking tougher than I really am. You had to keep a balance. I'd always had to do that. Out on the streets it was important to look tougher than you were, and talk dumber than you were. If you talked too smart, then people got it into their heads that you were all head and weak everywhere else. But with *him*, I knew I just had to look tough, but I couldn't let him think I was dumb. His eyes were green and he had really long white eyelashes. "A very young woman," he said.

"Not as young as you think," I shot back, but that wasn't true. I was sixteen and pregnant, and I looked like a twelve-year-old who hadn't lost her baby fat.

His thick white eyebrows rose a little, and he said, "Interesting." During the next months I would hear that comment from him countless times. It was the only compliment he ever paid any of us, and it always surprised me how often he used it, how many things he still genuinely found interesting, after all the years he'd lived and all the years he knew he still had coming.

"I saw your ad," I told him.

He nodded and stepped back, bowing slightly and making a welcoming gesture with one hand. I remember thinking that his hands were elegant, long and pale and thin, except that they were so hairy. "Come in, my dear."

"'My dear'?" I laughed. I'd figured he would talk like that, and I wanted him to know right away that it didn't impress me.

Except, of course, that it did. Not so much his fancy accent or old-fashioned language, but the way he noticed me, the fact that he really did seem to think it was interesting that I was there. That was new for me, and as soon as I got a little of it I wanted more. I went in, noticing the gold dragon under the gold cross on the door.

Against the bright, trendy pastels of this penthouse office suite, he looked like something out of a black-and-white movie. The only colors on him were his green eyes and the red of his mouth, so red I thought he might be wearing lipstick. He was dressed in crisp, creased black, although he wasn't wearing a cloak; I'd been expecting a cloak, and that threw me a little. His face and hands were so white that I wouldn't have thought anything could be whiter, but then I saw the tips of his teeth pushing out over the edge of his lower lip. His curly hair went past his shoulders—black, when I'd imagined it would be white—and his moustache was as white as his eyebrows, so that I could hardly see them across his skin.

"Sit down, my dear." When he soundlessly shut the door, it was as if we were the only two creatures in the world. "What can I do for you?"

"I'm answering your ad," I repeated stubbornly. I didn't like it when people made fun of me, and I heard mockery everywhere. I'd punched people out, scratched their green eyes, for less. "I'm applying for the school. The ad didn't say you needed an appointment."

I wished I could think of things to say that sounded more intelligent. People on the street were easy to impress; even Oliver didn't take much. Though at first I'd thought he would. But this guy would be a real challenge; I'd known that before I came. He'd be like my grandmother, only more so—able to see who you really were and what you really wanted when even you didn't know. I sat down on the gigantic couch that took up one whole wall of the room. The couch was that peculiar yellow-green color they call chartreuse, and the walls and carpet were mauve. Who'd have thought that mauve and chartreuse would go together? Who'd have expected this guy to be an interior decorator? But then, he'd already lived long enough to be anything he wanted.

The guy had *power*. Once you had power, nobody could hurt you. I'd learned that much on the streets. And before. Power might have kept my grandmother alive. It didn't really matter how you got it, because once you had it nobody much cared about the how. I'd been around the powerful people in my life—my mother, a social worker or two, PDs and DAs and juvenile court judges, Oliver. But they were little fish. They had power only in relation to utterly powerless people like me. This guy had real power, and he could teach me how to have it, too. So I could pass it on to my baby.

I shivered in appreciation, then stiffened my body to still it and hoped he hadn't noticed. He had, of course; I saw the amusement in his eyes.

My jeans were dirty and smelled of the streets. It pleased me to think I might be soiling the fancy upholstery. I squirmed on the couch, moved my butt around a lot, just to make sure.

"Pregnant," he observed. He was standing too close to me, and he was really tall. I hated it when people, especially men, towered over me like that; too many times, at home and in juvie and in foster homes and on the street, some guy had stood too close to me like that and had ended up fucking me over.

I wasn't about to let him know he was making me nervous; you didn't dare let them know. I yawned, hoping my breath smelled as bad as it tasted, and put my filthy tennis shoes up on the arm of his elegant sofa. "So," I demanded, looking up at him as insolently as I could, "what do I have to do?"

He sat down in the enormous armchair that faced the couch. He crossed his legs, meticulously adjusted his pant leg. He wasn't a very big man; he was as thin as anybody I'd ever met under a bridge or in a shelter, as if, like them, he was always hungry—though I doubted it was because he couldn't afford food. For some reason, I'd thought he'd be bigger. I wondered what Oliver, who thought he knew everything there was to know about him, would think of him in person. "I ain't smart enough to go to some hot-shit yuppie school," Oliver had sneered. "You're the schoolgirl. You go, and then you come back and tell us." But I was never going back. I hadn't loved Oliver; I just let him think I did. He wasn't very powerful; for awhile he could keep me safer than I could keep myself, but now I was ready for more.

There was a long silence. I noticed that I couldn't hear anything from the street or from the rest of the building, only his breathing and mine. Wondering about that, I pressed the back of my fist against the wall over my head; the wall was spongy and gave a little, like living tissue, and before I could stop myself I'd gasped and jerked my hand away.

He saw me do that, too, of course, and I knew he was keeping score. This was some creepy kind of exam. He sat there quietly with his thin white hands looking very thin and white against the wide chartreuse arms of the chair, and he looked at me calmly without saying anything. I was used to that. There was this chick in a doorway up across from Columbia who looked at you that way; you knew she saw everything about you and kept a list in her head, but I'd never heard her say anything, even the night she came after me with her nails and teeth and stole my sandwich—whole, still wrapped in wax paper—that I'd found on a table in a sidewalk cafe that lunch-time and been saving all day. The next day I went to her doorway and just sat on the stoop beside her and stared at her, to see what she'd do. She didn't do anything, so finally I gave up.

I didn't give up this time. I sat as quietly as he did and stared back at him. I didn't exactly look him in the eye; his eyes were too much for me. But I did stare at his face, and all of a sudden I was seeing a tiny drop of bright red—blood, I supposed—on the point of one of his teeth.

He spoke first, but not because I'd won anything. "What is your name?"

I couldn't think of any reason not to tell him. "Marie."

"And your surname?"

That was none of his business, and I wasn't part of that family anymore anyway. So I said, "Bathory," just to see what his reaction would be, sort of the way I'd sometimes shit on the sidewalk in front of some snooty restaurant.

He chuckled. He was laughing at me. "And why do you wish to attend the *scholomance*, Marie Bathory?"

I was ready for that one. I said what Oliver had told me to say, although I didn't always follow his orders no matter what he did to me. "Hey," I shrugged, "beats living on a heat grate, y'know?"

His face sharpened like a blade, and in one swift sharp motion he had stood up. "You are wasting my time."

I panicked. I'd overplayed the tough and ended up sounding stupid. As usual, Oliver didn't know what he was talking about. I told him, too soon and too eagerly, "When my grandmother died they drove a nail through her forehead."

"Interesting," he said, and I relaxed a little. "Why?"

I was confused by that, and my temper flared. I put my feet down on the thick carpet, leaned forward, even raised my voice. "What do you mean, why? Why do you think? They thought she was a vampire."

He nodded. "And was she?"

I started to give him some smart-ass answer, but then I was remembering my grandmother and having to fight back tears. She'd loved me. I remembered a lot of whippings, a few times locked in a dark rustling closet, but I'd deserved that. I also remembered feeling safe with her, and noticed, and understanding that my grandma was the most powerful person in the whole world and that if I was good and did what she told me I could grow up to be just like her.

But she died. She hadn't been powerful enough. Some lady in a shawl came and hammered a nail through her forehead. I remembered the shiny nail head among the soft wrinkles between her eyes. My father had pulled her yellow-white hair down low, trying to hide the nail, but he'd made no move to pull it out. That's how I knew she was really dead, and no one would ever love me again.

Sometimes, though, I looked at the New York City buildings I'd lived among all my life, and saw them the way she must have seen them when her own grandmother brought her here from Rumania. Mountains, they became, and the alleys crevasses, and lightning could be made to strike from the lake in Central Park or from the crowded ocean beaches as powerfully as from any isolated Carpathian pool deeper than a dream.

"Yeah, she was." I'd never said it out loud before, though I'd always secretly believed it. Foolishly, I added, "I miss her."

"Interesting. And your grandmother the vampire told you about the scholomance, did she?"

"No. Oliver did." That was a lie, partly. She'd told me a little—about the scholomance, about the tenth scholar, but when I kept asking her about them she'd shut up, as if she was sorry she'd told me anything at all. Then Oliver came along, and he told me more, and I wanted to be that tenth scholar, and would be, because I *had* to be for me and my baby.

He didn't ask who Oliver was. It wasn't as if he already knew; he just didn't care. So much for Oliver's power; I smiled to myself. When Oliver died, I wondered, would there be a shooting star? And would anybody notice it among all the city lights?

"Who is the father of your child?"

"I don't know." That was the truth, but I wouldn't have told him if I had known. On an impulse, watching his face, I added, "You can be if you want."

His face changed. Not much, but enough that I knew I'd scored a point. He smiled, showing more of his teeth under the moustache.

"Nobody gave my grandmother a candle while she was dying," I heard myself say. "So she died without light. She always said that was the worst thing that could happen to anybody, to die without light."

He understood what I meant better than I did. "And that is why you want to study at our school."

"I guess." The tenth scholar wouldn't die without a light, I was pretty sure of that. It was hard to believe, but maybe the tenth scholar wouldn't die at all.

He was moving around the room. Gliding, really; I half-expected him to vaporize at any second. I wondered if he really could do that, and if he could teach me; I wondered what I'd do if he left me, too. "Not a bad reason to apply," he said. "But you must understand that you will be expected to study diligently. To apply yourself."

"I'm not stupid," I said, feeling stupid.

"Only ten scholars are accepted into each class."

"I know. And one stays. As payment."

"Correct. So far, I see, you have done your homework."

"I'll be the one to stay," I said boldly.

"Ah, my dear, but I make that choice."

"You'll choose me."

He came too close to me again and peered down from his great height. The drop of blood was gone; his teeth gleamed. "Marie Bathory, do you know who I am?"

"Vlad Tepes," I said, giving the first name Oliver's broad Brooklyn "a" and pronouncing the last name "Teeps," the way Oliver did.

He exploded into laughter and I was mortified. "Tsepesh!" he exclaimed. "It is pronounced 'Tsepesh'!" I tried and failed to say it right. He bent like a huge shiny insect and took my face in his cold hands. "Marie. Say it. Vlad Tepes, the Impaler."

I could hardly breathe, but I managed to say, "Tepesh."

"Very good. Now say nosferatu."

That was easier. "Nosferatu," I gasped. His nails were digging into the soft flesh behind my ears.

Then his sharp cold face was only inches away from mine, and I thought he was going to kiss me or to sink his teeth into my neck. I would have been glad for either. He whispered "Dracule," and I repeated "Dracule," and then he let me go. My face was numb where he'd held me.

"Classes begin tomorrow," he said. "You will stay with me tonight, and you will be prepared."

Later that night he sent me down to the alley with his garbage, as he would so many other nights during my stay. I suppose this was meant to be part of my payment to him. He didn't trust the service the building provided, he said. They were lax and inefficient, he said. He said he wanted something more private.

That first night when I reached the alley I couldn't resist the temptation to peer into the thick, black plastic bag. The bag had been so heavy, I couldn't imagine what he'd thrown away.

It was a Rottweiler, its throat torn open sloppily, the edges of the wound frayed as if the killer had been starving, hadn't been able to wait to do it right.

Somehow, I would have thought him above all that. It embarrassed me. I closed the bag up quickly, and tried not to think about it after that. And I never told anyone.

78

I never thought I had much competition. Although Dracula would comment once in a while that he found us "interesting," individually or as a group, it didn't seem to me that we were an especially strong class, compared to those who must have gone before.

I was the only female, the only student under twenty-five, of course the only one pregnant, the only one who lived at the school. The others all came and went, and they actually seemed to have lives outside. I couldn't imagine any of them staying. I was so sure I had a lock on Tenth Scholar that I didn't worry much about what I'd do if he sent me away, where I'd go, how I'd ever live.

Some of my classmates I scarcely remember now, and wouldn't recognize on the street. Some of them, though, I remember. Andy, for instance, was an accomplished serial killer before classes ever started, and I'm sure he's still going strong. Although Dracula never made distinctions based on how we'd come to the school, we all guessed that Andy had been recruited, and he never did quite grasp what he was doing there, what was expected of him, what opportunities there were. I lost count of how many whores and street people he killed and dismembered; for one thing, it was more every time he talked about it. I used to sit in class and stare at him, sometimes losing track of the lesson; I'd try to figure out what Dracula saw in him, and whether I'd have pegged him as dangerous if I'd just met him on the street. I doubted it, not because he looked innocent—nobody has looked innocent to me in a long time—but because he looked so dumb.

Conrad preyed on kids. I remember him. The official scholomance policy was that child-molestation and murder were inherently no more or less praiseworthy than any other approach, but I couldn't help taking special note of Conrad. He was old, maybe fifty, and he participated a lot in class. He stared at me a lot, too, at my belly as I started to show.

Then there was Harlequin. Actually, Harlequin might have been a woman. He might also have been an animal—a lizard, say, or a bat—or some alien thing nobody'd ever heard of. I had no idea, either, how old he was, or what race. He was an exotic dancer, a hooker, a performance artist, a beggar. By turns he was fey and crude, heavy-handed as a rapist in a reeking alley and light-footed as the eternally restless spirits my grandmother had called *strigoi* (restless, I remembered, either because of some great sin or because of some great unclaimed treasure). I never knew exactly what he'd done to be admitted or how he got such spectacularly high grades—except that, rather than stalking and terrifying his victims, he dazzled and seduced them, and they died not out of fear of him but out of passion.

What I remember most vividly about Harlequin, though, are thunderbolts and blood.

We were having our regular early-morning nature class in Central Park. The sun was probably just rising over a horizon we couldn't see; the bowl of the park, inside our horizon of mountainous buildings, was still pretty dark, the charcoal-rose sky like a lid.

Andy, as usual, was already half-asleep; he should have been in his element here. Conrad, as usual, was sulky because there were so few children in the park at this time of the night, and those who were out were already taken.

Harlequin was even more spectacular than usual. He'd been studying, I could tell. I always hated brown-noses. The first of us to master vaporization, he kept disappearing and reappearing all over the place, leaping in the fountain like water drops himself, slithering through the dewy grass to coil himself adoringly around Dracula's ankles.

Dracula always put up with more from Harlequin than he should have. But finally that morning he observed sternly, "All this is most entertaining, but you are only distracting yourself and the others from serious application to the matters at hand."

Harlequin laughed like the cry of a gull, made himself very tall and thin, and swept both cupped palms across the paling sky. A shower of stars fell into the city, stars I didn't think had been ready to fall yet. Souls leaving this world, my grandmother would have said. Souls pulled from this world before their time, I thought, and grudgingly I acknowledged to myself Harlequin's skill and style.

The baby kicked. I could feel it drinking my blood through the umbilical cord, and I knew it was transforming me into something I didn't want to be. I imagined sinking my teeth into its not-yet-developed little neck, through the layers of my own flesh and blood.

Harlequin raced to the lake, the rest of us following. He found a rock the size of a baby, raised it above his glittering bald head, and threw it in. The splash wasn't very impressive in the noisy city dawn, and the surface of the water had already been deeply rippled, but there was a dragon in there and it awoke. Two, three, four long thunderbolts leaped out of the lake and crackled through the air to the sky, where they lit up the craggy top floors of the buildings. There was the immediate odor of burned hair and flesh, and from the shadows on the other side of the lake somebody screamed.

Beside me, always beside me, Dracula murmured, "Interesting," and jealousy licked like a fetus at the bottom of my heart. But Harlequin got on everybody's nerves, and just before the end of class, with the sun about to show above the buildings and Andy all but snoring, Dracula finally lost his patience. "Harlequin, enough. I have had enough. This morning, right now, you must prove yourself or leave the scholomance."

I was shocked. I hadn't known you could be expelled. Scared, I tried to move close to Dracula, yearning to touch him openly, to claim him in front of the others and put an end to the pointless competition for Tenth Scholar. But Dracula was watching Harlequin and took no notice of me.

Harlequin stood absolutely still among the moving shadows of the sunrise, looking small and frail. I hadn't realized until then how sick he was, and always would be. Immortal now, of course, like the rest of us, and eternally wasting away. The disease was his curse and his power; his kisses brought to his victims, who were his lovers, immortal sickness, too.

From behind the bushes that separated us from the path, we heard voices. We all sat up straight, even Conrad, who I knew was hoping for the sweet voice of a child unattended. Even Andy tried to rouse himself, but the sun was too high for him.

I started to move but Dracula held me back, his cold hand across my belly. Harlequin paused for maybe five seconds, centering himself as Dracula had taught us to do before an approach, and then stepped through the bushes. Conrad and a few of the other students repositioned themselves quietly to watch, but Dracula stayed where he was and kept me there, too.

There was almost no noise. Harlequin made none, of course, and his victims never knew what happened. That was the way it should be; Dracula loathed noise. I remembered how quiet my grandmother had been, too: how peaceful. We waited. Daylight had started to seep into the park and class was almost over when Harlequin stepped like a dancer back into the clearing among us.

His face and clothes were scarlet with blood. His teeth dripped. He looked stronger than he had in a long time, more substantial. His movements were more fluid and directed, less flighty.

In outstretched hands he carried two tall ridged silver thermos bottles, apparently taken from the victims. He dropped to his knees, bowed his head as if in offering, and passed one of the bottles in each direction around the circle. Dracula drank first, his eyes closed in pleasure and his long throat working. At last, without opening his eyes, he passed the thermos to me.

The blood was warm and sweet. Obviously the victims had been virgins, barely so, a young man and a young woman on the verge of becoming lovers when Harlequin had intervened. The mouth of the thermos was wide enough that the blood spilled over my nose and chin, bathing me in its vitality. I knew some of it was reaching the baby and I was glad, then I wished it wouldn't because maybe there wouldn't be enough left for me, but there was nothing I could do about that. I drank until I felt renewed, and then, reluctantly, passed the bottle on.

When Dracula said, "Prove yourself" to me, we were making love on his red silk sheets. The others had gone home for the day, or had gone wherever it was they went when they weren't at school; I couldn't imagine. City daylight came through the high window gray and pale blue, and it was exciting to be awake.

He was straddling me on all fours, and under the huge mound of my belly his penis entered me easily. It thrilled me to think of his penis pushing back and forth past the fetus like a fang.

I would turn seventeen soon. The baby would be born soon. Soon we would be graduated.

"Prove yourself," he said, and I thought he was talking about something sexual.

Although I couldn't guess what there was left that I hadn't already done, I gasped, "Tell me what you want."

He buried his face in my shoulder. His teeth grazed my neck and found a spot, but they didn't go in yet; he was playing with me. "Prove yourself," he murmured again, "or leave the scholomance. Now."

I stiffened with fear and outrage and frantic desire. I tried to wrap my arms and legs around him, but my stomach was too big, the baby was between us, and Dracula was moving down my body. I spread my legs and waited for his sharp tongue, but he stopped at my navel and I felt his teeth.

"You are not the Tenth Scholar," I heard him say.

"Why not? Who is? Harlequin? Shit, I thought you were smart enough to see through him—"

"The baby is the Tenth Scholar."

A fang went into my belly button and withdrew again. There was the suggestion of pain.

I struggled weakly to get out from under him. Of course I couldn't, and, anyway, I didn't know where I'd go if I got free. "You mean I can't stay?"

"I have taught you as much as it is possible for you to learn."

Betrayal made me light-headed, as though he'd already bitten through. "No," I cried, foolishly. "Please."

His voice came up to me singsong, seductive, and cold as immortal blood. "If you give me the baby now, you may stay to raise it until it can take its place at my side. Twelve years, perhaps, or ten years, or fourteen, depending on its nature and inclinations. If you do not give me the baby, you will leave. Tonight. I have lost interest in you."

"Take it," I said.

A vision of the dog with the butchered throat came into my head. A vision of my grandmother, dying when I'd been sure she'd never die, leaving me. I bit my lower lip hard to drive the visions away.

At first there was no more pain, really, than during any normal bite, except that the nerves in my abdomen were exquisitely sensitive. He sucked and drank a lot of blood. Before he was done I was so dizzy I could barely see, and he, obviously, was stoned.

His hands went all over my body—cold skin, sharp nails. His tongue went all over my body. He had started to sing as if to himself, to croon, and his laughter was sweet and smooth. Unable to fathom what I'd be like in fourteen years, what the city would be like when I had to go back into it alone, I paid attention only to him, only to the perforations his teeth were making from my navel to my pubic hair, only to his promise that if I did this he would let me stay.

Now pain and blood gushed. I lost and regained consciousness and lost it again; stars fell. When I awoke, the light was the same blue-gray it had been, but I was sure time had passed. There was a terrible, wonderful emptiness in my abdomen, and the wound had already started to close.

I heard Dracula's odd crooning and the gurgling of an infant, but for a while I couldn't find them. The colors in the room—chartreuse, mauve, blood-red—gave around me like living tissue. Then I saw the tall thin form by the window, blackened by my blood and the baby's and the rich nourishing blood of the placenta and afterbirth.

"It's a girl," he told me.

I was dizzied by a peculiar kind of pride: I'd borne a healthy daughter who would be the Tenth Scholar, even if I could not be. I'd carried on my grandmother's line. I'd given Dracula something he'd wanted, something that, apparently, no one else had ever given him. And fourteen years was a long time.

It was, of course, a trick. "Go now," he said, almost casually, staring at the baby in his arms.

"What?"

"Leave. The scholomance is filled."

"You said I could stay. You said—"

"I saw no point in exerting myself to take my daughter by force when you would give her to me out of love."

"She's my daughter!"

The baby in his arms curled and stretched. Somehow, she was feeding. "I am her father," he said, and I understood that it was true. He looked at me then, green gaze forking like lightning, and said, "Go. You have no place here."

My daughter is fourteen now. I look for her everywhere and see her nowhere. Probably I wouldn't know who she was, anyway, except for her resemblance to him.

I kill for sustenance; there is no pleasure in it. I infect some of my victims with immortality in hopes that they will be my companions, but they always leave.

I know that my classmates are out here, and they've been taught by the Master; I try not to forget that. I try to protect myself against them, but it's unclear to me what danger there is, what pain there could be left. The city seems full of scholomance graduates and wannabes, and it's hard for me to believe these days that Dracula accepts only ten students at a time.

THIS ICY REGION
MY HEART ENCIRCLES

H E HAD COME BACK. She had always known he would, because she had imagined it so.

She had imagined his form: moving slowly from shadow to shadow, as one with the weathered faces of the brick and stone, at times almost indistinguishable from pillar or hitching post. Sleeping in an abandoned stable space or beneath a tree in Hyde Park.

Once she had imagined his face, too, but she could not re-imagine it now. She could be sure only that, as always, it was a live visage properly dead. A too-vivid dream. Once before she had dreamed such a thing: that her firstborn and first-dead babe had come back to life, that the sweet little thing had been only cold, that she and Shelley had rubbed it before the fire, and it had lived. But when she'd awakened there had been no baby; her Mary Jane was still dead.

How was it she had so long survived this beautiful and monstrous Imagination, when with regularity it repulsed and wounded her?

Her own dear Shelley had not survived. It seemed to her now that he had been little but Imagination in its purest, most beautiful, most dangerous form, inspiration for both Victor Frankenstein and the Monster, neither of them wholly recognizable after all these years.

Shelley's features would not have been recognizable, either, that July day on the beach off Via Reggio. They had tried to keep the details from her, but she had persisted. There had been his green jacket, and in the pockets his volumes of Keats and Sophocles. His beautiful face had been bloated and pulled apart by the dark sea. But she would have recognized him by his form, by the shadow his soul had cast.

During the past few days she had glimpsed such a shadow stretched out across a neighboring rooftop on Chester Square, and once in a distant garden stiff and erect as a giant scarecrow. This shadow was soulless, and she knew at once who cast it. She almost welcomed him, although she was so afraid.

He had come back, and with him he'd brought some of the icy regions of his exile. The weather was extraordinarily cold. She had lain down in January, and now she thought February must be fast approaching. She had always disliked the English climate, but she could not remember a London January ever quite so cold.

But why call this creature a "he," unless this was, indeed, Shelley returning to her, making his way back out of the icy emptiness, the wasteland beyond passion and poetry? Such thoughts filled her with guilt, as if she were the abomination. She was a foolish old woman.

The Monster wrapped the cold about itself like a winding sheet, as if for protection. She had touched the window glass once but could touch it no more; the distant shadow beyond it had burned her fingers with its ice. The air in the street appeared solid, full of light, and much too cold to breathe. She wanted to warn her son Percy not to go out but could not quite manage it. She had never been able to keep her children safe.

90

Birds froze on the branches. Their dark bodies littered the pavement. Each day the dark form seemed closer. She wondered if she should warn the Queen, Buckingham Palace being only a short distance away. But even if she could, what might she say? She could talk to her of Shelley, but not of this other bringing its ice deep into the heart and soul of England. Victoria's strong affection for her Albert was widely known, but what did the Queen understand of spirit and Imagination?

Out in the square dogs grew heavy with sheaths of ice and collapsed into their fur. Mary saw that the glass in the window had begun to crack, the fissures so crisp and definite that she wondered if they might lie across her eyeballs instead. Warm, wet fingers tracked the cold of her throat. What could it want?

"What do you want?"

Outside her window, ice thundered and moaned with the Monster's cries, and London paid no heed.

The Monster had come for Shelley's heart. It was hers. She would not give it up.

Mary knew her husband's heart more intimately now than ever when he was alive. It was as though, without referent during the more than twenty-eight years since Shelley's drowning, she had recreated his heart for herself, endowed it with a new kind of life.

Imagination, Mary thought, and, although her body ached with new pain and her spirit with old, "the beaming face of Imagination peeped in, and the weight of deadly woe was lightened." She smiled. Some twenty years ago, when she'd written those words, she'd been amazed and distressed to discover even moments of happiness, and she'd thought she knew everything about both woe and Imagination. How strange, she thought now as she'd thought all her life, how strange a thing her life had been!

Kind, gloomy Edward Trelawney had first presented Shelley's heart to Leigh Hunt, snatched unconsumed from the flames of the beach pyre which Mary had been unable to bring herself to attend.

She'd been told, and had not been surprised, that the body had been slow to burn, had finally separated after three hours, the unusually large heart apparently impregnable to the fire. Again and again her Imagination had conjured vivid, not entirely unwelcome visions of the scene: hand bandaged, eyes glistening with tears from smoke and grief and pain, Trelawney saying nothing as he passed Shelley's heart to another, though far lesser, poet.

At last Shelley's heart had been returned to Mary, and she had kept it with her all these years. She had wrapped it in linen and in the lines of his poem "Adonais," and—although written as an elegy to a man he had not much liked—they had come to speak to her as if they'd always been closest to her beloved's heart:

I am borne darkly, fearfully, afar!

In the miserable little house at Pisa, always so vulnerable to flood-waters and now suddenly and permanently flooded by Shelley's absence, the heart had been as agitated as she was, had never been able to find a place. It had rested briefly on table, shelf, rain-grayed corner of the floor, for Mary had been unwilling to believe any surface capable of supporting it for long and had worried that the baby would somehow stumble on it and would know what it was, or, equally horrible, would not know.

At Albaro, her dreadful first home alone, the wrapped heart had reposed on her desk. His heart, then, had occupied very nearly the same space as her own while she set about what was to have been her one life-task: commemorating the only creature worth loving and living for, the essential being who had been both trapped and enshrined in a fragile image, now shattered, now freed, while she was left to go on as best she could.

But with each move thereafter, the package containing Shelley's heart had become simply a part of the household furnishings. In all the London flats—Speldhurst Street, Somerset Street, Park Street—in Putney, now here at 24 Chester Square, it had been scarcely more remarkable to her than this mirror or that chair. And yet still his words would come back to her, as if the pressure of his heart had rubbed them from the manuscript and launched them into the air:

...*a grave among the eternal...*

The words came into her like a whisper from his heart. Sometimes it seemed a desecration to her, and dangerous, that Shelley's heart had not been burned, sometimes a miracle.

Waking from dreams she could remember if she wanted to, Mary found herself staring at the cold mantel where, in this room, the heart package had always sat. Her own habitual unmindfulness of it disgusted her, and she said aloud, "Monster." It was a name she'd often used for herself in the journals no one would ever see, and now, halfway to the grave, she dared say it aloud: "Monster!"

As if in reply there was a shifting outside her window, a shadowy fall of snow, a cracking as of long-unused limbs bending and seeking purchase on the outer walls. It had come back. Fear had descended now into weariness, and Mary rolled over, away from the mantel and the window and the heart, and thought to go back to sleep, for there would be nothing again today worth waking to.

Something was in her bed, something small and solid and very still at about the level of her waist. Mary reached down among the bedclothes and touched the object, gasped and pulled her hands back, forced herself to find the thing again and extract it and hold it up. With great effort of will she did not drop it, held it at arm's length and stared. Mary Jane, dead in her bed again. Her baby girl, dead.

The baby was not really there. Mary's hands were empty. Trembling, she lay back on her pillow and thought how alone she was, how alone she'd always been, estranged from her fellows and estranged from herself. Those who accused her of having a cold heart were wrong: her heart was hot, searing, but the core of her was protected by layers and layers of ice that had allowed her to survive.

Outside her window the city cracked beneath the weight of ice, and a hungry, half-imagined shadow made its way awkwardly toward her room. Shelley's words provided no comfort:

He had adorned and hid the coming bulk of Death.

Mary struggled out of bed and crossed the few steps to her window. The sun had risen into a painful glaring of snow-filled sky, turned the room and her white nightgown gray. The birds were silent, their beaks packed with ice. Toward her from among the skeletal trees was coming a very small figure, with the wide-legged toddle of a child just learning to walk. As Mary watched, mesmerized by a horrible and impossible hope, the sun rose another sliver and illuminated the child's face. Mary's throat constricted as though a hand had closed around it. "Clara!" she cried aloud. Her little girl—dead these thirty years, her health sacrificed for her father's who had died anyway—looked up at the sound of her name, and Mary, though unable to move, was frantically thinking how she might open the window and climb out and run across the cold blanket of sunrise and this time save her daughter, when the child was gone.

But another child was there. Older, sturdier, closer to her, blond hair glinting in the early sun. William. Willmouse. Willy Blue-Eyes. His death foretold by three years in the book of the Monster: William is dead! That sweet child, whose smiles delighted and warmed my heart, who was so gentle, yet so gay. Victor, he is murdered. And foretold, too, the mother's culpability, inescapable no matter what the circumstances of her child's death: "Oh, God. I have murdered my child!"

Mary was not surprised to see William after the others. But her heart stopped at the sight of him, long enough for her vision to fill in with blackness as though the sun had never risen, would never rise again, or as though its rising made no difference anymore. What cruelty was this that sent her dead children to her now, to remind her that she had taken for herself, however unwillingly, years and years

94

of life that should have been theirs? To remind her, too, monstrously, that she would sacrifice them all again, even darling William, for one more day with Shelley. She managed to get the window open, skinning her knuckles on the ridge of ice, and to thrust both hands out into the frigid air, but her gesture sent William away again and she was alone.... *earth's shadows fly...*

Shelley's heart had known it all.

She was not alone. When she turned and staggered toward her bed—thinking she might sleep at least until her surviving son and his wife began to stir and she must accept another day for living—her bed was already occupied. A female figure, head thrown back halfway off the mattress, black mouth open and marked throat exposed, features blurred and mingled, skin yellowed and taut in the slanting light so that Mary said aloud, "Fanny!" and then, "Harriet!" and knew that it was both. Her love for Shelley and his for her had murdered them both; the marks of her hands and his were on both their hearts, and, given the choice, she would without hesitation do it again.

From where she stood with her back chilled by the icy breeze from the half-open window, the bed was between her and the door. At the foot of the bed was a space just wide enough for her to pass through sideways. She pressed herself against the wall and began to sidle along it, hoping she could escape from this room with the specter in the bed, into the early-morning liveliness of her son's family, which was as bright and open and unencumbered by genius and shadows as he was. But the figure reached for her. "Fiend!" Mary shrieked. "Leave me alone!"

The face was a monstrous composite of the women Mary had killed—her sister, Shelley's first wife, and someone else she could not quite name. "You will always be alone," the woman murmured, "until you take me in."

The woman was holding her hands out palms up, obviously in supplication. The woman wanted something from her, and Mary was moved to a primal kind of pity, but horror and revulsion were stronger and she took a few more steps along the wall toward the door.

"Don't deny me, Mary."

Her breath already short and wheezing, Mary bolted. Too soon, though, or too late, because the woman slipped between her and the door, like a shadow when the light has shifted. Arms encircled her waist. Hot breath like smoke, sweet as the grave, misted her eyes and took her own breath away. There was an explosion inside her head, a burst of exquisite color and then the rush of darkness, and in that moment she saw who the woman was. "Mother!" she cried.

Her mother, whose life and very name she had taken for her own, embraced her so tightly that Mary felt her heart and her skull split open. Her mother rushed into her mind and body and reclaimed them. "You created me!" her mother was whispering, but of course that wasn't true; Mary was her mother's creature, given life and then abandoned.

Mary fell sideways and struck her temple on the corner of the bed. Thinking there must be blood, she meant to raise a hand to the wound, and discovered she could not. She managed to drag herself up onto the bed and turn herself over so that she could breathe. Her entire left side was paralyzed. The apparition was gone, and she was alone in the room, hearing the household waking around her and knowing it had nothing to do with her anymore, staring quite without intention at the packaged heart on the mantel over no fire.

Once, very young, she had come upon a gray cat nibbling yellow roses. "Shelley!" she had called in delight to her not-yet-husband. "Here is a cat eating roses! She will turn into a woman!" And Shelley, charmed, had written it down.

Mary tried to sit up, and found she could not. She could not reach the wrapped heart on the mantel, and could lift only one hand to press on her own heart which was, remarkably, still beating. She had lived with Shelley—breathed the same air, dreaded and courted the same shadows, watched the same cat eating the same roses—for a brief, whole lifetime; she had lived without him nearly four times as long, a lifetime that was not yet finished. She suspected that, by now, he was more real and present to her in his absence than he'd ever been while physically alive in this corporeal world.

Now as she was preparing at last to join him, Mary thought she should unwrap the linen and, for what would be the last time, encounter Shelley's heart directly. Touch it. Smell it. Take measure of what remained of it. Observe its color and shape. Hold it against her breast (her nipple an eye that had so frightened him at Diodati, seeing the future, suckling the past) until her own heart stilled. She did not think she had much time.

She could not reach the "Adonais" with Shelley wrapped at its heart. She could not get out of bed; the mere thought of trying to move all those muscles in concert and sequence was ludicrous. She thought to summon Percy or his Lady Jane to fetch the heart for her, but the bell had been placed on the table at her left side, where last night it had been perfectly accessible, and now she couldn't raise or lower her fingers to ring it.

Someone came anyway. There were purposeful footsteps and harsh, rapid breathing. Mary tried to speak her relief and gratitude, and to tell what it was she wanted. For some reason, she was afraid. For some reason, she was weeping, and she herself could scarcely make sense of the guttural sounds that came from her throat.

It was not kind Jane come to do her bidding, nor her son. It was not Shelley at her door, inside her cold room with the sun-rise, at her deathbed, although she had more than half expected him as guide. It was not any of the spectral women who had appeared to her earlier. She knew, suddenly, who it was.

"Monster!" she whispered, and knew that no one listening would comprehend the greeting.

It was her Monster, first given form in that long-ago, tumultuous,

97

companionable summer at Diodati when everything had seemed possible if only fate could be avoided. Death and grief, then, had been mere words, with no true echo in her heart, although she, like the others, had thought she knew all the grand emotions of the world. After the first nightmare and the subsequent fugue-like fever of creation, Mary had come to think of the Monster as idle, foolish fancy, nothing more than a toy of a girl's Imagination. Now here it was, more real than she was; she was aware of an odd tingling sensation in the parts of her body that had been paralyzed by the touch of her mother's shade, and of a terrifying warmth in the icy region around her heart.

The Monster made as if to touch her, to caress or attack. Mary tried to shrink away, but the Monster was very close, as if their feet were attached, or the tops of their heads, or—like the infant Siamese twins she and Shelley had seen in a traveling freakshow one autumn in Genoa—their breastbones, sharing one swollen heart.

Mary rubbed her eyes with her right fist and tried clumsily to shake her head. Although the light in the room was steadily growing brighter as the sun rose over ice, she could hardly see. But the peculiar and oddly familiar odor of the Monster overlay the old-woman's-sickroom smell, a mix of acrid human sweat and chemical bitterness unexpectedly, disorientingly, lightened by a flowery fragrance.

She stared, and the Monster took form before her. The boundaries of her body were no longer clear. The Monster was so near to her now that it might have been inside her.

As always, the limbs of the Monster were perfectly proportioned, the features beautiful. Cumbersomely, Mary surveyed her own body and visualized her own face, first as in a mirror and then from the inside out. She had always thought of herself as plain, and years without Shelley had made her ugly; although she could not specify an appendage or a feature out of place, she had long thought of herself as deformed.

98

The pearly yellow skin of the Monster lightly, almost delicately covered the network underneath of muscles and arteries. Mary was able to lift her right hand enough to inspect it. Her own skin was grayish, wrinkled, mottled, stretched too tightly in some spots and hanging loosely in others; the underlying bone structure and pattern of blood vessels looked wrong, as though they could not possibly function, and, indeed, on the other, distant side of her body they no longer did.

The creature's hair was lustrous black, and flowing. Mary twisted her head crookedly on the hot pillow, and remembered that her own hair was tangled, dirty, dulled by age and sickness and too much sorrow.

All these characteristics of the Monster were familiar to her. She remembered dreaming them, imagining them, writing them down, reading them aloud to her appreciative if somewhat distracted first audience. But there was something new this time. Creation, once turned loose upon her chaos, had not stopped. Horror had vivified. During its ice-bound exile the Monster had changed much as she had changed; its long period of corruption had dropped its disguise and exposed an entirely new face. The mask of the Monster had rotted away. Shelley's heart must have always known:

...*he hath awakened from the dream of life...*

Now she knew what had always been true: her Monster was female. She had not created the pendulous breasts, the delicate hands, the shadowy and concave region between the thighs; she would never have been able to bring herself to allow such thoughts into her mind, much less to set them down on paper or, dear God, read them aloud to the three intense young men who had not in the first place truly regarded women as real. But her Monster was and had always been female, a woman like herself, and Mary did not know how she could bear this revelation.

And she knew why the Monster had come to her now. If she did not somehow protect Shelley's heart, the Monster—her own orphaned creation, the one so long denied—would discover and devour it, would claim it as her own. But how could one protect a heart?

"Go away from me!" It was more a wail than a shout, more a plea than a command.

The Monster drew back a little, her beautiful face contorted with the bitterness of the eternal outcast. Mary had imagined that the Monster's face would look like that to Victor Frankenstein but she had never expected herself to be the agent of such unhappiness. She knew her own features were twisted, too, and she could not smooth them anymore.

"Why are you here? Why have you come to me now?" It was a senseless question, for she knew the answer, but she held her breath painfully for the other's reply.

"You summoned me," the creature said, and Mary recognized the voice as more like hers than hers was now.

She did not deny it. "Go away, then. I have changed my mind."

"I have nowhere else to go. I belong to you. I am your creature. No one else will have me."

"I will not have you, either, you hideous thing." Her own cruelty amazed her and was, she saw, utterly ineffectual.

"I am your creature." The Monster pounded her chest. "And I am empty. I am in need of. . ." She stopped, her neck turning awkwardly as she gazed about Mary's room.

Mary stopped herself from finishing the plea, and said instead, audaciously, "Bring me that bound poem on the mantel, then. There is a linen-wrapped parcel inside. Bring me my husband's heart."

Her Monster smiled in childlike pleasure at being asked to do something for her, and Mary's stomach turned. The Monster did not seem surprised by the request, or in the least confused. She turned stiffly and made her way directly to the mantel, her strides much longer than Mary's would have been so that she crossed the room in two steps. Her hands around the bundle were steady; Mary could hardly bear to see them there and, indeed, could see only their outline in the icy brightness of the room.

The Monster lifted the package from the mantel, pivoted, and brought it to her. Mary could raise only one hand to take it and the Monster would not release it to her, as if knowing she would drop it and the contents would spill. She bent from the waist and set the bundle on Mary's lap. It was remarkably light. That was distressing. Poems should be heavy, Mary thought, and Imagination. Shelley's heart should be heaviest of all.

My spirit's bark is driven far from the shore...

Mary fumbled with the brittle pages of the "Adonais." The beautiful lines tore beneath her trembling fingers and she wept....*fed with true love tears instead of dew ...*

The linen bindings were stiff and tight from the years, and with only one hand she had no hope of manipulating them. *One with trembling hands clasps his cold head...*

The Monster put her hand over Mary's and Mary recoiled, but she was held fast, and the Monster's longer, stronger fingers pried apart the linen, carrying Mary's fingers with them like shadows. *A tear some dream has loosened from his brain.*

Mary could not see inside the stiff old cloth. Its shadows had deepened, its wrinkles roughened. Her probing fingers felt nothing but grit and dust. She looked at her Monster, and for a long moment they were both motionless and silent. *Grief returns with the revolving year...*

Mary cried out. The Monster cried out. The cloth was empty. Shelley's heart was gone.

Mary scrambled for an explanation. Perhaps the heart had never been there. Perhaps Hunt, aided by her own mad fantasies, had tricked her, or Trelawney been crazed by his own grief; per-haps all these years she had kept herself in the unmindful presence of an empty piece of cloth.

More likely, the heart had simply disintegrated. Like every-thing else in her life, it had likely faded away from her, been reclaimed, altered its form and substance so thoroughly that she couldn't recognize it anymore. The Monster was weeping, her hot tears melting Mary's flesh.

Or someone had taken it.

Mary and her Monster shrieked at each other at the same time, "You have stolen the heart!"

The Monster's hands came around Mary's throat. The powerful thumbs pressed into her vocal chords so that she had no hope of crying out. The Monster's frenzied thoughts exploded in her own brain, and her whole body was paralyzed now, although she seemed to be moving very fast. Her heart was being consumed by the Monster's flame, as Shelley's had not been; there was a curious sensation of wholeness and warmth. As she hurtled into the dark caverns of this new journey, her Monster came with her, holding high the torch.

Mary Wollstonecraft Godwin Shelley died in her London residence on the first day of February, 1851. Paralysis had set in during the last month of her illness. She was buried at St. Peter's Church, Bournemouth, in a tomb with her father William Godwin, her mother Mary Wollstonecraft Godwin, and Shelley's heart.

MASK OF THE HERO

— for *Mark*

Mark wasn't sure they were dreams.

He did not, in fact, believe they were dreams, although he knew everyone else would think so. They came to him at night when he was asleep, pretending to be dreams, but when he woke himself up and turned on the bedside light, got to his feet and walked around his room, they were still there. Grinning at him. Nodding at him. Weeping. Snarling. Crowding around him.

Masks.

Bodiless heads.

Bodies without spirits. Or, he thought, spirits without bodies.

They always made an eerie sound, a humming on the very edge of what he could hear, sometimes high-pitched and thin as a hair, sometimes full-bodied and low. The music always came to him before the masks did and lingered long after they'd disappeared. By the time he was eighteen years old, Mark was hearing the music almost all the time.

Sometimes he'd reach out in an attempt to touch the masks. When he was a child, he'd thought they were toys, or friends, or monsters come to eat him alive, or the faces of his parents whom he remembered so dimly he thought they probably had been dreams, too. Sometimes he did touch the masks—the corner of one's eye, or the mouth hole. When that happened, both the mask in his hand and his hand on the mask showed themselves to be made of small bits and pieces, building blocks, he supposed they were molecules—smaller hands, smaller and smaller masks.

When the masks disappeared altogether, as they always did, without revealing what was behind them, Mark would raise his hands to touch his own face. Every time, his face came off, peeled away. Sometimes the pain made him cry out, and sometimes there was no pain. Either way, no one heard him. Then he would hold his face in his hands for as long as he could while the music hummed high and low.

By the time he was eighteen, Mark had come to think of himself secretly as the Prince of Masks.

In the real world, which didn't always seem very real to him, Mark went to school, went to work, went home to the group home. Now and then he fell in love with a girl, but he always talked too much or didn't talk enough or said the wrong thing. At school he had to think about things that really weren't very important. He could get interested in a poem or a science experiment, but then he'd find he'd discover hidden meanings in the way the words were used, secret questions in the data so that when the experiment was finished you had hundreds more hypotheses to test than when you'd started. A few teachers tried to talk to him about what he was going to do when he graduated; sometimes Mark thought about nothing else, and sometimes he couldn't bring himself to think about it at all.

The group home was okay. Although none of the counselors understood him, most of them were kind, and although the other boys weren't his friends he didn't have any trouble with them as long as he stayed away from them. There were times, though—across the dinner table, watching the game on TV in the living room, shooting pool in the basement—when he'd look up and see the masks they were all wearing.

One wore a mask of a wolf, which showed he couldn't be trusted. Another wore a mask of a bird with lifted feathers; she was gone in a week. They all thought they were wearing masks to conceal their real selves, but Mark was the Prince of Masks and he knew that the masks revealed who they really were.

Then their faces would go back to normal. The wolf-man would be just some guy who thought he was cool, baring his pretty white teeth in a smile that was supposed to be friendly but made Mark sick. The bird-lady would be looking down in a way that was supposed to keep people from hurting her or she would fly away. As far as Mark knew, nobody hurt her here, but she flew away anyway.

Mark's job as a bicycle messenger took him to parts of the city he'd never known existed and brought him into contact with people he would never have met. He got lost a lot; he was sure he was going to get fired. Almost every day he came close to having an accident; he'd be riding along as fast as he could, zipping through crowds waiting for the bus, leaping over curbs, and suddenly there'd be a car right in front of him or an old lady slowly pulling a two-wheeled cart with grocery sacks in it. Mark would swerve and drag his heels to stop, and the driver would blast the horn or the old lady would glare at him over her shoulder, and Mark would see that they were wearing masks.

On the Sixteenth Street Mall one afternoon, a lady in a gray business suit and carrying a briefcase waited with him at a corner. Mark was thinking about quarterback Joe Montana, who never felt out of place, who belonged in this world, ruled this world. It was a long light. The lady half-turned toward him, the sunshine struck her face from a different angle, and Mark saw her mask. She lifted her hand as though to smooth her hair, which hadn't moved at all in the slight breeze, but instead she slipped her oval pink nails under the edge of her mask, peeled it off, and put it into her briefcase. The face underneath was rosy and younger; with it, she smiled at Mark as though they shared a secret now, and then the light changed and he lost her in the rush hour crowd.

"Hey, kid," said a man in a dirty flannel shirt, stepping in front of him as he went up the steps of an office building he'd finally found on Champa Street. "Spare a quarter for the bus?"

Mark gave him a quarter, even though he couldn't spare it. The bum grinned at him and held out his hand. Not knowing what else to do, Mark took it. The bum shook his hand hard and for a long time, and when he finally let go he left a tiny mask in the cup of Mark's palm, a mask so tiny that it had no features except glittery little eyes.

Mark had been thinking about Diana, whether she was really going to break up with Rick, and he didn't know what to do about the mask in his hand. The bum was shuffling off down the sidewalk now, muttering to himself and looking for somebody else to hit up for "bus money." Finally, Mark rubbed his hand on his jeans and the mask fell off onto the concrete like a fingernail paring or a piece of his own skin. He wondered what the man would leave in the hand of the next stranger who didn't just ignore him or tell him to go to hell.

Mark's boss was Dave, a tall man with many chins. Dave always hired boys from the group home, so you were representing the whole program every day you went to work, and he talked loudly about how he was giving these boys a chance to turn their lives around. He also talked loudly about why he fired them, so Mark knew that Jake had stolen money and Bobby had gotten high on his lunch break and it had turned out that Kevin couldn't read so he'd delivered stuff to all the wrong addresses. Kevin had only lasted three days. Mark wondered what Dave was saying about him. He did get lost a lot, because he'd be thinking about Diana or about Joe

106

Montana or about what he was going to do when he emancipated from the group home next summer. Also because sometimes when he looked at the letters on street signs or the numbers on buildings all he could see was that they were symbols for something else, codes, masks over some other meaning that he couldn't grasp anymore.

It took several months for Mark to get a look at Dave's mask. The man smiled a lot. He clapped your shoulder and said your name a lot. He thought his mask of friendliness hid how he really felt about the boys from the group home, but the open mouth and squinty eyes and puffed-out cheeks just accentuated his contempt. Realizing that each of Dave's chins was the chin of a mask, Mark wondered how far down you'd have to go to get to the face.

"Hey, son, how ya doin'?" Dave greeted him when he came in one chilly Saturday morning.

"Okay."

"Got a LoDo run for you. Warehouse down there under the 23rd Street Viaduct. Think you can find it?"

"Sure," Mark said, although he'd never been into Lower Downtown, had no idea where 23rd Street was, and didn't know what the term "viaduct" meant. The package to be delivered was an oversized manila envelope, very lightweight and a little stiff.

The downtown streets weren't busy on a Saturday morning. Mark pedaled briskly along the Mall through the crisp sunshine and shadows, weaving among the mostly-deserted benches and empty waist-high flowerpots. He was nervous about finding this place. He was nervous about what to do now that Diana had broken up with Rick and was obviously expecting him to ask her out; he really didn't think they had very much in common, although he often fantasized about marrying her, making love to her, spending the rest of his life with her. He was nervous about what he'd do when he emancipated, where he'd live, how he'd support himself, whether he'd ever have any friends. There was a guy playing saxophone in the streaked shadow of the bank building with all the black glass; as Mark went past he nodded, and his horn glinted sweetly, and Mark didn't see any evidence of a mask. Maybe, he thought, the music was a mask, concealing and revealing the guy's true self.

Wind swept along the streets and alleys between the tall flat buildings, faster than he could ride. Stuff blew across his path and under his wheels: newspapers, plastic bags, hats, sections of orange mesh fencing, masks.

Masks. He almost fell, almost rode out into the street against the light. Masks, blowing along the streets and sidewalks like all the other debris, piling up against the curb in complicated little piles of grins, frowns, tongues sticking out, eyes winking and bulging, ears pointed or flapping or no ears at all.

Following what he remembered of Dave's directions, he turned right onto Blake Street and there, the only big building in the block, was the warehouse, faded red brick with only a few windows. Proud of himself that he'd found it right away, he turned right again into the alley to go into the back door off the parking lot. The alley was so full of masks that he had to dismount and push his bike. Masks bit his ankles, lifted themselves high enough to kiss his hands.

There was only one door in the back of the building, so he didn't have to figure out which one to use. He couldn't see anything to lock his bike to so he just left it leaning against the building; already he was worrying that it would get stolen and he wouldn't have any way to get out of here. Debris, most of it probably masks but he tried not to look, skittered around the parking lot like living creatures. Something hit the back of his leg and fell off; he didn't turn around to see what it was. Carefully carrying the manila envelope in both hands so as not to drop it or bend whatever was inside, Mark tried the door. It was unlocked and swung inward. He took a deep breath, stepped inside, and closed the door behind him.

"Quick service," a quiet voice said. "I like that."

There were a lot of lights in the building, but they were all dim and uncovered and they were hung up among the rafters of the very high ceiling, so they didn't cast much light. Mark thrust the parcel in the direction of the voice. "Here's your package."

"No," the voice said softly. "That belongs to you."

He'd made another stupid mistake. Somehow he'd gotten confused and brought the wrong package. He was going to get fired for sure.

Mark's eyes had adjusted to the dim light enough now that he could see something of the owner of the quiet voice, could tell at least that the person was about his own height and weight and was dressed in ordinary clothes—jeans and a plain gray sweatshirt. He couldn't make out the age or sex or race of the person, though, because the whole head was covered by the most elaborate mask Mark had ever seen.

The mask must have been three feet tall and nearly as wide. When the figure turned a little sideways, Mark could see how far the mask extended above the top and beyond the sides of the head. There looked to be dozens of eye sockets, and the opening for the mouth changed form as he stared at it, from grinning to frowning to grimacing to a scream. Protuberances that might have been noses or ears or tongues pushed out all over it, and myriad iridescent colors swirled with black, so vivid that they weren't confined by the boundaries of the mask but bled into the air itself.

"Open it," the muffled voice told him.

Mark was already shaking his head. "I'm not supposed to—"

"Open it. It belongs to you."

Knowing he shouldn't be doing this, Mark made a deliberate decision to do it anyway, to see what this adventure would be. He loosened the sealed flap of the envelope and straightened its metal prongs. He hesitated, then slid his hand inside.

Something soft and warm was in there. Something moving. Something fleshy.

He gasped and tried to pull his hand out, but whatever was inside the envelope wouldn't let him go. There was no pain, he didn't feel teeth, but he had the vivid sensation that the thing had taken him in its mouth.

"Take it out," commanded the voice from behind the tall mask.

Slowly Mark withdrew his hand from the envelope. With it came a mask. He knew it was a mask before he'd even seen it completely, and his heart raced.

"Put it on." He would have put it on without being told.

He raised the mask in his hands. Immediately it swelled, sent out feelers, and adhered itself to his face.

It was so pliant and fit his features so perfectly that he could hardly feel it once it was in place.

Now the masked figure was backing into the darkness of the huge warehouse room. First its body disappeared, leaving only its face, which was a mask, looking empty, lifeless, unoccupied. Then the mask disappeared, too, and Mark was staring at a blank warehouse wall, a wide mouth-like loading door, two dingy windows above like cracked eyes.

Mark was afraid he would be left alone here, and he would remain a misfit, an alien for the rest of his life. "Wait!" he shouted, and followed the guide through the murky warehouse.

It seemed to take much longer than it should have, many steps and a great deal of pushing through some sort of viscous material before he reached the wall and the door that he thought the masked creature had gone through. Telling himself that he was a masked creature, too, he kept reaching toward the door. Finally he had it at his fingertips, but he couldn't seem to force his hand through the last few inches. He was stuck. It seemed to him he'd always been stuck, always heard calls he couldn't answer, always waited for someone to claim him and feared he wouldn't be able to follow.

He cried out. No one answered. He tried to break through with fists and feet, but his flailing was pointless. He gathered himself and flung his whole masked body headfirst against the door, but he only bounced back.

Finally he gave up. He sat down on the floor, lay down on the dirty warehouse floor and waited. Maybe he fell asleep. He didn't think he was asleep, but his mind felt viscous, too, and was full of masks and music.

The floor, the wall, the door began to dissolve around him. Momentarily he was half-in and half-out of the mask they'd put on him, and then it snapped back into place as if elastic, wrapped completely around his head, pulled and pushed at him until it altered his shape.

Then he was through to the other side.

Where half-formed faces floating in midair fought each other with fangs coming out of their nostrils and with swords held in ears that looked like hands. Where distorted humanoid figures frantically traded clothes, appendages, skins. Where heads disintegrated and totally different heads filled in the empty shoulders.

His own face floated. His own head disintegrated, re-formed in a new configuration, disintegrated again. His own clothes and skin were sloughed off and replaced by clothes and skin that had belonged to somebody else.

As far as Mark could see were rows and rows of other creatures, not unlike himself, masked and constantly transforming. Some of the masks looked too heavy to bear; others looked lighter than skin. All of them thoroughly covered their wearers; Mark would have thought they were nothing but masks if he hadn't been so aware of himself under his own mask.

"We have been calling you for a long time," someone complained.

"I'm here now." His voice felt different from behind the mask. From all around him rose a murmur of relief.

"You have been a long time coming."

Mark said, "All my life," and nodded. His mask moved in ways of its own.

He didn't need to ask where he was. This was the other world he'd always known existed, intertwined with the world of school and work and girls and loneliness. This was the world he'd glimpsed all his life, between letters and numbers when they skittered around rearranging themselves before he could put them to any use. This was the land he'd begun to perceive among the molecules of objects most people thought were solid: trees, mountains, cars, people. This was the place the masks had been telling him about for years.

"All my life," he said again. "I've heard you, but I didn't know how to get here."

"There is not much time. You may have waited too long." The tall creature wearing the giant mouth mask trembled and swayed, and its voice was weak.

Mark hated having to ask, "Not much time for what?" He should have already known. Maybe he would make stupid mistakes here, too. He might not understand what he was supposed to do. Maybe it wouldn't be so easy to fit in here, either. "What am I supposed to do?" he forced himself to ask, and answers formed everywhere, murmurs and mutterings, sighs and shrieks.

"The enemy."

"The enemy makes us wear masks that change who we are and make us do her bidding."

"The enemy grows stronger and we grow weaker. For a long time she has been sending forays into the other world, gauging its strength, changing pieces of it with her masks. Now she is ready to invade the other world completely and claim it for her own. Without you, we cannot stop her."

"But I'm wearing a mask, too." Confused, he put his hands to his face and, for a dizzying moment, thought maybe he wasn't wearing a mask anymore. In only two small places could he distinguish the edge of the mask from his own flesh: under the point of his chin and at the base of his skull.

"You are part of both worlds," they told him. "You are the only one who can save both worlds from the enemy."

"Why would I want to?" Suddenly Mark was furious. "Why should I care what happens to this world or that one? I don't belong in either one."

The masked creatures swarmed around him. The music hurt his ears. "Because if you do not," they screeched and sang, "if the enemy wins, nobody will ever be anything but a mask and nothing will ever be what it seems to be."

Mark was grabbed from behind. The masked creatures moaned and howled, but none of them came to his aid, except that someone thrust into his hand a sword, as pliant and sharp as the edge of his mask. He twisted away from his attacker and swung the sword backwards in a wide swift arc.

The sword connected with something semi-solid that came apart under the blade.

Something was pulled over his head. Another mask, he thought, heavy and with no apertures for seeing or speaking or even breathing. He couldn't breathe. Desperately he brought the sword upward in both hands, its tip perilously close to his own face, and split the mask apart. Its pieces fell at his feet, piece after piece dividing, until the ground was littered with countless infinitesimal masks.

Mark whirled. A figure in a soldier's uniform and a featureless khaki mask was lunging the short distance between them with a dagger upraised. Mark kicked at the descending fist. The dagger flew upward and then plummeted, clattering onto a dark hard surface far beneath them. Mark leaped after it, groped through thick sticky layers of some substance he couldn't name, and brought the dagger back up. He grabbed the front of the uniform and held the point of the dagger to the soldier's throat. "Take off your mask," he ordered.

The soldier shook his head violently and struggled in Mark's hold. "I cannot! The Queen has decreed—"

Mark thrust the dagger into the heavy khaki fabric at the soldier's throat and ripped the blade upward. A dark blood of dust and shadows spurted and the soldier shrieked but Mark, as if unable to stop, cut and slashed at the skintight mask until it was completely stripped away. But the soldier's face had been stripped away, too, and all he could see was blood and sinew and gaping moving holes.

Shocked by his own violence, Mark dropped both the dagger and the unmasked body of the soldier. "I'm sorry!" he breathed. "Oh, God, I'm sorry!" He backed away, then blindly turned and fled.

Light fluctuated around him, altering the shapes and textures of things, replacing shadows with reflections. He didn't know where he was heading and he couldn't tell where he'd already been. The surface under his feet might have been ground or floor or street; it undulated randomly, shifted wildly under his weight. Sometimes he heard such a cacophony of noises that he couldn't sort them out; sometimes he heard nothing at all, a huge and almost painful silence; sometimes he heard only the piercing music of the masks. The air was freezing cold and then so hot it nearly burned his skin. It smelled of flowers and then of acrid smoke, of mint and poison.

He had the vivid sensation that he was moving between and through masks. This whole world was masked, designed to confuse and trap him. Or maybe this whole world was nothing but a mask. Maybe it had been forced to wear masks for such a long time that there was no longer anything real underneath.

He walked for a long time. After a while he was not really aware of his legs moving or his feet coming into contact with anything solid, and he thought he might be flying, swimming, crawling.

Mark had felt alien all his life. He was more alien now than he had ever been before.

Something wrapped around him, its long thick body pulsing everywhere as though it had a thousand hearts. Strong muscles coiled tighter and tighter around his chest; fangs—so tiny he could hardly see them and then, suddenly, longer and thicker than his whole body—poised dripping above his head.

Mark dug his fingers into the pulpy skin of the serpent and

pulled hard. A layer pulled away, scales the breadth of his finger. The serpent shuddered and contracted; Mark's shoulders and hips ached from the pressure of the huge coils. He pulled himself inward, made himself small and narrow, and, still clutching the monster's skin, leaped downward into the inverted cone made by the sinuous body.

He slid and fell, down and down, and the skin came away in his hands. He saw that it was a mask, and under it were revealed more and more masks—smooth, with diamond shapes; rough, with a gelatinous substance in the pits and crevices; iridescent and mottled. He fell and fell, into the dark pulsing pit made by the body of the snake, and the mask he was pulling away grew so large that it folded over him, adhered to him, wrapped him up. He was becoming the snake, or he was becoming the snake's mask.

But then he had fallen out the bottom of the serpent's coils. He stopped suddenly, his nerves jangling. The slough of skin covering him dried rapidly, cracked, and split open. Breathless and dizzy, Mark emerged into dazzling saffron light, the sweetest mask-music he'd ever heard, and the presence of the enemy Queen.

"Mark," said the enemy, and his name bespoke her power. "I am delighted to have you."

Mark was dazed by his long fall, half-blinded by the brilliant light and nearly deafened by the music of the masks. He tried to say something to her, to tell her that he wasn't here for her and that he knew her tricks, but he couldn't find his voice.

The enemy Queen was leaning over him. She was so vast and so near to him that she had no features, but the cold radiating from her was paralyzing and her overwhelming odor entangled his thoughts. "Ah, Mark," she breathed into his face, into his lungs, "You wear the mask of the hero well, as if you had been born to it. Stay with me and you will continue to be a hero, bold and daring in the hero's mask I will construct for you. You will make a fine, strong warrior. I will use you well."

She didn't grasp him; he doubted she had hands. She enveloped him, her entire body over and inside his entire body, for such a long time he thought he had ceased to exist. When she removed herself, something had been grafted to all his surfaces, so that nothing about him was himself anymore.

One plane of the enemy Queen's body turned reflective long enough for Mark to see what he had become. A warrior: face transformed by a hideous mask of violence, red and blue slashes seaming his face, long jagged teeth bared and eyes aflame; weapons literally growing from his body, daggers at his waist and guns growing out of the flesh of his hands and iron-like bands of muscle studded with spikes circling his heavy thighs.

The Queen gave a great sigh that made everything in Mark's consciousness heave and billow. "Perfect. You are perfect for my purposes. We will conquer the worlds."

"No!" With strength he'd always suspected he possessed but never had had a chance to test, Mark kicked high, so that the many spikes and daggers ripped into the mass of the enemy Queen. She shrieked, a terrible noise like the wind that would end the world, and he recognized her pain as his own, as part of the music of the masks.

He aimed the pistol of his right hand toward the place where he imagined her heart would be, and pulled the trigger again and again and again. In the tumult raging around and in him, he couldn't be sure when the gun stopped firing, but finally he flung it as hard as he could upward and outward. A machine gun rested as if glued to his left forearm, and he swung it back and forth and fired it for a long time. The enemy Queen roared and shuddered. Mark found himself sorry for her pain and frightened for his own, but he had no doubt what he had to do.

Suddenly the Queen quieted. Mark held his breath. The mask-music was a very faint keening now; he felt it more than heard it, and its sweet sharp sorrow slid between his flesh and his bones. The enemy Queen was singing now inside his heart, and for the briefest of moments he surrendered to her. In that instant, she melded herself to his mind and body and became part of his flesh. He realized, too late, that she was even stronger and more clever than he had imagined. She had meant for him to attack her so viciously, to rip into her body. She had known he would be trapped there. She had intended all along to become his new mask, the hero's mask.

"You are the enemy now." Her seductive voice moved like fire inside him. "You have become me. You have the power to use other people for anything you like, and none of them will ever know who you really are."

"No!" Mark screamed, and pulled from his belt a dagger whose blade curved like the curve of the world. He inserted its point into the base of the enemy Queen's throat, where her pulse was strongest, and ripped the blade downward through the Queen and through himself, through all his different selves, through all the masks he had collected during his lifetime.

All his masks came off. Layer after layer after layer of them, down to the bone. Masks that Mark had never known he wore, some that looked exactly like him and some he never would have recognized as himself. The enemy Queen wailed; Mark wailed; the music of the masks wailed. Mask after mask stripped away, and when it was over Mark was nothing and nobody but who he was. In unmasking himself, he had destroyed all pretending, and destroyed the enemy Queen who had trapped him as well.

Creatures gathered around him, none of them masked anymore, all of their faces looking new and strong. "You have liberated us," they sang to him, a song he'd never been able to hear before because of the music of the masks. "Now we will take you home."

They made a sack for him and ferried him through the iridescent viscosity, took him back through the fear and wonder of his dreams and out into the chilly Saturday morning of the other world. The warehouse was empty. His bicycle was where he'd left it. His package had been delivered.

BEAUTIFUL STRANGERS

A T FIRST MARY WAS SURE she'd known him before. There was something so familiar about him, at the same time that he seemed odd, different.

In the dim light of the bar and through the alcohol haze she'd finally managed to induce, she tried to stare at him, although it was hard to keep her gaze focused. She wondered, briefly, if maybe she'd left her protective lenses in, then remembered they were back in her room's supply chest. He was paying no attention to her. Men often didn't notice her until she made the first move.

He faded into the shadows and smoke, and she thought he might not be there anymore. Then he slowly slipped into focus again, as if he'd moved, or as if the light had changed. She didn't think either of those things had actually occurred; it was just that she was drunk, or not drunk enough.

He was beautiful. Seductive. Terribly familiar. Surely she'd known him somewhere before.

Maybe it had been as long ago as her second week out with the company, her first drop. The vague impressions she seemed to have of him now could well have come from some of those early fantasies she'd had of the kind of men, or non-men, she might find out here. Back then she'd been naive, desperate to please, willing to become anything anybody wanted her to be. The stewards had nearly driven her planetside that first day in port. Perhaps in that first port there had been a man like this man: watching, waiting, familiar in this unfamiliar landscape.

Mary shivered and rubbed her eyes. She was tired and lonely, conditions so characteristic of her life that she was surprised she even noticed them anymore. Remembering how she'd been in those early days, which were not really so long ago, made her ashamed, made her call for another drink. The bartender pretended not to see her; he sometimes did that when he wanted to slow her down. For now, Mary let it go and stared again at the beautiful dark stranger at the door.

Maybe she'd known him in Brotskyville or Smithport, one of the innumerable little frontier towns with aluminum-alloy shacks and hydroponics and not much work. Mansfield, Stellarton, Unity, Quest. With fancy names or pedestrian, they were all nothing more than stops on the line for the big interstellar subs.

This one, planet and town, had—with foolish nostalgia or failed wit—been dubbed Wheat. Since she'd been here she'd seen nothing growing but nameless weeds, dun-colored and frayed like the last of her grandfather's sickly Kansas grain, but thicker, sharper at the edges, ready to slice through garments and skin.

Suddenly the man looked at her and, she thought, smiled. Mary's skin tingled, and she realized she couldn't possibly have known him or anyone like him before. He was breathtaking.

She'd dreamed about him, though, and he'd given a form to her longings when she'd been drinking alone or when she was finishing with a particularly boring customer. He wasn't of this world, or any other she'd physically lived in.

But now he'd walked through the rickety door of this nondescript establishment in this dull little backwater town as if he were a regular. She couldn't tell whether he was looking at her or not.

She'd met enough men in this place that some things were second nature by now; she looked him over, tried to meet his gaze. His skin was dark but gave the impression of being transparent, like night air almost too thin to breathe. His eyes were empty. And yet she knew he was staring at her.

Then he wasn't. He moved from the doorway, and Mary caught her breath at the primal beauty of his body in motion. In ways she couldn't specify, his movements were unlike those of any man she'd ever watched before, yet somehow she knew what to expect. He took a stool at the far end of the bar.

This time the bartender came when she signaled, but he made no move to draw her another ale. Mary tapped her glass impatiently on the bar and demanded, "Who's he?"

The bartender glanced in the direction she'd indicated. "What are you talking about?"

Very deliberately, knowing he was being difficult because he thought she'd had too much to drink, Mary persisted. "The guy at the end of the bar. The stranger. Who is he?"

The bartender did an exaggerated double-take. Then he took the glass away from Mary and patted her hand. "No more for you tonight. When you start hallucinating in my establishment, you've reached your limit."

"What are you trying to do to me?" She heard the rising panic in her own voice and knew he was right, she'd had too much to drink. A woman in her situation couldn't afford to be afraid of anything, and here she was, afraid of the beauty and strangeness of this beautiful stranger and equally afraid he wasn't really there. She grabbed the bartender's substantial wrist and demanded, with considerably more belligerence than she felt, "What are you talking about, hallucinating? Why are you playing with my mind? I'm not that crazy. He's right there."

That was true. Although she didn't dare turn her head to look at him again, she could see his reflection, or a suggestion of it, in the glass over the huge primitive painting above the bar. Fragments of his face hid in the shadows surrounding the stalks of wheat. She saw his dark hair with the odd scalloped hairline, his eyes that seemed to be no color at all. He was real. He was right there.

But suddenly she was also seeing—in the glass, in the painting itself—suggestions and reflections of other beautiful strangers. Suddenly she wasn't in this lonely bar on this barren, lonely planet, trying to figure out reality, wasn't clutching the bartender's wrists with both hands to force him to admit what she knew was real. For a long, wavering moment she was somewhere else, not quite in the world of the painting either, but in a space between which was populated by creatures, suggestions of creatures whose forms and voices and names weren't like hers but with whom she was quite at home.

She knew these creatures. She remembered their names and their functions in the heavy Russian accent of her Great-Aunt Sonia, who had believed in them the way people who'd travelled the dark between planets believed in the stars when they were back on Earth looking at pinpoints of light in the night sky.

Domoviye, who lived behind the stove and would ruin the house if they weren't kept content. One-eyed Lishiye, whose whispering often lured men off the path into the dark woods. Rusalky, slender and beautiful as summer grain, dancing in the wind to induce the grain to grow. Dark and handsome Poleviki, who altered their height according to the growing season, and who would silently strangle the drunkard careless enough to trample the crops and fall asleep in the fields.

Sonia had often appealed to the fairies when times were hard on the Kansas farm, and times were often hard. Barely realizing it, the child Mary had waited for the fairies to speak to her, too, and sometimes she thought they had. She'd liked to think of them living in miniature behind the stove, or so tall between the growing green and yellow stalks of wheat. Living, like her, in the world, but, like her, strange to it all. Living in the spaces of the world, the parts in between. Alien and beautiful.

For a long, whirling moment, Mary was now one of them. A creature not factual but profoundly real, whose existence made sense and had a clear purpose, with an unspoken mythical name of her own.

But then the long moment passed, and the painting—antique, a little sloppy, part of the bar's self-conscious and tacky "atmosphere"—was again only a depiction of a simplistic Kansas wheat field. Mary had often sat and stared at the painting when business was slow. Now, like an irritating tune she couldn't get out of her head, it snapped back into focus and she was clearly outside it, an observer, much as she'd been in the world it represented, much as she was on this sickly little planet that ironically shared its name.

Nearly in the center of the landscape, atop an old-fashioned diesel tractor, sat a shirtless young man; muscles were inexpertly shaded under improbably bronzed skin. The spidery legs of an irrigation machine rolled away toward the low horizon. The picture was dominated by a warm, rippling, gold color, and heads of grain that were finely detailed in the foreground blended into waves to suggest distance. Across the bottom quarter of the painting was its title in elaborate gilt scroll: "Wheat."

This was the country where Mary had grown up. The wheat fields had still been vast and golden like this, although no people had worked them since the prolonged drought and series of economic depressions around the turn of the millennium. Her grandparents and Sonia had operated one of the semi-private co-ops whose machinery, along with the even more sophisticated and efficient machinery of the agro-industrial conglomerates, had by then dotted the prairies, foreground and background. Back then it had never occurred to Mary that eventually somebody would paint a foolishly nostalgic painting of it, which would then hang in some

123

atmospheric bar somewhere in the populated universe and make people feel homesick when they had no reason to be.

All her life there, Mary had felt lost. Hating the vastness of the prairie, she'd yearned for the vastness of the stars. She recognized every detail in the crude painting, but none of it felt like home.

The bartender had leaned his elbows on the bar and brought his face very close to hers. At this proximity, he almost didn't look human. Each of his features separated from the rest and took on a life of its own: the nose a bulbous snail, the eyebrow a serpent. Mary found herself a little afraid of him.

The antique home-video unit in the corner blared dissonant, surprisingly disturbing music Mary knew had been called punk rock. On the white wall, indistinct forms gyrated and mouthed the lyrics out-of-sync. More atmosphere.

The place had filled with noisy patrons, almost all of them from the company. There was little else to do in this place. The stranger at the other end of the bar was almost lost in the crowd, but Mary knew he was still there.

"Mary, listen to me," the bartender said earnestly. She thought she must reek of ale, then told herself he must be used to that by now as she was used to the various odors that came with her job. "Mary. You're in trouble. You've got to get yourself some help. The company doctors—"

She stopped herself from jerking away from him only because she was afraid she'd tumble backwards off the stool. "Just get the hell out of my way, will you? I've got a living to make here."

The bartender guffawed. "This should be interesting. I don't believe I've ever seen a hooker put the moves on a figment of her imagination before." Shaking his head, he went to wait on another customer, passing right by the handsome stranger as if he weren't there.

Mary sighed and checked herself in the mirror above the end of the bar. The combination of ship's inventory officer and whore still jarred her. Blonde hair cut regulation length just above the collar, and thick blue makeup in an Earth style that she knew must already be out-of-date. As the days and nights accumulated here, she took less and less care with her appearance, and it didn't seem to matter at all to her customers. Sensory drugs and stimulation machines were readily available all over the frontier, and there were probably equal numbers of men and women, but actual whores were rare and easy money was always passing through. Mary's customers didn't care what she looked like or how much she charged; they cared only that she didn't try to get to know them, or expect them to be interested in knowing her.

Someone sat down between her and the stranger, then waved to a friend across the room and went away. Mary moved several stools closer to him. Like closed tents on the gleaming, cracked surface of the bar, his hands were thin, long-fingered, with delicate skin and gleaming nails. He reminded her of things.

The voice of the computer in Sonia's kitchen: On Sunday mornings she used to wake up to the peaceful, orderly chatter of the computer as Sonia prepared all the meals for the coming week, all the homemade cookies and breads and lunches, and filed them in chronological order.

The tiny fuzzy spores—she'd settled for calling them spores because everyone else did, but privately thought of them as having a touch of sentience—which had invaded her shack during one of the early pit stops on a close-in planet. She still dreamed about them sifting into the pores of her skin and, waking, thought they probably were still there.

A mentally retarded laborer aboard ship, whose mouth twisted when he laughed at nothing and whose eyes were so slow to focus that they looked hollow. Her Intro to Astrophysics prof at school, who'd had six fingers on his left hand. Aunt Sonia in the year before her death, refusing all the hormones and mental stimulation therapies, joyous in her senility, clutching at Mary's hair, eyes turned inward to some other reality that had made Mary restless with curiosity and envy. Shadows on the low, distant Kansas horizon, drifting in and out of the silhouettes of wheat.

She didn't know why he should make her think of such things, but the images came immediately, hungrily. Suddenly she was sure he'd said something to her, something so soft and intimate that it might have been the wind shifting sand outside or a dry clump of weeds rustling across the metal wall. But the sound had been articulated; she was sure there had been words. He wasn't looking at her yet; he still faced forward, looking at nothing as far as she could tell, face devoid of any expression she could read.

Mary huddled over her glass, which was full again with the acrid brown ale made of whatever vegetation grew in this place; the bartender, she thought with some regret, must have given up. She took a long swallow of the stuff, thinking how stupid she'd been to join the company in the first place. She'd wanted a survey ship, and she should have held out. She had the training: fluency in several Earth and simulated languages, advanced degrees in interstellar anthropology, honors in research. But she hadn't been willing to wait. This transport company had seemed a good way to sample many different worlds in a short time.

So far, though, all she'd seen were Earth outposts and a crew of humans whose customs and languages were essentially the same as hers, although she felt no kinship with any of them. And, anyway, reports from the survey ships indicated they were discovering nothing but new species of tiny flora and fauna. Mary longed to find a being she could engage with, fundamental alienness she could struggle with face-to-face, someone she could come to understand and who would understand her.

Hearing the whispering again, she slid impatiently off her stool and stood beside the stranger. "Hello. Would you like a little company?"

126

His eyes were half-closed, yet she thought they looked dreamy, unfocused. His hair fell oddly across his forehead and grew very low down his temples and neck, heavy black on dusky skin. He didn't acknowledge her presence in any discernible way, but Mary knew he was aware of her as nobody had ever been, and that he understood what she wanted from him.

She touched his shoulder and bent closer to him, wondering if maybe his auditory perceptions were different, thinking that he might not have heard her over the blare of the nostalgic music and the shouts of the war-games players in the corner. His odor was startling—not unpleasant, certainly, but unexpected, a fragrance she was sure she'd never smelled before. "Hey, stranger," she said, because it most often met with the response she wanted. "Can I buy you a drink?" It was something they might have said in an old vid; in any other bar she'd have felt silly, but here the anachronistic cliche was part of the ambience, and with this stranger nothing was out of place because, clearly, she was inventing the rules.

He looked up at her then—or, she interpreted his head movement and the peculiar scanning of eyes which appeared pupil-less as looking at her. He slid his narrow mouth into a gesture that resembled a smile. Afraid to break the connection, she kept her hand on his shoulder longer than she would have otherwise. She didn't know what to expect, was as nervous as if this were her first time.

Finally, when he still said nothing, Mary sat on the stool beside him and signaled the bartender for another round. This time he came, but when she said, "Bring one for my friend here, too," he said, "Mary, I can't do that," and would fill only her glass. The stranger didn't seem to mind.

She had downed almost half the bitter ale in her glass before she thought of anything to say. "I haven't seen you around here before. I thought I knew everybody on Wheat by now."

"I've seen you," she thought he replied, although his voice had such a startling timbre that she almost didn't understand his words. Rapidly, she reviewed everything she'd learned in school about accent and dialect and idiom, trying to place his origin.

Finally she asked him, "Where are you from?"

He gestured with his long hands, a round sweeping double motion obviously intended to convey information to her, to answer her query. She had no idea what it meant, but she didn't ask again.

Sipping the ale, Mary remembered the first time she'd approached a man in this bar—her awkwardness and shame, the skill she'd discovered in herself, the ability to keep a man at a distance safe for both of them while doing the most intimate of things. Dumped on this seedy backwater planet by a chief steward she'd turned down once too often for reasons that were obscure to her now, she'd had to make her way somehow. Whoring turned out to be no more distasteful than anything else she could think of, although there were days when it didn't seem worth the effort.

On those days she'd appealed to the fairies, who might as well live in the in-between spaces of Wheat as Kansas, and apparently they'd answered her, shown her the way, because here she was, trying to pick up this strange and beautiful man. He was so beautiful that she could hardly look at him, so strange that she hardly dared understand what was happening between them.

Outside, the wind was picking up. The seams of the metal building whined, and weeds scraped across the walls. Mary huddled closer to herself, recognizing the tendency toward introspection that sometimes interfered with her work, the preference for her own thoughts and her own company to which she sometimes succumbed. The stranger sat quietly beside her, neither looking at her nor looking away. His posture on the stool, the way he held his hands, the tilt of his head all made her feel slightly disoriented.

She often felt disoriented, here and elsewhere. Nights on Wheat suggested to her travel through subspace. In training, Mary had secretly found it hard to imagine subspace as a real phenomenon; science notwithstanding, she'd been able to accept it only as metaphor. But now she understood it as the in-between, the country which is neither here nor there, the terrain where dreams take place once the props and backdrops and references to the waking world have dissolved. The land where the dark Domoviye live forever behind the stove no matter what you do, and the exquisite Ruselky dance the night and the dawn and the dusk away in whatever wheat fields there are. The place where Mary might at last feel at home.

If she were to step out of this bar alone, she would find herself in thick gray darkness without features—no trees, rivers, mountains. Although the wind was constant and she always felt the grit and force of it, she could never see anything blowing. To find another building on Wheat at night, she looked for lighted windows, like other ships, alien sparks of life. But by this time, when everything but this bar was closed and everyone but patrons of this bar was asleep, she wouldn't have the lights; if she went outside alone, she'd have to travel from one building to another by dreamlike memory, as though sleepwalking or making her way through someone else's imagination.

She glanced at the stranger again. He was leaning back on his stool at an impossible angle, hands peaked and still in midair in front of him. Usually by now she knew whether a man was interested and didn't waste her time on somebody who, for whatever reason, didn't respond; she had learned early not to take personally either interest or the lack of it. But with this man she couldn't tell.

Deliberately, she raised a hand and put it over one of his, so that their two hands hovered in the air between them. His skin was cool, and of an odd texture. She noticed how long his nails were, and shaped in asymmetrical triangles. He didn't move his hand or make any other response to her, but Mary was somehow aware that something had altered in the relationship, the exchange, the space between them.

Then she and the stranger were walking together toward the

door. Together, but not touching or even speaking. There was none of the businesslike haste she often experienced with a customer, both of them eager to get on with it, to get it over. Mary felt as if she were floating free.

The wind was directionless, blowing from all sides at once. She shielded her eyes and threw her head back, trying to glimpse the expression on the stranger's face even if it wouldn't tell her anything about what he was thinking. But he was too tall, the night was too dark, and his face was shadowed by the high collar he'd pushed up around his neck—some kind of soft fabric, or maybe, she thought, skin. They matched stride for stride, as though both of them knew exactly where they were going.

Between the bar and the place where she lived—between almost any two objects on the surface of Wheat—was an expanse of weeds, knee-high and tough, bulging with sap that made your skin itch. Mary thought this was probably the source of both the locally-brewed ale and the acrid liquid that passed for coffee, although she'd never heard a specific name for the plants other than "sap weed" and never seen any indication of either cultivation or harvest. As she and the stranger pushed among them, the stalks snapped against her shins and, she imagined, wrapped themselves around his thin ankles. Although it was impossible to distinguish one patch of weeds from another, Mary had the curious sense that, in the dense darkness or the daytime glare, they were landmarks to guide her home.

Her body was moving in ways she was sure it had never moved before, although it was a profoundly familiar sensation. The stranger was with her, around her, matching every motion she made, leading and following. They were dancing, she realized, and the plants were dancing with them. The plants were growing to their rhythm and to the silent music that sustained it.

He was singing. His mouth moved very slightly as he sang sounds that she didn't think were words. His hands were at the small of her back, the long feathery fingers reaching almost all the way around her.

She lived in a single room in a distant, narrow two-story barracks. It was as much "home" as anywhere else she'd ever lived, certainly as much as the Kansas farm. This time she'd remembered to leave the red light on (the color satisfied her occasional need to make fun of what she did); a few nights sleeping under a windblown bush or, at the home of the somewhat horrified customer, had finally taught her to make sure she could find her way home.

The main door had come open in the wind, as it often did, and was banging back against the corrugated wall. She held it open for him, tried to capture a sense of him as he slipped past, then pulled the door tight. But it swung open again and the wind swept in.

He had already started up the stairs, and she studied him as she followed. His torso was very long in proportion to his legs, too long according to any conventional aesthetic but enormously pleasing to her. Scanning the hallway, he turned his head too far from one side to the other, as though his neck was more loosely jointed than hers. When he reached to open her door, and before she could intervene, his forearm and elbow stayed stationary while his wrist pivoted so far that it should have snapped. Mary was sure that she had locked her door.

He preceded her into her room. She saw how broad his shoulders were, but sharply angular. Under his thick coat, his shoulder blades created more movement than she'd have expected. As though he had extra ones there. Or maybe, she thought on the verge of a nervous laugh, wings.

She had a sensation of flying, of falling into the subspace. He turned and looked down at her, a glance that didn't hold and that could have meant anything or nothing. Mary reached up, fitted her hands to the unlikely contours of his face, and brought his lips to hers.

He resisted a little, as if he didn't know what she was doing. The possibility that she might teach him something, too, added to her excitement. Drunk, aroused, she could barely stand, and his arms came around her in ways no one had ever held her before.

She was falling. She had no thought to catch herself. His arms opened for her and closed around her, again and again. Some part of him—his tongue, maybe, if he had a tongue, or the tips of his long thin fingers—flickered in her throat until she thought she must have wandered off the path and fallen asleep in the field, and now for punishment would choke on her own carelessness.

His skin opened for her. Almost effortlessly she tried on the dark veil of him, slipped him on and stood before a mirror she knew from memory was there although she couldn't see it in this alien night. She saw her own reflection, and the reflection of the place where he had taken her, and it was home.

With altered eyes, she stared through him into a vast field of thick black plants that glistened from hidden sources of light; they grew and shrank and grew again, and her height shifted accordingly. Hearing acutely and in a different way, she listened to the wind's directionless moan, which had become the voices of everyone she'd left behind on earth, everyone she'd never found.

Suddenly she was terrified that she would fly the in-between forever, that she'd lose herself altogether in the spreading country of this man's imagination. She tried to stop, to say no and push him away, but it was too late and she'd gone too far. He entered her from underneath her own skin, from among the folds of her brain. It hurt, and she cried out. But it was what she'd been waiting for all her life. Other things happened then, but she forgot them even as they occurred. She slept, but without sleeping.

And then, in the morning, he was gone. As usual, Mary woke up alone in Wheat's harsh early daylight, and knew before she was fully conscious that she was more profoundly alone than she'd ever been, that the alien had made her more alien. She lay on her bed for a long time, but the heat in the little room soon became unbearable and the glare through the high uncurtained window cast sharp shadows.

"So," said the bartender by way of greeting, bringing her unasked a mug of coffee as bitter as last night's ale, "how was your night? I didn't see you leave."

"I went home alone."

He looked at her guardedly. "Mary, do you remember thinking there was a tall, dark, handsome man in here last night? And you were determined to pick him up?"

"I was drunk," she said. Already her head was spinning and her hands shaking unpleasantly from the coffee, and her words had an edge to them. She drained the mug and pushed it across the counter for more.

Refilling it, the bartender said, "I told you this last night, Mary, but maybe you don't remember. You need to get yourself some help."

"What I need," she told him, "is to get off this damn planet. When does the next ship come through? Headed anywhere?"

"They were talking in here last night that most of the subs coming through here anymore are automateds." He shook his head. "Bad for business. The Outliner II is due in a few months, but they'd already have a full crew. You got any passenger credits?"

"I can't wait a few months." She rested her forehead on her fists. Even as she gave in to the panic, she knew it was pointless. She was almost sure the stranger would be anywhere she went, would make her dance among the stalks of any alien grain, would live behind any stove and, when she was sufficiently unhappy, would destroy any house. Still, she muttered, "I have to get out of here right away. Tonight."

"You know that's impossible." He put his hands on her hunched shoulders. "Mary, what are you so afraid of? What happened last night?"

She pulled away from him and stumbled out into the reddish

glare of broad daylight. In her path rose the suggestion of the alien; she saw him only out of the corner of her eye. He made no move toward her and didn't say his sweet version of her name, but shreds of him clung to her as she ran and finally she stopped trying to shake them off, stopped running altogether and waited for him.

Where are you? he whispered. Come back to me.

Leave me alone, she sang. Wherever she looked in the sun's glare she saw red circles with white edges and dark centers, like fairy rings.

All day she stayed out in the sun, and she neither found the alien nor escaped him. The heat made her dizzy. The glare hurt her eyes and, she knew, was probably damaging them, but she would never wear the protective lenses again.

People stared at her. Some said hello. Some of them she'd had sex with, slept with, spent a night or more with. She didn't know which ones.

As the short day ended and the short night came on, Mary slipped between buildings, between weed stalks, into the border between light and shadow. She searched between things for the lover who had so frightened her, who had claimed her from all others. He wasn't there, and yet he was.

In the darkness then there were lights all around, but none of them hers. She didn't know whether she'd left the light on in her barracks room; that wasn't the way she'd ever find her way home again.

Instead, she wandered off the path and fell asleep in the fields. The shadows separated then, as though choosing sides, and she was neither asleep nor awake but in between, and his hands were around her neck, his fingertips in her mouth.

Mary heard the song he sang, felt it in her own throat, and sang it back. Her body moved as his did. In his empty eyes she saw her own eyes, her own perspective. She thought of him entering her, but of course he was already there.

134

They travelled together, between the stars. Between the places where everyone else lived. Into the country of his dreams and hers, the in-between. Into the Kansas of memories of a life she'd never lived, into a future on a planet among life forms she would never discover.

Ground moved in waves, separated to reveal another sky beneath it. Great pools of sunlight changed their borders slowly, eventually becoming the size and shape of her eyes. Fallen animals, which were parts of her body, buzzed with decay and turned her into something else that was neither alive nor dead. Tall plants of every color, bursting with poisonous hallucinogenic sap, rose so high and so quickly that she couldn't imagine the scope of either their branches or their roots; high above her head and deep under her feet, they spoke of things she'd never dared speak of before.

He reached for her. His hands were not hands. He would embrace her, make love to her, devour her. "Leave me alone!" she cried. "I don't belong with you, either!" But she knew it was not true.

She heard them calling her name, a search party made up of all those others she'd slept with, all those others she'd never known. She heard the bartender calling her name, telling her they'd come to help. She could see their hands reaching toward her through the burnt haze of her damaged eyes.

But his hands, which were not hands, reached her first.

My love, he said, and his face was so close to hers that she thought the sheer vision of him would consume her, this is not me, his voice pulsing with her breath and her heartbeat, this is you.

SAFE AT HOME

"Mindy.
"Touch me. Here. Like this.
"You like to touch me, don't you?
"That's a good girl. Oh, that's right."

Charlie was incredulous. "You want me to take you to another horror movie? But you hate that stuff."

"The monster in this one has long sticky tentacles that come up out of a dark pool." Melinda squinted at the newspaper ad and gave a short, brittle laugh.

"Let me guess. It has a particular affinity for pretty young women." Charlie's laugh was easier, fuller than hers.

"Don't they all," she said.

Charlie took her to the movie because she wanted to go, and also because he knew there was a good possibility of sex afterwards. She didn't begrudge him that. Charlie was a good guy, and Melinda felt bad about using his baser instincts to get what she wanted. But it worked. It had always worked.

She didn't love Charlie, not yet. And he didn't love her. She hoped he didn't love her.

"I love you, Mindy. You're my favorite niece, did you know that?
"You want to make your Uncle Pat happy, don't you? Let me show you how to make me happy.
"Oh, you are such a good girl."

Charlie was a tender, considerate lover. He went slow. He'd never hurt her. She knew he thought what they did together in bed was beautiful.

It made her want to throw up.

Monsters made it possible for her to throw up. Monsters in horror movies especially, with sticky appendages or gaping maws or formless bodies that oozed from everywhere and never went away.

At some point during every show she'd get up and hurry to the ladies' room, hoping there wouldn't be a line. She'd crouch over a toilet and vomit for a long time. If she'd been able to force herself to eat any popcorn or candy, it would come out of her in recognizable chunks, but everything else being expelled from her body was whitish and viscous, like semen. For a while then—sometimes minutes, sometimes the rest of the night—she wouldn't be sick to her stomach.

"Oh, no, Mindy, this isn't wrong. We love each other, so how could anything we do together be wrong?
"Show me that you love me, Mindy.
"That's right. That's my girl."

She hated having to chew and swallow in front of people.

138

Sometimes she caught herself imagining that if she opened her mouth too wide a sticky, sinewy monster would slide out and wriggle into the darkness under the house, under the streets, under the world.

She watched Charlie eat. She wanted to see what his teeth did to the food, how his tongue rolled and humped to get the food down. Sometimes in the middle of a meal she'd reach over and very lightly rest her fingertips on the hinge of his jaw, where she could feel the bones and muscles, sinews and tendons all working together in one building rhythm.

"You're weird," Charlie said the first time she was brave enough to do that. Mouth full of spaghetti, he leaned across the table and kissed her.

Melinda had thought he was going to say he loved her. He'd had that tender, passionate, self-absorbed look on his face that had nothing to do with her. Relieved that he'd said something else, she didn't pull away.

She tried hard not to imagine the spaghetti in his mouth. For some reason it scared her.

Then she gave up and set herself to imagining it as vividly as she could. Whitish sticky tendrils, viscous sauce. Charlie's mouth caressing it, taking everything from it, the inside of a kiss.

"Sweet," Charlie said, still looking at her more intently than she liked. "And very beautiful. But definitely weird."

"Your mommy and daddy didn't mean me. I'm your daddy's brother.

"They asked me to babysit this weekend, remember? They asked me to take care of you while they were gone. Don't you think they must trust me a lot to let me take care of their precious little girl?

"So you can trust me, too.

"Come here, Mindy. Come to Uncle Pat."

After the movie they often rode the bus across town to Charlie's house. When she rode the bus alone, Melinda watched all the men waiting for her, in the other seats, at stops, on street corners, on billboards and movie posters. During heavy rains there were so many people in doorways that she couldn't tell which ones were waiting for just her, and in the wet shadows she usually couldn't see their hands. There ought to be a law requiring men to keep their hands exposed at all times in the presence of females. Especially girls. Especially little girls.

A man with a narrow face, or maybe with only a penis for a face, stared at her from a narrow passageway when the bus stopped for a light. His long pale tongue slid out of the shadows and down his coat, down one leg and across the sidewalk, leaving a slick, steaming trail. The tongue was wiggling its way toward her when the bus pulled into the intersection. Charlie hugged her and whispered a soft alien language into her ear.

In Charlie's bedroom she took off her clothes, forcing herself to move slowly, holding her breath, hoping the bile in her stomach wouldn't rise into her throat. Charlie watched her adoringly. "You are so beautiful," he kept saying, and Melinda flinched that he would say such a thing out loud. "You are so beautiful."

Melinda could barely let herself hear such nice things about her body, but she liked hearing them, was relieved each time that he didn't say how ugly she was, how pale, how skinny or how fat, how wormlike smooth or how hairy. If she didn't trim her bikini line her pubic hair would just keep growing, would spill out of her crotch and rise above the waistband of her shorts, would wrap itself like monkey tails up and down her limbs.

A woman was never safe. Like all women, Melinda had a wet, hairy hole in the middle of her body. A hole in the middle of her life. Where awful things might enter.

Charlie invited her to stay the night. Melinda said no, she wasn't ready, and Charlie didn't push. He insisted on accompanying her on the bus all the way home. He was so sweet. Gratefully, she kissed him good-bye at her door, although she really didn't want to touch him anymore. She didn't ask him in.

Alone in her apartment, she sat naked in the dark, all the bed-clothes pushed well away from her. Cloth would burn her; her bare flesh was already aching with nothing touching it at all. It hurt her to be exposed like this; it would hurt more to try to cover herself up.

Then she waited until she was too tired to wait anymore. She waited, as she did every night, for something to break her door down or to seep in under it. For something to drag her or coax her into the sticky dark outside.

Safe. Safe at home.

"Mindy, Mindy, you are so beautiful."

That July the annual invasion of miller moths was the worst any-body could remember. They bred somewhere in the South and would go up into the mountains to die, Melinda read, or maybe it was the other way around; when she was afraid of something she tried to find out as much about it as she could, but often she had trouble keeping her facts straight and that just made her more afraid. It didn't matter anyway; the truth was, they came from everywhere, bred everywhere, and they would never die.

Miller moths were monsters, and she was terrified of them. They swarmed so thickly around the lamp on her bedside stand or the hood light on her stove that they looked like clots of curly hair. They got stuck in her food, drowned in her coffee. They flew into her face, into her mouth, into the hole in the middle of her body, leaving everywhere the dust from their wings. The dust from their wings was poisonous. It was also what enabled them to breed.

They were in her bed. When Charlie wasn't there she felt them all

141

night long, flicking against the back of her neck, kissing the insides of her thighs, crawling into her vagina.

Finally, after three virtually sleepless nights, Melinda danced around her bedroom in a frenzy, with a rolled-up newspaper in one hand and a flyswatter in the other. She smashed every moth she saw or thought she saw, until the paper was tattered and the flyswatter was covered with pulpy wing dust and she was faint with exertion and fear. But in the end she was helpless against them. There were miller moths everywhere.

And they would get their revenge. They would pass stories on from one generation to the next about what she'd done to their family, or tried to do, and someday when she thought she was safe at home—in the winter, say, when there weren't supposed to be any moths—one or a dozen or a million of them would lay their eggs inside her.

Monsters were everywhere. Great hairy things with eyes and teeth, miller moths with poisonous wings, squirmy creatures with tentacles that caught and held. All the monsters communicated with all the other monsters—the moths with the beasts, the caterpillars with the men. They spoke a language Melinda frequently understood but could not quite use herself. They talked about her. They watched her every minute of every day and night.

Everything was a monster, monstrous and magical. Everything was family but her. Everything talked.

"If you tell, they won't understand."
"If you tell, they'll be mad at me. And at you."
"If you tell, you'll get us both in big trouble."
"If you tell, you'll tear our family apart."
"If you tell, Mindy, I'll go to jail, and then I won't love you anymore."

Charlie lay back in her arms. He was so sweet, so patient and good to her.

142

He was watching her. He watched her all the time. Even when they made love he didn't close his eyes; she'd open hers during a long breathtaking kiss and find him looking at her, his eyes so close they didn't look like eyes anymore but like dark pools out of which anything might rise. Even when she let him spend the night (at her place, at home, never at his where she wouldn't know where the monsters had bred in the night) and she woke up from her habitually fitful sleep, she knew he was watching her in his dreams. Every minute of every day and night.

"Sometimes you're such a little girl," he observed. "Like when we go to horror shows and you get so scared you have to run to the bathroom and throw up."

Melinda hadn't realized he knew about that. She felt her face and neck go hot.

"And other times," he persisted, "you're like a beautiful wise old woman. No, not old. Ageless. Like you've been alive forever. That's how you seem when we make love."

"Sex is older than we are," Melinda said. "It's older than anybody. It's so old and so powerful it's like a god, or a monster. People will do anything, tell themselves anything to make what they do all right, just so they can hold onto it for a split second."

She saw Charlie's eyes widen, heard him catch his breath, saw an appendage with a searching eye and clinging membranes slither toward her as he started to say, "Love's like that, too, you know."

She stopped him with a kiss. The tentacle went into her mouth, into her throat. She sucked. The hole in the middle of her body filled up with viscous whitish fluid, and she ran to the bathroom to vomit it away.

"You're growing up now. You're becoming a woman.
"Why do you treat me like this? Why do you hate me?
"I don't understand why you want to hurt me. We've been so close.
"I don't understand.
"I love you."

143

Charlie sneaked up on her. They were in her bed and she was relaxing in his arms, feeling pleasantly hungry, thinking that even if that furry shadow in the corner of the ceiling was a moth it wouldn't hurt her, it was as afraid of her as she was of it, when Charlie said before she saw it coming, "I love you."

She was going to throw up. She struggled to get up, to free herself of him, but he wouldn't let her go.

"Melinda, wait. Please don't go. I love you."

The miller moth elongated and swelled and inserted itself into her mouth. Its poisonous dust was making her choke. It pushed its way down through her body; she felt it circling her heart, winding among her intestines, nudging the inside of her vagina, but it didn't come out.

"I know you're afraid. I know somebody has hurt you. But I won't hurt you. I love you."

The monster was godlike; the god was monstrous. It had a single wet eye and a bifurcated heart. She would do anything she had to do to keep it away from her, anything to make it forever her own.

But not now. She wasn't ready now.

"Mindy. I love you."

"No no no!" She pulled away from his wet tongue, his hairy hands, his single eye. She sprang from the bed and ran, the monster who loved her stumbling after her.

She ran down the hall, painfully aware of her nakedness, of the hairy, wounded hole in the middle of her body, that wanted to be filled, that wanted to be protected from the crawling, slimy vermin that filled the world. Even as she ran she frantically considered what she might use to plug it up.

She ran into the bathroom and slammed the door, locking it. Outside the monster panted, out of breath. "Mindy, Mindy…love …" And then fell silent.

She crouched on the cool tile in the corner, her head pressed against cold porcelain. It was too late to vomit. Too late to escape. Under the edge of the door, black hair was spreading toward her.

Melinda tried to pull herself into the hole in the middle of her body, the hole in the middle of her life, the hole she had become. She knew she wouldn't die there, although sometimes that's what she wanted. She hoped she wouldn't have to eat there, that nothing would have to enter her body ever again.

There, she knew she could be the monster who never needed to love. She could be the god.

Safe. Safe at home.

THE MARRIAGE

H E HAD CHOSEN HER AS HIS MATE because of her ability to renew her emotions again and again, however thoroughly he might deplete her. Even after long periods of hysterical grieving, she would come to him and he would be surprised by her ability to smile, to love, to rage and to endure serious pain. From the start he had known, of course, that it could not continue forever, for she, like all the others, was mortal, and sooner or later would die. He had thought that most likely he would kill her with his need, all the more ferocious because it would not be satisfied, and then he would be forced to find someone else or to content himself entirely with strangers.

Not that the variously-flavored emotions of strangers lacked attraction, not that the surge and substance of their bodies were any less sweet, but even he liked someone familiar to come home to.

She knew, of course, of his predilections, what he did with his days and most of his nights. Sometimes she would request a particular detail, worrying the painful morsel in order to expand her passion in interesting ways.

"We all need our daily tickle and rub," the guy next door was fond of declaring coarsely. He wouldn't have been so cheerful about it if he'd known about certain late-night and mid-afternoon visits to his sad-looking wife and his brittle but equally sad-looking daughters.

Not that he had been the cause of any of this sadness. The neighbor himself with his anger and his appetites was sufficient cause for any degree of sadness. He had only found the well and chosen to drink there. Taken a taste of the family's miseries by way of blood and vaginal secretions. And—when he finally got to the paternal source—by way of semen.

But the passions of that particular family, the passions of all the mundane sorts he met, sorted through, and tasted each day, paled in comparison with those of his wife. For this part of his life, for the last eighty-four human years, she was by far the most intense person he had met.

Just now, on her deathbed, she was in considerable pain, and her pain was his for the taking. Nearing a hundred in human years, her body was frail, the pain very close to both the surface of the flesh and the marrow of the bone, and he could have sucked it out of her with scarcely any effort, relieving both her and himself in a single easy act.

Instead, he lingered. He teased. He kissed her gently, his lips and teeth closed, all over her aged body, while she moaned and writhed under him in the titillated passion of her suffering. He bared his penis, entered her dry vagina, and probed, curious whether he could increase either her agony or his arousal, seeing that he could. She cried out, begged him. He waited as long as he thought he dared, then drew the pain out of her and into him in one swift current.

She was spent, crumpled against him like a used paper sack. He was, as always, disappointed. He should have waited longer. She could have held more suffering for him. She could have given him more.

So he left her, though she tried feebly to hold him back, and in a bar full of dark music and dim light although it was mid-afternoon he came, without warning or foreplay, upon a woman who almost at once asked him to tell her he loved her. Readily he took her away from the eyes of that place, out onto hot asphalt and into heady automotive perfumes, where he professed his love for her with perfect, borrowed sincerity. She nodded, licked her lips. "Bite me," he whispered. "No, there." He experienced only a distant discomfort, no true pain, as the tiny mouth-shaped ovals of skin disappeared from his arm.

"Now, my turn," she insisted, too eagerly. She did not care that he had not received pleasure. She did not feel for him.

So he took too much from her too quickly, gorged himself on the pain he had spared her, a mercy which she did not deserve. "Love me," he urged, and shook her. But by now she could feel no more than he could, so he left her in the parking lot and went back home.

Tonight his wife was afraid of dying. She was not always so. Sometimes she approached death with a giddy sort of readiness that he found insubstantial, difficult to hold onto, and utterly unsatisfying, like spun sugar. At other times she seemed not to be aware at all that the end of her life was near.

But tonight she was profoundly frightened, and fear was among the sensations he savored most. He surrounded her with arms and legs, tongue and teeth, anxious for the fullness of her fear to descend upon them both, and when it would not come fast enough he found himself nibbling at her dry skin, licking every orifice for any available secretion. She'd been incontinent for years, and to allay any suspicions he had accepted the doctors' prescriptions for catheters and adult diapers, but of course he would never apply such ugly contraptions to her flesh, insisting instead to clean her in his own way, and to keep her clean with his appetites, several times each day.

Tonight he lay in their marriage bed with her in his arms, waiting for her fear to ripen, and he reflected that, although it went without saying that he did not love her, he would indeed be sorry when she was gone.

Which was not to say that she was or ever had been enough for him. Nothing was ever enough, no one could keep him full. Strangers had provided him with some memorable experiences, however. Vivid enough that even in his long life they might make an impression he could dessert on. Just last week, was it, or last month:

"You don't have to tell me you love me," the man with the crooked teeth had assured him magnanimously.

"Maybe I will anyway," he'd said with a borrowed feminine smile.

"You will," the man had agreed, stroking his woman's cheek, gliding a hand down under the lacy collar and pulling away the blouse, unhooking the satiny brassiere to expose his woman's nipples.

He'd wrapped his female arms around the man, who had assumed, no doubt, that the scratches in his back were being made by long scarlet fingernails mining for passion when in fact the fingertips themselves were sharpening and lengthening as his famished body and soul realized the imminence of a meal. "Love me," he'd begged the man in his breathy female voice, with his woman's shortness of breath, and pushed himself into him until skin interpenetrated. Disoriented by his own paltry lust, the man had perhaps thought this some strange undergarment when actually it was a thin layer of his own skin peeling away. The man kissed, sucked, thrust, struggling to remove all real and imagined barriers between him and the object of his desire, all the while causing himself to bleed. Ultimately, it was pain which made the man's erection rise, fear that thrust itself past his labia, lubricated by the man's free-flowing blood as they writhed together. The man's passionate desperation probed and scraped until tidal spasms of horror washed both their minds clean, so that they could feel nothing, for once again he had taken and used it all.

150

But he always came back to her, and she was always waiting for him, welcoming. Willing, eager, often frantic for him to siphon off the emotions that were too much for her and never enough for him.

"Hold me," she pleaded now. Thinned and cracked with age, it was still the importuning and caressing voice that he had been hearing for what now seemed like such a long time but would reveal itself, once she had died, as only the most fleeting instant of his interminable existence. "Take it. Take the fear. Death is a natural part of life. Everybody dies. Everybody has always died. I don't want to be afraid."

Through her toothless kiss she spat in a hot stream into his throat the acrid roiling broth of her terror. Though she was more than willing, and he was expert, and their give-and-take had been the core of their marriage for more than eight decades, it took a deliciously long time for him to get it all. By the time they had both achieved a transitory calm, he was already not thinking much of her anymore but of his next foray.

Rather recently he'd discovered the accessible pleasures of hospital emergency rooms. Even the most commonplace passions were magnified within families, and in an emergency room a family was opened and left bleeding, especially when one of its children was hurt or ill, dead or nearly so. He would go again tonight, when his wife was asleep. He could tell by the way she breathed against his shoulder that she was nearly asleep now, and his mouth began to water in anticipation of what this night was likely to bring.

"Noooo!" The mother wailed her denial. That sort of hysteria was filling, to be sure, but hard on the finer nerves if taken by mouth, so he'd developed a method of taking it in through the nostrils. He'd dallied pleasantly with images to describe the particular odor of frenzied despair: Vaguely, it smelled like a child's soiled shirt, and also like the kind of sunlight that can be trapped only in a child's hair.

He'd seen the teenage daughter, the older sister, hovering around the edges of the knot made by the rest of the family. She obviously wanted to be part of the high drama of grief, but—so typical of her age—could not quite permit herself to join them. Her grief was tinged with embarrassment at her mother's noise, with resentment over having lost the center of attention, with fear that her father might grieve himself insane.

Eventually the daughter detached herself from the palsied fist of pain which the other brother, sister, father, mother had become, and sought out a quiet dark corner. Where he waited, had been waiting for more than an hour.

"Everybody's dying," she said softly to the wall, as though she knew he was there. Her tongue played with sadness as though it were prey, a mouse that might escape the damp chamber of her mouth. Inhaling deeply, he immediately knew that her vagina was moist, and he stepped into her smell. He then allowed her to smell him. He heard her pulse quicken. He felt his spirit soar, then, and change.

Via his own and her desire and shadow and lament, he willed buttons and fasteners to fade, fabric and elastic to dissolve. As he pressed against her he momentarily permitted her to see him, encouraged her youthful fantasies and her senses engorged by shock to create the bare-skinned youth of him, the long and impossibly thick black hair that became a creature all its own, and the dark penis down there in the shadows, because she wanted only a glimpse.

At that moment she began to weep, not so much a child's cry as the cry of a child departing, and the depth of it actually surprised him, made him gasp. He was quickly engulfed in this young woman's exploding emotions, gliding into the turmoil of her, feeling himself alive in the orgiastic brevity of his taking, taking, until she was irrevocably emptied and he, however fleetingly, was filled.

When he returned to their marriage bed he found his wife still asleep. Comatose. Her withered face looked blank, stripped.

Perhaps she was dead. He held his breath to listen for hers. He peered at her, laid his ear against her hollow chest. She was not dead.

He slid his arm from under her shoulders and crept out of their room, out of their house. He would leave her for a while, and then he would return to take whatever else she had for him in the last hours of her life.

This time in another emergency room he waited afterwards, and was gratified that he had thought to do so. Numbly, this other teenaged girl rejoined her family, her body spent, her eyes glazed. They would think perhaps that sorrow had overtaken her, and after a few hours there would be speculation that drugs were the cause, and the passions so exhibited would have been as nectar to him, and only after days or months had passed would they suspect that something was dangerously amiss. That she had given away her ability to feel.

The parents' despair would then be doubled. They would brood over how they had considered the adolescent daughter selfish. They would berate themselves for not understanding how desperately attached she'd been to her little brother, how fervently attached she was to them. They would try their best to reach her, then, but she would be beyond them. At still another emergency room vigil it was the father he determined to stalk and court. The father welcomed him, grasped him in a savage embrace, wanted to kill him. The father's rage was a sweet surprise that lasted well into the morning hours, and so he was late getting home.

This time his wife did not respond to him at all when, already wincing from the pangs which he had learned to term "hunger," he presented himself at her bedside. Her eyes, nostrils, mouth gaped, but it was obvious that she neither saw, smelled, nor tasted him. Her fingers clawed, but she was not touching him.

He knew her, though. She was his mate, his wife, his companion for this stretch of his endless life. Since she'd been a headstrong beauty of fifteen, renowned for her intensity and reputed to be

153

untamable, she had belonged to him. She had loved him beyond all others. She had given him everything she had, countless times, and replenished herself in order to give him more. She would not fail him now. He knew how to take what was his.

He pulled her to him. Her body and mind were flaccid, but she was not dead, for he could feel her heartbeat and her faint rattling breath. He kissed her, bit into her, but she gave him nothing.

He entered her. At the surface and for many layers under the surface there was nothing—no fear, no pain, no passion, no love for him.

Trembling with hunger and with the anticipation of an even greater hunger—starvation, famine—to come, he thrust deeper into her with nails and teeth and penis. So deep, distant and all but closed to him, was something. Joy, he thought. Profound peace. But he could not reach it.

She died in his arms. Reluctant to let her go, he lay there for a few minutes with the emptied body. "More," he pleaded. He stroked the creviced face. "I am not finished with you. I have not had enough. I need more." He lifted her in his arms and shook her. Her head lolled back across his forearm but her throat was motionless, did not pulse. Her lips hung slack but did not part for him. She had given him all she had, and it was not nearly sufficient.

Eventually he sighed and rose. Wearily he prepared himself to go out again, wondering whether he would find another mate as good for him as she had been. As he shut and locked the door of their home behind him, it came to him that he had loved her. He was shocked and—for a few, brief astonishing moments—full.

MORE THAN SHOULD BE ASKED

"JAKE NEVER WAS AN EASY CHILD." Mrs Klein always started stories about her son in just that way. It didn't matter whether the occasion was that Jake had exhibited bad table manners at a dinner party she had given for friends, or that Jake had just been arrested for robbing a convenience store. Even if she were talking to any one of a succession of teachers, social workers, lawyers, police officers. "It was a difficult delivery." As if that explained everything.

"Evelyn…" Mr Klein always tried to stop her, smiling at the officer, social worker, person-in-charge, as if this were an old joke. An old joke that was killing him. He loved his son; he loved him very much. But to say that Jake was never an easy child was the grimmest of jokes.

"I'm just trying to fill the officer in, George," she would admonish him, in a feigned whisper that never failed to embarrass. Then she would turn back to the official with a conspiratorial wink, as if George couldn't possibly understand what they knew to be obvious, that Jake was a good boy, just currently experiencing some bad luck. A problem of timing, was all. "In the first place, he was nearly a month late, taking on this world in his own good time. All along, he'd been so active in the womb kicking, punching, tossing and turning, even (I swear) biting that my poor insides were bruised and torn from his occupation of them, and they never have fully healed."

George always turned his back at that point, sat down, or went outside. No doubt they considered him the unconcerned parent, perhaps even the root cause. Not that it mattered. He just didn't want a stranger see him shudder, or cry.

Baby Jake had been more than a demanding infant. He didn't whimper or cry; he roared. He howled. He raged. Nothing they could do for him was ever enough. Especially, he never got enough to eat, either breast milk or formula. Evelyn's nipples were always so sore she wept when Jake reached for them. Often they were bloodied—George had never imagined such a thing as possible—he was appalled as Jake managed to make holes in an endless supply of rubber nipples. Jake never did sleep through the night.

To this day, George knew that Jake was up at all hours. Often George would get up in the middle of the night and drive by the apartment building where Jake sometimes stayed, and the lights would always be on, and sometimes there would be this form pacing by the window, motioning wildly with its arms as if arguing with itself. George never told Evelyn about that. He himself didn't sleep deeply after all those years of Jake racing down the stairs on all fours, Jake singing and yipping at the top of his lungs, Jake leaping out a window or climbing back in. After all, he had never been an easy child. In fact, he had never been a normal child.

When he was three, George had found him carefully laying broken bottles in the road. When he was seven, their neighbor informed them he'd been beating chickens to death with rocks; the man was almost apologetic when he brought a struggling and utterly unchastened Jake to the door, and George couldn't tell if he was sorry he hadn't told them before or sorry he was telling them now.

Even then, Evelyn hadn't believed a word of it. He was never an easy child, but somehow he would always be perfectly normal to her.

"He needs help," George had warned her. "And we can't help him by ourselves. Really, this is more than should be asked of any human being."

"Pre-natal care is vital," she replied. "I was young, and I skipped some visits. I was too busy. It's not your fault, George. It's dangerous to expose a developing fetus to any toxins, especially during the first trimester. It's in all the books. And I was still smoking, some, hiding it from you, and remember I took up oil painting that summer? All those toxic paints, and the heat?" She began to cry.

"For heaven's sake, Evelyn! He was nine years old when he burned the goddamn house down!"

Show me an arson fire in a house, one of the firefighters opined, almost jauntily, apparently trying to comfort them, and I'll show you a nine year old boy with a match. And Evelyn had nodded as if it were practically the wisest thing she had ever heard. Then she'd looked at George as if he should have known this essential bit of trivia all along.

But this hadn't been just a curious kid; Jake had deliberately built piles of old clothes and newspapers at strategic locations, doused them with gasoline he'd pilfered from the can in the shed, and set the fire. The house had been completely destroyed.

By the time he was thirteen, Jake had discovered the short-lived but gratifying thrills of stealing cars and doing drugs. At fifteen he was declared incorrigible and institutionalized. George and Evelyn had visited him dutifully twice a week, and each time George had told his son he loved him, loved him more than almost anything. That had not been a lie, but the smile on George's face as he said it was.

Between children's homes, reform schools, and jails, Jake never lived at home again. Now, at twenty, he was out, and going to be a father himself. The thought was mind boggling.

"Jake never was an easy child," Evelyn said again. "But maybe being a father will straighten him out. Sometimes it does, you know." George had looked at her as if she were crazy, but he knew there was some truth in what she said. Being a father changes you, whether you want to be changed or not. It transforms you into another person. Because only another person can love a child as a child must be loved.

"The world is a dangerous place." George had told his son this when his son was seven years old. "I know you don't know this yet—maybe you're not meant to know. But parents know this, and believe me, it drives them crazy."

Jake had looked up at him as if he—the father—knew nothing about it, could know nothing about it. George could see it in his son's eyes: the wildness. His son's eyes were saying that the world was a wild place, a hungry place, and although to the father that meant dangerous, they weren't really the same thing at all.

"I have never been afraid the way I have been afraid for you." George had told his son that the last time he ever visited him in jail. Jake had looked back at him with eyes that borrowed darkness, and from that silence held so long at the back of Jake's throat had come this murmuring, a sound George had been unsure of at first, but which later he knew to be far older than anything from the human families he knew anything about.

In a rare moment of confession, Evelyn once told George, "Sometimes he changes who I am. I have never been as angry with anyone else as I have been with my son. I look at myself in the mirror and I don't recognize the shape of my own face."

They never dared have another child because of Jake. Evelyn was as committed to that as was George. Now this would be their first grandchild the first, at least, that they'd been permitted to

158

know about. They couldn't just stand by. They had to do their best to help.

"Children will bring up all kinds of unresolved issues for parents," they warned.

Jake stared at them for a long moment and then laughed. "'Unresolved issues'? Jesus, speak English, at least," he snarled, and lit another cigarette. George imagined the lungs of his unborn grandchild corroded with secondhand smoke and felt silly, and obsolete.

"Children will change you," Evelyn promised, but Jake wasn't a father yet. He had no way to understand.

"Being a parent is the toughest job you'll ever have," George told him, even though none of his lectures had helped over all the years before. So why was he trying now? "You're expected to have the patience of Job and the wisdom of Solomon, not to mention a sense of humor and the ability to make critical split second decisions a hundred times a day, plus you have to give unconditional love without requiring anything back. Being a parent is more than should be asked of any human being. Sometimes it seems like more than any human being can do. It changes you, son."

George had waited twenty years to deliver that speech, and Jake adroitly dismissed him with a wave of his hand, walking away with the comment, "You guys think too much—that's your problem."

The baby was born with an excess of body hair. George had worried over that until Evelyn read to him from one of her huge baby-care books about how that was perfectly normal, and that the baby would lose the hair over time. It had something to do with evolution apparently, something to do with our animal selves. George wondered how sane parenting could have possibly taken place in the centuries before Gutenberg.

The baby was a fierce little thing, just like his father, George thought. Fussy. Ravenously hungry. No easy child. Sometimes when George held his baby grandson up to his chest he was actually a little afraid, suddenly nervous that the child would try to bite him. Not trying to hurt his grandfather, really, but out of a natural fierceness and a natural need. A hunger that could not be satisfied, especially not under the rules parents and grandparents would feel compelled to lay down for him.

So then George would kiss his grandson nervously, and hand him back, and feel his neck for scratches.

One Sunday evening they stopped by Jake and Melinda's apartment on the pretext of taking them an extra chicken that had been on sale 2 for the price of 1 at Safeway. In truth, as their son almost certainly knew, they were there to monitor how the new parents were doing with their grandson. George could hear Jake yelling and the baby screaming before he even got out of the car.

George and Evelyn looked at each other. Their worried gazes had met in just that way hundreds of times over Jake helpless, enraged by their helplessness, furiously longing to do the right thing. George wished they could just drive off and come back later when this crisis was over, one way or another, and they could pretend they hadn't known about it and therefore bore no responsibility. But that wasn't so. Their son may have been beyond their reach, but their grandson wasn't as yet, and they had to do something.

One after the other, they made their way as fast as they could, on legs that weren't young any more and with lung capacities that showed themselves to be alarmingly limited, up the unlit and musty smelling steps to the apartment. Their footsteps clattered and echoed. The door at the top landing was ajar. George could see through the young couple's minuscule living room into the tiny alcove that served as a bedroom for all three of them. But Jake didn't seem to know or care that they were there, even when Evelyn said his name.

In the few seconds that passed while George caught his breath and took stock of the situation, he saw his son with his son in his hands. Not in his arms, for he held the baby well away from him, but in a two handed grip such as you would use on a basketball. His hands seemed unnaturally large, much larger than George remembered them—in fact, George remembered Jake as having relatively small hands. Jake was roaring. The baby was roaring. They were having some kind of yelling match.

Evelyn said, "Jake!" again, but he didn't hear. "Shut up!" he bellowed at the baby. "Shut the fuck up, you little bastard!" and he shook the baby, too hard. Thinking of the soft infant brain skidding around inside the skull, George stepped forward.

Jake lifted the squirming and bellowing baby over his head. George was sure he was going to throw him.

Both George and Evelyn reached for the baby. Jake twisted away. Now he had folded his son in against his chest. As if he loved him, which George believed he did. As if he owned him. As if he could do with him whatever he wanted.

George couldn't let that happen.

Jake twisted his head and looked fiercely at his aging parents. George could feel his son's disdain. As if they were too old, too weak, too wounded to be of much use anymore. Jake threw back his head and howled. "We were just…" He laughed uncontrollably. "The little cub and I were…"

George tried to say something to his son—some small lecture, some bit of easy wisdom—but discovered that his body, however aged, had rushed past his voice, his words lengthening into a growl that solidified in front of his face.

With the intuition and unspoken communication that parents often develop when they've worked for years to present a united front, George and Evelyn sprang at once.

Without thinking George's jaws closed on the back of his son's neck and snapped it.

Evelyn's clawed nails went through Jake's shirt and the skin and bone of his chest, into his heart.

Jake dropped his son. George caught his grandson in his mouth.

MAMA

E LIZABETH'S MOTHER WAS DEAD.

Which was a shame, because right now Elizabeth wanted to kill her herself.

She guessed she didn't mean that. She guessed it wasn't Mama's fault that she'd gotten the cancer. No, that wasn't true either. Mama deserved the cancer because she'd always smoked, smoked in secret in the bathroom and in the garage but everybody knew about it—they just pretended they didn't know. That was the kind of power Mama had. Dad had pretended so well that one time he smelled cigarette smoke outside Elizabeth's room and he yelled at her, accused her of it, until he realized it was Mama who had done it and he'd looked all embarrassed, and then he'd looked angry and he'd said, "but someday it will be you, Elizabeth. You're just like her!" And then he'd stomped away and Elizabeth felt like she'd been slapped in the face.

163

That was another reason for being mad at Mama, she guessed. Everybody said she was just like her Mama. She had her Mama's face, her Mama's temper. Dad said he couldn't tell how she was going to feel about anything from one minute to the next. Dad said she was "moody" like Mama, too. That meant she got depressed like Mama.

Sometimes she wondered if maybe it had really been Mama's depression that had given her the cancer. Mama had been depressed as long as Elizabeth could remember. Sometimes she'd stayed in bed for days, just lying there like a dead person, with no interest in anything. The only reason Elizabeth knew she wasn't dead was because Dad took Mama trays sometimes, and sometimes there'd be a little bit of food missing. But lots of times that was the only way to tell, and that had scared Elizabeth bad. What if Mama had been dead for days and Dad just hadn't been brave enough to tell them yet? They'd never know. Parents never let kids know anything, even kids as old as fourteen.

When Mama got depressed, it was like she wanted to be dead. She was just waiting for somebody to notice and bury her. It was scary because Elizabeth knew exactly what that felt like.

It was all so dramatic. Like a soap opera. All that gave Mama lots of power. Before anybody in the family did anything they first had to figure out how it might affect Mama. There was no telling what might make her mad, or make her depressed. Everybody got exhausted trying to figure out what Mama wanted, until finally they didn't have any life left for themselves.

Some days Elizabeth wanted to be like that. To lie down, to give up. To be dead and still have everybody focusing on you. To use up their life because you didn't have any of your own left to use. Mama had been selfish. She'd deserved to die.

Which was a terrible thing to be thinking. It made Elizabeth feel awful, which made her even more furious with her mother.

Not that she hadn't thought that same thing lots of times before.

She'd even said it in a couple of their fights when she'd said everything else she could think of. "I hate you! You're the worst mother in the whole world! I wish I didn't even have a mother! I wish you were dead!"

That wasn't why Mama had died. Elizabeth was fourteen, and she knew better than that. Everybody she knew hated their parents, and their parents didn't die. Leave it to Mama to do something that would embarrass her and make her feel bad all at the same time. Mama was always on her case. Nothing she ever did was good enough.

One time Mama'd started crying and said she felt the same way, like nothing she ever did was good enough for Elizabeth. It had made Elizabeth feel so guilty to see her mother cry, like she was supposed to do something and she didn't know what. So she just walked out of the room and then out of the house. She wasn't running away or anything. She just needed to get away from her mother.

I'm sorry, Mama. You were good enough. Please come back. Please don't be dead.

Elizabeth was also old enough to know that, just because she'd wished so hard and so often that she had a mother again, just because she kept having those dumb dreams that Mama came back to life, that didn't mean that Mama would come back to life. Stuff like that didn't happen except in the movies. Once your mother died and left you, she was gone forever.

But now all of a sudden Mama wasn't dead anymore. Just like all those times she'd been too depressed to get out of bed. And Dad had kept her back in the bedroom, and hid her, and fed her like he was in her power and had no other choice. Now here she was, yelling at Elizabeth for coming home late last night, and Elizabeth was really pissed, just like always, and her mother was dead. Dead six months.

Mama had had her way again. She'd turned everything upside down.

"You're grounded!" Mama yelled.

"You're dead!" Elizabeth yelled back, and the power of saying that took her breath away. She wanted to tell Mama she was sorry but she was too scared. She'd gone to a memorial service but she actually hadn't seen Mama's body. Had Dad been keeping her in the bedroom all that time? What was Mama trying to pull now? Just because she was her mother didn't mean that she could do anything she damn well wanted. It made Elizabeth hate her dad, just for a minute—it was too scary to hate him any longer than that—but he should have told them. They had a right to know, even if they were only kids. He was just so weak where Mama was concerned. Sometimes her dad was so weak she thought she would die.

She stormed out of the room and on out of the house, making a show of ignoring her mother calling her name behind her. She was just going for a walk, for God's sake. She wasn't some little kid.

She went over to Stacey's house. Stacey used to be her best friend before that boyfriend of hers came along. Stacey didn't have much time for her after that.

"So do you like it better this way…" Stacey pushed up the back of her hair making it flop down in front. "Or this way?" She pulled down hard on the ends, straightening the curl out.

"Stacey, did you hear me? I said my mother's not dead anymore. She came back today."

Stacey looked at her out of one eye, the other one hiding behind a big fall of hair. "That's a sick joke, Liz. She was your mother, after all."

"Stacey, you gotta let me stay here. I'm scared."

"I can't." Stacey turned back to the mirror behind them, playing with her hair. "See, I got a date tonight… and Mom says I can't have girlfriends over if I'm just gonna leave…"

"Stacey!"

"I'm sorry, okay? My mom's a bitch sometimes—I can't help it."

"You're supposed to be my friend."

Stacey looked at her then, trying to look serious, and that just made Elizabeth even angrier. "Liz, really, this isn't real. Your mom's dead. I went to the funeral, remember? You oughta see somebody. I mean, your mom, she's been screwin' with your head for years, makin' you feel guilty about everything. I mean, you always said you couldn't please her. Now she's dead, and she's still doing it to you. Your mom, I know you loved her and everything, but she could be a real bitch sometimes…"

"My mama wasn't a bitch!" Elizabeth didn't mean to, but she slapped Stacey as hard as she could. Stacey fell back against the mirror with her hair flying everywhere, and she just started bawling, just like a baby. But it wasn't funny—Elizabeth felt like she'd just done the worst thing. She was so scared she jumped up and ran out of Stacey's house, and Stacey's mom was screaming behind her and cursing, and Elizabeth couldn't help it, but she kept wondering if her mama would still stand up for her the same way.

It was on the way home that she finally started figuring things out. Her dad and Mama had done something weird. They'd wanted people to think Mama was dead for some stupid reason, and because she and Mark were just kids they hadn't told them anything. Typical. It made her really angry. Like they didn't care how she felt. Sure—Mama stayed inside the house. In the shadows. So now Mama was some dirty little secret in the family. Something perverted. Elizabeth was already feeling dirty because she'd tried to tell Stacey about Mama. She wasn't going to try that again. She'd just pretend like Dad and Mama were pretending. Maybe she'd talk to Mark about it. They'd have some kind of a plan together. That would show them.

When she got back Mama screamed at her for being late, like she'd had permission to go in the first place. What a laugh. Elizabeth didn't even argue. That way Mama would know how really mad she was at her.

Dad used to really hate it when Elizabeth and her mother fought. Sometimes he'd go back and forth between them, trying to explain to each of them what the other one had meant or what the other one was feeling. Once in a while that worked, but usually they both just ended up mad at him, too, and Elizabeth would feel a little sorry for him. "You're so much alike," he'd say, kind of helplessly.

Everybody always said that. That was not what Elizabeth wanted to hear, although secretly it made her kind of proud. She knew it wasn't what Mama wanted to hear, either, and that hurt her feelings.

Dad would tell Elizabeth, "You know, a lot of girls your age have trouble with their mothers, especially when they've been close like you and your Mama have been. You guys love each other. You'll get through it." Now, of course, they never would. Even if Mama wasn't really dead after all, things couldn't be fixed. Not after they'd lied to her and her brother. Not after they'd made their family weird.

Tears burned her eyes, and she rubbed them away hard with her knuckles. She was not going to cry any more about her mother. She was not. She'd been crying practically nonstop for six months.

But she was crying when Mark came rattling up behind her on his roller blades, grabbed her around the waist and spun her halfway around so that she practically fell down, and whooped, "Yo, Lizzie!"

She loathed it when he called her Lizzie, which, naturally, was why he did it. At least he made her stop crying. "You little turd!"

"You big butthead!" he yelled, and then he giggled this silly little giggle like he always did, like everything was just one big joke to him, and the joke was always on her. He took off past her. For a twelve-year-old creep, he was pretty good on those roller blades. But she wouldn't tell him that in a million years.

She watched him speed around the corner and made herself not hurry up to see where he went from there. She was not going to worry about him. She was not going to take care of him. She was not going to be his mother. She'd figure out some way to tell him about what Dad and Mama had done, the right way so that he wouldn't freak out or anything.

Since Mama'd died, Elizabeth had felt so sorry for Dad that she couldn't stand to be around him. He went to work every day and he came home every night, and he tried really hard to take care of Mark and Elizabeth even though Elizabeth tried to show him she didn't need anybody to take care of her. The clothes got washed and the meals got cooked and as far as she knew the bills got paid, and he showed up at their school stuff and he helped Mark with his homework, but his heart didn't seem to be in it. But now that she knew the truth about Mama, she didn't know what to feel about Dad. He'd lied to her, lied to her for months. It was just so sick, the kind of sick only adults could do. It was scary.

Once, maybe a week after Mama'd died—after Dad said she'd died—when Elizabeth was just starting to realize what it meant, she'd asked him, "Are you ever going to be happy again?"

She'd expected him to say something like, "Sure, honey. Of course I'll be happy again." Even though she wouldn't have believed it, even though she'd have been furious to think he could ever be happy without Mama, it still would have been a relief. But he didn't. He'd looked at her with a sad face like she didn't know a human being could have and he'd said, "I don't know, honey. I don't know anything about what happens next."

But knowing now that Mama had been alive all along, she didn't know what to think about what Dad had said that day. She knew he'd been terribly, terribly sad—Dad had never been able to hide his true feelings about anything—but now she had no idea what he'd been sad about. Maybe the whole sick thing had been Mama's idea. Mama had done something to him, to make him like that. She'd been doing something to him for years. That was the only explanation. He had no back bone: he was like some kind of slimy jellyfish. He had no life of his own—he'd given it all to Mama. And he was so pale, depressed, and he moved so slowly anymore—now Elizabeth was afraid of losing him. Mama had come up with something terrible, and made Dad go along with it. And now it was killing him. She had to do something.

She went for a long walk. She thought about school. She thought about how all her friends were getting their ears double-pierced and some triple. She thought about how she was never going to get a boyfriend because she was dumb and ugly. She thought about how Stacey would never be her friend anymore. She thought about everything she could think of that wasn't Mama.

But Mama got in there anyway. Everything she thought about came back to Mama. Mama saying maybe they ought to get her a tutor for algebra—which was just what she needed, to have to think about stupid algebra even more, like she was ever going to need $x(x-y)$ in real life. Mama laughing and saying she didn't care how many holes Elizabeth got in her ears if Elizabeth paid for it with her own money, and not to worry about Dad, he'd get used to it. Mama telling her she was beautiful and smart and a nice person and interesting, and just wait, pretty soon she'd have to beat 'em off with a stick.

Missing her mother made Elizabeth's stomach hurt. She missed her mother. She wanted her mother to come back. That ought to count for something, how much she wanted Mama.

It didn't, though. Once somebody was dead, they were dead.

But Mama was back. It had all been a trick. She was in the house like always, making breakfast. And it was Dad who was looking pale, sick, and depressed, like he wanted to die. Like Mama had taken everything away from him. Like Mama had gotten her way again and he had taken Mama's place. But Elizabeth hadn't gotten Mama back either, because of the trick, and Mama had changed, and nothing would ever be right again.

Elizabeth kept walking and walking. Tears kept trickling down her cheeks, but she was determined not to cry any more.

"Elizabeth! Breakfast!"

She was right back by her own house, and that was Mama calling her. Elizabeth didn't know what was going on, but her mind refused to think about it any more, so she just gave up and went inside.

Mark was already there, sitting at the kitchen table reading the comics. He stuck his tongue out at her. She grabbed the paper out of his hands and it tore some, but she got it. Brat.

Mark whined, "Mama, she stole the comics!" and Mama, standing at the stove just like she always did, said over her shoulder, "Now, children, let's have some peace while we eat," just like she always did, and Elizabeth thought, as hard as she could, Mama's dead.

Mark was so dumb, just like a little kid. If he knew something was wrong with Mama being back and everything he sure didn't act like it. He acted like everything was normal. But then a little kid wouldn't know something was perverted even if he saw it. It was scary. Now she was afraid something was wrong with Mark, too.

She pulled a handful of sticky, linty gumdrops out of her sweatshirt pocket and stuffed them into her mouth. Mama crossed to the sink and opened up the window, just like she always did. Elizabeth hated that. Mark hated that, Dad hated that—the whole family complained about Mama's thing for fresh air. Dead of winter, middle of the night, first thing in the morning, it didn't matter. They could all freeze to death just so Mama could get her fresh air.

Elizabeth pushed the gumdrops out of her mouth with her tongue, the gross chewed-up mess into her hand. Mama would give her hell for eating sugar before breakfast.

Mama didn't notice, though. She was busy scraping the eggs out of the cast iron skillet. No aluminum for her. Good old-fashioned cast iron, which Elizabeth thought was disgusting because it had little grooves in it where bits of food could hide and black stuff came off on the dish towels.

Just like in her dreams. Mama cooking breakfast in the big cast-iron skillets. Mama raking the yard, ironing Dad's shirts, loading the dishwasher. Letting everybody else know what to think, how to feel, just by the way she looked at you. Doing all the stuff she always did that kept the house going and you didn't even notice until she wasn't around anymore to do it.

Except Mama was supposed to be dead. They'd lied.

Then Mama turned and looked at Elizabeth. Her eyes were as black as the skillet bottoms, and way too big. "Don't you feel good, Elizabeth? You look a little peaked. Maybe you should stay home from school today and rest? I'll take care of you, sweetheart," she said, and grinned.

Mama doesn't grin like that. Mama never calls me sweetheart.

"Hey," complained Mark. "No fair."

"Don't worry about it, baby," she said to him, not daring to say anything to her mother. She felt herself backing away, scared that her mother might touch her. "I'm going to school. I've got an algebra test."

Mama set a plate full of fried eggs in front of each of them. Elizabeth went to the bathroom to get rid of the gooey gumdrops in her hand. She heard Mark say, "Yuck! There's yolk in mine!" and it kind of gave her the creeps because he'd never, in his whole life, liked yolks and their mother knew that. *If she was their real mother. Which she shouldn't be, because their mother was dead.*

When she came back into the kitchen, Mama was standing behind Mark with her hands on his shoulders. Mama's face was tight and stiff like when she was really mad, and she was pinching Mark's shoulders hard. Then she grinned, and wrapped her arms around him. Tighter, tighter, so that Elizabeth saw his face go pale, as if Mama were squeezing the life and blood right out of him. He looked kind of sick, but he was still eating his eggs.

She should have done something. Gotten Mark alone and talked to him. But she didn't know what to say. He was just a little kid, really. She was alone in this. It was all up to her.

Elizabeth didn't even look at her eggs. She just grabbed her books off the counter and practically ran out of the house, mumbling that she'd get breakfast at school, she had to study algebra. Mama was paying too much attention to Mark to even try to stop her.

The algebra test wasn't that bad, and she thought she passed it. Not that she much cared. She thought about not going home from school, and she walked around for awhile, but Stacey wasn't her friend anymore—she didn't say anything or even look at her all day—and Elizabeth couldn't think of anywhere else to go. She wanted so badly to tell somebody what her parents had done—whatever they had done—but she knew it must be too dirty a secret to tell.

When she got home Mark was sick in bed. Dad was there, home early from work, taking care of him. She didn't see Mama.

"He's running a little fever, honey," Dad said, but it didn't look like a little fever. Mark was shaking all over. At first she thought maybe Mark was faking. But he kept throwing up. Even water made him throw up. His skin was the color of concrete. Dad said, too many times, "It's just the flu. Everybody gets the flu." But Elizabeth saw how worried he looked, and she didn't want to see, so she went to her room and shut the door and sat on her bed for a while, trying not to think about Mama.

She thought about whether she should tell Heather what Julie said about her. "You should be the one who stops gossip," Mama would have said. But maybe if she told Heather then Heather would be her friend and let her stay at her house.

She thought about Jeff. He was pretty much of a jerk, and she was sure he did drugs, and she didn't understand why she was so attracted to him. "He's dangerous," Mama told her. "Lots of women find dangerous men attractive. Nothing wrong with feeling that way. But you don't have to act on your feelings."

Elizabeth threw herself face down on her bed and covered her head with her pillow. Mama is dead. "It's not fair," Mama said, not loud but in a way that Elizabeth knew meant she was really really mad. "I've been cheated." I've been cheated, too, Elizabeth

173

found herself thinking, and fell asleep, and dreamed that Mama was in Mark's room, taking care of him, grinning, wrapping her arms around him, hugging him, hurting him, too, making him sick.

Mark died before morning. Elizabeth woke up because Dad was moaning, and she didn't want to go see what was the matter, but she couldn't help it. Dad was on Mark's bed, crying, with Mark's body in his arms, and Mama was standing in the shadows with her hands over her face.

"Oh, honey," Mama said softly, and went over to Elizabeth, and before Elizabeth could pull away Mama kissed her lightly on the cheek with lips as dry as dead leaves, lips that smelled of earth, and insects, but most of all, of copper.

"You should've called the doctor," she accused her father, then felt terrible for talking to him like that, for putting him through even more pain.

"I know, I know..." he said from his chair in the shadows. I don't know what's the matter with me. Sometimes I know what I should be doing about something, and I think about it, but for some reason I can't seem to do anything." His voice sounded weak, kind of crackly, as if he were speaking to her on a long distance connection. "I just want to sit here. I just want to sit, and do nothing."

"But, Daddy... you have to... have to take care of Mark. His body? Daddy, please!"

"Honey, it's okay. I... took care of things. They came for it while you were sleeping."

"But the funeral?"

"We'll have it later, honey. A memorial service, at least. With the neighbors, and Mark's friends. There'll be time. I'm... I'm going to ask them to cremate the body. I think that would be best."

"Daddy..."

"Hush now, baby. Hush..."

174

"Daddy, it was Mama's idea wasn't it? Having Mark cremated. So people wouldn't find out what she did…"

"Baby, oh honey…" Dad pulled her close. "I'm so sorry. I should have paid more attention. We all loved your mom very much. But she's dead, honey. She's dead."

Elizabeth pulled away and looked at him. He thought he was telling the truth. She could see it in his eyes.

"Daddy? Daddy?"

But he was crying and couldn't answer her anymore. Elizabeth got up and started for the door, but stopped when she saw her mother standing there in the shadows. "You don't feel good, Elizabeth. It's understandable. Maybe you should stay home from school today and rest? Mama will take care of you, sweetheart," she said, and grinned with something dark staining the grin, and held her soft mothering arms out to hug her, but Elizabeth pushed past, shuddering.

She didn't go to school the next day. Or the day after that. Her Dad understood, of course. He knew she was grieving. He'd just call her in sick and explain everything later. He'd take care of her.

But he couldn't. Sure she was grieving, but she was staying home because she had to take care of him. She tried to call Stacey to apologize but the phone was dead. She wondered if maybe her Dad had disconnected it so that he wouldn't have to talk to anybody. But then she wondered if maybe Mama had something to do with it.

She could go out, tell the police or something. But she and Mark were the only ones who had seen Mama, and now it was just her. She wasn't a kid anymore, but they would think she was. Nobody listened to kids. They treated them like crazy people. They'd put her in the hospital or something and then Dad would be all alone with Mama. She couldn't leave him alone in the house. Not even for a minute.

All day long Elizabeth's mother walked back and forth in front of her father's door. Waiting. But her father never came out. Not once. He might be dying in there, but if she opened her father's door then Mama might get in there. And then she'd lose her daddy, too.

Elizabeth knew she was going to be left all alone. All alone in the house with her mother, who was dead, who had been dead for months.

Over the next couple of days people knocked at the front door, but they always went away. Elizabeth was afraid to go to the door, afraid of what Mama might do if somebody else learned about their perverted secret.

Elizabeth tried to learn as much as she could about Mama's new routine. It made her feel a little safer. Every morning Mama shuffled slowly out of her bedroom as if she had almost no strength left for the day. Sometimes she had all her clothes on but sometimes she just wore a big torn slip. After an hour or so of standing in the hall outside her dad's bedroom door Mama started walking around the house, avoiding the windows and just walking like she'd forgotten what it was she was supposed to do. Sometimes she'd stop walking and stand there with her head kind of sideways like she was listening for something, but maybe she'd forgotten what it was she was listening for.

Sometimes Mama would fix something on the stove and then just throw it into the garbage. Sometimes Elizabeth would see Mama eating flies. Sometimes Elizabeth would see a mouse's head poke itself suddenly out of Mama's mouth before getting pulled back inside again. Sometimes Mama's chin would be covered with blood.

Elizabeth stayed out of Mama's way the best she could, and although she didn't exactly understand why, she figured she was pretty safe as long as Mama kept hanging around outside her Daddy's bedroom door. It wasn't too hard staying out of Mama's way—she seemed pretty sleepy most of the time, like she'd had too much to eat or drink.

176

Sometimes Mama would call out her name, though. Sometimes Mama would look into Elizabeth's empty room (she'd stopped sleeping in there days ago), and say, "Elizabeth? Elizabeth, honey? Do you need a hug? Let me give you a hug, sweetheart!"

And it would make Elizabeth depressed because Mama had never hugged her very much before—not like her friends' moms—and she'd always wanted her mama to hug her like those moms did. She did need a hug right now for sure, but not from Mama.

And after a while she started seeing Mark around the house, and then she knew her daddy had never gotten around to ordering the cremation. And she was almost glad, but not quite. Sometimes Mark would walk through the house, and eat flies, and call out to Elizabeth with sugar in his voice asking if she would give him a hug, too. And then he'd giggle, just like he used to, just like it was all a big joke he'd pulled on her.

Finally one night when she could hear Mama and Mark in another room moving around and bumping into furniture and chasing things Elizabeth slipped into her father's bedroom. He was lying there on the floor in the dark very very still but she figured if she could just get him off the floor she could help him out of the house and they could stay at a neighbor's house or in a hotel somewhere until they could figure out what else to do.

But then Elizabeth saw that her daddy didn't have a face anymore, just part of a tongue sticking out with teethmarks along the edges where it had been chewed. And most of one leg was gone. But still she kept asking him if he could stand up, if he was ready to go now but he didn't say a word. She'd let him down. Just like with Mama, she hadn't been good enough.

Elizabeth was in the house alone with Mama and Mark. They'd never let her go. Even if she walked out the back door nobody would believe her and anyway Mark and Mama would never let her go. And it was almost time for her period, maybe only a couple of days away. And Elizabeth didn't want to think about how Mama and her brother were going to act when her period came.

So that's why she's waiting in the kitchen now for Mama and Mark to come into the room and find her. Everybody always said she was just like her mother anyway. She guessed it must be true—they were always saying it and now look at Mama crawling into the room on her hands and knees and licking Elizabeth's feet, and there's Mark licking her hand and getting up, getting closer.

"I'm ready for my hug now," she says, trying to keep her voice steady as her mother and brother come closer and wrap her in their terrible long arms and squeeze her in her family's cold embrace until she isn't alone anymore.

"I'm ready," she says, smiling, thinking maybe that at last her Mama would be pleased, pleased that now she was so much like her. But the joke would be on Mama, Mama with her dirty little grown-up secret.

Because Elizabeth would be even better than Mama. Even stronger.

NVUMBI

"WHO NEEDS MEN?" Jamie's daughter Eliza demands with free floating adolescent vigor. "I mean, what good are they anyway?"

Jamie notices the light through the high kitchen window that opens onto the alley, a thin sliver like the slit in a door up to which, in another time and place, the sorcerer rode backwards. He notices the sounds of this particular city morning, the taste of the closely inhabited apartment air when he licks his dry lips.

Eliza's mother, Jamie's wife Danielle, is getting ready for work in the dark little bedroom off the kitchen. Through the door less opening Jamie catches flashes of her bright red uniform, her pastel underwear, her skin which is golden tan. Danielle is a beautiful woman. He loves her, of course, if love can be defined as owing someone both your life and your death.

Jamie's mother in law, Eliza's grandmother and Danielle's mother Claudine, stands at the stove with her back to them, frying bacon for breakfast. The black skillet that Claudine calls a spider is full, and more raw striped pink strips wait on the counter. All the appetites of all the Miller women are prodigious. Jamie, of course, will eat very little.

Claudine is a tiny woman, and old. No outsider would see her power, which is part of her power. To neighbors and family and friends her power is obvious, a given part of life. Of Jamie's life, certainly. Of his death. Thinking about how powerful Claudine is, how old, how small, Jamie is slightly unnerved.

"I mean, what good is he?" Eliza gestures toward Jamie with a sharp backward jerk of her head. Out of long habit, his hands stay with the abrupt movement and don't lose the braid. Eliza's hair is thick and coarse; it curls around his fingers like entrails scooped, prodded, divined. It resists the braiding, but pointlessly. Overt resistance is always pointless.

The dead do not resist.

Jamie spent months or years in the sorcerer's bottle. He remembers that time as pleasant: sitting up on a shelf with thousands of similar bottles, aging, collecting dust. Until Danielle was ready for him and Claudine and Danielle came to claim him, and his tired old body, so poorly cared for down in the sorcerer's cellar, was forced to inhale the contents of the bottle with those dry and tattered old nostrils. Forced to make the same mistakes over and over again.

A lifetime of hard labor, and then hard labor after death.

Eliza has hurt Jamie's feelings. He is dimly surprised. His hands want to tremble among the braids he has made in his daughter's hair, but they do not.

Claudine flourishes her spatula. The bacon sizzles. She mutters loudly, "Nvumbi."

"Nvumbi my ass," Eliza says brazenly under his hands. He stiffens and so does she, but she goes on recklessly, "Personally, I don't even believe in nvumbi."

Claudine whirls from the stove, spatula raised like the sorcerer's forked, hooked stick. Jamie wonders if she'll be buried with her spatula, what she'll take with her into the next world or her next life in this one. Will she take him? He wonders how she'll die, what he'll do when she does.

Danielle flies out of the bedroom. Her uniform top is unsnapped over her lacy flesh colored bra, her flesh a rosy brown and the nipples concealed from Jamie but still there, still soft until he raises them with his tongue. She slaps Eliza hard across the face. Jamie's hands stay with Eliza's head as it recoils from her mother's blow. He means to be gentle and steady for her, the father figure he's been trained to be, but he's sure he pulls her hair, and he's faintly sorry.

Danielle leans close. Her breath smells like her morning coffee. "You watch your mouth, girl," she says with quiet menace. Eliza is sobbing and leaning back against Jamie, against his groin. He can't protect her, but her hair is almost done. "No call to disrespect nvumbi."

Claudine observes, "Time to get her her own."

Jamie sees alarm on his wife's face and feels the surprising sinking of his own heart. Eliza has already stopped crying; she is, after all, a Miller woman.

Claudine nods twice and pronounces, "High time."

"Ma," Danielle begins. She glances at the clock and curses. She's having trouble with the snaps on her uniform. Jamie fastens the last barrette onto the last of Eliza's braids and crosses the narrow room to help Danielle. Her flesh is soft and pliant under his knuckles, her bones hard. He has touched her thousands of times during their marriage, and he's never noticed such things before. She doesn't look at him, just drops her hands and lets him dress her while she says to her mother, "Ma, she's barely thirteen."

Claudine takes the bacon strips out of the spider one by one. They dangle from her spatula, and drops of grease glitter. Jamie snaps the top snap of Danielle's uniform; her flesh gives a little under his thumb, and the unaccustomed clarity of the sensation makes him take a step back from her. She catches his arm, pulls him to her, kisses him, puts her tongue in his mouth and keeps it there long enough that he thinks he might have stopped breathing. That has happened before.

"You were twelve," Claudine points out.

"Yeah," Danielle says into Jamie's mouth. Her words, her coffee breath, her fat tongue make him want to gag, but she won't let him. "Too young," she says.

"Old enough for nvumbi."

Nvumbi. People with weak and sickly souls, souls that cannot carry their weight through the world. The world is full of them. Nearly empty eyes, blank faces blankly animated, voices thin and skittering, hands sliding away from handshake or caress they are easily identified while alive and easily turned after death.

Danielle was, yes, twelve years old when she got Jamie. He doesn't remember much of what she looked like then; for a long time, he was vaguely aware only of her smell, the taste of certain parts of her body, the feel of her around him. Hearing came next, the sound of her voice, the sound of her voice saying his name and what he was to do, the sound of her breath and her heartbeat. Sight came only gradually, for some reason, and he wasn't even aware of what he was seeing until he'd been seeing it for a long time. His wife Danielle is beautiful, of course. All the Miller women are beautiful. His daughter Eliza is the most beautiful of all.

There is danger in this.

Jamie doesn't know how old he was when the Millers came to get him for Danielle. He doesn't know how long he'd lived or how long he'd been dead, or whether there was any difference. He used to think he wouldn't remember anything about his life until the Miller women came to get him for the dead, they say, carry their memories like purses, easily stolen and easily spilled.

But now he does remember some of it, bits and pieces, like the silhouettes some old woman of his childhood used to snip out of thick black paper. Snip snip snip. Silhouettes of all the boy children.

Dozens of silhouettes of Jamie, one after another after another as he grew up, arranged in an eerily lengthening row across a wall somewhere. He can't remember whose wall it was, or where, or whether his silhouettes really were the only ones on it.

He doesn't know why the silhouettes stopped, whether the old woman died or whether she decided at some point, for unfathomable reasons of her own, that there was no more need to cut out flat shadowy likenesses of Jamie. He doesn't remember her name or what she looked like, only her hands and the small noise of her very sharp scissors, snipping, snipping.

He remembers a hot wet place, a country of shimmering light. Hot; he remembers being hot all the time, nights hot and hard to breathe, mornings and evenings hot, middays so hot that the earth itself shimmered and the rain turned to steam as it fell, rose back from the shimmering earth to fall again, fall again.

He remembers exhaustion. The constant motion of bodies at work in the fields, his body. The same stooping, cutting, pulling, stooping motion repeated so many times in a day, so many days in a lifetime, that the motion and the heat and the exhaustion and the beating of a heart and the breath in and out became the life, became this day and the next day and the next hot wet shimmering day.

He remembers a tunnel. A country full of light. Her hands on the stiff parts of his face. Her taste at the edges of his lips where his tongue can just reach. A shadow growing in the palm of her hand, the silhouette of someone's face, someone's hand, snip snip, not his. The shadow flutters its paper thin edges, gently rolls to the center of the bed and opens its face to him. It is a veil. Vaguely Jamie knows that he likes to wear this veil over his face, but he's far from knowing why. He strokes it.

Danielle is shouting but Jamie can't....

Danielle is shouting, "He's not breathing!" She shouts it, shouts it, whispers it. "He's not breathing!"

This may be now. This may not be a memory; this may be now. Or it may already be a memory of now, passed away, passed on, passed over.

When Danielle rubs his face and chest, there is a painful burst of tiny bright bubbles. Danielle is crying, shouting. Someone else is in the room, in the bed. Jamie's eyes sting. He can't feel any part of his body except his eyes, and his penis, which hurts. He feels the...silhouette of her fingers, probing and caressing...spiderweb shockwaves...

...he is falling asleep...

...he is waking up.

"They do that sometimes."

Jamie recoils from the voice of Dr Lezare. He should have known Dr Lezare was here, but he didn't. He's afraid of Dr Lezare, and he owes him everything.

Afraid.

Danielle holds him, won't let Dr Lezare hurt him, won't let him go. "Like some babies," the doctor says, "nvumbi sometimes forget to breathe."

Jamie remembers Dr Lezare. It is like waking from a long dream.

He remembers Dr Lezare in that other life, watching him for a very long time. Watching him for months. Then bringing Claudine and Danielle to watch him as he worked all day in the fields. He remembers his mother taking him into their hut and hiding him, warning him to stay away from Dr Lezare and the two Miller women, not to do anything Dr Lezare says, for the man is a sorcerer, a magician, an evil man, and the Miller women were said to pay him well for his services.

And if you see him riding his horse backwards... run away, my son. Run as far and as fast as you can.

184

But Jamie remembers the night Dr Lezare came to his bed and kissed him, and put his tongue inside Jamie's mouth, and then he was in the bottle, and somewhere he could hear his mother crying over his empty body.

He remembers another night, some time later, when Danielle and Claudine came to pick him up from Dr Lezare. He remembers the way Danielle kissed him and pinched his flesh. He remembers how Claudine caressed him, too.

He remembers how they placed the black veil over his face and led him away, one on each side of their dark bride, holding his arms tightly as he got used to walking again. Leaning over and kissing, caressing the black veil, giggling like school girls every time he stumbled.

Jamie remembers these things without curiosity. The dead have no curiosity. You can do anything with the dead you desire and they will never ask you why.

The dead make the best of friends.

You can plant them in deep holes or store them in jars. You can stack them like logs in a cave and still they won't complain. You can pile stones on top of them to keep them in their holes, as if the dead really cared for escape, or if a few stones could stop them anyway.

You could eat the brains of the dead, and sometimes people did.

The dead asked for nothing and they permitted everything.

The small black bird flutters its thin wings, gently rolls to the center of the bed and opens its face to him. It is a veil. Jamie likes to wear this veil, but he doesn't remember why. He strokes it, treating it like some small animal. His veil, sweet veil: soft and loose like a lover's lingerie. Its cool embrace is comforting.

Danielle stands at the door watching him. Then she comes and joins him and his veil.

His life before was nothing like this. He worked the fields, and he lived with his mother, and he fought no one, and he disrespected no one.

Now he lives with the Miller women. He works all day. He makes love to Danielle. And he fights no one. He doesn't even raise his voice.

Sometimes he remembers his mother, crying over his empty body.

Sometimes he thinks he may be waking up, but he cannot hold that thought for long.

Danielle is upstairs in her bedroom playing with Jamie's black veil. She purrs softly through the ceiling, making coy, ritualistic comments about its properties. "It is thin and yielding, like the moist husk of a spider," she says. She holds it up to her face like a window to look through. The lines of her face darken, the veins in a leaf just turning brown.

Jamie stands at the bedroom door, watching Danielle play with his black veil. She pats the flat of the veil, puffs it up with her fist beneath, and moves it from her crotch to her navel. He walks over and sits down in the chair. He sits very still. She giggles and calls him to come look at her. But the dead are poor at feigning interest.

Danielle looks at Jamie intently and for the first time Jamie sees himself as she must be seeing him: the hard, rough mask of his face, the dry thin lips, the wrinkled eyes. The underlying decay only just showing. That is wrong, he knows. There is no decay but Jamie still insists on feeling it there.

Waking up is a hard thing.

Danielle insists that Jamie is darkly beautiful.

She examines his nose, ears, eyes, and throat. She checks his pulse. She watches his penis for signs of life. She rubs his flesh with creams.

She asks, "Don't you love me anymore?"

186

"Nvumbi ain't nothing but old woman jive," Eliza sneers, but only to him when her mother and grandmother aren't around. "I'm gonna have me a real live boyfriend, not some fake dead dude like you."

"I'm not dead," he wants suddenly to tell her, and, "Nvumbi are real, and they aren't dead, either. I am nvumbi." Then he thinks, with dim horror, that he might have said some of it aloud. He might actually have spoken.

Apparently not, because Eliza doesn't react, and surely she'd have noticed something like that, even about him, even though she does her best not to notice him at all. She's sitting with her back to him, towel bunched in her lap, wet hair dripping and wildly curling. He's supposed to be putting lotion on her back.

He has been warming the pink lotion between his pink brown palms before he lets it touch her skin. Danielle taught him that. He has become distracted by the slinky feel of the lotion across his own flesh, something he is not aware of ever having noticed before. He has become distracted by the sudden possibilities of all the things he'd like to say to his daughter.

"Would you hurry up?" She glares at him over her shoulder, still bony as a child's. "I ain't got all day. I got a hot date."

All the lotion has vanished through his own pores and he must start over. He squeezes a daub onto his left palm and cups his right palm over it. It is cool. But Eliza is so impatient that he has to put it on her before it is properly warmed. He lays both palms flat on the soft flesh between her shoulder blades and her spine. She yelps and jerks away from him and threatens to tell her mother.

"You know, someday she's just gonna get rid of you. She'll find some cute little stud who's even more zonked out than you are, and she'll just throw you to the trash. Or she'll just get sick of having a man around at all, like Gram did. Then what will you do?"

Smoothing the lotion into her warm skin, Jamie wants to say, "I'm your father," but he doesn't believe he can.

Jamie goes and stands in his place while Eliza gets ready. Nobody else is home, and he wonders whether Claudine and Danielle know about this date. He wonders if he should go and find them. He wonders if he should try to stop her. He wonders what to do.

The apartment is so hot, and the evening noises from the street are so loud. He thinks he might faint. He thinks he might run out into the street and make noises of his own.

Both of these are peculiar thoughts, and he simply stands in his place until his daughter is ready. She is wearing a short tight skirt and a blouse that shows off breasts he didn't know she had. She hasn't had him put her hair in braids this time; instead, she's picked it high and wide. Her face is vivid, masklike, oddly deathlike with makeup.

She leaves without so much as a glance at him. He stands still in his place until she is out the door, then follows the click of her heels and the clouds of her perfume down the dark narrow stairs and into the muggy, crowded evening.

A boy is waiting for her in the middle of the block. A man, really much older than she, much bigger. From a little distance, Jamie watches and listens. The man makes extravagant gestures, and his loud voice swings up and down the register, up and down. He calls her Liza. He kisses her, grabs her buttocks under the skirt. He is high. Eliza giggles and leans herself against him.

Jamie doesn't follow them. He doesn't think he can walk that far or that fast, and he doesn't think his eyes will focus well enough to keep them in sight. He almost gets lost just going back to the building the Miller women live in, and then he almost can't climb all the stairs.

But he is quietly waiting in his place when Danielle comes home and wants him for a while. And he is there, waiting, when Eliza comes home much later, smelling of weed and of sex.

Her mother and grandmother look at her, look at each other, and together they say, "It's time," and Eliza says, "No," but Jamie knows it is.

Claudine and Danielle take Jamie with them when they go out hunting a nvumbi for Eliza. A nvumbi for this youngest Miller woman. For granddaughter and daughter. His daughter.

He doesn't know why they make him go, and he doesn't want to. It surprises him to have an opinion, but he definitely doesn't want to go. For one thing, it seems even hotter to him in the city at night than during the day, even hotter outside in the open streets than inside the cramped and airless apartment. The heat makes him feel ephemeral.

And, for some reason, he's afraid to go with them. Afraid they'll find a nvumbi, afraid they won't. Afraid he'll get lost. It took him a while even to recognize what he feels now as fear. It's been a long time since Jamie felt fear, since Dr Lezare rode backwards on his horse up to Jamie's house, and rode forward to take him away. It's been a long time since Jamie felt anything.

Now he does. Now he feels a distant call of fear. When he hesitates and Danielle pulls him roughly along, he scrapes his knuckles against a brick wall and it hurts. She pays him no mind. She thinks he doesn't feel anything. That's why she keeps him. He and all nvumbi act as if they will never feel anything again.

It is very hot. The streets teem with heat, and with loud voices and music. So many people congregate on the street corners that the corners have become hard to locate; they seem to have melted in the body heat and vivid clothes and rich flesh of all those people. Jamie tries to stay close to Danielle, to hang onto her, but she brushes him aside, making him trip over a curb and hurt his ankle, and points something out to her mother. "There's one!"

Jamie's gaze follows the line of her extended arm and forefinger and long pink nail. She's pointing to a conglomeration of young men around the next spilled over corner, but he can't tell which one she means because four of them are nvumbi.

Claudine squints, considers, finally decides, "Nope," and moves on.

Danielle lingers. "Oooo eee, don't he have a cute little ass, though?"

"You want him then?" her mother snaps.

Danielle laughs throatily. Jamie has heard her laugh like that countless times during his life with her, and now suddenly he doesn't like the sound of it. "Nah. Ain't done with this one yet." She jerks her head toward Jamie without really looking at him, and he feels dimly relieved.

In this neighborhood there are nvumbi everywhere. The boy who mows the grass for the projects where the Miller women live is nvumbi; Jamie has seen it in the cut of his eyes. The gaunt man who always sits at the back of the church with his womenfolk never any expression on his face no matter how het up the preacher gets, no matter how many times he himself stands up and sits down to pray or sing with the others is nvumbi.

Here is an impromptu band impromptu on the part of the young women who circle and clap, since nvumbi don't make any decisions at all, let alone one on the spur of the moment. The young men on the bongo and harmonica and the child rapper are nvumbi. Their music is technically smooth and rather pleasing, but it has no life, no soul. Jamie feels an astonishing urge to join them. Danielle pauses to consider the harmonica player, who is very tall and dark. Claudine doesn't even glance their way.

"Gimme a break," Danielle protests. "Ma, she ain't but thirteen. This is her first. Don't have to be perfect."

"Has to be right," Claudine insists, and keeps going.

A figure darts out of an alley so full of stink that even Jamie is bothered by the smell. Jamie thinks he hears the old man say, "Claudine," but there is such a cacophony in the street and Jamie's ears are so unaccustomed to perceiving sounds not specifically directed at him that he isn't certain the old nvumbi said anything at all.

As he has learned so well to do, he looks to his women for clues. Claudine pays no attention to the old man at all, doesn't even shake his hand off when he clutches at her sleeve. Danielle looks at him, looks away again, but Jamie catches a flicker across her face that might mean something. She knows this man. She has some sort of feeling for him. Jamie wonders if this is how Eliza will look at him when he is of no more use to the Miller women and has been set free.

For this is Claudine's nvumbi from a long time ago, and Danielle's father. Jamie has been shown pictures. The man in the pictures was much younger, of course, far more handsome and far less animated than this one, but it is the same man. Jamie would like to speak his name, but he thinks he has never known it.

The nvumbi tries to block their path, but is no match for Claudine. Jamie wonders what this nvumbi could possibly want from the Miller women that he didn't already get. Then Jamie wonders what he himself will someday want from them. The old man says, clearly this time through the din, "Danielle. Daughter." Danielle stops.

Jamie doesn't know what to do. He doesn't know where his place is now. His wife has stopped and is facing the nvumbi, her father, as if she intends to have a conversation with him, while Claudine small, bent, utterly purposeful is far enough ahead in the crowds now that Jamie can hardly see her. He doesn't know what he should do. Unfamiliar anxiety makes him dance, and there are any number of rhythms and tunes in the street to which he might be dancing.

"What do you want?" Danielle demands. "Thought I'd never see you again."

"I know why you're out here," the nvumbi tells her. Jamie looks at him, listens to him carefully, his body twitching with the unaccustomed effort of concentrating. Something is wrong. This man is nvumbi, but he is awake. "I know what you're hunting."

Danielle nods. "Ma says it's time. Eliza's thirteen and she's got hormones."

"Well, look."

The nvumbi gestures, and from out of the stinking alley behind him comes a parade of pretty boys. Dark skinned, fair skinned, tall and small, they all have the slack faces and blank movements of new nvumbi, not long out of the bottles. Steadily more frightened, Jamie glances furtively around for Dr Lezare. There are so many people he could be anywhere.

"Ah," breathes Danielle beside him, and he feels the temperature of her body rise. "Not bad."

"Just out, too," the old man says proudly, reaching out to prod the gleaming buttock of one boy and tug at the curls of another as they go by. "These won't wake up for a long time."

"That one," Danielle says, pointing. "Let me see that one."

The man grasps the arm of the boy Danielle has indicated and pulls him out of line. The next boy closes the gap and the procession continues. The man sets the boy in front of Danielle and steps back. "Pierre. He's eighteen."

"Ain't no eighteen," Danielle objects. "Twenty one, maybe."

"Pretty, though, don't you think?"

Pierre is taller than Jamie and broader shouldered. His skin is truly black, highlighting in blue. He stands so still that Jamie can hardly see him breathing, and wonders if he has been given back his breath yet. As Danielle slides her hands over the virile body, the boy groans softly, involuntarily. "Nice," she murmurs, and the old nvumbi cackles.

Jamie wants to say something to this sleeping boy, or to the awakened old man. He doesn't know what he would say. Behind the old nvumbi he catches sight of Claudine. She is watching the transaction intently, but allowing her daughter to handle it. Jamie doesn't know why, but that makes him shiver.

"He sings, too," the old nvumbi declares, and slaps the boy's bare rump hard, playfully. "Sing, boy!"

Immediately, with no warm up or pause, the boy hits a perfect high C and takes the melody upward from there. It is a haunting, simple, repeating chant that Jamie knows he has heard before. It makes him remember things he does not want to remember: Heat that shimmered across fields rather than collecting among buildings. Someone he loved, vaguely. Vaguely he remembers love.

But the song Pierre sings has no soul. He sings it on pitch and with perfect inflection, but his face doesn't move, his voice doesn't change, and when he is finished he simply shuts his mouth.

"How much?" asks Danielle.

The dead eat very little. But Jamie resents the minuscule nourishment that Pierre requires.

The dead have no politics. But Jamie looks for things about which to challenge Pierre.

The dead listen to music even when the radio isn't on, and watch television for hours without moving. One night the Miller women leave Jamie and Pierre in the room with a television on. Movies play all night long. Bela Lugosi: White Zombie. Lugosi's staring eyes, dozens of white crosses on a dark hillside, and the pale thirties beauty of the woman Madeline. A large castle on the cliff.

"Nvumbi make good actors," he heard the old doctor say once. "I trained one to play a corpse for a director I once knew."

The dead trust too easily, and are readily deceived. Jamie will not be deceived by Pierre, nor by Danielle any more.

Sometimes Jamie watches Danielle as she sleeps. The pale eye of the moon washes her body with its gaze, washes the softness of her body away, leaving sharp angles and leveled out planes.

193

In the heat and yellow darkness she has kicked the covers from the bed. Her flesh is like moist wax, pressed into the recesses of the sheets, the simultaneous motion picture flicker of hundreds of bleached out corpses: pulled out of Belsen, Auschwitz, Nam Penh, Diem Bien Phu.

Jamie does not know how he knows these names, but the dead know all the names. The dead have time for names. More and more, Jamie thinks he needs a new name. All the dead need new names.

Danielle will no longer sleep in the same bed with him. She is afraid of waking up with his body lying beside hers. The singing of Eliza's nvumbi starts and stops all night long.

Sometimes the Miller women leave him and Pierre in the house alone. He sits and watches the electric can opener. He starts the clothes washer and stops it again. He takes off his slippers, throws them into the dryer, starts it, stops it, then puts his slippers back on again. He sits by the window and watches the children on their bicycles.

Pierre sings. Jamie dislikes Pierre's singing and wants to tell him to stop.

Jamie thinks about the dark tunnel with the light at its end. It will not let him go. It grows inside him, becomes his throat. When he opens his mouth wide he feels the light inside.

Danielle takes Jamie to the grocery store. There is little he feels he can eat: grains, a few vegetables. The thought of raw, dead meat makes him sick. She is careful what she buys; she tells him she will go on a diet just so he won't suffer watching her eat. She tells him this shows how much she cares.

Jamie knows he must agree. He knows to nod; he forces a slight smile across his lips. But it bothers him.

He picks up a tomato and examines it. Danielle looks at him curiously as he picks up each vegetable in turn and looks at them.

Danielle is angry with him again. She pushes the grocery cart

194

swiftly through the aisles. People stare at Jamie when he chases her, his arms full of vegetables.

Jamie tries but he cannot use the phone. When a voice comes out of the wire, out of the tabled receiver, he cannot pick up the receiver. He cannot touch that detached, lost voice.

Jamie smiles the way he imagines mashed potatoes might smile. The dead can imagine anything.

"I do not want you leaving with that man," Jamie says hesitantly. "He is no good. He will hurt you. You are too young for him, daughter."

Eliza looks at her nvumbi father with scorn. Her scorn is so heavy that she doesn't appear surprised to hear him talk. "Say what? You're telling me what to do? Nvumbi!" She almost spits the word.

"I am your father. And I don't… I do not want you to be hurt."

She looks at him for a moment, as if seeing him for the first time. But then the calm passes, and it is as if the veil has suddenly crossed her face. "Ma told you to say that, right? Make me keep Pierre? Well, ain't no way!" Pierre stands in Jamie's old spot, grinning and grinning and grinning. "Stupid nvumbi! I'm gonna get me a real boyfriend!"

Jamie and Pierre watch as Eliza gets in the car with the dark, older man. He cups her breast with his long, slender hand. Jamie can see him putting his tongue into her mouth. He can hear her laughing as if she is flattered, as if she is loved. She is just a child. She knows nothing. She is his child.

Pierre sings a cheerful song. But the dead cannot laugh.

Jamie watches as the car takes his daughter away from him. Pierre sings and sings and sings. Jamie can do nothing. His daughter belongs at home, but Jamie can do nothing. He rubs his hands together slowly, thinking of her beautiful braids.

The dead cannot weep.

For a week Jamie watches over Pierre—feeding him, putting him

195

to bed, covering the nvumbi's mouth with his hand when Pierre will not stop singing. Danielle and Claudine come into the room now and then to observe the two nvumbi, and are sometimes puzzled, sometimes amused by what they see.

One day a huge yellow Cadillac backs into the alley behind the Miller house. Jamie has been watching it from an upstairs window—it has been backing up toward this house for many blocks. The car door opens and Doctor Lezare climbs out. He opens up the trunk of the car and goes to pick up the singing Pierre from his spot on the back porch. Dr Lezare sticks his tongue into Pierre's mouth and eats his song. Then he removes the bottle from his pocket.

In the window above them Jamie watches as the Cadillac drives away with Pierre and Doctor Lezare. He would do something. He would do something.

But the dead do not weep.

Jamie stands quietly in his spot waiting for his daughter to come home. He has stood here many months. He feels the dust collecting on his skin, a sensation like powder, or a butterfly's brittle wings. He is fully awake now, but still he waits, and thinks of the song he will sing for his daughter, the sweet lullabies his dry lips will kiss into her hair. His wife and his mother-in-law pass in and out of this room but they pay him no mind.

For the dead do not speak. And the dead do not weep.

But the dead will wait forever.

THE PERFECT DIAMOND

for Chris

CHRISTOPHER WALKED DOWN THE STREET, a free man. Actually, what the guard processing them out of prison had said was, "Free to go." As if he could go anywhere he wanted, do anything he wanted.

He'd looked to see if the guy was kidding or had an attitude, but he couldn't tell and it wasn't worth finding out.

In his mind he'd seen the guard holding a red bird, sort of like a cardinal but really not like any bird he'd ever seen. Then letting the bird go, saying, "You're free to go!" and the bird trying to fly but falling, falling, until it got so mad about falling all the time that it exploded into a rainbow of trailing colors, a shower of splintered diamonds.

He almost stopped in the middle of the street. He wanted to stop and think about the bird, and, especially, the diamond. Was it part of the bird? Did the bird spit it out? Did the same person or thing that made the bird fall also break the diamond? Or did the bird itself break it, falling, or thinking it could fly in the first place?

But it hurt too much to stop and think about anything, and stopping in the middle of the street was dangerous, so Chris kept walking. He also kept watch, tried to see everything and everyone at once, before they saw him. But he still had the feeling that something was in his face or tailing him, always just one step ahead or behind.

Which was the truth. Which was not his imagination, or him being crazy and he needed to see some shrink, or him being paranoid after almost two years in prison for probation violation when child molestors got maybe six months and his big crime in the first place was taking some hundred-dollar radio from some guy who owed him money anyway. Something was always one step ahead or behind, something with claws and teeth or with a blade thinner and sharper than most people would have thought possible, waiting for its chance to screw things up.

Christopher had known that all his life. At least, as long as he could remember. At least, ever since the diamond got ruined.

He kept his hands in his pockets with his fists lightly closed. In one pocket was his money. After rent and food, there wasn't a lot left; they didn't really give you enough to make much of a difference.

In the other pocket was his diamond. He tried to hold the diamond a lot more loosely than he held the money, but he could still feel the flaw. It made him sick. Ever since he was old enough to realize that the diamond was something perfect that had been ruined, the scratch had made him want to puke whenever he let himself think about it very much.

The diamond was all he had left from when he was a kid, and he hadn't really been a kid for very long. His mom (his birth mom, his real mom, his first mom, Sandy—he didn't know how to think about her) had given it to him when he was a baby, he guessed, or maybe somehow he'd been born with it, come out of her body with the diamond already there. Sometimes he'd imagined that she was a foreign spy and the diamond was meant to buy bombs or change the balance of power. Or maybe it had belonged to an evil magician and she'd stolen it to protect the world from the magician's madness. Or maybe she'd taken it from a world-famous jewel thief she'd been dating, and when the time was right she was going to give it back to the museum or the princess it belonged to, and then she'd be famous herself.

Kid stuff. Actually, she'd probably just ripped it off herself, or found it somewhere. She probably didn't have any idea how much it was worth. She probably thought it was nothing but glass.

Christopher knew how much it was worth. Even as a kid he'd known it was just about the most valuable thing in the world. He'd kept it under the mattress in his grandparents' house, and every time his mother came she'd say she wasn't ever going to leave him again and she'd remind him not to tell Grandma and Grandpa about the diamond; he didn't know why. He always made the bed up himself and they never figured it out, even though they should have been suspicious because making his bed was the only chore he'd ever been willing to do around there. Sometimes still it made him mad that they'd never figured out he had a diamond.

He'd taken the diamond out only when nobody else was around. That was dumb, leaving a little kid alone in the house like that. But when they were all gone he'd take the diamond out and hold it up to the light and look through it. It was already scratched. If his mother hadn't kept leaving him it wouldn't be scratched. But even past the ugly scratch he would see a whole different world, a world where kids lived with their mothers and knew who their fathers were, and there was plenty of food and friends to play with, and you didn't have to steal—you didn't even feel like stealing. And you could count on things staying pretty much the way you wanted them.

He didn't know exactly when or how the diamond got scratched. All he remembered was the terrible sick feeling when he'd reached into his pocket and taken the diamond out to look at in the light and seen that it was spoiled. Ever since then, for almost as long as he could remember, he'd been trying to fix it or at least to make the scratch not matter to him anymore.

It almost made Chris laugh to think of all the stupid things he'd tried. He'd tried being good, because just before he went to his first foster home when his grandparents didn't want him Sandy had picked him up and whispered like a secret in his ear that if he was a real good boy the judge would let her have him back again, but it didn't work and the diamond was still scratched; if his grandparents had kept him it wouldn't have been. He'd tried being bad, and he did manage to get himself hit a lot and sent to a lot of different foster homes, but the scratch just got deeper and wider and uglier. He'd tried drugs and booze; cocaine especially could sometimes make it seem that the diamond had never been hurt, but no matter how much coke you did or how high the quality you always had to come down sometime. He'd tried stealing, but he never had found another diamond anywhere near as beautiful as his own once had been.

He went into some bar and ordered a beer.

"Chris?"

Damn. Gina was standing in front of him. Looking so good it hurt. In prison he'd tried to imagine her away, to dream that she'd never been. And here she was. It figured that he'd run into Gina on his first day out, in a city of half a million people. He went and sat down, didn't say anything to her, drank the beer.

"So, how are you, Chris?"

"Hey," he said. His stomach felt weird, making him mad. "Doin' terrific, you know? What do you think? Hey, I want my stuff back."

He saw that she'd been going to sit down with him but now she'd changed her mind. He couldn't see much of her face, but her body was outlined by the afternoon haze of the bar. She never had been really good-looking, at least what most guys would call good looking, but she was looking good now the way she always had.

He'd quit smoking in prison—not because of any strength of character or concern about his health, but because just his luck they'd passed this stupid law while he was in there, no smoking in public buildings, he was sure it was unconstitutional—and now the smoke in here made his throat hurt, made him crave a cigarette. Gina smoked, or she used to, but he wasn't going to ask her for anything. It had been a long time, and now, against his will, he missed her.

"What stuff?" she demanded. "What are you talking about?"

"My chair. The kitchen table I made. My gray winter jacket."

"You gave all that to me, you jerk. You said I could have it."

He'd never much liked it when girls called him names. He wanted to hold her and slap her at the same time. "Yeah, well, I'm out now and I want it all back."

"Go to hell," she said, as she'd said a lot of other times, and walked away. Then she stopped, and without turning around—as if she was talking to the door—she said, "You got the perfect diamond. What else do you need?" Then she left.

Chris didn't follow her. It wasn't worth it. She spoiled everything. When she treated him like that, he couldn't imagine her ever loving him, or him ever loving her back. He'd never hit her, no matter how mad she made him. He'd never hit her.

Gina'd had two abortions while they were together, maybe more that he didn't know about. She hadn't told him she was pregnant until it was already too late. Not that he could have talked her out of it. Not that he was ready to have kids, either. Usually he could keep himself from thinking about how she'd killed his kids.

He finished his beer and ordered another one. Beer was one of the things he'd looked forward to in prison—for a while he'd imagined that getting out of a prison would be like starting all over, like a second chance at all the little pleasures of childhood. But beer wasn't cutting it, because when he put his hand in his pocket he could still feel the scratch across the face of the diamond, and he couldn't stop thinking about how perfect it once had been.

He and Gina had been together for over a year before he'd told her about the diamond, a lot longer than that before he'd showed it to her. She'd touched it with her fingertips, then kissed it, very gently. She'd whispered give her time, she'd smooth it out. For a while the scratch hadn't seemed so deep, and Christopher had dared to hope she really could make it go away.

When he got sent up he'd hidden the diamond and wouldn't tell her where it was. And he'd been right, because after a few months she'd written him a letter that said she'd always love him but she had to get away from him because he was bringing her down. Then even though he couldn't see it he'd imagined how the scratch was deeper and uglier than ever, and in order to stop imagining it he'd assaulted a guard and spent thirty days in the hole. Gina had just made things worse.

Christopher could remember—almost consciously, the way some people said they could remember being born—when his diamond really had been perfect. Perfect to look at: silvery and snowy, with rainbows if you held it in the light just right, and hundreds and hundreds of tiny reflections of anything you put on the other side of it. Perfect to the touch: so smooth that your fingertips left their own patterns on it, like pictures in clouds, like shapes made by your own steady heartbeat or your own warm breath. Once he'd looked inside it to find warm rooms with fireplaces, a lazy dog that slept with him every night, a mother who held him with arms that were magical in the way they wrapped around him, a father who read him stories like his dreams.

Finally Chris left the bar. He had a buzz on, but he was not drunk. It was hot. Heat swelled up from the pavement. He'd lived in this town all his life except the two years in prison and the six weeks he and Gina had tried living in Phoenix but neither one of them could stand the sand or the heat or being away from their families. There was nothing for him here, but there was nothing for him anywhere else, either.

"Christopher!"

He glanced around but didn't see anybody who should know him.

"Chris!"

He peered into a store window, as if the voice could be coming out of the glass. He squinted into the confusing reflection and saw his dad hurrying toward him, waving. His dad who'd adopted him, the only person he'd ever called dad.

Turning around so he could see better, Christopher wondered, briefly, what it must be like to meet your son downtown who'd just gotten out of prison. No son of his was ever going to prison. He'd see to that.

Before his father could reach him, three kids went between them on skateboards, maybe nine years old. One of them came back, walking, walked up behind Christopher and offered him a joint, grinning at him in the window. Christopher took the joint without turning around. The kid held out his hand. Chris slapped it away. Kid wasn't even ten years old. Bad things happen to kids before they were even ten years old.

By the time he was ten years old Chris had been left more times than he could count, and his diamond was a mess. Then when he was ten he got adopted. His parents (adopted parents, real parents, forever parents—he didn't know how to think about them either) had loved him. They still loved him. He loved them, too, and he loved his adopted brother and sisters. Because of the love, he'd kept waiting for the diamond to be made perfect again, for the scratch to be taken away. But it was already too late. His perfect diamond had already been spoiled, and his adoptive parents hadn't loved him enough.

His dad stopped a step or two away. Taller than he was. Paler. They didn't look anything alike. Not knowing what else to do, Christopher held out his hand, but his father put his arms around his waist in a hug and Chris hugged him back. He noticed right away that his dad had put on weight. He wasn't taking care of himself, wasn't eating right. He always did drink too much pop.

"Good to see you," his father said over his shoulder. Then—as if he didn't know what else to do, or as if it was really true, he said again, "It's good to see you."

Christopher stepped back, looking at his dad, who had this silly grin on his face, like a clown or something. And he was shrugging his shoulders as if he had no idea what more to say. And his eyes looked funny, as if he was about to start crying.

Chris twisted his body away so his dad wouldn't feel the diamond in his pocket. Wouldn't steal it—although he didn't really think that was likely. Wouldn't ask about it. Wouldn't even know about it.

His dad had always known about the diamond; abruptly now, Chris admitted it to himself. The same way he'd known Chris had put the nail under the front tire, had shoplifted the pack of Trues. Had known stuff, but hadn't been powerful enough to stop Chris from getting himself into more and more trouble. Had known, but hadn't been able to fix the diamond.

Christopher pulled back from his father so roughly that he might have pushed the man away, might have been furious with him, might have been about to cry himself. He ran down the street toward his room, for a minute not exactly sure which direction it was in. He thought about throwing the diamond away while he ran, for all the good it had ever done him, but he didn't.

That first day out of prison, Chris had managed to find a place to live, which was a relief. A hot yellow room in one of those rundown apartment buildings/hotels that hadn't been renovated yet in lower downtown. He'd lived in a lot of those hot yellow rooms in his twenty-two years, where the sun turned the window shade brown and the lightbulb hanging from the ceiling never had a cover. There was a stove and a sink in one corner, a battered wardrobe in a second, his single bed with the stained mattress in the third, and in the fourth the door, the transom hanging open over it to let in some air and the sound of somebody's constant fighting.

For all the ugliness of this room, for all that it looked like every other hot lonely yellow room, Christopher could see where people had tried to make little improvements: A picture from a magazine of a red flower had been taped to the top of the dresser and varnished over; it was a tacky picture and the varnish had bubbled, but he kind of liked its flash of color. In the back of the wardrobe he found white lace curtains, a little brown on the edges but still okay; when he tacked them at the window they made the sunlight seem softer.

Before he'd gone to prison, he would have thought stuff like that was stupid. Now, he had a moment of imagining that these were messages of hope from other people miserable enough, poor enough, lonely enough to have lived in this room before him. He had to remind himself that none of them had had a perfect diamond ruined forever.

Coming up and down the stairs, he had to step over drunks who smelled like vomit and pee, but he didn't care. Every night he couldn't sleep from the heat and the thumping next door and over his head and under his floor, but he didn't care. He had nobody in the whole damn place to talk to but he didn't care.

But gradually Christopher began to realize that he had neighbors. Whether he wanted to or not—and he didn't want to—he started meeting the people who lived in the other rooms. Sometimes he'd look up at his building as he came home, and its two dozen eyes would be flapping in the winds of its dreams. In each of those windows a face would be staring back at him, a gray oval or triangle or pyramid. People whose lives had been ruined by something somebody had done to them a long time ago, and who, like him, were damaged now, imperfect.

In the room under the stairs on the first floor lived the fattest guy

Chris had ever seen. He couldn't possibly get through the narrow door; Chris thought of prison. He'd lost his face inside all that fat, but he hadn't lost his voice. He called out to Chris by name: "Christopher! Come in and see me!"

The first time, Chris pretended he hadn't heard. But the next time, the voice came up the stairs after him and he turned around and went back down to stand in the doorway of the fat guy's room. "You talking to me?"

"Your name's Christopher, ain't it?"

"How'd you know that?"

The guy was laughing and crying at the same time. "I know things. Please come in. I'm lonely."

"I'm busy," Chris started to say. "I gotta go look for work."

"Nobody ever visits me. Nobody ever talks to me."

"You're lying." Chris hated it when people made their problems worse than they were. "Somebody comes two or three times a day and brings you food."

"That's my mother. But she doesn't visit me. She doesn't talk to me."

Chris stepped just inside the room. The guy was so huge he was pushed into every corner. It reeked in there. Food was smeared all over his face, if that was his face. His mouth was almost buried in the flesh, and Chris could see only one of his little eyes.

"Why do you let her shove all that crap into you all the time? Why do you let her keep you trapped in this room?"

Chris wasn't any more surprised by the fat guy's answer than by his own questions, and he knew they were both telling some version of the truth. "What I eat won't come back to hurt me."

"Sure it will," Chris said, exasperated. "It'll hurt you from inside."

"What's that?" The guy was suddenly eager, afraid. "What's that in your hand? Did you bring me something? Something to eat?"

Chris opened his hand. His diamond was in it. He hadn't realized he'd taken it out of his pocket. "That's my diamond," he said, reluctantly. "It used to be perfect, but now it's ruined."

"Let me have it."

"Why?" Chris laughed. "You think you can fix it?"

Part of the enormous fleshy creature in the room with him simply swelled up around him and took the diamond away. Chris swore, thought to fight. But he watched the glittering gem disappear inside the wet mouth, heard gurgling noises, and then, horrified, saw and heard and smelled it being excreted at his feet.

"There you go," the fat guy said with a flourish. He howled with laughter. He sobbed. "Good as new."

But it wasn't. When Christopher bent and picked his diamond out of the disgusting mess on the floor, it smelled of the fat guy's insides, and the scratch was longer and dirtier than ever.

He backed out into the hall. The voice oozed out into the hall and up the stairs after him. "Come again, Christopher! Come visit me again!"

At the head of the stairs, where you couldn't help looking right into it before you turned right to Christopher's room or left to the bathroom, was a room full of furniture, neatly arranged and probably pretty expensive. The door was always open. He kept hearing a soft voice, just a little louder than a whisper, but for a long time he never saw who lived there.

The day he'd moved in he'd walked right into that room, not to steal anything (but that's what they'd think if anybody saw him, and it made him shake, thinking about being locked up again), but just to see who lived there, to say hello. And somebody had been there because he'd talked to them, he'd had a long conversation with them about what they did all day (dreamed), what they ate (air and dust), what they looked like (whatever you like, just don't hurt me). But he'd seen nobody, no matter how hard he'd looked. He just kept hearing this wonderful sweet voice, a young woman's voice.

Maybe he could love somebody in his life besides Gina. Maybe he just hadn't found the right woman who could make his diamond perfect again.

It wasn't hard for Chris to find jobs, but it was hard for him to keep them. He got bored. He didn't let people push him around. The morning he got fired from the dishwashing job, he came back to his hot yellow room, thinking he'd sleep for a while, watch some TV, maybe smoke a joint to relax. The door at the top of the stairs was wide open, as usual, but he didn't hear the woman's voice. Maybe it had left.

Christopher walked into the room of the voice and sat down in a rocking chair with a brocade seat. Everything in here was so ordinary, so perfect. As if the place had never been lived in.

"So," he said, "how's it going?"

No answer.

"Want some company?"

No answer. He was starting to think she'd tricked him. It wouldn't be the first time.

He picked up a bowl with a pale blue Indian design and threw it down. On the thick rose-colored carpet it didn't break or even make much of a noise. "Talk to me," he insisted, trying not to raise his voice very much. He knew she had invited him in here, but now she wouldn't talk to him at all.

He stood up, walked across the room, kicked at the gleaming leg of a sofa. The sofa didn't move. "Why don't you talk to me, dammit! Nobody talks to me!"

Then—he couldn't believe he was doing this—Christopher had squatted on the floor and was holding his diamond in both hands, holding it out as if offering it to the girl with the disembodied voice. "It used to be perfect," he heard himself pleading. "You could make it perfect again."

He talked and talked then, telling her his story of the perfect diamond and all the ways it had been scratched and marred and hurt over the years. He talked and talked, but the woman's voice never came back.

After he'd been in her room a long time, talking about his diamond, Chris thought he understood. She'd been hurt a lot; she'd probably been invisible most of her life. Now she was afraid of him, afraid that he and his diamond would hurt her, so she'd deliberately lost her voice, too.

Retrieving the diamond from the pile of the rug where he'd laid it, he immediately felt the hole. The scratch had been turned into a gouge, that ate way into the stone.

Chris said he was sorry and walked out of the room, carrying his diamond in the cup of one palm and gently shutting the door behind him.

Then there was the guy who was all hair and a growl that seemed to start in the bottoms of his feet. And the girl who wore so much make-up all the time that Chris thought at first she was a painting hanging there on the wall. These two must have sat in the drab, dirty lobby all day and all night, because every time Chris passed through they were there. He never said anything to them and they never said anything to him.

One night, late, he came in a little drunk, a little stoned. He'd run into Bobby at the pancake house. Bobby was probably his best friend, outside of Gina—who, he reminded himself, wasn't his friend anymore. He hadn't seen Bobby the whole time he was in prison, had heard from him once and that was to borrow his tools that Gina still had; Chris had written back yes which was beside the point since Gina had probably already let Bobby take them; they always did have the hots for each other. All night at the pancake house and then at the bar and then at Bobby's old lady's place, neither one of them had mentioned the tools or Gina, and Chris drank and smoked more than he should have, more than he meant to, waiting for Bobby to say something. He had six days to get the crap out of his system before he saw his parole officer and took a UA.

So when Christopher staggered into the lobby of his apartment building that night and saw the hairy man and the made-up woman sitting there like always, he just went over to them without thinking about it and held out his diamond, noticing how badly his hand was shaking and supporting it with the other hand, and said, "Can you fix my diamond?"

Even to his own ears his words sounded so slurred that he wasn't sure he'd said what he meant.

They didn't even look. He couldn't tell exactly where their eyes were, but he could tell that they didn't look at his diamond, which appeared dull and worthless in his trembling hands because the hurt part was bigger than the good part by now.

The made-up woman shrieked with laughter that sounded angry and mournful. A growl passed from the soles of the hairy man's feet up through his hairy body and out his mouth in a stream of rancid breath. "We all got diamonds, son, and one way or another they all get ruined."

Christopher stayed up night after hot night, watching stupid horror movies where no matter what you did the monster didn't stay dead. The people in the movies were always so dumb; they'd walk alone into the house where they'd heard the weird noise, or they'd try to pretend they hadn't seen the ghost when they knew as well as he did that they had, or they'd decide they could beat the thing when nobody else in the entire two-hour movie had lasted five minutes against it. Chris wanted to yell—sometimes he did yell, since there wasn't anybody around to object—"Don't go in there! Turn around!" But the people in the movies didn't listen any more than he would have if he'd been in their situation, and the monsters and ghosts and nameless creatures didn't pay any attention to him either.

During the days he slept a lot, ate a lot. He didn't look for work. He missed his appointment with his parole officer—at least, he thought he did; he had a vague sinking feeling and he thought that might be why, but he'd lost track of the days and nobody came after him so maybe not.

Sometime during one of those half-asleep days or half-awake nights, Christopher left his room and went up all the flights and half-flights of steps to the attic. In the part facing the alley a person lived. He'd seen them at the window, a gray oval or triangle or pyramid.

It wasn't really a room. It was just a place under the eaves, cobwebby and riddled with mouse droppings, without any floor or ceiling or walls. Christopher stepped carefully.

It wasn't really a person, either—or maybe it was some new kind of human being, a third sex since it sure as hell wasn't a man or a woman. It had no arms or legs and not much of a head. It was propped up in a rickety hard wooden chair. It looked young as a dead baby not even born yet, and at the same time so old Chris couldn't imagine getting that old. It wore veils that could have been skin; Chris actually touched some of the soft fluttering lace.

"So what happened to you?" he asked, surprised by his own boldness. Somehow without planning it he'd sat down on the other uncomfortable wooden chair, crossed his arms and legs tight against his body and tucked in his chin. Somehow the diamond had tumbled onto the dusty floor between them. It looked bigger than it should be, and it glimmered. Christopher dared to hope that the terrible scratch had been smoothed away, but he couldn't think how to find out.

He didn't know which part of the body the voice came from, but it was as sharp and clear as any voice he'd ever heard. "I paid someone to cut everything off."

It was a minute or two before Chris could bring himself to ask, "Why?"

"My mother and father would have done it anyway. I saw them

with the knives. I heard them sharpening the knives. I heard them making plans for me. I was not going to let them hurt me anymore, so I beat them to it."

"That's crazy."

The torso with the foreshortened head laughed. "You think so? Really? You think I am crazier than the rest of the people in this hotel? Crazier than you, say, obsessed with finding someone who can make your diamond perfect?" Chris knew it would have used its hands to wave in the air, to indicate him and the rest of the hotel, if it had had any hands.

"You didn't have to do that," Chris muttered. "You let them ruin your life."

"Of course. Why not."

"You didn't have to let them turn you into a —a damned monster!"

Atop its lace-draped torso, the flat head shook fiercely from side to side, all grin and bony forehead. "No!" it screeched. "Do you not see? I turned myself into an angel! I am not of this world anymore!"

Chris had started to ask, "Can you fix my diamond?" when the torso stretched upward as far as it could, the lacy torn skin fluttered, and the creature rose through the roof of the building toward, he supposed, heaven.

"I hear you have a once-perfect diamond that has been spoiled."

Christopher stirred in his bed. Hot yellow light bathed him. He was sweating, drowning.

"I can help you make it perfect again."

Christopher opened his eyes. His head was pounding and his vision was blurred. Somebody was crouching too close beside him. He shouted, struck out with his fist, sat up, felt for the diamond under his pillow. It was still there. The scratch was so deep against his frantic fingertips that he was afraid the stone would split in two.

"Let me have it. I'll show you how to make it more beautiful than ever."

"No." Christopher's voice was hoarse and his throat hurt. He cleared his throat and said again, "No."

"Okay, okay." The guy backed off a little, sat down on the floor, and Chris saw that it was a woman, beautiful, sweet-smelling, taller than he was, stronger than he was for sure. "Okay," she said again. "I'll stay here. I'll work on it in this room with you. I brought my tools. Let me have your diamond just for a little while, and we'll fix it right here. You'll see, We'll make it more valuable and more perfect than it ever was before."

Chris already knew he was going to give it to her. He roused himself enough to ask her, "Why would you do that? Why are you here?"

"Because I love you," she said, and Chris was more afraid than he'd ever been in his life.

He couldn't take care of the diamond. It was too much for him. He wished he'd never had it in the first place. The woman would probably steal it. If she stole it, he'd die. That was okay with him. "Take it," he said miserably, and she smiled and reached over with her long sweet mother's fingers and took hold of his hands with the diamond cupped inside them.

She stayed there with him and worked on his diamond. She held and guided his hands as he did the work. Chris thought it took a long time, but it might not have. Her tools whined and whirred. She sang lullabies while they worked. Diamond dust got in his eyes and nose; he tasted diamond.

And it hurt. What they were doing to his diamond hurt him. Pain made him cry. His chest hurt. His heart hurt. He thought he was dying and to his surprise he didn't want to die, but it was beyond him now, it was out of his control.

Finally, she came close to him again, lay down on the filthy mattress with him and took him in her arms. She pressed the throbbing diamond against his dry lips and called him by name. "Christopher. Look. Look at your diamond now."

He didn't want to look. He hid his face against her breast. "Did we take the scratches away? Did I make it perfect again?"

"It's better than perfect. Look." She eased his eyelids open with her fingertips, and he looked.

He cried out. He'd marred his diamond past all hope. He'd actually extended and connected the scratches so that now they covered almost the entire surface of the stone. Tendrils curled and twisted. The layered center, where he'd always suspected the hurt had started, had been layered even more.

Then he saw that it was a flower. The most beautiful flower he had ever seen.

LOST

FRANK DIDN'T KNOW THE DATE he arrived in Los Perdidos, or even the day of the week, not having paid attention to such things for some time. Couldn't have told you who his congressman was, either, or what he himself had had for breakfast that morning, though chips and Coke would have been a safe bet, depending on what you called breakfast, what counted as morning; Frank was just as likely to nap at high noon and be driving and snacking when the sun came up, having more or less deliberately lost conventional demarcations of a day or a night.

The ancient Dodge decided for him where he would stop; he made a point of having no opinion. Just over the New Mexico line, he lost two hubcaps virtually simultaneously, and chuckled and cursed at how things had a habit of disappearing from his life. When he got out to check, he saw he'd lost a lug nut, too, which made him laugh out loud, though without much mirth. He doubted he had much mirth in him anymore, if he ever had.

He'd never been out west before, knew it only from movies and gaudy paperbacks his dad had left him in a battered suitcase. He'd been amazed and amused to discover that the desert was exactly what he'd been led to expect: growth and destruction masquerading as nothing. From the books and movies, Frank knew to look under the surface, to take in the broader picture, and he found what he'd known he'd find. Endless sky. Marks of heat and cold, drought and flash flood, perfectly plain to anyone who knew what they signified. Eyefuls of land and then some, land that wore down whatever humans could put in it—cars, wagon wheels, arcane farm machinery, rotting fence posts and rusting barbed wire spiraling into nothing. Torn and shattered bits of things, the debris left after some other's fortune or misfortune had finally run its course, sucked up by the wind and scattered hundreds of miles, spread out over the land so that after a time you couldn't tell it from natural rock, dirt, vegetation. All this stuff didn't deface the landscape, and it wasn't junk, for the land had made it its own. There was something immensely and dangerously appealing about that.

What he didn't think he had expected were the street people in the western cities, the hitchhikers in shabby clothes out on these long, dusty roads. It made sense when you thought about it, he guessed—they'd be drawn to warmer climes, some place where they wouldn't freeze to death sleeping in a doorway or under a bridge. Or maybe he noticed all these ragged figures in the shadows of not-very-tall buildings because already he'd come to expect them, the ones who had lost everything, or who had left all they'd had.

"The wolf is at the door," he'd whispered to the shadows moving past. They would know exactly what he was talking about. So what could you do? There was no way to get rid of the wolf, so you got rid of the door, of course, on the well-proven theory that you couldn't lose what you didn't have.

Losing the house to the bank had been almost a relief, although Monica didn't think so. She'd never understood what a prison it had become, with all the things inside he'd had to protect. Better to be outside, wandering from place to place, taking only what you had to take, and keeping nothing for very long. Better to be the wolf than to be afraid of the wolf.

Frank didn't know and didn't care how many miles he'd traveled since escaping his home state of Virginia; he'd never looked at a map, his route hadn't been anything like a straight line, and he hadn't kept track of the zigs and zags. Though he didn't trust his own judgment, just before the car died he'd been daring to think he might have gone far enough, because the civilized world had begun to recede, worn and rubbed out by the persistent land. Passing through cities, which became rarer and smaller the longer he was on the road, he experienced the long fade, streets and buildings growing more faint, figures in gutters and ditches less definable, faces less organized, until they were just a recent memory, lost in a backsplash of dust. He'd known to expect that, too; it was why he'd come here.

Here at last, a vast flatness had swallowed every sign of human habitation but this skeletal little settlement, and the flatness itself had about it a powerful sense of place. Once he'd entered it, he thought maybe he'd reached the beginning, beyond which there'd be nothing left to lose. But then more of the car fell off: the rear bumper and some anonymous but clearly important piece of the exhaust system, one of the side views and the red plastic cover off his right tail light. A fat spider crack appeared on the driver's side of the windshield, though he hadn't seen or heard anything hit, and with grim satisfaction he watched it spread. Then finally some bit dropped out of the cooling system, so that he came into town trailing smoke.

Situated with ironic convenience just inside the town limits was a service station. The Dodge limped in and rattled and wheezed to a stop. A small man in his mid-sixties, gray coveralls, ambled out as the car collapsed into its own steam. "Howdy, mister, you lost?"

Frank grinned; they actually said howdy. "Well, I don't know where I am, but I'm not exactly lost. Knowing where I am is not high on my list."

The attendant leaned against the single pump, sizing him up in a way that Frank suspected was a lost art, like phrenology. "Well, sir, be a week minimum before I can get to your car. Only mechanic in town. You might wanta call one of the big places in Albuquerque or Flagstaff, if that wait's gonna make you suffer."

"Use it or junk it," Frank said on an impulse. "It's yours."

"Chrysler makes a good car."

"I won't need it anymore." Frank made his voice go soft, insinuating more meaning than there was in his statement.

"Deal," the man agreed mildly, as if he'd had this conversation before. Indeed, as Frank got out of the car he saw three or four other junkers around the station, left, no doubt, by other newcomers who'd made it only this far on wheels. Not a few western towns had gotten their start in this very way, only back then it had been wagons heading for California.

"What's the name of this place?"

"Los Perdidos." The Anglo mechanic, already squatted behind the Dodge to pry with a screwdriver at the rusted screws on its license plate, pronounced the name with such a complete lack of Spanish accent that at first Frank, who spoke only a very little Spanish himself, didn't catch what he'd said. Grunting, the mechanic pulled the plate off and held it up like a trophy. "I been needing one of these. Didn't have a Virginia. Glad you came by." He grinned slyly at Frank and repeated, more slowly but still with no linguistic acknowledgment that the words were not southwest American English, "Los Perdidos. Means 'the lost ones.'"

Frank chuckled in appreciation. Back East, colorful place names tended toward the florid, poetic, or suggestive: Blacklick, Virginia; Two in a Bush, Pennsylvania. Out West, the most creative names people'd given their towns, mountain passes, rock formations, were more on the wry and desperate side: Last Chance and Purgatory,

Colorado; the Devil's Backbone; Death Valley. Los Perdidos, the Lost Ones, was perfect.

Before he could stop himself, he was hearing Monica, whose once-familiar voice he'd swallowed and held hidden in some deep place inside himself: "You were moaning and crying in your sleep again, Frank. I know, I know, 'nothing's wrong.' I can't get past that. I swear you push everyone away before you have the chance to lose them. But I've got news, Frank—in the end, they're still lost."

Actually, he didn't try very hard to keep from remembering Monica. Like the books and the movies, she'd taught him what to expect.

The town's only mechanic directed him to the town's only grocer, who readily agreed to provide him a cot and meals in exchange for light manual labor. Frank settled in, as much as he needed to. It brought him great satisfaction, feeling like a monk or even a saint: no possessions and even the food and sleeping place belonged to someone else. They could steal everything else, but not your soul. Wasn't that true? Hadn't some great thinker promised that? He used to know things like that, a long time ago, but he'd lost the knowledge somewhere down the road. They could steal your books, but they couldn't steal the ideas inside them, right? But you could lose those ideas over time, he'd discovered, in a gradual falling-out process not unlike losing your hair.

It took him no more than a day to learn the town: who served the best food, where to stand for the best view of the distant hills, where the prettiest girls lived (to look at, not to speak to), which people to ask for favors, which people to avoid. Each scene and piece of information became part of a mental collection with "Los Perdidos" inscribed on the cover in bright red dust letters. He'd study it again and again, he knew, caressing each item lovingly, but he also knew that someday he'd be ripping those pages out, losing them to the wind.

Soon he began walking at night. He made no conscious decision to do so—he simply fell into it. Suddenly it seemed such a natural thing: he breathed, he ate, he excreted, he walked at night. Out past the diner and the hardware store, through the broken circle of an abandoned corral to the dark desert beyond. Learning the place at night would, he saw, require much more time and a different kind of attention.

Los Perdidos had no streetlights or traffic lights, but houses were usually illuminated and there were occasional headlights, motorcycle singles as common as the doubles of cars and pick-ups and RVs. Away from town and off the road, there was no light but the beam of the flashlight his boss had let him have.

At night the desert seemed to have far more features than in daylight. Under his sneaker soles Frank felt bumps and cavities, undulations and rough spots, and once in a while he would sense a solid mass nearby, protruding from the ground just enough for him to have tripped over if his path had been slightly different, or shoulder-high, or looming over his head, almost but not quite touching his flesh as he passed.

"You oughta take care," the storekeeper advised. "Don't wanta go too far from home in the desert at night. Might get good and lost."

Frank almost couldn't speak, having been ambushed by the word "home," which, with any luck, he'd never be in a position to use again. "Right," he managed, hoping to sound nonchalant.

The storekeeper wasn't ready to let it go. "It's happened, you know. Folks wander off and don't come back. Fellow from Santa Fe four-five winters ago, car broke down too far outside town to make it in to Brady's, started walking and got off the road somehow and froze to death in the desert."

"Stay in your car," Frank recited solemnly. "Don't start walking in the middle of the night in winter."

The other man regarded him evenly. "Tourists from somewhere back East, newlyweds, thought it would be romantic or some fool thing to do it under a desert moon. Rattlers got 'em."

220

Belatedly realizing to what "do it" alluded, Frank agreed, barely suppressing a guffaw, "Damn fools. See what love'll do to you?" He clapped the storekeeper's shoulder. "I promise you, my friend, I won't do it in the desert. Okay?"

"We got ghosts, too."

"Why am I not surprised?"

"Spirits. Kids who've gotten lost out there. Run away. Or been left. We lost another one, a young boy, just a few months ago. Seems to me we lose more folks to that desert than to anything else. Don't always find 'em, either, but we keep looking. Sometimes we find stuff, clothes or toys or something. That desert must be just full of what people left behind, forgot was theirs, or couldn't see the sense in anymore."

"Now don't tell me." Frank struck a pose, hand over his heart. "Those ghosts, those kids. They're doomed to spend the rest of eternity wandering the desert out there, searching for parents. Right?"

The man scowled. "Hell, no. They don't want to be found any more than the rest of us do. Any more than you do, smart ass. 'Los Perdidos,' you know?"

Now Frank dropped any pretense of playing along. "You believe all this crap?"

"They're sad stories," the man shrugged. "I like a sad story as much as the next guy. Sort of collect 'em, if you know what I mean."

Despite his scorn, Frank found he was slightly spooked by the tales, and, though he didn't stop his nighttime wanderings, he did make an effort not to stray too far too soon from town. Each successive night he deliberately widened his circle just a bit, always keeping a sense of the town's tether, playing at getting lost but not quite getting there.

During the day, when he wasn't stocking shelves or sweeping up in the store, he wrote letters he knew he would never send. If he let himself be cute about it, he might even decide to stick them in odd places, in a book or under a potted plant or in a pants pocket headed

221

for the wash. Then he'd forget what he'd done. Sometimes he really did forget. Sometimes he lost just that much of his mind.

By the age of three or so, Frank had already begun what had turned out to be a lifelong pattern of giving away, losing, dismantling, destroying, or otherwise relinquishing his most prized possessions. Naturally, it drove his parents crazy. His earliest memories were of his mother's rushed-morning frustration when, once again, she couldn't find some necessary item of his clothing, and of his father's helpless bafflement when a favorite book or toy was nowhere to be found at bedtime and Frank was, quite genuinely, inconsolable.

When Frank was a little older, his beloved grandmother had made for him, as she had for all the grandchildren, a doll as big as he was, brown eyes like his embroidered on the tightly stuffed head, black hair like his under a jaunty green cap Frank coveted for himself but was relieved the doll had, firmly stitched on. For a period of time Frank found gratifying now that he knew something about the attention span of a six-year-old, he and the Frank-doll were inseparable. Then he gave it to a kid in school he barely knew, an Army brat who promptly moved out of the country. Frank had made no attempt to hide what he'd done, whether because he didn't understand it was shocking or because he did, and Granna, maybe to teach him about the power we have over those who love us, had made no attempt to hide her hurt. Now, in Los Perdidos, Frank thought about how much he'd loved his Granna and that doll she made for him; he wrote unmailable letters to them both.

For a while there, Frank mused, things had gotten a trifle bizarre. Sometime in junior high, he'd eaten the stuffing out of the belly of the blue-and-white panda he'd had since he was a baby, piece by cottony piece, then cut the rest of it into little chunks he could flush sadly down the toilet. He disassembled scores of action figures, snapping off every appendage he could and reattaching them backwards, in the wrong positions, mix-and-match; it gave him the creeps and, at the same time, made him really proud when he got the head of a GI Joe to fit in the shoulder socket of a Tarzan. He found old toys and decorated them with awful colors and strange designs. He mapped out the parentage and tangled relationships of each piece. Then he would leave them bunched together for weeks at a time, checking back periodically to see if they'd changed anything on their own. Sometimes he'd whisper nonsense into anything passing for an ear, and he'd wait for anything passing for a mouth to reply. Everyone thought his sweet black Lab got lost, and technically that was true. The whole truth was that he'd left her sniffing weeds at the side of a country road, so confident he was right behind her that she didn't even look back, and he'd sped off as fast as he could with his brand new driver's license in his chewing-gum-and-chicken-wire truck. "I hope you found a good home," he wrote now to the dog, wincing at the memory and at the word, and, shaking his head at himself, buried the single-line note behind the store where years of scraping garbage cans had softened the dirt.

In college he was known as a ladies' man, a heartbreaker, though that wasn't exactly accurate. His fraternity brothers took to accusing him, admiringly, of bringing out the worst in women; hey, thanks, little brother, his friends were ready and willing to lend a sympathetic ear to some girl's complaints about how Frank had mistreated them. None of them had stayed friends with him long. He'd brought out the worst in them, too. Barely recalling any names, of his buddies back then or of any of the girls he'd loved and lost, he wrote a sort of generic apology and thought he ought to let it blow away in a high desert wind, but settled for throwing it into a cluttered drawer.

Every night now he went walking. During the days, while he did his little jobs at the store, wrote his truncated missives, or made small talk with the storekeeper and the mechanic and the morning waitress at the diner where he ate breakfast, his mind worked on ways to increase the risk and, therefore, the thrill. He went out later. He stayed up all night and went out just before dawn, giddy from

This used to be a river, and near here there used to be a garden, Frank decided confusedly, gazing at the jumble of toys and hard-ware and electrical supplies and articles of clothing and glittering amalgams and conglomerates both organic and inorganic. They surrounded him to form a dust-laden bed many yards across at the bottom of this dry wash providing passage through the desert. There appeared to be soft, wave-like movement as well. A sighing undulation. A waltz of many pieces.

Nearby a baby doll's head rocked rapidly, a flutter of movement until it at last righted itself. It turned and pointed its painted eyes at Frank, who found he could not bring himself to look inside them. Its smile obscured by a film of dirt, it edged itself up on a roller skate, and used this to ease slowly across the surface of pipes and wires, ball bearings and coat hangers and pill bottles and broken shoes and plastic guns, darts and dinner plates and the thrown-out innards of thousands of happy homes.

Near here, in some world shared with here, there used to be a garden. Frank remembered that there used to be a garden, full of wonderful things. Full of toys, he thought, full of flowers and friends. Monica had been there, for a little while. Now there was nothing, and the bad things that grow when there is nothing.

You should never throw away your toys, Frankie. Some day you may need them.

He followed the doll's head on the skate, down the river of jumble, joined now and again by clocks with stuffed arms and steaming trains with dolls' legs. Legless tin monkeys and headless soldiers, spools with mouths full of copper gears, and all the unfathomable activity that still bore his mark, the result of his handiwork, the product of his whims. He'd been near a genius, he mused, in his waste.

Now the busy river thinned and the exotic conveyances began losing all their parts. Dust swallowed up the skate. The doll's head rolled and winked, the cavity in its head filling with a nest of determined insects. He sank deeper into the riverbed, which faded and lost its features until it was only outline, only surface.

Barren outcroppings loomed all around him, giving the strong impression of being porous and pliable but not alive. Something like fungi, or an underwater growth. A devolution.

Right here, there used to be a garden. This sharp, gritty wind used to smell of flowers. Children used to play here. People used to love. But the garden had been too beautiful, too good to be true, too frightening to cherish, and so it had been lost, disassembled, given away, destroyed.

The crescent moon, so enormous now he wanted to call it something other than a moon, dominated the swath of jet sky in a way Frank found threatening. The air here was breathable, though he wasn't confident from one inhalation to the next that it would be. He became aware of a repetitive sound he'd been hearing for a while, slightly different from what he was used to but recognizable as footsteps, quick, light, almost musical, and coming toward him. The taste in his mouth could be blood or dread or only sudden thirst, or something he'd touched and carelessly transferred to lips and tongue; it could be poisonous.

Moonlight, if that was a moon and not some foreign body fallen too close, and the peculiar perspective of this place allowed him to make out that the approaching figure was a small, naked, long-haired boy. He hadn't seen Frank yet; Frank didn't know why that should seem to give him the advantage, but the feeling of relief was keen that there was no connection between them just yet. He was not ready for this. But he got to his feet.

The possibility occurred to him that the boy had been aware of his presence all along, and that he was being toyed with. The thought of himself as a toy made him smile. Or maybe the child was afraid of him; there was reason to be, though Frank meant no harm. It was possible, too, that the boy didn't believe Frank was real, or took him for only a part of the landscape.

The child wasn't wandering, or stumbling, or playfully skipping along. He strode, small sturdy arms and legs swinging purposefully, strong little back erect, head high. Frank wanted to stand still, but his legs shook violently. He sank to his haunches. It wouldn't be long before his thigh muscles protested this position, too, and then maybe he would just sit down. The boy was carrying something in his hand. Frank balanced himself with a tent of stiffened fingers on the dusty ground, propped the other forearm on his unsteady thigh, and waited.

The towering formations pretended to make a path between themselves, but it wasn't a real path because it didn't lead anywhere. The boy made the last turn in the false path, and he and Frank were face-to-face.

"Hi," Frank said. Then, because he couldn't think what else to say under the circumstances, "Are you lost?"

The boy didn't speak, but he grinned and nodded and was about to go on his jaunty way right past Frank.

"What have you got there?" Frank was suddenly, coldly, furiously suspicious.

Just out of reach, the boy held up—in both little fists, so as not to lose it—a small blue-and-white panda bear with a hole in its belly. Quickly, then, he brought it in to his bare chest, where he cradled it lovingly, peering up under long lashes at Frank.

"Hey." Anger rose. "That's mine." He found he was making an imperious "gimme" gesture with fingers curling toward himself. "I lost it. A long time ago. I really didn't mean to give it away."

The little boy's wide dark eyes were radiant with tears. Staring at Frank and vehemently shaking his head, he took a faltering step backward and stopped. Through gaps between the small fingers the piquant face and stubby paws of the blue bear poked, and one round ear with a white inside flapped against a grimy thumb. Tendons stood out in the plump wrists from the fiercely tightened grip on the toy.

"I lost him," Frank insisted. Incredibly, he felt on the verge of tears himself. "I want him back." Amazed, he could hear the whine in his voice.

Tears were streaming down the boy's round cheeks now, glimmering in too much moonlight. The child took one hand away from the bear, and Frank's heart leaped, but swiftly the other hand with the bear in it disappeared behind the boy's back.

Frank was crying now. The salt of his tears was startling, and their wetness on the dry backs of his hands. A great and hungry mouth was opening up inside him, showing its teeth, desperate for what had escaped it.

The two of them stayed that way, staring at each other and crying, the toy and the memory of the lost toy connecting them and setting them against each other. Then, with no warning, the child shrieked, rushed forward, and thrust the bear into Frank's chest.

Frank wasn't ready. He didn't get his hands up in time, and the bear tumbled off his lap. He lunged for it and so did the child, howling in outrage or horror. Neither of them found the toy at first and then both of them did, and then they were clawing at each other, holding each other's hands, scrabbling over and under each other until the boy had the bear again and, breathing heavily, clutched it to himself.

Panting, crouched low in the dark dust now, Frank was still considerably taller than the boy, and much bigger, of course. But the boy was faster, and more acclimated to this place. He simply scampered away, tucking Frank's blue bear under his lowered chin so Frank couldn't see it anymore. His rapid footsteps vanished on the hard ground. Frank had nothing.

He looked around at the endless desert. The lost ones chasing their own paths. The long shimmer of the thrown away river, sliding and clicking and chattering across the emptiness. Frank in the place he'd been heading for all his life, alone. The dying wind. The wolf at the door. The moon too big for the sky.

NORTH

HE WAS ON HIS WAY NORTH. He could have just as well gone south, he supposed; like most faux choices people were faced with, this one wouldn't have made much difference either way.

But after the divorce hearing he'd set off north—out of town, across the state line, over the Canadian border, eventually up the Alaska Highway—and it was as good a direction as any. Better than some: despite the earth's spherical nature, lines of longitude were not the same as lines of latitude, and eastward or westward would have led him in endless circling. This way, north, there would come a point past which he couldn't travel without changing direction, and when that happened he'd stop. For no good reason, except that maybe, at the very top of the world, he would be alone.

For now, though, he was stuck in the company of an Eskimo guide allegedly named George. Surely that couldn't be; he must have a secret, real name, studded with k's and q's, and "George" was for scamming tourists. Jay had briefly considered telling the smug bastard that his name was, say, Vlad, but he'd paid with a personal check for an exorbitant amount—not many guides would go into the interior this time of year, George had pointed out calmly. The check was rubber, but by the time George discovered that, Jay would be unavailable.

When he'd left the Lower Forty-Eight he hadn't thought about needing a guide because he hadn't thought he was going anywhere in particular except north. He should have known better. Coincidences did not happen, at least not for the likes of him. His life had always had a direction. There had always been a pull.

There had turned out to be another reason for coming up here, and this was probably what kept him going, what woke him up every morning to utterly lightless dawn. He was searching for someone he didn't even believe in, whose relationship to him was mythical at best—and of whom, astonishingly, George claimed to have heard.

Jay didn't have to believe, it seemed. Just the idea of the man had weight, gravity. Wherever Jay tried to go, all roads would eventually lead to him.

He had never told Rachel about his fairytale great-grandfather. But then, there were plenty of things he'd never told her about. Vietnam, for instance. His refusal to talk to her about Vietnam had upset her because, she'd accused, it meant he didn't trust her. Of course he didn't trust her, and he'd been right not to, as the divorce had proved. What had unnerved him was the thought of how close he'd come, a few times during those sixteen years, to taking a real chance with her.

But he'd had the sense and self-discipline to restrain himself, said about Vietnam only that it was the reason he would never be responsible for bringing children into this world, and about Dracula nothing at all. Never let her even guess at certain tastes and pulls. Which was why, when the judge had declared it done, he'd been able to walk calmly past the tearful Rachel and just head north.

In Nome he'd said to this George only that he needed a guide through the interior, that he was headed north above the Arctic Circle, that his great-grandfather had once made this trip. This last part he'd made up, of course, but then he'd become convinced it was true. George had nodded once, and Jay had been left with the unpleasant impression that, despite his intentions, he'd been too loquacious, had somehow revealed something.

"You like stories about my people," George was saying now, nodding in an offensive, knowing way.

Jay had no interest at all in folklore, but when George was talking he wasn't, presumably, listening, and there wasn't dangerous silence between them. Jay took a modicum of satisfaction in having fooled the man, but satisfaction was risky if it caused you to let your guard down.

"Especially you like the bloody ones, I think. One man eats another man. A woman eats her husband's second wife. A ghost sucks all the blood out of an old woman and leaves her skull to go rolling across the ice. A child drinks so much of its mother's milk that it explodes all over the village." George laughed, too loud and too long. "You think we Inupiak have the big appetite, eh?"

"Well," Jay mocked, turning his head in his bedroll to look pointedly in the direction of George's belly, which he could see dimly in the firelight reflected off the cabin walls. This caused the Eskimo's hilarity to increase, and Jay's irritation with it. "Hell," he all but shouted, "you guys don't have any more of an appetite than anybody else. You just talk about it more."

"The White Man Who Doesn't Eat? The man you're looking for? He's here, you know."

Jay caught himself before he actually glanced around. "Why do you call him that? His reputation is that he eats a lot. Speaking of appetites."

George's face glowed, a red ball in the light of the fire. The walls were a duller red, and beyond them, Jay knew, was absolute dark.

Under the crack of the flames and George's blubbery voice, ice moaned. Jay burrowed into his parka, letting the hood come forward to shield his head until only a small gap remained, completely filled by George's burning face. There was a rustle as, apparently, the Eskimo shrugged. "I guess he ate all he could eat. Maybe all he needed to eat."

"He's a mythical creature. Not real."

"Lots of Outsiders think ice worms aren't real, either."

"Ice worms?" Jay guffawed.

"Tiny little black buggers live in temperate glaciers. Eat debris that falls through the cracks. If you touch one, your body heat burns him. Shrivels right up."

"Probably doesn't happen very often," Jay said mock-seriously. "Living in glaciers probably doesn't bring them into a lot of human contact."

George laughed heartily.

"What are you talking about, he's here?" Jay demanded, though by pursuing it he was exposing himself. "Where?"

"In the Brooks Range somewhere. Some people say here, some say there. The Brooks Range, though, somewhere."

Jay's heart had quickened. Not to let George guess at his eagerness, he growled, "I thought you were going to tell another story."

"This is a true one," George began happily. "A true story about my own great-grandfather, who had many children and grandchildren, and who ate at least two of his grandsons during the times of starvation. Now, my own father has said these two boys were sickly and would have died anyway and that my great- grandfather had no choice if he was to survive, but others have told how he always had this taste for human meat, liking it better than fish or walrus fat. Who can know what is true?

"But the story I heard was that he beat my great-grandmother when he was angry, and he was angry most of the time. Bad weather or stupid dogs, poor hunting or a broken tool, all of these things

232

made him angry and he would beat her. This is an ugly part of the story, but I knew this man when he was very old and I believe this part at least to be true.

"Finally one day she left him, travelling into another village, leaving the two grandsons behind. At first the old man was nice to them, feeding them walrus fat and the belly of the whale, even when they made mistakes and angered him, which was often. He himself ate almost nothing, except a few caribou turds, sitting most of the time watching his grandsons grow fat and happy.

"Then one night he fed them all that remained of his store of food and told them stories of the paradise that exists in a deep valley surrounded by ice, and when they were asleep with smiles on their faces he beat them over the head with stones and ate them. When my great-grandmother returned she found him with blood and fat still dripping from his mouth."

George paused for such a long time that Jay felt compelled to ask, "And then what happened? What did the people do to him?"

"Nothing. My great-grandmother went back and she never said a word to him. No one said a word to him. Maybe it was because it was a time of starvation, maybe it was something else, who can know? Things follow their natures. When I knew him he was very old, and very fat, and my father wouldn't let me near him. I remember that every night someone in the family had to stay awake if he was there."

Jay found himself beginning eagerly, almost before George had stopped talking, "my great-grandfather once impaled a woman for making her husband's shirt too short. This was a long time ago, in another age. But I believe the story. I think he used a hot stake of iron, thrust into the vagina, through the body, and out the mouth. He had a strong, if peculiar, sense of morality. Unfaithful wives were skinned alive. Nipples were sliced off, that sort of thing." Jay paused, a little surprised both that he was telling such things at all and that he wasn't much bothered by them, as if the tale had nothing to do with him. "Sometimes children were roasted, I believe. And fed to their mothers."

He looked up. Regarding him intently, George demanded, "Your great-grandfather did these things? Truly?"

Jay shrugged, feeling a peculiar sort of pride.

George nodded slowly. "'A hunger worse than any Inupiak hunger'—that is what they say about The White Man Who Doesn't Eat."

They talked long into the night. When finally George's breathing deepened into snores, Jay was incensed. At this price, the least the son-of-a-bitch could do was be polite. He lay awake for a long time then, thinking about how dark darkness could be when you knew the sun was not going to rise in the morning, and he was not aware of falling asleep or of sleeping but of waking up to find George gone.

No note. No kiss-my-ass. Cash, half the amount of his worthless check, stuck in his boot. No directions. Shit, Jay chided himself as he pushed out into the morning cold and dark. What did you expect? Just go north.

He'd walked and climbed maybe ten minutes before he could think about anything but George's treachery and how it proved, as if he'd needed more proof, the general and individual calumny of humankind. Then certain details of his situation floated up into his consciousness, and he cursed himself for a fool to have been distracted by yet another scumbag.

For one thing, he saw that the darkness was not total now; a faint ring of what could only be called paler black hinted—falsely—at sunrise. This slight illumination threw rocks, snowfields, his own stumbling feet into a disorienting relief, making him wish for complete darkness again, and, because it limned the horizon all the way around, it helped not at all to find north.

He also realized suddenly that he was a step or two away from

234

the edge of a crevasse. It wasn't so much that he could see the crack but that he could hear some alteration in the ambient silence.

Caught between powerful eagerness and strong aversion, neither of which he could quite justify, Jay set his right boot down carefully, almost soundlessly, on the frozen ground a wide pace ahead. Stalking in the tundra was different in technique from stalking in the jungle, but the attitude, the relationship with the environment and with the prey, were the same, and something in Jay welcomed the chance to do this again. His body remembered how to move, his lungs how to breathe, his mind how to think of himself. His gloved hands were clumsy around the flashlight that ought to have been a weapon, but the single assaultive motion—shifting his weight and bringing his left foot forward, crouching, swinging the beam out and down—was practiced and still sure. He continued it down the sloping lip of the crevasse, stepping carefully, checking himself with each footfall. Going north. Going down.

He'd found the children just this way, a sliver of light on their pale, bloody faces. Barely breathing, they would have died anyway, had been about to die. After all, hadn't they crawled off into the jungle, their bodies chewed by bullets and shrapnel, to die in peace? He'd only helped them—that had been his intention all along. And all he'd wanted for his trouble had been the taste.

At first, when the shaft of light hit something large below him, Jay thought the crevasse must not be very deep after all, which would, if true, belie what his senses had told him. So, scanning the beam back and forth and, with each pass, picking up more detail, he felt a grim sort of relief to discover that, indeed, this enormous crack in the ice and icy ground was stuffed with something. Something alive, and huge.

As he climbed and then slid down the steep incline, two surprising thoughts, apparently disparate, occurred to him: that—as with the children in the jungle pit—he'd hardly even paused to consider whether he'd go down or not, and that streams in the Brooks Range flowed north-south while their trellis-like tributaries flowed east-west, so by heading along this fissure the narrow way he had a fifty-fifty chance of still traveling north.

The air grew noticeably warmer as he descended, which was contrary to what he'd expected, and peculiarly soggy. Any trace of daylight vanished. Snow flew up at him, and darkness.

Gradually, though, he began to discern features, first only those very close to his eyes—an outcropping to steer himself against, a line left on rock by summer algae, the zipper on his own right sleeve. Now the sweep of hard snow on the other side of the crevasse came clear, and numerous footprints across it, and now the huge human body below and ahead of him. Whether his eyes were growing accustomed to the barely perceptible light or whether there was actually increased illumination from some source unknown to him, he could now clearly see a massive naked human being, supine between the sheer icy walls.

Jay wedged his feet and braced his elbows to keep from going on over the last little ridge between himself and the enormous creature, and he stared. The body, many yards across at the widest point of its belly, all but filled the fissure, stretched and bloated like many he'd seen drowned but ruddy, almost scarlet, instead of pale. It was male; the huge erect penis, so engorged it was almost purple and looked painful, made Jay wince. Caucasian; the skin was florid, but unnaturally so. Old, probably, with hair two or three times longer than Jay was tall, white and dirty as glacial ice.

Mostly the man looked hot, and his body heat radiated in all directions. Sweat was raised uncomfortably inside Jay's parka, and the permafrost had melted slightly so that under and alongside him oozed a steady, eerie dripping.

He crabbed along the wall of the fissure, northward. Before he'd gone very far he was overheated and exhausted, and the slippery

236

ground under his hands and feet threatened to give way with every inch of forward progress he made.

The heat and luminescence of the gigantic swollen torso helped him keep his bearings, distorted as they were. The gelatinous hump of the belly nudged up against his flank, then receded slightly to the moraine-like expanse of the chest braided over with that icy hair from beard, moustache, scalp, brow. An arm rose and fell like ruddy dough. A hand flexed and clenched like rubber. The man's great moist inhalations and exhalations seemed to express both passion and pain, and Jay, who had long regarded sex as a release not much more intimate than passing gas, felt a strange excitement.

As he crawled along, glancing down now and then to keep track of where he was in relation to the giant, Jay became aware of dark patches on the reddish flesh, then realized that they were fur. Suddenly shivering violently, he wondered what their purpose could be since their relative proportion was inadequate for either warmth or modesty. Oddly, his right glove rubbing his left sleeve, he found himself wishing for some of those warm little spots himself. They were moving, too, he saw—massaging, kneading. His chill passed, replaced by a wave of prickly, itching heat.

Finally he was perched directly above the vast face. At first his fascination with each individual feature—wet and bulbous nose, bulging eyes, cheeks like hillocks implanted with silicon—that he had no sense of the visage as a whole. The mouth, especially, riveted his attention: pillowy lips, tongue like a gargantuan worm, and fangs.

"Dracula," Jay whispered.

The countenance billowed up toward him and he recognized it—distorted in color and shape, but still the face he'd been shown once in a dark old portrait, told once was his great-grandfather, and never seen again.

He lowered himself over the final drop and, as his boots hit ice and rock that didn't give and flesh that did, he sank to his knees, bouncing slightly. Aware of a dozen pools of warmth and motion around him, he realized with a not altogether unpleasant shock that the spots of fur were heads, the dark hair of Eskimo women whose clothed bodies blended with the old man's flesh but whose heads stood out like hairy moles. And they weren't massaging; they were sucking. Dozens of enthusiastic slurps and swallows punctuated the arctic silence, in dizzying counterpoint to Dracula's panting and his own.

The face had turned toward him, setting off small avalanches, and the dark head clinging to the flabby underside of the jaw squirmed off. The bloodshot eye on this side focused with some difficulty on Jay.

"I'm Jay Eric Bucher," Jay explained, feeling ridiculous. "I think you're my great-grandfather."

Dracula snorted, showering Jay and heaving him onto his side. "The same could be said by countless hordes. What are you doing here?"

Not bothering to right himself, Jay mumbled into the springy flesh under him, "I—don't know. I was just headed north."

"Keep going, then. North."

"I don't think I can." Jay despised the whine in his own voice, but it was the truth; he was incapable of continuing as far north as north went, to the end of the world. "I've gone as far as I can."

"I want no company but my ladies. I came here to be alone."

"I'm not company. I'm family."

Dracula sighed. Jay stretched his arms and legs out over the shifting breast on which he lay. "I grew weary with both the individual and the massed lives of humanity," Dracula declared. "The petty concerns, the tediousness of their every breath and movement. The very pulse of them became an irritant I could no longer bear."

"I know," Jay murmured, thinking of Rachel.

"My body refused to process any more of their fluids. The regular movement of my bowels, once redolent of massive quantities of blood and the sweat of lives cut short—the stool of a hunting beast—all but ceased. It all collected in my gut."

Thinking of the child with no legs, the pit full of blood and flesh, the woman with a razor blade in her vagina, Jay breathed, "I know."

"I grew in proportion to the blood I drank, the lives I took away, the evil I caused and consumed. The ocean of blood which had always made an island of my mind now became the ocean my skin could but barely contain. I hardly eat at all anymore. I cannot stomach the thought of coming close enough to eat."

Jay felt a touch at the small of his back and stiffened.

"My concubines can never consume enough to reduce me for more than a brief spell. But they give me momentary relief as nothing else can do."

Jay slid over onto his back. A dark-haired, round-faced woman was smiling at him, clearly offering herself. Teeth glittered. He must have seemed willing, for she lowered her mouth to his in a long kiss that had pain in it and, quickly, blood. He struggled to free himself but only sank back into Dracula's flesh, and the woman followed him without ever breaking contact, sucking.

Panicked, Jay flailed to look for his great-grandfather's eyes. The Eskimo woman bit into his back and he howled. Then above a mass of flesh one gargantuan eye peered darkly, bloodshot. Like the eye of one of the children at the end of the trail of blood across glistening green leaves. Begging for relief.

When Jay buried his teeth into Dracula's flesh, murmurs of approval rose like steam from the women around him. Murmuring. Biting. Sucking. Trying to eat his way through an ocean of flesh into an ocean of blood below.

The child's eye stared up at him as Jay first dug for, then found, its fist-sized heart.

But when he found his way to Dracula's heart he was amazed at the enormity of it: a heaving, impassioned, great side of beef of a heart that exploded with the first tug of Jay's teeth.

"And so the grandson drowned in the blood of the great- grand-father's beast of a heart," George said, winking at the solemn Eskimo children gathered around him. "For hunger is a wonderful thing, and a terrible thing, as every Inupiak young and old must know."

EMPTY MORNING

A LL EVENING, BEFORE SHE STOOD UP and found her balance and began a slow journey across the small room made to seem smaller by multicolored smoke and by the impression of many bodies not entirely visible, before she stalked him and called out his name, she had been watching him. Through the opium haze so dense it did not drift but pulsed, pooled, coagulated, she had traced and traced again his features, his profile, the outline and contours of his head and shoulders and arms, the occasional glimmer of his hands on pipe or glass.

Having wizened considerably, he could no longer be said to be of medium weight and strongly built. His head, though, was still noble, large behind the ears in the shape currently imagined to indicate superior intelligence. His nose, when she caught it in profile, was still straight, the two ridges at his hairline still prominent above bushy brows. Dim blue and violet lights had the intended effect of obscuring the true colors of objects they illumined, but she knew his hair would be gray now rather than red. His eyes would still be large, dark blue, set wide. She had looked into his eyes before, and would do so again, this time with very different purpose.

He sat hunched over his folded hands. He leaned back, rested his head against the pillowed edge of the chair, folded his hands across his abdomen. He looked up to exchange words with someone who paused beside him, then gazed distractedly after the figure as it went on.

He lifted the thin green glass, sipped, set it down, did not drink again for a long time. Others approached him, spoke, drifted away. She had watched him.

Through the fluted syrupy cylinder of her own glass, his silhouette had floated and blurred, emerging into transparency and then sinking once again into emerald murk. Having drained and replenished her drink far less often than he had, she was indeed inebriated. This establishment prided itself on serving only Swiss absinthe, the finest available; the far better and stronger liquors she had once known were now by her own choice lost to her. This was and forever would be the best she could do. With the help for which she had hunted him down, it could perhaps become enough.

An immense holiday was at hand, the turn of a century, but neither the measurement of time nor the celebration for which it provided excuse had relevance to her. She guessed, however, that it would mean something to him.

He was an old man, besotted by opium, absinthe, no doubt laudanum, no doubt memory and dread and all the other maladies she understood were associated with mortal aging. He would be weaker of body, mind, spirit than during their very brief encounter long ago and during the many years thereafter when she had followed him by reputation. But from the throbbing at the base of her belly when he glanced her way, she knew he would still kill her if he knew who she was. And she also knew he, he alone, could save her.

All but certain she recognized this man, she dared not trust what she knew, about this or anything else. "Who—is that?"

Her companion was a long-haired young man who spoke, moved, drank with such studied languor that his recurrent sexual overtures surprised her, and of whom she would soon divest herself though not with as much dispatch as she once would have done. Mistaking the object of her query to be the girl on a nearby chaise whose hair across her face and fingers around the pipe were themselves like smoke, he uttered a name as if it were an obscenity.

"No," she interrupted, suddenly very tired and very bored. "The man behind her, at the corner table, alone. The old man."

"Van Helsing." Supercilious and sure of himself, he quaffed the last of his absinthe, sighed and licked his lips, reached for her.

She pressed her fist into his chest. It was easy enough to keep him at bay without really hurting him, though under other circumstances and in another time she'd not have resisted the urge. "Abraham Van Helsing?" Her constricted throat had turned her voice husky.

"Yes." The young man caught her fist, brought it to his mouth, grazed her knuckles with his teeth in what she supposed he thought was a daring caress.

"The physician and metaphysician?" Blood coursed hot through her arteries and veins, pounded at her throat and wrists, reddened her vision, coppered her tongue. To be so close.

"And world-famous slayer of creatures vampiric." Thrusting her hand away from him, he stood, laughed, swayed. "What utter rubbish." The declaration was meant to be haughty, but he lost his balance and collapsed against the next table, spilling the liquor of the patrons and attracting the attention of those charged with maintaining the decorum of this place. A large man escorted him out. Blue and violet smoke instantly oozed into the place he had lately occupied.

Testing herself, she took time finishing her drink, smoked

another pipe. Since her vow—an indefinite span, as was all time for her kind, though for humans it moved and had shape in ways she could only yearn for—she had tested herself on countless occasions, and had not always passed. Now, though quavering, she did hold firm.

At last, fortified as best she could be within the condition she had set for herself (blood was thick here for the taking, blood to satiate, blood to transport, but she would not take it, she would not), she thought to approach him. The smoky girl on the chaise cried out and flung her legs wide, skirt raised. The stalwart guardian of public propriety went to her, momentarily obscuring the view.

Van Helsing was gone from his table. Panicked, she rose, then saw him slowly making his way toward the door. He was the only hope she had of turning away from the thing she had been for so many years. She had little choice but to follow him.

Sick in stomach and head, unsteady on his feet, he stumbled as he left La Fee and reentered the teeming night. Almost immediately he was seized by the sharp cough that lately beset him in the London streets. A hack driver cursed at him, the horses kicking rubble against his shins. A street urchin screeched in his general direction for tuppence, and dropped into his hand a filthy apple he knew better than to eat but absently ate anyway. His head ached, and he noted his hands shook more than usual.

He noted also, and not without a certain sad amusement, that the malaise and despondency which had brought him into La Fee had been deepened by his time there. This was nearly always the case, and yet he went there nearly every night, a typical addictive pattern. As he steadied himself against a grimy wall before turning the first of the three corners between the opium den and his flat, he mused that, for a man of science in all its forms, he had become decidedly irrational.

Once he'd believed the turn of the century would herald the dawning of a cleaner, more scientific era. But now approaching his dodder age, and mere weeks away from that most anticipated event, he saw little evidence of it. England was at war once again, this time with the Boers. The summer had seen the death of his beloved Strauss. And if anything these streets were darker, dirtier, more chaotic. He would not be surprised if the Ripper himself returned. He would not be surprised if Dracula himself returned from the dead.

"Sir? Kind sir?" A woman hailed him from behind. Irrationally, he turned. Heavy perfumes did no more to mask her other unsavory odors than did layers of rags to disguise her gauntness and filth. Even in the near-darkness her trembling was evident. He knew her for yet another harlot desperate to feed the very habit he himself was well on his way to acquiring.

Searching a pocket and then another, he grew light-headed, and his vision blurred a sickly version of absinthe's emerald. Needing both hands now to support himself, scraping his palms on rumpled brick, he shook his head and turned his face away from her. But she came closer and said his name. "Dr Abraham Van Helsing." It was not a query.

Drawing in his breath caused him to cough again. "Yes, yes, I am Van Helsing. What do you want with me?" Being thus recognized in public had become increasingly rare; he was both grateful and disappointed.

"My name is—"

He thought she hesitated, although the various substances he had taken into his body this evening and many previous evenings had the attraction of making perception unreliable.

"—Katherine Harker." Another hesitation, as if she expected some response. "We have met."

The surname was familiar but not uncommon, and he discerned no physical resemblance to the Harker he had once known. Doing his best to be, if not quite gallant, at least polite, he reached to tip his hat and discovered it not on his head. Perhaps he had not worn it, or perhaps he had left it at his table where another patron might find and wear or discard it. "Please," he said, "forgive the memory of an old man."

"It was a long time past and a very brief encounter," she said, "and not under the most favorable of circumstances. But it changed my life." She gave a harsh laugh. "More accurately, it caused me to want to change my life."

Social protocol dictated he inquire as to the particulars, and he wished not to be impolite, even to creatures as unwholesome as she. But a wave of sickness overcame him. He swayed. When she caught and held him, he saw her more closely.

No taller than his shoulder, and he was not a tall man, she had dark greasy hair and dark complicated eyes shadowed by dense lashes. Her cheekbones made high cliffs, her lips were cracked and slightly parted, her teeth broken. By nature she might be beautiful, but obviously her current situation was extreme. Her hands shook where they clutched his arms.

"Miss Harker." Saying the name, he suddenly felt as if he could have known her very well. "How nice to see you again."

The doddering old fool did not know who she was, nor did he care. Although using the name Harker had been a risky self-indulgence, she need not have worried; clearly, he was well past his heroic prime. But she knew of no one else who could turn her into what she longed to be.

Again he stumbled and she caught him, then pushed him away, afraid of her own instincts, afraid of what he might smell on her though she thought she remembered the Master scoffing at human olfactory capacity. Van Helsing looked like a man pondering whether he had wandered abroad in his nightshirt; the image was not as amusing as it might once have been.

"Pleasant to see you as well, sir," she mumbled, glancing about. When a man grinned and beckoned, she took ridiculous offense.

"You ought to be escorted," Van Helsing slurred into her ear. "All

246

manner of rough creatures about. Believe me, I am versed in such things."

Revulsion flooded her throat, belly, groin. The Master had talked like that. "I love you," the Master would whisper or snarl through endless nights of food displayed and denied, through long hours hiding from the daylight, when the hunger he induced in his countless brides kept them awake and nearly drove them altogether out of the dark. "You, most beautiful and most hungry. All manner of creatures are abroad in the night and day. Such as this one, my darling!" flinging bones of cattle or wild dogs and making his arousal clearly visible as the chosen bride scrambled to mine for the little blood still in the marrow.

Often his favorite and his favorite victim, she had at his leering behest more than once trawled like a pig the bloody waste pits behind hospitals for sustenance and, indeed, for pleasure. His and her own. She could taste it now. She could taste it. She bent her head to the old man's neck.

Rather more easily than she would have expected, he extricated himself from what had become almost an embrace as though he knew already what she would beg of him. He still slurred, however, and shambled as he took a step or two away from her. "The night does have its appeal, though, does it not, my dear?"

Was the most honorable Abraham Van Helsing making a dishonorable suggestion? Nearly as weak now with memory and unholy desire as this weak old enemy she desperately needed, she nonetheless caught up with him in a single stride and in the light from a grimy streetlamp examined his face for intention. He looked wasted and ill; she detected no lechery in him, only relief, bafflement, despair. Her fate was in the hands of a baffled, despairing old man.

He was still talking, perhaps not to her. "A woman should not be left to manage the darkness alone. I would rush the night's passage myself if I did not feel such emptiness in the mornings."

"Ah, the mornings," she agreed. "I manage the nights better, too."

A passing hack driver cut his horse with the whip, and although the animal reacted not at all, she nearly swooned to the quick odor of its blood. And to the odor of human blood as well; perhaps the tip of the whip had flicked the driver's forearm, or perhaps she was smelling Van Helsing's blood through thin flesh and vein, a thought she dared not long entertain.

Since the Master's blessed, cursed murder, she had managed a base survival with small meals of rats and bird hearts, once or twice an addict with blood so diluted it was almost not blood, the occasional newborn and its afterbirth, the occasional child weakened by disease. Hunger had made her delirious, and out of that delirium had come yearning for life without the sickness. The blood fever had distorted all memory of her life before the Master had come to her, but what she remembered, what she must have again, surely was better than this. Eventually out of her desperation had come: Be like him. Be like the destroyer, the only one in the world more powerful than the Master. She had not since tasted live blood.

Scurrying at the base of a building. Blood, blood everywhere, and the terrible need. The need to eat. The need to keep her vow. The need.

Van Helsing turned into an alley. She followed him.

The woman seized his face and brought it close to her own to stare at him. Van Helsing shuddered, reminded not only of the madness of his own late beloved wife but also of a butcher appraising a cow. Vehemently she whispered, "I require your assistance, Dr Van Helsing. Your protection, if you will."

Too tired and inebriated to articulate a refusal, he shrugged and went on. When he missed the grimy doorway to his building, he turned back abruptly and they collided. He felt the surging desperation of her, the decadent ardor. She seemed remarkably strong for a woman, especially a woman in such straits. No doubt she was dangerous. But perhaps for once he would not be alone in the morning, not quite so empty.

At some point on the many stairs up to his flat, he realized she was supporting him with a hand at the small of his back, and he asked himself who was protecting whom. But when she gasped at the rat bright-eyed and -fanged on the landing, he put himself between her and the vermin. He had seen much worse.

Dimly he recalled she had more than once spoken his name, so perhaps she knew who he had been. Dimly he recalled that the name she had given him for herself—he doubted it was truly her name—had meant something to him, suggested something, but it eluded him and he made no effort to chase it down.

The gray cat that now and again shared his flat—which sometimes he indulged himself by thinking of as Fee Verte for its liquid green eyes—hissed and put its back up as they entered. Van Helsing had received aloofness from this scrawny creature as often as affection, but he had not before been the target of its hostility, and he wondered at it. Behind him, she gave a small cry. Pitying what he took to be unreasonable fear, he shielded her from the cat as he held the door open for it to slink out into the stairwell, perhaps to dispatch or be dispatched by the huge rodent gnawing there.

Uninvited, she settled herself onto the settee his wife had, in her calmer moments, so enjoyed for its prim elegance. It was slovenly now and unsteady. He made a vague, belated motion of hospitality, then realized the disorder that had overtaken his living quarters, as if a tide of filth and misery had seeped in under the door, spread and ruined everything. Papers lay scattered like ashes, books sprawled half-devoured. Stench rose from soiled plates and utensils, rotting meat and soured milk and moldy bread and fruit nearer liquid than solid, clumps of stiffened and odoriferous clothing, spilled and long-unemptied chamber pots. He should be ashamed.

He should offer her refreshment, could not think what food or drink he had that would be fit to consume. He should offer her a place to sleep, his own bed the only choice and he would spread a blanket on the splintery floor. He should ask her again for her name. Green smoky unconsciousness overcame him, and he was dimly aware of falling.

Someone laughed outside the battered door, and she started. The hunger in her, tearing at her brain like insects in a feeding frenzy, sometimes made her hear things. Sometimes she felt pursued, and when she was aware enough to know that nothing pursued her but what had taken life inside herself, she was not soothed. Men shouted and cursed in the noisy street below. Church chimes announced the eleventh hour. The despair of the night was young, and, worse, the hope.

Stiffly crumpled at her feet, Van Helsing could not truly be regarded as sleeping, able to be awakened by pleas or threats or by any sort of touch. She considered touching him. She considered kneeling beside him, lying upon him, touching him with open mouth and tongue and then with teeth.

She must move quickly away from him, but her strength was insufficient; she shuffled as far as the confines of the flat allowed. He was her only hope, small and despairing as it was. More than any other creature not like herself, he knew about creatures like herself. He had studied. He had come close. He had destroyed the Master. He could destroy her. She had allowed herself the fancy that he could also save her, teach her how to change her essential nature or at least bear witness while she did so herself. Turn her.

The journey to London had taken a heavy toll, but she had maintained her vow along the way, keeping her distance from villagers and shopkeepers, able to imagine their veins filled with substances other than blood, minimally sustaining herself with raw meat pilfered through unfastened kitchen doors and buried rags from women's monthly bleeding she smelled and unearthed and forced herself to suck. She had heard he was in London and had developed a mighty opium-laudanum-absinthe habit. But once in the immense, crowded, odoriferous, clamorous city, she had been baffled by the search. This evening's serendipity had been a long time coming, and had cost her dearly.

Now here she was, and here he was, and he was unavailable to her. He well might sleep through the night, and the first light of day—even the gritty, overcast, nearly sunless light of London in winter—would cause her further anguish. She would have to find some corner to cower in, and cover herself against the sun's direct and accusing gaze.

She kicked him. He groaned and twitched his shoulder. She hissed his name, shrieked it. He stirred. He began to retch and she stooped to turn his head so his own vomitus would not choke him, thinking she might vomit herself, wondering as she watched the noxious puddle sink into the floor whether there might be anything in it for her. When he seemed to have finished, she wiped his mouth with the end of his own rumpled shirt and sat back away from him. He sank into oblivion again.

Something scratched at the door. She nearly lost her balance as she scrambled to her feet. The scratching came again. She opened the door. Instantly the scrawny gray cat sped past her yowling, claws raking her ankle. The roiling of its small reservoir of blood made her tongue swell. She did not see where in the flat it hid itself, but it would not be difficult to find. Its odor pulsed. She shut the door carefully and turned back into the room.

That night Van Helsing's opium dreams were convoluted tales of intrigue and adventure, loss and mourning, evil and great good and the vast territory between. They gave the illusion of meaning. Mostly, they were deep green. Mostly, he was alone.

He emerged to find himself choking on bile, hands turning his head so that his neck seemed in jeopardy, foul breath in his own foul face.

He emerged to the sensation that his flat was underwater, under blood, detritus from his life floating in the viscous fluid.

He emerged to the instantly clear sight of the woman who had called herself Katherine Harker. Crouching near to him, she held the green-eyed gray cat Fee Verte stretched long and flat across her indecently exposed thighs, its throat and belly slit wide. Her long teeth dripped.

He sank again, knowing it to be delirium. He had seen so much worse.

He awakened again, clutching the petrified claws of a woman whose name he should know as well as his own, but try as he might he could not bring it to his lips. Then he looked out to see it was the paw-like leg of a chair he gripped from where he lay on the floor. His wife howled from her crouch on the other side of the room, tongue out and mouth slavering, her once sweet nature parodied in mad laughter.

He struggled to his feet. Surely he could summon sufficient will and strength to stop what was happening to her, even if it meant beating the demons from her body, driving them out of her heart with that symbol of everything she'd once held sacred.

But he was falling. The gravity of all his failures tore him down.

"Van Helsing! Are you injured?"

Her hands were upon him, helping him to stand, the capable hands of this good woman. But it was that poor woman he'd met out in the street. What was her name? He wanted to say Harker but that couldn't be.

He saw the redness in her eyes, her gaze flitting away to the corner like some winged thing, then back again, trying to force him to see only what she wanted him to see. But he turned his head just enough to find the gray fur pressed behind the curtain, the streaks of red visible even in the clutter on the floor, and that crimson kiss on the back of the hand soothing his face.

He felt a moment of true sadness before realizing the death of his only companion was not the most important implication of this gruesome discovery. He struck her across the face.

She howled. Her back pulled her upward until she was almost his height, her eyes slitting as the skin of her face tightened.

But instead of attacking him she sprang backward. The shelves behind her splintered, book spines ripping and paper exploding into the air as if a cage of birds had been let loose in the room. She threw herself over the chair and into the small table by the window, knocking off his only photograph of his wife. With a cry he reached for it, but it cracked the window pane and fell.

"Demon!" he shouted, and scrambled toward the bed for the leather physician's bag he had not seen in months. He pawed frantically at the bed linen, threw garbage and sour garments behind him at the creature he'd invited in, hoping to delay her until he could once again feel the confidence of the spike in his hand and the power of the mallet that could send her back to Hell. For he knew now what she was. Expecting her on his back at any moment, teeth ripping out his throat, he found himself slowing, ready. More than ready.

She thrust her hand against her teeth, which instinctively bit down. Her own meat was tasteless and pale but she could not let go. Having come this far, having at last forced herself into his presence, she had been unable to deny herself a simple meal of his pet cat. She was lost. Meaning to call his name, she howled wordlessly around her own bloody flesh.

He was coming for her with mallet and blessed spike heavy in his hands. She wrenched her hand out of her teeth and crooned, "Van Hel-sing! Don't be shy, Van Helsing." He stopped. "Please!"

With tears in his eyes, he shook his head. "I cannot. I haven't the strength to raise the mallet anymore. It might as well weigh the world."

Diving into the garbage, sewage, wreckage in which he stood ankle-deep, she fed. He groaned but he stood by. With fingernails and teeth she tore out fibers of the threadbare rug, then bits of half-dissolved wood. There was blood in all of it. There was blood in everything. In him, too.

"Stop! Stop it, woman!" Lowering himself to his haunches and then to his knees, he stared her in the face. His broad forehead looked animalistic now. His mouth contorted. "Such a pitiable pair we are." He ripped his shirt down the front and pulled away his collar. "Drink if you must. I myself have drunk quite enough for one evening, and now self-pity inebriates me past enduring."

In the decimated and dingy little flat, a clean space of silence formed. The pair of them were alone in this place at the end of this human century, which would bring neither of them release. Street noise pulsed at the broken window but had little to do with them. Something cleared in her head: a memory of life before the Master. She had sat alone in a room above a street like this one, sat by a broken window letting too much of the cold in, her lover long gone and herself reduced to whoring. And then the Master had come. Despair, preceded only by despair.

"Would you," Van Helsing inquired pleasantly, "like a cup of tea?"

By the time he had brewed their tea, set it in chipped china cups in a space he cleared with his elbow on the rickety table, tipped the trash off two flimsy chairs and dragged them into an arrangement simulating companionability, she had put the flat into a semblance of order. Having already rid it of much debris, she had only to set its remaining objects right and gather or conceal broken things she had no idea how to organize. In lamplight, presentability was easy to achieve; daybreak, even through the small sooted window, would make more noticeable the hidden things. Daybreak was not far off.

Shakily but with practiced elegance, he gave a small bow and held a chair for her. She nearly curtsied. Disheveled from their earlier exertions, both of them bearing stains of various external substances and bodily fluids not mentionable in polite company, they sat together politely, even comfortably, and sipped their tea. He did not wish for absinthe or opium. She granted no notice to the steady pulse of his blood.

When after a while he stood up, she thought he would leave her or order her away, and she felt a vast sorrow. Instead he leaned, with some difficulty, across the table to pry open the window. The cracked pane wobbled but did not fall out. The air that burst in was almost violent in its sweetness. Sitting down again, he swayed and she reached to hold his arm until he was settled, then eased herself back into her own chair and folded her swollen, shaking hands in her lap.

"A fine morning, my dear," he observed. When she said nothing, he continued, "Uncharacteristically clear and bright."

"Empty," she said.

But it was not yet empty. The sky was pale blue. The sun would very soon rise above gray and brown roofs. Light would stream between buildings and into the room. Then, the morning would be empty.

He was aware of what was happening before she was, although they had both expected it. He saw the first ray of sunshine fall across her tangled hair and set it on fire. He saw her fingertips begin to disintegrate, and then she felt the first pain. "My dear," he said sadly, but he did nothing to try to stop it, knowing he could not. He did not flinch or look away. For that, as long as she was aware of anything, she was grateful.

PIT'S EDGE

ON HIS LAST NIGHT IN THE BELOVED CITY where he'd lived his entire adult life, Alan rode the bus from downtown to the edge of the eastern suburb where his home had always been. He used to do this all the time, while he was finishing grad school and then when he'd worked on Seventeenth Street. Some colleagues and neighbors had warned he was taking a risk. That was true, even then, but Alan had gone out of his way to scoff. Over the years it had grown increasingly difficult to pinpoint exactly where danger would be coming from.

He didn't know why he was riding the bus now. There was no good reason to have been downtown. It was a foolish risk. By his very presence he was daring them to get him. They would, of course. Maybe they already had. He wasn't sure he'd know.

For now he was permitted—or sentenced—to wander more or less at will, and to immerse himself in what had happened to his city. Terrible as it was, maybe it was better than staying at home. Yet he yearned to be at home, and was afraid of that yearning, and was also afraid to be out here.

This is a fucked-up way to be, he thought, and considered saying it out loud. But he didn't. He'd heard stories about how they sometimes reacted to profanity.

The No. 10 bus still stopped across the street from his office, although the office itself, like almost every other establishment in the center of the city, was closed. His house was at the end of the line, if the route hadn't changed. He waited, shivering, on the always-windy corner of Seventeenth and Bank Streets, nostalgic for the people who'd waited at the same bus stop, relieved that no one else was here.

The bus was only a few minutes late. The driver nodded and offered him a pleasant enough, "Hi there. Nice evening, isn't it?" and he looked all right, but Alan knew better than to trust his own perceptions. Early on, people were known to look and act normal, even though they'd already become monsters. That was, in fact, one of the worst aspects of this—what? Plague? Moral decay? Invasion? Alan found any metaphor unspeakably coy, but there seemed no words capable of directly naming or describing the change that had swept through the world.

Except that it wasn't really change at all. Things were as they had always been. Only more so.

He hadn't noticed anything peculiar about Nan, other than a certain edginess not unlike moods she'd put him through practically ever since they'd been married, until that night in bed when she'd nearly torn off his penis in the throes of what he'd expected to be familiar connubial passion. He shuddered at the memory, but it also

258

aroused him. He couldn't bring himself to think much about that, although he knew he should. Maybe he just hadn't known her very well in the first place, his wife of nineteen years.

Eventually he'd had to strap her down, and he still worried over whether that had been the right thing to do. She'd never tried to attack him again, but she did awful things to herself. Once she'd eaten her own right thumb. If she wasn't monitored, she would chew great hunks out of her lips. He was far more bothered by this self-cannibalism than she seemed to be, and even Kelly seemed to regard it with a certain equanimity. Maybe he shouldn't try to stop her. He didn't know what to do. Certainly there was no one to consult. It didn't seem proper for a father to ask advice in such matters from his adolescent daughter.

The bus driver was holding out a gloved hand for the fare. That was suspicious; the procedure was simply to drop it into the fare box, unless you had or required a transfer, which Alan did not. He hesitated. In the bleeding incandescent gloom of streetlights and neon lights filtering through the big encrusted windows, he tried to be inconspicuous as he looked for a way to deposit his two quarters without coming into personal contact with the driver and also without making a scene. The driver's brown-uniformed forearm rested across the fare box, completely obscuring the slot. He was trapped, unable to move, staring at the driver's arm.

Alan very nearly backed down. He began shaking his head, considered muttering "wrong bus," and retreating down the steps. That would have taken him back into the city evening, which was full—though not nearly as full as it should have been, considering what was going on there—of screams human and inhuman and the howling of sirens whose effect was not to rescue or to relieve but to add to the general hysteria.

He steeled himself and managed to drop the coins into the shiny cupped palm with only minimal contact. Wiping his hand on his pants, he hurried along the aisle into the tubular metal vehicle. He tried to take the measure of his fellow passengers without seeming to, because sometimes nothing more provocative than a passing glance triggered an attack.

When this thing had been going on for a while, unfazed by legislation and neighborhood patrol groups and social reform plans however radical, the police chief had held a news conference instructing the populace on how to avoid conflict. Don't argue over a parking space. Don't answer back to an insult or a smart remark. If they want your money, give them your money. Whatever you do, don't make physical contact. Don't let them smell you. Unstated: because then they're going to want to taste you. "Your pride isn't worth your life," the chief summed it up, in what Alan had at the time considered a rather catchy slogan and had repeated to his children. Now it seemed ridiculous and smug.

Of course there was no sense in trying to outguess them. Their violence was random, impersonal, and without motive. Still, the instinct for self-preservation, surely vestigial or downright dysfunctional by now, kept working to come up with some way to keep the organism safe and its environment predictable.

Alan took note of a stout middle-aged man sitting with big knees wide apart and taking up most of the sideways seat behind the driver which ordinarily could accommodate three people. Midway back on the other side was a woman with a preschool child; Alan particularly hated it that current circumstances made him wary even of the children. In opposite corners of the shadowy back seat, two thin young men wore earphones out of which beat, stripped of melody, seeped loudly enough to be felt throughout the bus.

He took the seat directly across from the back door. The sense of available escape this position afforded him was, he knew, utterly illusory, since the door would open only to the driver's command and not to his own. He sat next to the aisle so as not to appear inviting to a potential seatmate, and found himself thinking about

Kelly, who had ridden the bus to school and to work since she'd been a young teenager and had always elaborately scoffed at his paternal urgings of caution. In an ironic way, she'd turned out to be right; he never would have thought to warn her about the form the real dangers would take. Fathers needed to warn, caution, elucidate, but by now it was obvious to everyone that fathers didn't have a clue.

The two kids with the boom box got off at Magnolia. They didn't stare at him or flash any arcane signs or bump into him as they swaggered past, and Alan was so grateful he trembled. Such gratitude was infuriating.

The back door eased shut almost noiselessly, but the bus gave a great wheeze and belch as the driver shifted gears and pulled back into traffic. Both the smooth, silent motion and the loud, jarring one were unsettling.

Thinking about Kelly produced so much anxiety that Alan could hardly bear it. That made him angry, too. He crossed his legs, crossed his arms over his chest. He should not have left her alone with her mother. Kelly was nineteen, hardly an age that should require a babysitter, and she'd always been more independent than he was ready for. Under ordinary circumstances, he'd have tried to dismiss his uneasiness as Nan once would have, affectionately or impatiently: He was too protective and doting for either his or Kelly's own good. He did her no favors by teaching her to live her life in fear.

Even tonight, under what they both knew were circumstances so far from ordinary as to be virtually incredible, Kelly had laughed at his hesitation and pushed him gently out the door. "I'll be fine, Daddy. We'll be fine. I know how to take care of her, and I've got some packing to do, and I have to wash my hair. Go." Feeling foolish and old, Alan had turned in the doorway and kissed her, so glad there was someone left whom he could touch without fear. His daughter had patted his cheek and said lightly, "Take care, and don't be too late or I'll be worrying about you."

Alan had been touched by that, but the bittersweet pleasure of it hadn't lasted long. He'd seen things about Kelly that he didn't want to understand. He'd seen the way her top sometimes fell down, exposing her breasts, and how she didn't always pull it up right away. He didn't want to see his daughter's breasts. He didn't. But he didn't dare say anything to her about it, and he was afraid to reach over himself and cover her.

It was almost easier to think about Scott, he told himself. But it wasn't. Scott could be out here anywhere, still his son but only because Alan insisted on it, no longer his son in any recognizable form. Scott never had had much common sense. He had always wanted to go out at night, wander around, just to see what he could see. He said it was "like, inneresting." No matter what Alan told him about the dangers, he'd felt compelled to be out there. With them. Alan couldn't help wondering if Scott had eventually joined them of his own free will.

He had not seen his son since the night Scott had come home. With his new friends. By the time Alan had been willing to listen to his own misgivings, it had been very hard, cost him a great deal, to keep them out of the house and away from Nan and Kelly. Kelly had been a little insulted that he'd protected her.

"He's my own brother," she'd objected. "He wouldn't hurt me. Anyway, I can take care of myself."

The child in the middle seat stood up and tugged at the bell cord. Delighted by the sound he'd made, he tugged it again, and the driver frowned irritably into his mirror. Hastily the mother pulled her child into her lap. The child protested loudly. The mother hushed him, surreptitiously watching the driver. The two of them were down the steps and out the door before the bus had completely stopped. Alan saw her look over her shoulder at him, as if he might be some danger to her and her child, and that embarrassed him, hurt, angered him.

The end of the line was at the bottom of the steep hill on the outskirts of the city. Alan was the last passenger on the bus. The driver waved but didn't speak or smile, and Alan couldn't see, for all his furtive glances, into the eyes that must surely be under the low-pulled cap.

Trudging up the hill, Alan pulled the flashlight out of his briefcase, and then the gun. You couldn't be too careful. He'd come to live by that credo. He'd always told his family that, even though he knew they never listened. "Be careful," he'd whispered gently each night, just the same.

Kelly would be all packed by now. She was a good girl, a good daughter. He counted on that. She always did what she said she was going to do. He neared the top of the hill. He could see the edge of the silver halo cast by the huge lights mounted evenly around the pit in order to illuminate the rim. The Manager of Public Works had insisted on that, when there had been a Manager of Public Works. Alan had never quite understood the purpose of the lights: To scare them away? To keep away the rest of the public, that other "them"? To stop the adventuresome and the careless from falling into the pit—as if falling into the pit could ever be accidental? In any case, the bright lights only made the pit itself and the darkness around it seem darker.

Alan reached the summit and stared down the rim line of the pit to where his dilapidated little house perched on the pit's edge like some elderly, would-be suicide. All the lights blazed inside. Kelly always liked plenty of light, especially when she was home alone with her mom. She would be done packing by now. Maybe she would be feeding Nan. He didn't like to think about that.

Tomorrow they would leave for his home town, a hundred miles from here. The numerous reasons he'd left still grated, and he'd had no contact with anyone there in all the years since he'd moved away, but he was hoping things might not be so bad there yet. With the bogus certainty a father can muster when speaking to his child, he'd said as much to Kelly. only he'd put it without hesitation: "We'll be safe back home."

Alan meant to hurry around the rim of the pit without looking in, to reach the crumbling shack he and his family were trying to live in—but only for one more night, only for a few more hours—without having to acknowledge what lay outside it, at its very door, under the lip of its foundation. But the pit had widened and deepened again just since he'd been gone on his self-indulgent bus ride, and in order to keep from sliding in he had no choice but to look.

It was usually the crane cranking up each morning that awakened him, diesel engines roaring to life as if the pit were spreading its jaws in a hedonistic yawn. Hardly awake, he'd stumble outside to watch. Sometimes when he stood outside his house on the edge of the pit, the crane operator waved to him: slowly, mechanically. And some mornings he almost waved back, and then he was awake enough to remember that the crane operator was one of them.

Some of them had talents. Or a sense of routine that substituted for talent. They could be quite dependable, that way. They could be tolerated, from a distance.

Behind him, his family would begin to stir. His wife's jaws would crack like a snapping turtle's, and her lips would smack. Embarrassed, he would hear Kelly coming out of sleep, lips making a wet noise like sex.

He would force himself back into the shack as the operator started adding more bodies to the countless piled below. More body parts. Some of them still moving. Hands rising out of the piles of meat to applaud the operator's performance, then dropping back into sleep, folded across the chest of another body, the mouth of a third. Legs idly kicking at nearby heads. Disconnected hips gyrating obscenely in time with the thrum of the engine.

264

As the plague had worn on, the dead had become more difficult to kill. Not that Alan believed in death anymore, for anyone.

"Morning, sweetheart." He would gaze at Nan strapped to the chair. She would gaze back, opening and closing her mouth over and over he worried that maybe it was wrong to confine her like that; she hadn't been a danger to anyone but herself. Maybe he was imposing his own values on her. But until he could think of what else to do, he kept her like that and endured her faintly longing looks. He'd always loved her. He loved her now.

When Alan heard the crane roar into life in the darkness, he jumped, frightened by how far into reverie he'd been. For a long moment he was disoriented, sure he was falling. It was nighttime. He hadn't known the cranes worked at night. Things must be getting worse. Of course things were getting worse.

The steel jaws rose into the glare of the lights, and he saw the operator: eyes shiny, mouth opening and shutting as if in mockery of the crane's. Kelly naked astride the operator, pumping her body up and down in time with the thrum of the engine, turning to look at her father with eyes lifeless but not dead.

The jaws of the crane rose out of darkness into obscuring brilliance once again. Alan saw the body of his wife trapped between its teeth—still thrashing, her face nearly skinless from beating against its jaws, her mouth a blur trying to eat the metal.

Alan worked his way to the pit's edge. He was terrified, but stronger than his terror was his determination to save one, at least one, of his family. The crane swung down. Desperately he reached up, and was just able to catch Kelly by the waist. He forced himself not to recoil from the touch of her flesh and pulled her backwards off her lover, who would destroy her, into his own embrace. "Kelly, Kelly, don't. What are you doing? What have you done?"

She said, "Daddy," and it was an endearment he could accept. She twisted in his arms to nibble obscenely and painfully at his earlobe.

IN CONCERT

ost...I am lost was suddenly in her mind, the words and a terrible sensation of freefall. But it was not her thought. She'd never have thought the word "freefall." It didn't come from inside her head. It came from very far away. *Lost...* That could have been her own thought—she certainly felt lost a lot of the time—but it wasn't.

She sat still and waited. Most of what she did at this stage of her life, because she couldn't do anything else, was sitting still and waiting. Usually not waiting for anything in particular, just because there was nothing else to do. A thick, dull sort of waiting that stretched out and deepened time until it was just about unrecognizable. Now, space seemed to be deepened and stretched out, too, and she had the sensation of being weightless, almost formless, moving without any direction or reason, and very afraid.

A bird was singing in the apple tree, a pattern of three notes and then four and then three again. From what had become her accustomed place on the couch, Inez Baird whistled along, whistled in call and response, as if the bird might be sending her a message or receiving a message from her. "Whistling girls and crowing hens are sure to come to some bad end," Mama used to admonish, which had only made Inez whistle more.

The apple tree was leafing out. It almost filled the window. The apples never had been any good—small, sour, wormy—and it was fine with her that the birds and squirrels got most of them. She'd have liked to think this bird was thanking her, but it wasn't. It was just singing. And the *I am...lost* call was gone without a trace.

Well, that wasn't true. Every time her mind was invaded like this, which by now must be thousands and thousands of times, something was deposited. This time it was hopelessness. She didn't want it. She had no choice but to just let it be and try to think about something else.

The kids' tire swing had hung from the thickest branch long after they'd both grown and gone. Inez tried and failed to remember the moment it had come down, the dividing line between existence and non-existence. Year after year the swing had hung there, its graying rope loosened and retied to accommodate the growth of the limb. Maybe somebody had taken it down without telling her. Maybe it had finally just slipped away without her being aware of it. Or maybe it hadn't seemed important at the time; she'd been noticing how some perfectly ordinary events and the perfectly ordinary absence of some events stood out in relief now that she looked back on them.

She did clearly remember the day Ken had planted the tree, no taller than he was and its trunk no thicker than his thumb. The house hadn't been finished yet. They'd just had their first anniversary. She'd been pregnant with their first baby, though she hadn't known about the baby or the miscarriage yet. She'd been painting the kitchen, pleased by afternoon light across new sunflower-yellow, when someone else's thought had fluttered among her own like a swatch of bright ragged fabric. There had been words and an actual voice, *...get this damn thing in the ground*, so she'd known it was Ken, *get loose, go to her.*

Embarrassed and excited by the pictures that accompanied the words, she'd come to a stopping point with her painting and climbed down from the ladder and gone to get ready for him, bathe and change clothes and dab cologne behind her ears. Only when he'd shouted to her from outside that he was going into town for something, and then hadn't come home till after midnight, did she realize it wasn't her he'd been thinking of.

Still whistling half under her breath, though the bird had stopped, Inez noticed how the stripe of the tree shadow crossed the sill, the brown-and-beige oval rug, the dusty floor. Vaguely she wondered whether the bright blue sky sectioned by the tree was the same sky she'd seen for forty-three years from this window, or whether sky could be said to be one thing sometimes and then another while still being sky, like a river, like a life, like a person's mind.

You could get lost in ruminations like that, and why not? More and more it seemed to her that she didn't altogether live in this world any longer, that time and space were changing shape, that she was floating even as her body grew stiffer and slower by the day. Maybe this was what it meant to be old and getting ready for death.

Focus was seldom required of her anymore. Even with all her visitors, some more welcome than others though their visits felt like acts of charity or job assignments, she still spent many hours a day, a night, a week, alone with her own thoughts and the scattered thoughts of others—a mental soup, sometimes thin as broth, often a glutinous porridge shot through with shreds and chunks and lumps of foreign matter.

Inez drifted with this cloud of speculation. There was no reason not to.

Some time later, loud chirping brought her back. Bossy and strident, it was probably a jay. Not for the first time, Inez wanted to know more about the mental processes of other species, regretted she'd never swum with dolphins or worked with gorillas, wished she could have tapped into the minds of Dian Fossey or Jane Goodall.

But she'd never had anything to say about what alien thoughts passed into her mind, could neither invite nor refuse them. As she used to grumble about menopausal hot flashes—too bad you couldn't order them up while you were waiting for the bus on a cold winter morning--it was too bad none of Mama's thoughts had ever come to her that she'd been aware of, or maybe knowing what was on Mama's mind would have just made her feel worse. Too bad she hadn't been able to pull answers to the eleventh-grade algebra final exam out of the mind of the smart girl who'd sat behind her—although she'd probably have felt guilty about cheating for the rest of her life. Too bad she hadn't been able to read ahead of time her son's decision to invest in that fly-by-night company, or Ken's intention to keep up his wanderings. More an annoyance than either a gift or a curse, telepathy, if that's what it was, had never been what it was cracked up to be.

For a long time as a child she'd assumed everybody else got those snatches of words and songs and images, too. During her teen years she'd decided it was just her over-active imagination, or maybe a sixth sense she'd developed in a botched attempt at self-defense from growing up with Mama that told her something was wrong but never what or why and so made her more nervous than if she hadn't known anything at all. Often, she'd worried about her own sanity, but consulting a doctor would have meant telling someone about it, and of course she couldn't do that.

No matter what she called it, it kept happening. Single words and phrases would appear, so truncated and out of context they made no sense, mental pictures of places and faces she'd never seen, entire paragraphs in what might have been foreign languages or just gibberish. Once she'd picked up part of a plan to blow up a train; she'd never heard that this had actually happened, but the saboteur could have been anywhere in the world so maybe the news just hadn't reached her. So many spouses toyed with the idea of infidelity that it got boring. Other people's love and loyalty and courage and compassion buoyed her through the times when she had little of her own.

She'd known that Papa knew he was sick. She hadn't known he'd be gone that day when she came home from school. For a long time, and again these past few years, she'd tried to keep herself open to communications from him, but none had ever come.

The jay was complaining. She didn't blame him. The birdfeeder was always empty now because she couldn't keep it filled or take it down. Even at this time of year when the birds could find their own food, it was a constant reproach.

A train went by, its diesel hoot nowhere near as expressive as a steam engine whistle, but still nice to hear. When that had been a passenger train, and then when hobos rode the freights, Inez would try, just for fun, to snatch thoughts from the people speeding by, but she never could.

She thought she was a little hungry, as hungry as she ever got these days. What did she feel like eating that she had the energy to fix? Maybe just the spaghetti from the Meals-on-Wheels lunch, not half-bad, and easy. Absently whistling, she sat and considered what to do.

Thousands of miles away in south-central Florida, Daniel entertained the idea of suicide.

Like everything else these days except her own fundamental loneliness, Inez's sense of alert was muted. Her body, already stiff from age and Parkinson's, didn't clench. Her heart didn't beat any faster, adrenaline didn't spike, her ears didn't perk up. But she stopped whistling and her mind was spattered with residue like a cold white comet trail, a few disconnected words and random images (*rope*), music all beat and no melody.

The thoughts not her own that came into her head were not always this clear. As a child she'd almost never known what they meant or whose they were, though from the vantage point of adulthood and experience she'd been able to identify some of them—numbers from Papa's store ledgers, a few musical notes she recognized much later in a Duke Ellington release all full and new and quite beyond her, once a terrible detail which, when the truth about the concentration camps came out, she'd had no choice but to believe had been flung into her mind from a Nazi's.

Usually these weren't messages and she didn't have to take any action, though she still worried over that Nazi thought, whether she could have stopped something. They just came and went, bubbling up or zipping through, and she'd learned to live with them.

This time, though, it was her own great-grandson Daniel to whom she'd once been very close, and Daniel was considering suicide, and Inez had Daniel's phone number. She eased herself to a sitting position, placed her feet side by side on the floor, stood up, exhaled, and, whistling thinly, began the labor of walking the twenty or so steps into the kitchen where her address book was in the drawer.

But it wasn't. In the drawer were rubber bands and paper clips and thumb tacks—all tools for attaching one thing to another, she noted wryly. But the brown spiral-bound book—with years' worth of names, addresses, phone numbers, birthdays, anniversaries—had vanished.

The panic that threatened whenever she couldn't find something, which was often, made her clumsy now as she dialed her daughter. The machine answered, so at least Inez had remembered Donna's number right. "I was just sitting here looking at the apple tree and I got to thinking about Daniel," she said as if the apple tree and Daniel had anything to do with each other. Acutely conscious of her voice being recorded, she wished she could edit. "I don't seem to have his number. Have you heard from him lately?" The chain of connection that would have to work here, down through the generations from

274

herself to her daughter to her grandson to her great-grandson, was almost more than Inez could keep straight in her mind. And she didn't have to—once set in motion, it would happen or it wouldn't, without her. She finished as always with "I love you," hung up, and stood there for long moments not even whistling, frozen in place by Parkinson's and fear.

Inez had long experience with being wrong about this. Nothing had come of what she'd taken for that young soldier's attraction to her. Neither of her children had ever shown the slightest real-life interest in missionary work despite what Inez had picked up. All the music that had appeared in her mind during her lifetime had not made her, as she'd once hoped, a composer or a musician or even a respectable shower-singer or whistler. So she was probably wrong about Daniel, too.

The day moved forward without her. Time stretched behind and—a much smaller distance—ahead. After a while, through no effort or will of her own, she was again able to move.

She took the spaghetti out of the microwave too soon and ate it tepid from the carton. Like most things with tomato sauce, it was better the second time, quite good, in fact. She ate it all and finished the green beans, too; spaghetti and green beans were a funny combination, but it tasted fine. Having started with the gingerbread when the meal had been delivered, for dessert she happily chose chocolate-chunk from among the four flavors of ice cream in her freezer and savored half a dozen tablespoonfuls without bothering with a bowl.

Neither Daniel nor his father nor his grandmother had called back. Maybe the phone was out of order. Inez picked up the receiver and was both relieved and worried to hear the dial tone going strong. She had email addresses for them, too, but had given up on the computer her grandson had set up in the spare bedroom and several times tried to teach her to use. The idea of messages flying through space should have made perfect sense to her, but did not. Daniel had told her he could stream music through his computer, too. She didn't have to understand it to like the idea of streaming music.

The day outside seemed lovely, and Inez had been thinking she might take a walk to the corner and back. But, as so often happened after she ate, her energy had plummeted. It seemed particularly cruel that such a basic necessity as eating should make her feel so terrible, that the very act of sustaining life made life so hard to live.

Fatigue was fast overtaking her. To protect herself against waking from a nap into a silent house, Inez managed to find the TV remote among the couch pillows. No sense in changing channels since she didn't know what was on at just after four on a weekday afternoon and it didn't matter anyway. There was music of some sort and that soothed her. But worry about Daniel and about what would become of her in these last years of her life was with her as she sank into heavy sleep and busy, vivid, meaningless dreams from L-Dopa and her own subconscious that would leave her even more frightened and fatigued.

It was 6:22 when she awoke. Her back hurt and her need for the bathroom was urgent. Working to get herself off the couch, she registered that the news was on and the light was wrong. It was not until she was washing up and changing clothes that she realized it was morning and she had slept for fourteen hours. Suddenly clear-headed, she stood still, awestruck by the sensation of having one foot in this world and one in another.

"...lost in space." The TV announcer was chirpy even in his attempt at solemnity. Inez turned on the electric toothbrush, gratified to find the switch easier to work this morning than usual. "...casualty of humanity's quest for knowledge," she heard when she flipped the switch off, and then, clearly, a name: "Casey Liebler," such a young-sounding name. She'd seen it in print but couldn't recall having heard it spoken aloud before. Probably she had, though — this was the current big story, the latest public tragedy.

Already Inez had forgotten his real name, the one a pair of loving parents had given him. She'd think of him as The Lost Astronaut. What was lost could be found. There was always hope. Almost always.

What broke her heart was that no one waited for him, no one cared in a very personal way that the astronaut was lost. His parents were never mentioned. A year before he'd gone into space the lost astronaut's wife and little girl had been killed in an amusement park fire. Everyone knew this the way everyone knew George Washington had had wooden teeth and a wife named Martha. Everyone knew this sort of the way Inez knew things—from words flying through the air.

She became aware of dampness. In the mirror her hair and clothing appeared dry, but her cheeks were wet, her eyes red. Obviously, she'd been crying. But she never cried, even when she wanted to, even when what she needed to do more than anything was start crying and not stop. She couldn't cry. It was a personal failing. And right now, she hadn't been aware of even feeling sad. She was whistling soundlessly in what she recognized as a nervous habit but saw no reason to break.

A man's pale face precipitated out of the depths of the mirror, somewhere back of her head, his features distorted under plastic shielding. She started to look behind her. *That'll do no good.* Had the thought been hers or his?

"You worry too much, Nezzie." Ken had been talking with his mouth full. She'd told him a thousand times how much she hated that. It wasn't just the mastication itself, but the thoughts that went with it, and with sex, going to the bathroom—primitive wordless mental processes of desire, hunger, relief, anger. Being on the receiving end was beyond uncomfortable. Ken had been filling himself, and spitting some of it out at her. "Stay out of other people's business." His biscuit had dripped gravy onto her best tablecloth. If she said he was criticizing her, he'd just deny it and twist it into another example of how she took things too seriously. But she knew the truth—more than a few times she had heard the aggression in his mind when he said things like that. He waited for her to answer. She just looked away and whistled very softly. That drove him crazy.

Ken faded from view, and she was alone at her dining room table, staring at his empty chair. He'd died—she wanted to say twenty years ago, but she'd been saying "twenty years" for the longest time and it must be much longer now. He'd had a heart attack. She hadn't known it was coming. He'd had many secrets, though a lot fewer than he'd imagined.

"...yellow roses... bells... why can't I say what I feel... alone so long... goodbye..."

Someone somewhere was lost and desperate. Inez had the familiar and pointless impulse to cover her ears. She could feel lost and desperate just fine all on her own, thank you very much. Now the actual ringing of bells came to her, which might be her own memory—she couldn't place it, but she'd heard a lot of bells in her life. Donna, in fact, had been in a children's bell choir for a while; Inez floated in that happy memory until it was interrupted by music she didn't recognize, surely from a place and time she'd never visited, strange instruments and strange voices and alien language and tune. Music was always nice. During the periodic long stretches when she'd had no thoughts but her own, Inez had most missed the alien music.

"... hope her mind... didn't take a turn..." Inez recognized the particular warmth: that sweet girl from the agency who did shopping for her. The girl was about to knock on her door. Wasn't she a few days early? Or had Inez lost track of time? It was her biggest worry, that she would lose time, the idea of it, the working of it, and she'd be wandering through space with no clear memory of anything, until death made her land.

Whistling, Inez made the mistake of opening the door before the visitor had a chance to knock. "Oh!" said the girl.

278

Dotty old woman. . . Which of them had thought that? Inez resorted to talking with no thought at all. "I came out to, look for the paper and see the flowers and that silly barking dog across the street? And what do you know? There you are?"

"Hello, Inez. How are you today? Are you doing okay?"

Inez made herself laugh. "Oh, fine, fine. I... don't think I expected you today, did I?"

The young woman gazed at her, no doubt evaluating. "It's your grocery list, hon. There are some things on it I don't quite understand. I just thought I'd better check."

"Let me see it." Inez held out her hand. Was she being a little snappish?

The list was in her handwriting, so she knew there hadn't been a mix-up between clients. She studied it.

Cheese
Furniture polish
Stamps
Bottle orange juice
Glittering dust
Crackers
Faulty navigation
Raisins
Distant
Wheat bread
Tea
Signal
Cream
Lost

"I'm so embarrassed."

"Oh, honey, it's okay."

"Why, my penmanship is atrocious!"

"Is it?" She touched the list, and when Inez didn't let it go, gently pushed one corner of it down and twisted her head and shoulders around so she could read. "I didn't think the handwriting was so bad."

"Well, look here, does that look like 'Signal' to you?"

"Yes. Yes. It does."

"Well, that's supposed to be 'Cereal.' My 'C's and 'R's, especially, are terrible. Parkinson's, you know. And that last word on the list, can you read that?"

The girl started to say something, stopped herself. "No, I guess I can't."

"Well, that's supposed to be 'soap.' Hand soap? It looks like 'lost,' doesn't it?"

"Yes, yes, it does," she said again, and smiled.

"You probably thought it was my mind that was lost!"

The answering giggle was uncomfortable, the protest unconvincing. "Of course not!"

Inez corrected the list for her, adding glass cleaner, a mop, detergent, none of which she actually needed. The girl promised to bring the items in a couple of days, then asked to use Inez's phone. Thinking she might be calling in a report on her, Inez went just around the corner and listened, but it turned out to be just a call to the next client apologizing for being late.

When the girl left, she walked right past a sad-looking man standing in the middle of the front sidewalk. The sun was suddenly too bright and Inez raised a shaky hand for shade. But by the time she adjusted her eyes he was gone and she closed the door, only slightly more aware than usual of the many things outside her comprehension in this world and, maybe, others.

Sometimes at the end of the afternoon, on days she expected no guests, Inez would venture past whistling into outright singing. Usually she didn't remember entire songs, just choruses, beginnings, occasional other lines. She did the best she could, making up her own lyrics to fill in the gaps. She would have been embarrassed if anyone were to hear, but, alone, it was a pleasure to make these songs into songs about her life.

"My life is an endless river!" she sang now, even though there was an outside chance that a sad-looking, glowing man might be standing in her driveway. "Which does not know it flows!"

"Why so many ter-ri-ble secrets!" she sang. "That tear the heart within!/Why so many beau-ti-ful secrets/That would fill the heart with joy?"

Silly as she knew this to be, it softened the loneliness. The central fact of her talent for receiving other people's thought was that, like being the unattached person in a crowded party, it only made you lonelier.

"There are stars beyond number!" she sang. "My journey has no end!"

Her face felt damp again. With the back of a shaky hand she wiped her tears away. Then she stared at the hand: it was wrapped in a shiny, plastic-looking material, some kind of glove. The fingers moved, but felt much too big. There was something vaguely sad about such large fingers, such a clumsy hand not made for grasping other hands or for touching another person's skin.

Fear gripped her, along with a certain intense interest. Was this a Parkinson's symptom she hadn't been told about? Now her hand looked and felt perfectly normal again. Was she now going to start having physical hallucinations in addition to auditory ones?

"Oh, for God's sake, Nezzie, don't be a little fool."

Ken had been gazing at her sleepily. Sometimes he nodded off in the middle of a conversation, or dropped his fork during a meal, suddenly unable to grip, unable to remain fixed in the here and now. During those last few years his thoughts had become less and less present, like a radio station whose transmitter had begun to fail, and the management couldn't afford to have it fixed or replaced, so they were just going to let the station fade away and die. But he always seemed to have a firm grip on that awful nickname. "Nezzie, Nezzie, Nezzie."

"I've been trying to tell you for years," she'd said. "A wife and a husband aren't supposed to keep secrets from one another."

His eyes had blinked on the word "secrets," but other than that his face had remained a mask. She'd tried to think that maybe he wanted to come clean with her but he'd waited too long and could no longer move his frozen muscles enough to reveal the honest truth. "You say crap like that to the wrong people and they'll lock you up in a padded cell," he'd said. "I don't know why it hasn't happened already."

The hinted threat had made her mad. "You know something, Kenneth? I really don't care. I've been living with this all my life. I should be able to talk to my husband about it—that's what husbands are for."

"Hey..."

"Shut up, Kenneth. The least you can do is shut up and listen!"

He'd looked away then, somewhere beyond their dining room, perhaps beyond his own life entirely, perhaps to his own idea of heaven. She couldn't know, but she thought she was on the right track, had finally after all these years reached her husband's sadness. His face was a shade paler, and something glistened there in his eyes.

He'd turned back to her, his hands on the table on either side of his plate. "So you're telling me you can read minds."

"No. Not like in the movies or TV. It's more like sometimes, I feel them. And a few words or pictures come through. And sometimes I pick things up, like a radio, but a radio whose frequency selector is broken, and it's just scanning rapidly, and the channels clarify for just a second or two, and then they're gone." She hadn't told him she thought of him as a broken radio, too.

"Okay. Tell me what I'm thinking right now. And don't say I'm thinking that I don't believe you. That's cheating. Tell me something else."

"But I can't. You don't understand me. I told you already that's not the way it works."

He'd opened his hands abruptly, giving up on her. "Then it's not very useful, now is it?"

His hair washed into lighter shades of gray. Fat began to disappear from under his skin, his cheeks sank and his teeth became more prominent. His skin dried and broke into intricate wrinkles. Then from inside Kenneth's vaporous image another image grew, the chest broader, the shoulders higher, the head bigger, the figure finally born as the rest of Kenneth shredded away.

She recognized the uniform first, then the piercing green eyes, close-cropped blond hair, handsome nose, fine cheekbones, the sad eyelids dropping into place. She'd seen his picture a dozen times.

Finally. I see you. The voice inside her head was weak, but she could tell that once it had been strong.

"I... this is an honor." Light-headed, Inez meant to touch the counter for support but missed. He looked vaguely puzzled. His eyes flickered back and forth. "I'd recognize you anywhere. From the news, all your photos. Casey Liebler." She was so pleased to have remembered the name.

Then they...know...I've lost... my way?

"They actually think you're dead." She was sorry she'd said that.

I heard...you singing.

"Not very well, I'm afraid. I've never had a voice for singing, and especially now, but I do love to sing."

I heard...you singing.

"Well, well." She smiled. "I am very glad you did."

The Lost Astronaut went away then, passed out of her awareness, dissipated—whatever the right term would be for the reverse of whatever the process was that brought other people's thoughts into her mind in the first place. Throughout the afternoon and into the evening, Inez waited for him to come back. She tried to make her mind especially receptive. She thought inviting thoughts. She put his name into her own thoughts: "Casey! Casey? Lost Astronaut?" No strategies like this had ever worked before either to bring thoughts to her or to keep them out, but she couldn't help trying. She so wanted to be in contact with him, this other person floating out of time and space away from the rest of the world.

This was very odd, she couldn't argue with that. But no odder than, say, the time when, amid the hectic hodgepodge of everyday thoughts decidedly her own about the kids' after-school schedules and Ken's socks that needed darning and her sister's impending visit, she'd discovered in her mind unuttered cries of anguish in a language she'd never heard but years later would encounter among traditional Alaskan Tlingits. No odder than, during Daniel's eighth-grade band concert, hearing a conversation about quantum physics so loud she'd turned to shush the people behind her and found no one sitting there. No odder, really, than countless things everybody took for granted every day—being born, giving birth, dying, falling in love, falling out of love, getting old.

When Donna called, Inez didn't wonder what the sound was or mistake her voice for the voice of the Lost Astronaut or anything like that. It was perfectly clear who was who, and she understood as much about how Casey Liebler was communicating with her as about how her daughter was. More and more, understanding didn't seem to be called for.

She said hello. Donna said, all in a loud rush as had become her habit after having been such a placid little girl and even-tempered teenager, "Hi, Ma, how you doing, I got your message, I haven't heard from Daniel, but then I don't, he doesn't call me, James says he's on spring break on a camping trip somewhere, how are you?"

Breathless, though her daughter was not and could have gone

284

on for paragraphs, Inez managed, "I'm all right. I was just thinking about Daniel," though in truth it seemed a long time since she'd been thinking about Daniel. That scared her, made her feel disloyal. What if she'd been right, and Daniel—whom she'd known and loved since before his birth—had killed himself while she'd been distracted by the Lost Astronaut?

And the Lost Astronaut had been receiving from her. Wondering over the years whether other people picked up random snatches of her thoughts the way she picked up theirs—whether maybe everybody's mind was spattered with other people's thoughts and it just wasn't talked about—she'd sometimes tried to be careful what she let herself think and other times deliberately put silly or nasty or fanciful ideas in there just to see what would happen. Nothing, as far as she knew.

But Casey had told her straight out: "I heard you singing." That was the part Inez couldn't get over—that and the terrible, lovely picture in her mind of him floating all alone in a place she longed to be able to imagine. "I heard you singing," he'd told her. And that was another thing: Never before in her life, as far as she knew, had anybody deliberately sent her their thoughts.

To her daughter she said, "Has James heard from him?" which sent Donna off on a long, loud, rapid monologue about how much money James was making now and how his wife didn't appreciate him and how Daniel was breaking his father's heart by not going into the family business. Though she'd heard it all more than a few times before, Inez knew not to tune it out because the answer to her question might be in there somewhere. But empty space and tiny little pieces of other people's thoughts instead of deluges looked more and more appealing. Eventually she gathered that no, no one in the family had heard from Daniel since he'd gone back to school in January.

"Isn't that just typical," Donna sneered. "He's got his 'own life,' you know."

"Oh, I hope so" was unquestionably Inez's own thought, and, in the interest of avoiding a diatribe from her daughter, she kept it to herself.

Donna was full of stories about the assisted living place where she lived. Some of them Inez would have found entertaining if they hadn't been so mean-spirited. Not for the first time it saddened her and made her feel guilty that her daughter's main pleasure in life seemed to be criticizing while pretending not to be so you couldn't even object. Having a child in senior housing no longer seemed strange. "Some folks'll get used to any damn thing," Ken would often say, just as snide as Donna talking about Daniel. Inez thought what he said was true, but admirable.

Over Donna's strident chatter she layered a silent, wordless plea for Danny to contact her. Though she knew better from years of experience, she closed her eyes and willed it to go to him.

"Does he still play the drums?" she heard herself asking.

It took Donna several beats to register that her mother had said something. She skidded to a halt mid-sentence. "What? Who?"

"Daniel. Remember how he played drums when he was a little boy? And cymbals? James used to complain about the noise?"

Donna's voice was syrupy with exaggerated patience. "No, Ma, I never heard about him playing drums."

"Oh," Inez sighed, "maybe I'm wrong," and maybe she was. It wouldn't be the first time she'd had a vivid impression that turned out to be totally false.

Donna said she had to go, and provided a long detailed list of all the things she had to do today, iron and get her hair done and make a lemon meringue pie for the ladies' potluck and clean her venetian blinds. Though none of these activities would ever have interested Inez enough to be conversational topics, the fact that she couldn't now do any of them depressed her.

When she could get off the phone with Donna she called Daniel again and left another voice message. She didn't like leaving voice messages. She always wanted to go back and edit.

Now she was exhausted. As she was making her way step by careful step back to the couch, she got dizzy and fell, just like that, hard on her hands and knees, grazing the coffee table with the side of her head.

She fell about once a month these days and hadn't broken anything yet, though it always shook her up a little. The few times it had happened when somebody was here, there'd been a flurry of activity to get her up, really quite foolish since what she wanted was to stay a few minutes where she'd landed, get her bearings, catch her breath, and she never did see what the rush was. The falls while she was alone, which was most of them, she could handle to suit herself, and that was what she did now, pulling the pillow off the couch, easing herself onto her stomach and then onto her side with one knee cocked in an undignified but more or less comfortable position, settling down on the rug in the sun and waiting to find out what would happen next, like that lovely summer morning speeding along the Haines Highway singing Broadway tunes at the top of her voice and then saying to herself, almost singing to herself, "I'm flipping the car. Isn't that interesting. I wonder how I'll get out of this one?"

Time passed, or she passed through time. She slept and half-slept. The urge to use the bathroom came and went. She was a little thirsty for a while, but not enough to get up. She wasn't hungry at all.

She started whistling "Some Enchanted Evening" and then sang it all the way through to the end, screeching but hitting the high notes, words so effortless it was more as if they were sliding through her than being remembered.

"Ne...ver...let...Her...GO."

But everybody had to let everybody go. Sometimes that broke her heart. Sometimes it soothed her from the inside out.

"I...sang...that song...in...high school...choir."

Already in her mind, her reply flew to him without any act of will. "Sing with me."

Together they sang most of the score of *South Pacific*. Both of them faded in and out. It embarrassed her a little to be singing "There Is Nothin' Like a Dame" with a handsome young man. "Cockeyed Optimist" still choked her up. More than once she got tired and let the Lost Astronaut take the lead, but she never stopped singing altogether and on "Bali Hai" she held the melody while he made harmonies around it, and she got chills.

When they'd sung all the songs in the show, there was what Inez hoped was a companionable silence and not loss of contact. She wondered what time it was, and wondered why it mattered. If she sat up she could probably see the clock, but she didn't want to sit up, she didn't want to move at all. It was sometime during the night; the picture window framed only darkness and the inside of the house was full of darkness, too.

Usually she could gauge the time of day by the nature of her hunger. If she felt slightly queasy, phlegmy and acidic, it meant she hadn't eaten breakfast yet. If she was relatively comfortable and the idea of hunger suddenly occurred to her with no physical longing to back it up, it probably meant lunchtime, and lunch was always a hard decision, because if she ate she'd often pay for it with drowsiness the rest of the day and if she didn't eat mid-afternoon vertigo could make her sit down wherever she was. Being absolutely famished indicated she was late for suppertime, and someday she might not even bother with cooking—she'd devour her evening meal raw, chicken and eggs and corn meal and all.

As far as she could tell, she wasn't the least bit hungry right now. Maybe she was dead. That would be interesting. Maybe she was floating in space with the Lost Astronaut, or toward him. Did you experience hunger differently when you were lost?

Her body let her know she wasn't dead and she was still right here

288

on earth and it was time to get up off the floor. After several false starts and much struggle, she managed to hang onto the edge of the couch and get herself to her knees, noticing her own thin arms like warped Q-tips pulling and pushing. Waiting to catch her balance, she glanced over at the window again.

At first she thought it was just the dark of the yard, but the black went deeper than that, reminding her of long vacation trips at night, gazing through the windshield at the yellowed edge of the road and the dizzying nothing beyond. The view through the window had that sad taste of nothingness, but streaked through with shimmering colored dust, floating gray stone orbs, distant suns flaming, a rushing through panicked breath and beyond.

This, this is what you see?

She waited a while, not so much for an answer as for the strength and courage and balance to go on with the process of getting to her feet. When she got there, she worked her way into her room, noticing how she was shuffling and swaying, and changed the clothes that she had soiled while she lay on the floor. All of this would be exceedingly distressing if she thought about it, so she didn't.

Instead, she thought about Daniel, and tried calling him again, dialing the number several times and getting all sorts of recorded messages about disconnects and full mailboxes and other numbers you were supposed to dial that made no sense to her.

When had she last cleaned the dingy yellow phone? It struck her how bits of everyday life—sweat from a palm, peanut butter and syrup from fingers, dirt from under nails—came off onto other pieces of everyday life, transferred into other people's lives without anybody really being aware of it.

The phone was dirty, and it wasn't working anyway, and she didn't want it in her hand. Maybe, she told herself bitterly, a message from Daniel would just fly into her head. Or maybe she'd just never hear anything of him again.

The list of emergency numbers Ken had so many years ago taped to the wall above the phone gave her an idea. Did emergency numbers ever change? She punched the buttons carefully but without confidence. A flat voice answered, and it was the right number after all.

Inez spoke quickly because she didn't know what to say now that she'd made the connection. "Yes, officer? I have some information? About a missing person?" Hearing how all her sentences were ending in question marks, she resolved to correct that if she got a chance to speak again.

She waited as she was transferred, then waited some more as the officer got her papers and pen ready. Was this really the proper response to an emergency? The world was landmined with peril, even when you went to those designated to help.

"Yes. Well, his name is Casey Liebler." Now the words were overly declarative. She was sure she must be frowning; Ken used to tease her about frowning whenever she tried to concentrate. "They call him the Dead—" She stopped. "He is the lost astronaut, the one the media is so obsessed with." This last sounded ridiculous, as if there were more than one lost astronaut the world had to contend with.

She needed no special talent to divine the police officer's change in attitude. It was plain in her voice as she asked a series of irrelevant questions no doubt meant to test a caller's competency. Inez tried again to provide the important information about the Lost Astronaut, in different words this time.

The woman was using that awful "active listening" technique. Eventually Inez just hung up. Well, she'd tried, she told herself desolately.

Then her fingers were pushing the numbers again, quite involuntarily, quite beyond her ability to stop, the very thing she'd been dreading since she'd been diagnosed, the wild spasms of Parkinson's. But it wasn't that. It was those oversized metallic fingers guiding hers to the right buttons. She saw them, felt the slick pressure against her knuckles and nails, and wasn't scared then. When the number was complete the gloved hand rudely shoved the receiver against her head, warm damp plastic carrying debris from other lives onto her skin and hair.

"Clarence Eng, Operations," said the voice on the other end.

"Yes, well. Please excuse my interruption, but I have, well, a little information concerning your Casey Liebler." Astonished by her own brashness, Inez made herself stop whistling and then from giddy speculation about what time it was where Clarence Eng was still at work.

"How did you get this number?"

Startled by the question and the aggressive tone, especially after she had been polite, Inez managed, "I beg your pardon?"

"I asked how you got this phone number."

"I looked it up," she told him petulantly.

"Impossible. This is a secure number. Who gave you this phone number?"

Ken used to say, *No good deed goes unpunished*, and he'd had a point, though she hadn't admitted it to him. All too often stray thoughts had demonstrated to her that people were annoyed by the kindness of others. "I lied," she said, her face burning. "I didn't know how to explain. He gave me the numbers."

"Who?"

"Casey Liebler." Closing her eyes, she saw the face of the Lost Astronaut.

"This isn't the least bit amusing, you know. Who is this?"

She took a breath and gave him her name, her full address including zip code, her phone number and social security number. "I would not be giving you that information if I was just some sort of—prankster." This was a bluff; they both knew a prankster could make up or steal all that information.

"Then maybe you're just crazy."

"Maybe I am. I am open to that possibility, I assure you." At least he hadn't said "senile."

The room tilted sharply. Inez grabbed the rolled edge of the kitchen counter. Light smeared across her vision like glare on a window. Nauseated, she wondered a bit wildly whether she'd had breakfast yet.

She swore she heard faint music, nothing she'd ever heard before yet almost familiar, mythical or mechanical. A wide band of glistening particles roared by like the wing of a dragon. Where it had passed through the wall she saw metal sanded thin, random corrosions, exposed tubes and wires. She found herself gripping nonexistent controls. *Nothing works. . . anymore.*

"What was that?" Mr Eng's annoyed, officious voice brought her back, but vast ribbons of dust, radioactive winds, smoldering suns, planets with the life turned out of them still filled her kitchen and living room, passed in and out of walls and furniture. Vista after dark vista overlapped her back yard where the children's tire swing used to be and just last year, when she'd still been able to venture that far on her own, she'd found a little bell in the weeds, tarnished but with clapper intact, and she'd stood in the middle of the yard and rung it, amazed to be making the music of the ages. She didn't know where the bell was now, after she'd rescued it from the weeds. She didn't need to know in order to have the music.

"What do you mean?" she asked Mr Eng, stalling for time, and with her other, silent voice seeking the Lost Astronaut's ear, screeching *Please! What do you want me to tell him!*

"You said, 'Nothing works anymore.'"

She sighed. "Well, Mr Eng. That pretty much sums it up."

Suddenly narrow blue and green lines segmented her walls, spreading in a curved pattern across ceiling and floor, passing through furniture and those astronomical artifacts she was coming to see as more and more like furniture, the interior décor of some endless strange room where Casey Liebler now spent his days and nights. Then the writing arrived like the words floating up into the window of one of those fortune telling Magic 8-Balls. Numbers mostly. Streams of numbers in a variety of colors, broken here and there with brutal words: *malfunction, unreadable, unknown, error, lost location.*

"Well, I'm really quite busy. I'm going to hang up, Mrs—"

"It's Miss now, I suppose. You were friends, weren't you?"

"What?"

"You and Captain Liebler, your missing friend. Your families knew each other." There was a long pause. Around her the great electronic display flashed violently in alarm. At some distance she heard the electric scream of the warning speaker, felt the trembling hand frantically seeking the spot, breaking something, silencing it. The most surprising and chilling thing was that she knew exactly what all this was.

Then Mr Eng spoke quietly. "We had regular dinners, all of us. Our wives, our children, all of us good friends. Companions. I played cello—not very well, mind you—not all of us are Yo-Yo Ma. He was much better at his violin. He led, I followed, sometimes all the way 'til dawn."

"But after the accident it changed, didn't it?"

"He was lost in a very dark place. Irretrievable. Look, how could you know? Who have you talked to?"

"He is full of regret, you know. He wishes it had not been that way. And he knows that you will seriously consider anything I have to say." This last was all her own and she sent a desperate apology to Casey Liebler.

"Yes. Okay. Please. Whatever you want to tell me."

And so with only a nudge now and then from the Lost Astronaut, Inez Baird described for Clarence Eng what had taken over her kitchen and living room and almost unbearably opened up her life which had become so constricted lately, so small, and now suddenly seemed to have no edges. Finally making use of that silly forty-foot cord James had connected to her kitchen phone because she couldn't keep track of a cell phone or a cordless, she wandered around the house and outside onto the patio, doing her best to describe the ways all that dust and rock moved, the actions and appearance of those flaming suns, the qualities of those sad floating worlds and a few that somehow seemed not so sad except that they were utterly out of reach. She almost told him about Daniel, but that would distract them both; the subject at hand was hard enough and she had to really focus. In conclusion she read off for him the cold words and numbers etched in midair, and she even tried to replicate the accompanying sound, as much like a musical chant as the alarm she guessed it was.

He thanked her. He said he had a lot to go over, various theories to consider. He said he would be back in contact. She hoped he would, but all this had taken a lot out of her so the hope was muted and weak. She had trouble getting the phone back on the hook and didn't even try to roll up the cord, just left it in a tangle on the counter and the floor. If somebody came to check on her they'd probably take that as one more sign that she could no longer keep her house in order, but right now Inez didn't care.

The need to rest was overwhelming. She managed to get into bed and under the cover, then got up again almost immediately because she thought she heard someone at the door, at the window. Finding no one, she went to bed again, to be roused by an insistent phone call, but there was only the dial tone when she picked up the receiver. Most of the night—it might even have been two nights, with a smeary day between them—she spent in semi-consciousness agitated and then soothed and then agitated again by music she could just barely hear.

At one point, she was standing in her living room, steadying herself on the back of the couch, feeling so tired, so lost and precarious, staring out the picture window into her dark and endless back yard, singing. And what answered her, low at first, then climbing in volume and sweetness until it made the hair on her arms stand out, was a violin.

"You brought it with you?" she asked the dark.

Only. . . in my memory, but I play it every day. The crying of his violin penetrated to nerve, but it was the kind of crying that made her happy to be alive, reminded her of every beautiful thing.

The darkness ran with pinpoints of light. Planets like bright coins spun. In the distance of centuries suns burst apart, seeding the universe with death songs and birth songs and songs about life just going on its way.

"I am here," she sang. "I am here." Radioactive wind warmed her to tears.

drum

the thought of a drum, the roll and thump, the beat in her blood and bones

drumming

had been going on for a while before she was really aware of it, as if she had come in during the middle of a concert. Did Casey Liebler play the drums, too? But of course it was Daniel

drumming

drumming, maybe sending her a message but she didn't think so, only drumming or thinking about drumming and she was picking up his thoughts. She made herself as open as she could.

The drumming had stopped, or something had happened to her reception of it. But it had been there, clear and alien as could be. She was shaking.

Daniel must still be alive, then. Or maybe not—for all Inez knew, the thoughts of dead people still floated around in the universe and sometimes into her mind. Given what she'd been experiencing in the past few days—or hours, or weeks, however long it was—anything was possible.

Nothing else remarkable happened for a while. Sun came in

through the picture window. A squirrel and a jay—maybe that same jay—were arguing; Inez smiled at their ruckus. She noticed now that her clothes were dirty, chose not to think about how long it had been since she'd changed them or how they'd gotten so soiled, decided to risk taking a shower. Closing the bathroom door and the shower curtain made her a little claustrophobic, and she was alone in the house (except for the Lost Astronaut, who maybe could see her anyway, which made her blush). She left everything open.

Forgetting how hard the faucets were to turn, she flinched at the too-hot and then too-cold water but managed to get it right and stand under the spray with one hand gripping the bar she'd told James not to install and the other awkwardly maneuvering shampoo, soap, washcloth. She dropped the lid to the conditioner, got shampoo in her eyes, and couldn't manage the looftah for her back, but the shower was luxurious and no catastrophes happened. It didn't matter that she couldn't get herself completely dried off. The clean clothes felt good.

Triumphant to have accomplished all that, and noting that during the whole process there'd been nothing in her mind but thoughts of what she was doing, Inez was combing her hair, so wispy now that it hardly needed combing, when she heard someone call her name. "Just a minute," she answered. But her voice didn't carry and the person came on in to the house as people often did. She didn't mind, it was better than having to get up and down to answer the door.

She emerged from the bathroom to find that girl from the agency with her groceries. Usually Inez had her put them away, but today for some reason she didn't want her to stay that long. It took a few repetitions of "No, thanks, I'll get it" and "I like to do for myself when I can" and "It's easier for me to find things when I'm the one puts them away," and she hoped she wasn't being rude. Finally the girl accepted the money for the groceries and left, promising to come back next week.

296

Only then did Inez notice the mop leaned up against the counter. There was a perfectly good mop somewhere around here. Was that a hint that her house wasn't clean? For a minute the girl's audacity made her mad, and she considered calling the agency to complain and demand a refund of the cost of the mop. But she let it go. She had other things on her mind.

Nobody came to see her the next few days, nobody called, nobody answered the phone when she called and she didn't leave messages. On TV, among Oprah and Dr Phil and news about the war that angered her and news about a spelling bee that made her proud and commercials that shocked her to laughter, there was one reference to Casey Liebler, not even a whole story, just an aside in a piece about the space program, as if he were already only a footnote in history. *He's still alive,* she visualized sending back across the airwaves to those glib announcers. Once she positioned herself right in front of the set in a stance she'd learned in a long-ago aerobics class, feet shoulder-width apart and weight over center. Holding onto the TV cabinet but still swaying, she informed them in her loudest, firmest voice, "He's still alive. He can still be found."

Yesterday's news. Who cares? Even though she knew she was flat-out imagining that mean thought, it infuriated her. She turned off the TV and when that wasn't enough bent at considerable risk of falling and found the cord and dangerously jerked it loose from the plug.

For the next few days and nights, Inez's mind was so muddled and so full she couldn't tell whether she was receiving any thoughts from anyone else. The streak of colored lights was probably a memory of Christmas, of many Christmases. The travel plans might have once been hers; she'd never been to Italy but for years she'd thought about it, read brochures, taken Beginning Italian at the community college.

She slept a lot and when she awoke could make no sense of her dreams. She was careful to retrieve the brown bags that Meals on

Wheels left on her porch, so nobody would worry about them accumulating, and she ate a little from them. She brought in the mail, changed her clothes at least once, did her best to keep track of when the shopper was due to come back. Right now, of all times, she couldn't risk appearing incompetent and somebody moving in to take charge of her life. She sat on the couch and looked out the picture window, waiting to see what would happen next.

What happened was that Clarence Eng showed up at her door. The minute she saw him she guessed who he was, because she didn't know anyone else Oriental; talking to him on the phone she hadn't realized he was Oriental, but with a name like Eng and the reference to Yo-Yo Ma, he could hardly have been anything else. And of course he'd be a smart one. Catching herself in that little bit of racism, she tried and failed to chalk it up to a stray thought from someone else's mind. Embarrassment made her awkward when she invited him in, made him some tea, worried that it wouldn't be good enough for an Oriental man who probably knew all about tea, spilled the water but didn't call attention to her clumsiness by wiping it up, just made a mental note of it so as not to slip in it later.

"I wanted to talk to you about Casey," said Clarence Eng.

Trembling, Inez set her cup down. "You believe me, then."

He didn't say yes or no, exactly. He said, "We're pretty sure where he is. We know his trajectory, the general area of space, his location within a million miles or so. Many of the readings you gave me make no sense, in terms of what the sensors were programmed for. But what they tell us provide us with enough clues, at least for a theoretical understanding."

"What will you do? You'll find him? You'll get him back?"

"He's too far away, moving too fast."

"I don't understand," she said, although she did understand, her head swam and her heart thudded with the awful understanding.

He wasn't looking at her. He wasn't drinking his tea, either. There must be something wrong with it. Realizing she was whistling, Inez made herself stop. "There's nothing we can do," he said at last.

"But he's still alive." She gestured vaguely, hands and arms both stiff and shaking. "Out there somewhere."

"I know."

"There's no hope of rescue, then?" The least she could do, in honor of the Lost Astronaut, was say the terrible words out loud and insist this man acknowledge them.

He met her gaze. She thought that very brave of him. "No," he said, and his voice broke. "There is no hope of rescue."

"What will happen to him?"

"He will just keep drifting until the systems shut down or there's some sort of collision."

"And then he'll die."

"Yes."

"Alone."

She thought he'd say some platitude about how we all die alone, but to his credit he didn't. "Yes," he said, and she saw that his cheeks were wet. "Casey must know that. He's no fool. He just wanted us to know what happened to him. He wanted me to know. I thank you."

They were silent together for a while. Inez's mind wandered as she imagined the Lost Astronaut wandering through endless space. After a while she thought she better bring herself back to earth, which was, after all, where she still lived. Almost coyly, she said to Mr Eng, "You weren't all that slow to accept what I had to say."

"We've seen something like this before."

"Really?" She found herself both pleased and disappointed that she might not be the only one after all.

"There are two hundred or so like you, registered. None, I believe, with your degree of control."

She snorted. "I have no control at all."

"We could register you, Inez, track your abilities. But I can't honestly recommend it. I've told no one about you. Believe me, I think that's for the best. And I must ask you not to tell anyone else about Casey. If you do, I'll have to deny it."

This was so like something out of an old movie that Inez actually laughed. "Lucky for you everybody would just think I'm a senile old woman."

"I'm sorry."

"Don't be. This is a secret I've been keeping all my life."

"Thank you," he said again.

They didn't have anything more to say to each other. She could see that he didn't know how to take his leave, so she helped him out. "I'm very tired," she told him, which was true. "I'm afraid I have to rest now."

Hours later when she awoke, a stack of mail was on her coffee table, alongside three newspapers in different colored plastic bags. Inez had long since given up trying to get the newspaper people to stop sending her the Sunday papers, but she had managed to get over feeling obligated to read them just because they appeared in her driveway. Whoever had brought them in, along with her mail, must have felt doubly good about doing her the favor, never mind that she'd rather have just let them accumulate out there than have to figure out something to do with them in here. Through the green and blue and orange bags—was there some sort of color code?—she didn't see anything about Casey Liebler, just comics and ads.

She hardly ever got letters anymore; practically every letter-writer she'd known in her life was dead by now, or had switched to email. So Inez almost missed the small brown envelope with an actual postage stamp instead of a meter mark. There was no return address and she couldn't read the postmark. The ridiculous fantasy flashed through her mind that it was from the Lost Astronaut. But when she opened it she saw that it was, almost as amazingly, from Daniel.

"Dear Grammy." None of her other grandchildren called her that.

Once when I was a little kid Mom said something that I think means you're the only one I can talk to about this. Maybe I didn't understand what she said, or maybe I'm remembering it wrong, but do you sometimes have thoughts that aren't yours? In languages you don't know, or about things you couldn't possibly know about? Because I do, I have for as long as I can remember, and it's driving me crazy. Literally. The other day I got somebody else's suicidal thoughts. I have never been suicidal in my entire life, but I got why it was attractive to whoever it was. And I'm getting drums, with some kind of chanting or calling in some weird language. Middle of the night, middle of class, walking down the street, hanging out with my girlfriend. This sucks. I tried to call you but kept getting a busy signal. Too bad you don't have IM or texting or at least email, or even call waiting. Too bad we can't just read each other's minds when we want to, but I've never been able to do that, have you? Please write back.

Love, Daniel

After his signature were his address and phone number. Below that was what had to be—she smiled—his email address.

Stiff and off-balance, she tried to make sense of it. Had Donna known about her peculiarity, then? Who else knew? Was it obvious, like a deformity? Did she act funny without knowing it?

Then the important details of the letter started to come into focus. Daniel wasn't dead. He hadn't been toying with killing himself. He hadn't been playing the drums, either. She'd evidently been picking up from his mind thoughts he'd picked up from somebody else's mind. On top of everything else, this was just about more than she could take in.

Then there was the real shocker: Daniel was like her.

Rousing herself, she searched a little wildly through bedroom, bathroom, kitchen drawers for paper and a pen, finally settling for a sheet of purple gift wrap she'd smoothed and saved and a not very sharp pencil she found in with the pots and pans. The wrapping paper had a white underside. The pencil tore the paper a little but did make visible marks. Inez lowered herself onto a kitchen chair and pushed aside the bowl of overripe oranges and bananas, ignoring the cloud of fruit flies that went with it.

She began with "Dear Daniel" at the very top of the page, then moved way down to the bottom and wrote, "I love you, Grammy," liking the look of it and the sound of it as she said it aloud. Then, whistling, she set about filling in the white space in between with her handwriting made cramped by Parkinson's and blurry by the dull pencil.

It took her a long time because she wanted to say it right, and because both her concentration and her grip on the pencil kept slipping. Finally, though, she'd filled all the space available to her and done the best she could to tell him what she knew. Carefully folding and smoothing the purple paper, she slid it into an envelope from one of the pieces of junk mail, re-sealed it with Scotch tape, crossed out the address and replaced it with Daniel's, crossed out the used postage and stuck on a stamp from the new book the shopper had bought for her. All this exhausted her, but she was determined to make the trek to the end of the driveway, put the letter in the mailbox and raise the flag before lying down again.

When she opened the door, Clarence Eng was standing there, carrying a cello case. "Oh," they said at the same time. "Hello." Suddenly aware of how unkempt she must look, Inez smoothed her hair.

"I thought you might like—I wanted to play for you." Mr Eng looked shy. "I wanted to play for Casey."

It took her a moment, but when she understood what he meant her heart soared and her eyes filled with tears. "Please," she said, stepping carefully onto the porch, "walk with me to the mailbox. My grandson is waiting for this letter. Then we'll have ourselves a concert."

He didn't quite know what to do, so Inez took the lead, leaning lightly on his arm and directing him with her own movements around the potholes, newspapers, boxes, lawn chairs, tires. This might well be her last journey outside, and she was glad for the slow pace so she could savor the smell of the sunshine, the squawking of the jay, the bright yellow house across the street that had been gray the last time she'd noticed. For just a moment she thought of telling Mr Eng that apparently Daniel was just like her, but she decided not to.

When they got to the top of the driveway he gallantly opened the mailbox for her while she laid Daniel's letter inside, then closed it again. She raised the rusted metal flag.

By the time they got back to the house Inez was weak and profoundly fatigued. Gentleman that he was, Mr Eng must have noticed, for he offered to postpone the cello concert until another day. But she could tell how much he wanted to play now, and she understood why the timing was so critical. "No, no," she protested. "I want to hear the music," and that was as true as anything she'd ever said or thought.

She lay on the couch and closed her eyes. Mr Eng sat in her rocker with his cello between his thighs. There was silence. Then music like liquid chocolate poured into her living room and into her heart. At first she sang along, the melody vaguely familiar. But after a while she just let it be.

Far away, drifting farther, just at the edge of where she would be able to reach him, the Lost Astronaut was hearing the music, because she was. Inez didn't try to send it to him. She just made herself as open as she could and let it pass through her to him.

She floated into deep space. Soon he would drift beyond her ability to track him. Soon, she thought, she herself would drift beyond her ability to come back.

Thank you, in her mind, moving with the music, back and forth.

The music was sweet, and sad, but Inez could not think of it as elegiac, exactly. More, it was resolute, solemn in its understanding. Her face was cold and wet.

The sound of a single string, played solo within the wash of music, caught her attention. It rose and fell in pitch, singing in concert like prayer. It was a solitary thought, a nerve, a vein, a narrow thread of muscle.

While the body and the world disintegrated around it, it lingered a moment, then dissolved. *Thank you.*

BEES FROM THE HIVE

He's remembering that first day at the new school, middle of fourth grade, agonizingly shy, overwhelmed by all the colors and sounds and motion and new people and new smells, crouched in a corner by the playground fence pretending to be interested in something on the ground but really just trying to control what he'd later learn to call sensory stimulation, when Molly called him over to where she was cross-legged on the ground peering and poking at something and writing things down in a green spiral notebook open on her blue-jeaned thigh. "What do you think?" she asked him right off, not even looking up.

He stood over her. The top of her head was velvety, very short brown hair. She had a gigantic bug in an open jar. Xavier flinched and tried not to make the noise he wanted to make. He hated bugs. All those legs, all that wriggling, the way they felt when they jumped on you or crawled down your back or flew into your mouth when you were riding your bike really fast. He didn't want to look but he couldn't take his eyes off her small square hands. Very carefully she pulled off one of the insect's legs. There were so many of them he wouldn't have known she'd already done this many times before if he hadn't then seen a pile of legs like thread in another jar. He thought he was going to be sick. She wrote something in the notebook, and then tilted her head back to glance at him. "Isn't this cool? I'm doing an experiment. I need an assistant."

"I don't—"

He has long since gotten used to hardly ever getting a whole sentence out before she grabs the conversation back. She didn't care whether he thought it was cool. She, and only she, was the arbiter of cool. She was the arbiter of everything. If he'd fully understood earlier what that meant, things might have turned out different. Or maybe not. Maybe he wouldn't have wanted them to.

That first day, in the first five minutes they knew each other, Molly stood up, taller than he was then and for quite a few years, and announced, "I almost died before I was born. I was in the hospital a really long time. And I almost died a bunch of times before I was six months old. Cool, huh?"

Not quite sure what to make of this introduction, but impressed, he sort of gulped and said, "Yeah. He's come to wonder whether these near-death experiences—assuming they're true—made Molly what she is. Not that he really knows what she is. Molly is many things."

That morning in fourth grade, her expression made it clear she knew what she was doing and he certainly didn't, which pretty much matched what he already thought. Her hands now in fists at her sides. He could hear her breathing, smell the sun on her blue cotton shirt. Even then, something about her solemn, unblinking stare made him a little afraid of her, more than a little smitten. Later he came to think of it, sometimes, as aggressive, sexually aggressive, "opposite sex" or "opposing sex."

The way she kept brushing at her velvety hair was surprisingly wonderful. He kind of got lost for a little while in the rhythmic

308

motion of her small hand and arm, the very soft swishing sound of her hair against her skin, the wafts of shampoo and sunny smells. He was almost nine; she would come to his birthday party—she would *run* his birthday party, override and charm his parents into taking the kids to the water park instead of the zoo because after all they were new in town and she'd lived there all her life so she knew what was best. Already he was hers.

"Hi, Xavier." Her very clear voice saying his name, and pronouncing it right without a stupid "eks" sound in front of the "z" sound, gave him goosebumps. She told him her name. "You just moved into 432 Baker Avenue. The big white house with the red roof. You've got two cats."

"Um, yeah." She'd been watching him. That gave him the creeps and flattered him at the same time.

"Well, we're going to be great friends, starting this minute," she said, and finally blinked, and walked off carrying her notebook, telling him over her shoulder to bring the jars with the bug and the bug parts.

He did, and they were great friends from that moment on. Xavier couldn't have exactly said *why*. Molly decided what TV shows and movies they saw, what video games they played, what they'd have for snacks, and the topic of pretty much every conversation. Never did she ask him what he wanted to do, although occasionally she did demand his opinion, which she used as an opportunity to explain to him how he had totally misunderstood things. Every thing she said he found utterly fascinating. He thought he could listen to her all day, and often he did.

Jillian became part of their group almost at the end of that fourth grade year. She'd been living in California with her aunt, was now to live here with her grandmother. According to Molly, she had strawberry-blonde hair; to Xavier it just looked light brown. He remembers how Molly approached Jillian her first day, the intensity of her posture, her determined nodding as she spoke. "Hey, I'm

Molly. You're Jillian. I almost died before I was born. Isn't that cool? We're going to be best friends." Jillian looked a little stunned. It was his first out-of-body experience, watching himself watching them.

Shortly thereafter Molly declared the three of them a team. Xavier always thought Jillian was much more like Molly's personal assistant than a friend. She ran her errands, carried her books, did the homework Molly considered beneath her. At least Xavier hadn't had to do any of that. He'd had other uses.

"Can you move?"

Molly is above him, shouting into his face, her voice very loud and very clear. There is a halo of tree limbs behind her head, dark against the sun like blood vessels from her skull, maybe from her brain. He's heard of tumors doing that, attaching themselves to veins and arteries so they have their very own blood supply. He can feel something scratchy against his neck and cheek, several hard things under his left thigh and shoulder blade, things warm and liquid which may or may not be part of him.

Coughing brings out new centers of pain. "I don't know," he manages to tell her, because it isn't a good idea not to answer Molly. "I don't think so."

"Oh, sure you can." It's been a long time since he bothered demanding why she asks him questions if she's not going to believe his answers anyway. The fact is, she's often right and he's often wrong. "Just rest a second, then we'll help you."

Jillian's face wedges in next to Molly's, those sinister veins piercing her head now as if Molly shot them at her. Both faces and Jillian's long curly light hair and the veins blot out the sky.

"Open your mouth."

That's Molly, giving orders. He's afraid to open his mouth for her, afraid not to. He opens his mouth and something is pushed into it, hard and sticky, a piece of hard candy. It makes him choke a little, but that isn't what interests her.

"Can you taste that?"

310

Desperately wanting to tell her the truth, he has some trouble sorting out his senses. "No," he finally decides. "I can feel it but not taste it, I don't think."

"It's hot cinnamon," Jillian prompts.

"I can't taste it."

Molly puts her hand over his eyes and then something is passed under his nose. "Can you smell that?"

"It's an orange."

"Interesting," she breathes, and removes her hand. Instantly he misses her touch.

Jillian is normally nervous and high-strung, but Xavier can't remember a time she's looked so scared. She covers her mouth with trembling fingers, her grandmother's star sapphire ring sparking. Xavier thinks how old she looks. But wait, she's only twenty-three, *they're* only twenty-three. He's lost some indescribable and immeasurable quantity of precious time. He's floating. Before he floats totally outside his body he says, to one or the other or both of them, "You pushed me, didn't you? You pushed me off the path?" It's a question. You don't make assertions to Molly.

Molly's gasp is so unlike her that he guesses it's fake. "Jesus, Xave, you're not fucking serious." Then, to Jillian, "He must have really smashed his head."

Jillian just nods, her hand still over her mouth and still shaking, the ring quiet and dull now. Xavier focuses on the trembling of her hand, on the hand itself, on the ring, and floats away on it.

"Xavier. Hey, Xave." He's at home now, in his own bed, alone in his own bed which is rare. Some *Tindersticks* song is playing through the speakers, looping back over itself. Jillian made that track for him. Jillian is beside him, her familiar sunny smell, her familiar nervous voice and the star sapphire ring, the unfamiliar sensation of something nudging at his lips. "You haven't had anything to eat in like twenty-four hours. Will you eat some yogurt? For me?"

The spoon taps at his mouth again and his lips open. He feels the yogurt slide in, thinks of all the crass jokes they've made about yogurt, welcomes the feel of it in his mouth and on his tongue, but doesn't taste it. "What kind?" he asks, sort of urgently.

It takes her a minute to get what he wants to know. "Oh. Uh—strawberry banana, it says. I think we've got some plain, too, if you—"

"I can't taste it."

"Oh," she says. "Bummer. Something happened when you fell, I guess. That's what Molly thinks."

His head hurts. She feeds him the whole carton of yogurt. He can't taste it. He doesn't think he can taste it—the cool, thick, mucousy feel of it is so intense that it seems like a taste sometimes and he can smell it which is a lot like tasting, but he tastes no hint of strawberry or banana or yogurt tartness. "Coffee," he says, then makes an extra effort. "Could I have a cup of coffee, please? With lots of sugar?"

"Since when do you drink coffee?"

"It sounds good right now. Maybe falling off a cliff changed my taste in drinks." He laughs, and she obviously doesn't know what's funny, and it really isn't anything to laugh about even though puns are the highest form of humor.

Molly was right in front of him on the trail. Jillian had lagged behind to look at something. They were all high, and the sun was warm, and the mountains were awesome, the weed smoothing out all his sensations so it didn't matter that there were so many of them. He was feeling good. Molly stopped, he almost ran into her, he was saying what the fuck when she turned around and punched him in the groin and he yelled and stepped backward and fell.

He remembers that.

He smells coffee, dust, plants on the windowsill, lemon-scented spray cleaner, rain, a shitload of other odors he doesn't bother to label. He's learned you can get tangled up in labels, and he can't always tell when it matters what some sensation is and when it doesn't. He likes the smell of coffee brewing, just not the taste. But it's the most definite taste he can think of off the top of his head. So to speak. There's a bandage on his head. Molly cleaned the wound and put the bandage there. He remembers that. Did they take him to the ER? They should have taken him to the ER.

Once when they were like thirteen Molly said they were all going to go around blindfolded for a week. Open-minded and so goddamn tolerant it could drive you fuckin' crazy, Xavier's parents said it was a good exercise in sensitivity. Jillian's grandma said it was the most ridiculous thing she'd ever heard of, why would you want to make yourself blind, and kept confiscating Jillian's bandannas. He didn't know what Molly's mom thought about it. Molly never said much about her mom, and Xavier only saw her a couple of times before she died, never actually met her.

"St Teresa of Avila said if you want to know the true meaning of life—well, actually, she said if you want to know God—you have to go inside and not be distracted by stuff from the outside," Molly told them while they were walking blindfolded around the zoo, holding onto each other, bumping into things, Jillian and Xavier giggling and exaggerating.

Guiltily Xavier could see pieces of things from under the scarf Molly had tied too tight over his eyes, and through it he could detect light and shadow. He didn't tell her that. "Who?" he asked, staggering around like he was more drunk than blind.

"St Teresa. Of. Avila," Molly enunciated. "She was a Christian mystic. She said our senses like vision and hearing and taste and smell and touch are like bees that go out from the hive and gather up information and bring it back. She said you have to keep the bees from leaving the hive if you want to really understand life and death and the universe and God and stuff like that. Actually, what she wrote was—" and here Xavier knew she was drawing herself up the way she always did when she recited something word-for-word; Molly was awesome at memorization. "'As soon as you apply yourself to prison, you will at once feel your senses gather themselves together: they seem like bees which return to the hive and there shut themselves up to work at the making of honey. God disposes them to a state of utter rest and of perfect contemplation.'"

"Prison?"

Molly punched his shoulder. "Asshole. I tell you all that and you get stuck on one word at the very beginning? See, that's why you'll never be great, Xavier. You've got a small mind, you know that?"

It isn't often that Jillian comes to his defense, but she did that time. "I don't get the part about prison, either, Molly. What does that mean? And whatever happened to this saint chick? Did she get to know God, or whatever?"

Xavier can't remember if Molly ever answered that, or about prison. He remembers her saying, but she's said it so often he's not sure which time he's remembering, "I almost died before I was born and when I was being born and lots of times after I was born."

He and Jillian probably didn't tell her yeah, yeah, she'd said that a million times already. She had, but this time—whenever it was—she said more. He didn't understand it at the time, he still doesn't, but it stuck in his mind.

"When you're dead," he thinks she said, "your bees don't go out from the hive anymore. That'd be cool. I want to know what that'd be like, not to take in anything from outside, just to be in there with yourself and God. Or whatever."

If he's right that all this happened on the same day, he and Jillian collided again about then and held onto each other laughing. They were in front of the gorilla cage, or maybe orangutans. The jumble of their odors and noises come back to him strong now.

At the end of the week when they met in their spot down by the river to compare notes from the experiment, Xavier and Jillian had lots of comically exaggerated anecdotes about falling over furniture, sticking their hands in disgusting stuff while trying to feel their way, running into people and accidentally touching private parts. They

314

both swore they were already hearing better. Molly listened avidly and asked questions and took notes. Xavier suspected she'd cheated, hadn't kept her blindfold on except when they were together, but he's never asked. Maybe he will now.

But he doesn't think Molly's here, and instead he croaks out, "Vinegar." It takes Jillian a minute to get that he wants her to put vinegar in his mouth. When she does, he can't taste it, although it makes his nose tingle and his tongue curl.

Over the next hours and months, Xavier tries fiery chili, limburger cheese, Tabasco sauce, lye. The cheese makes him throw up. The chili, Tabasco, and lye burn. But he can't taste them. He never tastes anything again.

He's recovered from the fall, except for a scar on his arm and one under his hair where you can hardly see it but you can feel it like a thin bunched string, and except for his lost sense of taste. Sometimes his balance is jacked up, too, but it's so subtle- —just a few seconds of dizziness here and there, the world swooning and then immediately righting itself- —he tries not to think too much about it, or to enjoy the trip, but what if it's permanent? Molly has always called him "a little dizzy." He hasn't told her about it now that it's literal, but he's not surprised that Jillian did. Molly is very interested. "This may be a long term issue," she says solemnly. "We may have to do something with your ears, surgery maybe."

"'We'?" He means, "What's this 'we' shit? It's *my* ears we're talking about here." But he's having a dizzy spell right now. Thoughts and words and sensations are swirling around in his head like loose marbles and he holds onto the doorframe, which is twisting and dissolving and reconfiguring, he can't think how to sit down, he doesn't want to lose all this before he can use it in his art. One of the careening sensations is of her saying "we" and "surgery" and "your ears" in the same sentence. He starts to slide down the curvy wall that massages him, wriggles erotically around him, heaves him away. It's awesome and it's too much and he wants to go as far into it as he can (oh, Molly) and he wants it to stop (Molly, stop, stop it).

She's talking. "...where we get our balance, you know, from our inner ears." Molly loves knowing things and telling you what she knows.

Everything clears up. Xavier sits down in ordinary motion, an ordinary person in an ordinary chair. Molly's talking. Lately he's been paying even more attention to her, looking for clues, trying to understand her because maybe his life depends on it. Not the first time he's thought that. So for the moment he ignores how annoying it is when she acts like he doesn't know the simplest things. He also ignores his fucked-up memory of her hitting him and knocking him off that ledge on purpose. Molly wouldn't do that to him. They love each other. Ashamed for even thinking she'd do that, he tries to make himself feel better by touching the stringy scar under his hair, proof that he's had a head injury and no wonder he's paranoid. More for the sound of the word and the feel of it in his mouth, word as object, he repeats, "'We'?"

"Dude! I meant 'they!'" She giggles. Molly doesn't giggle. "Doctors, people who know what they're doing. But you don't have any health insurance, do you? You can't really afford a doctor."

She's doing what she always does, pulling the conversation back to where she wants it. He has the feeling he shouldn't let her do that this time. But he's tired and it's actually kind of a relief to be told what's real. Molly's good at that. That may be why he loves her.

You can live without taste. Having one less portal for sensory input to get into you is soothing, in a bizarre sort of way, and interesting, definitely interesting. Molly's spent a lot of time with him in these months, observing, recording, and she says he's doing great.

He keeps trying out stuff to see if his sense of taste might have come back. He pours salt straight onto his tongue; it makes the tissues pucker, but he can't taste it. He washes out his mouth with soap;

the strong flowery smell in the back of his throat seems like taste for a second but it isn't. Depending on the day, he misses the taste of Merlot, Burger King french fries, white chocolate, pineapple, peanut butter, Jillian. He always misses the taste of Molly.

He goes back to school, and he doesn't like it any better or worse than ever. He lost a semester to the accident so he'll graduate in August instead of May, but who cares. His senior project is visual and tactile representations of taste. He gets a C. They say it's immature, superficial. One of the jurors writes that the concept is interesting and "deserves further development and greater personal risk from the artist." Xavier would like to think he doesn't know what the fuck that means, but he's beginning to think he does, thanks mostly to Molly.

Sometime in there Molly starts nagging him to replace some light bulbs. It's his assigned job in the household. He always procrastinates, and she always nags him. This time she points out acidly that he doesn't need to taste a light bulb in order to fuckin' change it. He'll get to it. He's painting. He's an artist, can't be bothered with mundane shit like that.

Jillian steps closer to the new canvas, squints at it, grabs one wrist with the other hand behind her back and twists her grandmother's ring in her thinking-super-hard stance, steps back. It's Xavier who finally says, "Different, huh?"

Yeah. Something. What is it?"

"I can't taste it anymore."

"Taste the paint? What?" Jillian rolls her eyes at him. At least this time she doesn't say, "You are so *cute!*" When they're in one of their sex phases, that can make him want to kiss her. When they're not, like now, since the accident, it kind of pisses him off.

But this painting *is* taste. Fruit and seeds and juices, some of it warming in the light, some of it gone to sour and rot. The reds more like blood than fruit. The yellows, the oranges, more like pain. Berries the color of the darkness in the middle of the night, and you wake up all of a sudden, unable to see anything, scared shitless, deep inside yourself, your bees buzzing around not even trying to go out, getting everything they need from deep inside you. It occurs to him he's never tasted anything so intense as making this painting.

Because he has no clue how to explain what he means, or if he means anything, he says, like she's the dumbest chick in the world, which in some ways he's always thought she is, "Yeah, Jillian, taste the paint." She glares at him and stomps out of the room. If he said that to Molly, she'd tell him what he means. But he doesn't, and it's like a guilty secret.

"You've lost your sense of taste but not smell," Molly points out. As if he hadn't noticed. It makes him feel safer that she's noticed, too.

Her hair falls straight to her chin now. He liked it best short and velvety, but the silky look and feel of it this way are nice, too. He strokes it while she talks. She doesn't seem to notice.

"You've got ageusia but not anosmia. That only happens 0.5 percent of the time in head injury cases. Interesting."

"Quit saying that. Makes me feel like a bug."

"Usually ageusia doesn't occur without anosmia. Usually ageusia really *is* anosmia and results from injury to the olfactory nerve. But you can smell even though you can't taste. You're an anomaly, sweetie." She takes his face roughly in her hands and kisses him open-mouthed, a little tongue action, like she's rewarding him for doing or being something really cool.

Finally all the lights in the kitchen are out. It seems to him they burned out faster than usual. But he can't put off changing them any longer, and Molly's got a point when she tells him to earn his keep. Jillian offers to do it, but Molly shoots her a look and Xavier is a little insulted. He's not helpless. Hand over her mouth, grandmother's ring glinting, Jillian leaves the room, while Molly steadies the ladder for him. "Just quit rocking your feet," she orders.

He's stretching to get the globe loose. "I'm not rocking anything.

Quit moving your hands around." He's trying not to drop the light bulb or the glass globe.

"You're shaking the ladder, Xave."

"I'm not," he begins, feeling a flash of panic and anger, when he finds himself sideways, descending at the speed of nightmare, his feet gone. It's a short way down, but Before he crashes he's aware of something small and hard like a fist smashing into his face.

Jillian and Molly are standing over him, and he thinks he's just landed at the bottom of the drop-off from the mountain trail. Then he's aware of the pillows arranged on either side of his head, lumpy, pale, and huge (the pillows, not his head, or maybe in fact it's both). He wants to push them off the bed—he doesn't want them anywhere near him. But for the moment he can't make himself move.

"Oh, sweetie, you fell again," Jillian says, patting somewhere on his body below eye level.

"Yeah, we've really got to do something about your balance," Molly says. "But right now we've got to take care of your nose."

"By…bose?" he croaks.

Jillian lets loose a snort of laughter, apologizes for laughing, can't stop laughing, leaves the room. Molly explains, "Oh, yeah, you bled all over everything. Must have really cracked it when you fell. But I've packed your nasal passages good and tight. Good thing my grandmother taught me some great remedies for nosebleed. My dad used to get them all the time."

He is aware, now, of the stuffed, swollen feeling of his nose, as if his face has been taken away from him and she's grafted random meat to the underlying muscle. He can't smell anything but the bandages, a faint whiff of blood, and an odd metallic scent that reminds him of batteries.

"You're going to be fine," Molly pronounces. It scares him a little that he believes her.

After a week or so, not being able to smell starts to get to him. He bends over a simmering pot of Jillian's chicken soup until his face starts to burn, without capturing even a hint of aroma. He buries his nose in flowers and gets only their softness or prickliness or texture like tissue paper. Desperate, he sticks his face right down to his own shit in the toilet bowl and it might as well be a lump of clay floating there.

Now he can't taste or smell. It feels like more than that. The whole organic world seems denied him. He supposes this could be artistically interesting if he weren't so fucking scared and sad.

One night at dinner he is slowly chewing his way through a pile of shrimp when he becomes aware that Jillian and Molly are watching him closely from across the table. "What?" A couple of well-chewed lumps drop from his mouth. Jillian gags and covers her face. "What!" he shouts, spitting the rest of the shrimp out over the table.

"I'm sorry, Xave." Molly's face looks genuinely sorry so she's lying to him somehow. "I wasn't paying good enough attention. It looks like that batch of shrimp was spoiled. My bad. I am *so* sorry."

The shrimp starts up his throat. He barely makes it to the toilet bowl, hears himself retch as if his throat were turning inside out, dumps pints of colorful but remarkably odorless and tasteless puke.

"I don't think I need that anymore," Xavier says later that evening as Molly takes the packing out. Her hand on his forehead almost makes up for the tweezers up his nose and the sharp tug to get the cotton out. Breathing feels good. Then, seeing she's not done, he gets to his feet, swaying a little. "I don't think I need that anymore." When she ignores him, he tries, "I can't remember the last time there was any blood."

"There's still infection, and you appear to have developed a rash and some real sensitivity up there. You know how a doctor tells you to take all your antibiotics until your prescription runs out, even if you're feeling lots better? Same principle."

"What is that stuff you're soaking them in? It's dark. Looks metallic."

She hesitates, half a beat. Molly never hesitates, and it alarms him. Why doesn't he just get the fuck out of there? "My grandmother used this on my dad. She was a real natural healer, an actual expert. There's a little zinc, just a smidgen of lead, some other things."

"It's not toxic, right?" What a stupid question. Like she's going to tell him, yeah, Xave, I'm poisoning you.

What she says is, "Oh, Xave, do you think I'd give you something toxic?"

It's not a rhetorical question. She actually wants an answer, and he's forced to say, "No," and, when he says it to her, it's true, he doesn't think she'd do anything like that.

She nods. "It's fine in these amounts. You wait, you'll be better in no time."

"So it worked with your dad?"

"Well, for a while. But he had lots of other problems. He was a mess, actually. My grandma said he was like that from when he was a little boy."

She brings the cotton balls over and wedges them so far up his nose he panics a bit. He imagines them pushing up through into his brain. His nose feels like wood.

"I have to pack it really well," she croons. "In case it starts bleeding again." Then she wraps the bandage tight over his nose and under his eyes, standing on tiptoe to tie it at the back of his head. Xavier thinks he must look ridiculous, monstrous, but finds he isn't entirely displeased by the idea, especially when Molly kisses him long and hard. He has the definite impression he should be smelling some strong, terrible odors, but he smells nothing. Ever again.

For seven and a half months right after high school, he didn't see Molly at all. He didn't return her messages and, when she wouldn't quit calling and texting, he changed his cell number. He treated Jillian like shit when Molly used her as her messenger. He moved to San Diego, for no good reason, and his parents paid his art school tuition, relieved that he had some direction in his life, which he didn't except to get away from Molly. He made them promise not to tell anybody where he was. "Not even Molly and Jillian?" His parents had always liked "the girls" (or sometimes "our girls"), mostly because they were his only friends.

"Especially not them."

His dad said something approving about striking out on your own. Really what he was doing was running away. His mom went still and tilted her head—"You know you can talk to me, honey"—but the only person who'd have had a chance of getting what he might say was Jillian and Jillian was part of it, Jillian would tell Molly, he had to cut himself off from Jillian, too.

It sucked. He hated Molly for that more than all the other shit. And he did hate her. And he loved her. He never stopped loving her. When he came back home he paid for both hating her and loving her. Which was actually kind of fun, in an S-and-M sort of way.

"Why'd you come back?" Jillian whispered to him that first night. Then they were clinging to each other with Molly sound asleep—or pretending to be—between them.

"Didn't know what to do with myself," he tried, very aware that Molly could be listening to every word and recording it in her mental notebook. "Wanted to see what would happen next."

What he didn't say then, because he didn't quite know it yet, was that being in the world without Molly had been like being in a sensory shooting gallery, constantly bombarded, constantly on overload, not sure about which of the barrage of stimuli were foreground and which background, exhausted from trying to pay attention to them all. Molly kept things straight.

Now Jillian is in his arms again and he asks her tenderly, "Remember the paintings I did with patches over my eyes?"

"Sick shit," Jillian murmurs, probably meaning both sick like "disgusting" and sick like "very cool."

"Totally." Drawing his hand down her body, so familiar and sweet, he wonders what happened to those paintings. Molly probably has them cataloged somewhere, along with all the photos she takes of him and Jillian and the three of them and herself with him and with Jillian and herself with herself. And the pictures of the black cat with the cauterized eye sockets, which was what pushed him over the edge into leaving.

Shuddering, he wonders aloud, "Whatever happened to the cat?"

"Homer." Jillian burrows her face into his chest. They hug each other and chorus, "for the blind poet!" like Molly always said even before the cat showed up with both eyes gone, they assumed from some mother of a fight. When she brought him home, she'd already named him Homer because she was a fan of the *Iliad* or something, though Xavier didn't think she'd ever been much of a reader.

Then Xavier and Jillian get it on for a while, and even though he can't taste or smell her, even though they're both crying, it's incredible, the best it's been between them for a long time. Actually, being fucked up like this—no smell, no taste, sobbing hysterically when he comes—makes the sex a lot better for Xavier, and it occurs to him that Molly probably knows that.

They fall asleep for a while and then they both wake up at the same time and rush around so they won't be late to meet Molly for the moonlight nature hike she's decided they're going on. Hogging the bathroom as usual, Jillian calls out to him, "Homer did okay blind."

"Yeah," he grins. "Dude wrote awesome poetry."

She must not have heard him because when she comes back to get dressed she says, "He got so fuckin' independent he moved out. We saw him around and he'd let us pet him and he'd eat from Molly's hand but he wouldn't come home. Didn't need us. Seriously pissed her off. Remember?"

Xavier does remember that and Molly's files of notes on her laptop. Gelling his pompadour even bigger than before Jillian messed it up, he thinks to ask, "How did Homer lose his eyes, anyway? Did we ever know?"

Jillian takes a toke from the pre-concert joint and passes it to him. Tightly she answers, "Catfight, wasn't it?"

He sucks in the smoke and says in that same cartoony voice, "I don't think so," but she waves him off and they hurry out the door. Molly doesn't like to be kept waiting. It's a huge relief on the train when Xavier realizes he's buzzed, just like always, even though he can't taste or smell the weed.

Living without two of his senses turns out not to be all bad. That in itself is weird; he doesn't know if it's pitiful or admirable that a human being can adjust to any damn thing.

Things he doesn't see coming can seriously depress him — odorless wood smoke that still makes his eyes water, pumpkin pie slimy and sickening without the taste he's never liked anyway, his parents' messy Christmas tree that might as well be fake now that he doesn't get the pine fragrance. But he's doing okay, better than okay. Most of the time he's calmer than he's ever been. He feels safer, which is bizarre. He can follow conversations better, organize stuff like grocery lists and his checkbook, and stay with his art for longer periods of time without getting distracted. All that is of great interest to Molly.

He graduates, takes a few additional computer courses over the summer and finds a computer graphics job because no one makes a living in fine arts anymore, gets into collages and assemblage pieces that seem to actually come out of his odorless and tasteless new world, or out of how his vision and hearing and tactile senses are moving in to where smell and taste used to be, or something. He gets a couple of shows and a mention in the neighborhood paper. Three of his pieces sell.

At work and at the galleries he meets new people and starts doing things with friends besides Jillian and Molly or by himself, which is a first. He even has dates with a few new women, one of whom he thinks for a week or so he might be falling in love with until he hears from somebody else that she's moved out of town. Pissed off and embarrassed, maybe hurt, he builds a 5'x6' walk-in assemblage piece with all kinds of shit jutting out and thrusting up from the bottom and hanging down in your face, textures and shapes in juxtapositions he doesn't think about but just knows in ways he maybe wouldn't if he still had to deal with all five senses bringing him input from the wide world. That piece is a little hard to place, but a gallery downtown puts it in the building lobby and Xavier likes to lurk around anonymously watching people staring at it but hesitant to go inside it. He sympathizes. He never wants to go inside it, either, but once he does he doesn't want to come out.

He still paints now and then although it bothers him that he can't smell the oils. The oil smell wasn't good for you—his painting instructors used to harp on how you had to be careful and ventilate your studio well, or use acrylics, but he never liked acrylics. Now he's probably getting the brain damage without the odor. Whatever. These new paintings have huge electric arcs of color, faces with deep layers of tissue and bone exposed, starved bodies holding candles in amorphous dark corners.

"You seem happy," Molly observes in her very clear voice. They're looking at the big assemblage. It's the first time she's seen it. Jillian helped him construct it in the first place and then de-construct, move, and put it up here. "Why are you happy?"

"Why not?" He speaks quietly because she's talking too loud. Her voice echoes in the lobby and people on the other side of the assemblage look at her. Xavier suddenly doesn't want her here.

"I didn't say you shouldn't be happy. I want you to be happy. I just didn't think you would be, after all that's happened. And I'm interested in why."

"Why what?"

Molly turns to face him. To face him down. She sets her feet shoulder-width apart and crosses her arms in her don't-screw-with-me-asshole stance. "Xavier. You've lost two of your senses, so you should be getting only about sixty per cent of the normal sensory input. I'd have thought that would handicap you. But it seems to have made you more centered or at peace or something. Inspired you. How does that work?"

Enraged like he's never been at anybody before in his life, Xavier wouldn't mind having a scene with Molly right here and now—it's overdue—but not while there are people looking at his art. He grabs her arm and pulls her out onto the street, down the block, into an alley strewn with garbage he can't smell. Probably there are other odors in here, too, other tastes in the air, piss and booze and cooking smells from the back doors of restaurants. He expected her to resist, hoped she would so he could overpower her, but she didn't, and now she stands there against the stained brick wall half-smiling and watching him, which makes him even more furious. "Stop it!" he hisses. "Just stop, Molly, give it up!"

Her hair is short again and she runs a hand over it. His palm tingles with the feel of it, a cellular memory. "Stop what? What am I doing?" He knows her, has known her for a long time, and there's something wrong about the tone of her voice.

"You're such a fuckin' control freak! You always have been! You set people up, and you make things happen, and you take notes, and it's all so goddamn *interesting*, isn't it, Molly?" To keep from shaking her, he's pacing, kicking at things. He throws a half-full Corona can against a dumpster and beer splatters into his face but he doesn't taste it. Of course he doesn't taste it, or smell it, either.

Molly declares, "I don't know what you mean."

Xavier doesn't know what he means, either, and the anger seeps

326

out of him, leaving despair. He mutters, "Just leave me alone," and stalks off. He doesn't know what he'll do if Molly follows him. She doesn't even call his name. When he gets back to the house late that night, so stoned he can hardly walk and so depressed he hardly cares, Jillian is waiting for him. "What?" he mumbles, wanting nothing more than to collapse in bed alone.

She takes him in her arms and he thinks he might throw up but he doesn't have the strength to pull away. "We've got to get away," she whispers. "We've got to get away from her."

"From who?"

She claps her hand over his mouth hard enough that he feels slapped. "Shut up. I already packed your stuff. Let's go."

"You packed my stuff?" He's incredulous, in a fuzzy sort of way.

"I don't know where she is. She could be back any second. Come on."

"No," he says.

"Xavier, don't be an idiot. You're in danger. We both are, but especially you. She's fuckin' crazy."

"Who? Molly?"

"Shut *up!*"

"I'm not leaving, Jillian. You do what you gotta do, but things are going too good for me here." That's a lot of words for him to say in his current state, and he sits down hard on the floor.

"She hurts you."

"Well, yeah, but she doesn't mean to. It's just her way."

"She means to, Xavier. And she's going to hurt you more. I don't know how, exactly, but she's going to."

"Probably." This is all so absurd. He's giggling.

They hear Molly at the back door and Jillian gives one more tug at his hand, then drops it, grabs her backpack, and runs out the front. Xavier passes out right where he is and vaguely realizes Molly is putting him to bed. Vaguely, it feels nice.

Molly's sick with mumps. She says she never had it as a kid and Xavier knows this could be serious. "How'd you get mumps?" he asks her tenderly, not really to find out but as a way of saying he's sorry she feels so terrible.

"My cousin's kids all have it. I was over there the other day."

"Should've stayed home."

"I know. Wouldn't be sick and Jillian wouldn't be gone." She looks so pitiful. She puts her arms around his neck and pulls him down for a long kiss. He gets into bed with her and they make out for a while, have sex. He wouldn't think she'd feel like it and it pleases him that she wants him even when she's sick. She's feverish. She falls asleep and he tucks her in, only then thinks about contagion and calls his mom to see if he had mumps when he was little. He didn't.

When Molly's just getting better Xavier comes down with mumps, swollen glands like alien life forms under his neck, fever dreams, puking. Now and then he gets up to paint, and when he can't hold a brush anymore he dips his fingers into the paint and applies it to the canvas directly. He stands there, struggling to work, leaving only when he has to go to the bathroom. In the mirror he sees he has smeared paint all over his face and into his hair, raised rainbow squiggles and blotches adding to the hairline scar. Pleased with the effect, he wonders how long he can leave it there without doing damage to himself, and if he even cares about doing damage.

At some point he may have lost consciousness. When you're living the dream, you can never be sure if you're awake or if you're dreaming.

"She tried to take your hearing," Jillian says, above him. They're above him a lot, floating around like angels, closer to heaven than he can ever possibly be. It makes him jealous and sad. "Do you remember coming to the hospital?" Jillian holds his face still so that he has to look at her unless he closes his eyes and that's too much trouble.

He thinks he's shaking his head. Jillian is holding up a hand full of papers, scribbles like mouse droppings or worm trails, disgusting and hard on the eyes. "Are those love letters?" Trying to smile, he manages to close his eyes instead.

"It's her *notes*, Xave. She was trying to take your hearing, nobody would believe me, but now I've found her notes! Your own parents wouldn't believe me, but now we can both talk to them, and the doctors, and the police. We'll tell them everything she's done to you!" She starts crying. "And we'll tell them what I've done, too, how I was a part of it."

"No." He wants to say more but doesn't really get what more there is to say.

"Yes, yes! Just listen to this crap! 'Labyrinthine viral infection, from mumps or another viral illness, is one cause of Idiopathic Sudden Sensory Hearing Loss. Difficult to estimate the odds, or the danger to myself if exposed, but X is weak and susceptible, always has been, and the concerts we go to are loud, and I always insist we sit up front. He winces, but he's so inured to abuse, I don't think he even knows he's in pain. He has no idea I've been wearing ear plugs. But it's taking forever. I can't wait that long.' And, shit, here, at the bottom, 'intracochlear membrane rupture,' she's got in big letters, underlined! What do you think that means?"

"You're crazy!" Molly shouts, snatching the papers. Jillian tries to grab them back, and Xavier actually admires how strong and fast Molly is, keeping the papers away. "And stupid. And weak! Xave, she's lying. She pulled that stuff out of a magazine and wrote it down! I saw her out in the waiting room writing and looking things up—now I know what she was doing. She's resented my relationship with you for years-—she wants you all to herself! I think she always has—she just doesn't have the guts to fight for you like a real woman."

Molly slaps her. Jillian pushes Molly and they are fighting, throwing punches and scratching. Xavier is kind of excited but so shut down all he can do is watch from a distance.

329

Though Molly is a good three inches shorter and thirty pounds lighter, she has Jillian's hands twisted up behind her back. Jillian's hair streams over Molly's face. "I've already told your parents and the doctors about her—*nobody* believes her!"

"Fuck you!" Jillian kicks backward and Molly gets her onto the floor. "Xave, listen to me—"

From where she half-sits, half-lies on top of Jillian, Molly almost whispers, "I'm going to get you home, Xavier. I'm going to get you better."

His parents said they wanted him to come home with them, but Xavier didn't notice them arguing much when Molly said she would take care of him. They've never known what to do with him, and the truth is they're good with just visiting, bringing him tasteless food, chatting about crap that means even less to him now than it ever did, and leaving the rest of him to Molly. They trust Molly. They've always been clueless. So has he, in a different way, and that's why he needs Molly.

So he's home. "You're safe on my watch, good buddy," she says and laughs, over and over again until it isn't funny anymore, if it ever was.

She tells him Jillian is in a psych ward. Everybody says she needs lots of help, rest, time to get herself better. He misses her, but not very much.

Clay and sculpting tools were waiting for him when he got out of the hospital, a welcome-home present. Molly says it'll help his tactile sense. He's never much liked the feel of clay, the intense tiny-grained squishiness of it, the particles under his nails and in the creases of his skin, but now he's sitting up in bed with a newspaper-covered tray across his knees, in gray-blue twilight, pressing and digging at the gray-brown chunk, not thinking about what it is or what's in it, just getting used to the feel.

"I've made you some tea." Coming into the room, Molly is all smiles. She sees the clay, his fingers in the clay, the clay glistening and moving. "Ooh, that's sweet." She reaches toward the bulbous shape coming out from between his hands but she doesn't quite touch it. Kissing the top of his head, she croons, "You're so talented."

He leans his head back against her. After a quiet moment she takes away the clay even though he's not ready to stop, but once it's out of his reach he is done, she was right. She gives him a wet towel, helps him clean his hands. Another nice moment between the two of them.

Then she's businesslike and bustling again. "I'm dropping your antibiotics into this nice tea, see? So they're easier to take-—they don't taste so bad this way. You've got to take all your medicine, honey, okay?" When has she ever called him honey? "Here's your earphones. Just lean back against the pillow and sip your tea and listen to the nice music. I've put on something really soft-—you still like piano music, right? That New Age stuff? We always make fun, but it is relaxing. Dinner will be ready soon. I love you, sweetheart. You'll be better before you know it."

Sweetheart sounds weird coming out of her mouth. But Xavier likes it. He may have even yearned for it, just a little.

The music really is relaxing. It doesn't demand anything of you. As he's nodding off, Molly stands by the stereo, watching. Should he say something? Is that what she's waiting for? The music changes somehow, but Xavier is so relaxed it's like dropping into a deep hole, falling again but it's okay, it feels good, a nice long swooping slide.

When he wakes up he can't seem to open his eyes. He feels a soundless buzzing in his head. His head pulses like a too-full balloon, his hands and feet are tingling. He's done enough shit to know a drug hangover when he's got one. His thoughts are jumbled but finally he's thinking the stereo must have malfunctioned because there's just this buzzing, nothing remotely musical about it. Does Molly know? He needs to find Molly and tell her the piece-of-crap stereo's jacked up again. But why can't he open his eyes?

Light comes through his closed lids so at least, thank god, he isn't blind.

When he brings his hands up to rub his face, his eyelids start coming loose like they've been glued. On his fingertips is an amazing amount of what they used to call "eye boogers." He finds the dried mucous on his lips and chin, too.

He's starving. Did he eat dinner? He doesn't think so.

He looks around the room, sees the long cord snaking toward the stereo, realizes he still has the earphones on. He looks at the stereo, at the indicators flashing red, at the long bars pulsing. He looks back at the window, and sees it is half-open, the curtain blowing in. But he can't hear the wind, or the traffic noises outside, or anything else.

He reaches up to the ear cups. They're both vibrating hard. But he hears nothing.

He stares at the stereo, the indicators swinging, pulsing. Maximum volume. For how many days? Three? Five? A week? It would have been terrible for those expensive speakers. Shredding them internally. Good thing, he thinks, the sound had been diverted into the headphones.

And his ears? How many days?

He tears the headphones off and throws back his head to scream her name, so loud in his head but so silent. He rushes through the house. Where is she? Until he's thinking *I can't kill her if I can't find her*; he didn't know he wanted to kill her. She did this on purpose. She's done all this on purpose. What, exactly, has she done? Deliberately he bangs against something, tips something over, stops and waits for the sound to come to him delayed, but it never does.

In the studio a blank canvas is up on the easel. Did he put it there or did she? He wrestles the lids off jars of acrylic he's never used, sticks his fingers in, and throws gob after colorful gob at the expanse of pure white. In no time at all he fills it. He steps closer. The painting is telling him something, but what? He really wants to hear what it has to say.

Movement in the corner of his eye. He glances over. Molly is walking his way briskly, a notebook wedged under her arm, a pen in her fist. In her other hand a recorder pushed toward him like a weapon. She's speaking. What the fuck is she doing? She's babbling on. Suddenly she stops, laughing silently. She opens her mouth wide and speaks slowly, with serious exaggeration. Does she want him to read her lips? She's repeating it, again and again.

(say what you feel)

Is that it? He can still speak, so why wouldn't he be able to say what he feels?

He rips his mouth wide and screams, lunging for her. Noiselessly she stumbles backward, noiselessly scatters paint jars and brushes and equipment. He falls onto her and they both go down. She is a hysterical silent film heroine, struggling to get out from under him.

His hands are around her throat, squeezing the sound out of her. *Even trade!* But he doesn't know if he's saying it or just thinking it. Then her pen comes up and up, in slow motion, and then in the jagged speeded-up motion of a silent film. He didn't think about her pen.

So now he is blind.

Now he is deaf, too.

Now he is deaf and he is blind, too.

Are there words for people who can't taste or smell? For a while he panics because he doesn't know any. He's deaf and blind and he can't smell and he can't taste. That leaves touch. And terror.

333

Scratchy bandages bind his eyes, but loose enough he can still move the lids. No dim light. No shadows. Nothing but the deepest, darkest well of despair, and he has all the time in the world to stare down into it, to swim in it, to drink everything it holds.

Something squeezes his right hand. Again and again. How long has that been going on? Squeeze and squeeze again, regular, or irregular, as a heartbeat.

"Jillian?" he means to say. He can't hear the word or see it or smell it or taste it. For a while he gets lost in all this sensory confusion, and then realizing it could just as well be Molly squeezing his hand almost makes him black out, and he grabs wildly and flails and finds the hand with the ring. He's afraid to be relieved, to feel even momentarily safe, because Molly could be wearing a ring just to trick him. But it does feel like Jillian's ring. He isn't used to using his sense of touch like this—the only sense he has left—so he could be wrong, but it feels like the star sapphire ring with the ridged setting and the etched design on the band. He actually thinks he can feel the star in the sapphire, and he knows that isn't possible, and so he must be going crazy. A person can only take so much.

Squeeze again, then pressure, skin on skin, dampness, blood or tears? He thinks tears, but it could be blood. Not so long ago he wouldn't have thought about blood, but everything's changed.

"Squeeze once for yes if it's you, twice for no." There's a single, long squeeze. That means it's Jillian. But Molly could say "yes" that way, squeeze once for yes it's Jillian when it isn't. It doesn't tell him anything.

He hopes he says, "Okay, just a test. Squeeze twice for no."

Two hesitant, shaky squeezes. More tears. Or blood. Or piss or jiz. Or it's raining. Or there's a gigantic dog drooling on him. Or he's hallucinating, crazy-creating, filling in this sensory emptiness with any shit his frantic brain can make up. But it's probably tears. Tears make sense.

Whatever it is, Xavier is drowning.

334

Hands grab his. A man's. His right hand turned over and fingers unfolded, then movement across his palm, it tickles, it scares him, and he tries to close his fist and jerk his hand away but his arm is held still it hurts he panics, fights, the movement on his palm keeps on and on and he can't fuckin' stand it can't stand any of this and then he realizes it's writing. Like with that chick in that sappy movie what's-her-name Ellen something. Writing. A message.

With great struggle Xavier calms himself down enough to concentrate. He feels tiny scratching that must be the nails, roughness here on the skin and smoothness here, the trail of warmth on his own skin that fades so fast, his fingers wanting to close, the pulses in the fingertips and in his own wrist. He has to work really hard to bring his attention to the marks—he knows they're invisible, but everything's invisible to him now and he's goddamn going to think of them as marks—the lines and arcs being laid down on his hand. D. A. D again. He feels himself say, "Dad?" and he's drenched with his own and everybody else's tears. M. O. He likes the circle; do that again. M. "Mom."

One strong squeeze. Yes.

He fits his lips together and says, "Bee." There's a pause and then the letter B is traced on his palm. No way he can explain about the damn bees still going out from the hive to bring stuff back for him to make what he can out of it, honey and wax and shit. Persistent little fuckers. He's had enough of them. He just wants them to stop. He can't make anybody but Molly understand that. So he moves his mouth, lips, tongue, teeth, to say, "Where's Molly?"

D. E. A. D.

"Dad?" He knows that's not what was spelled, but he can't take in—

A long curve is traced on his cheek, a J, probably for Jillian. Then two fast squeezes on his hand, "no," and the terrible, beautiful word "DEAD" outlined again.

"Dead? Molly's dead?"

One squeeze and then lots of stuff written fast on his hand though he thinks he tries to pull it away, too many letters, too many words, too much stimulation. He clenches his fist over all that stimulation, imagining he's squashing the goddamn bees.

"Did I kill her?"

Two firm squeezes.

"Did she kill herself?"

A long pause, maybe he didn't say it out loud, he starts to say it again when somebody squeezes his fist once.

Molly is dead. She killed herself. She's freed herself from all sensory input. All he has is touch. He doesn't want touch. He's had enough to last a lifetime. He wants to know what Molly knows, after all this time.

He puts his mind to it. His mind focuses and slows like it never has before. He goes inside to meet God or the universe or whatever it is. To meet Molly. Who knows what happens, or when.

He stops being aware of the feel of air or a blanket or tears on his skin.

The sensations of food and liquid entering his body by mouth or IV are muted, then disappear altogether. Whatever passes out of his body is senseless, too. Xavier chuckles inside himself. Puns are the highest form of humor.

Stuff is written on his knuckles, the inside of his arms, his face. It's like insects crawling. Meaning goes away when he doesn't try to understand, doesn't answer, doesn't engage at all. Finally the touch goes away, too, whether they've stopped touching him or he just isn't taking it in anymore.

No sense of where he is in space. Or if he's in space at all. No sound, not even heartbeat or breath or the little plates of his skull clicking together. No smell or even memory of smell. No taste in his mouth or anywhere else. No light or shadow or shape or dull glow on the backs of his eyelids. And nothing tactile, nothing felt.

He might as well not be living in his body anymore. Maybe he isn't. That's the point.

It's peaceful here.

It's lonely here.

God comes to him, or he comes to God, or he sinks into the universe, or he rises into nothing.

Molly almost died lots of times, before she was born and all through her life. Molly's really dead now. Molly knows this place. She brought him here.

Xavier loves Molly.

THE MAN ON THE CEILING

Everything we're about to tell you is true.

Don't ask me if I mean that "literally." I know about the literal. The literal has failed miserably to explain the things I've really needed explanations for. The things in your dreams, the things in your head, don't know from literal. And yet that's where most of us live: in our dreams, in our heads. The stories there, those fables and fairytales, are our lives.

Ever since I was a little boy I wanted to find out the names of the mysterious characters who lived in those stories. The heroes, the demons, and the angels. Once I named them, I would be one step closer to understanding them. Once I named them, they would be real.

When Melanie and I got married, we chose this name, TEM.

339

A gypsy word meaning "country," and also the name of an ancient Egyptian deity who created the world and everything in it by naming the world and everything in it, who created its own divine self by naming itself, part by part. Tem became the name for our relationship, that undiscovered country which had always existed inside us both, but had never been real until we met.

Much of our life together has been concerned with this naming. Naming of things, places, and mysterious, shadowy characters. Naming of each other and of what is between us. Making it real.

The most disturbing thing about the figures of horror fiction for me is a particular kind of vagueness in their form. However clearly an author might paint some terrifying figure, if this character truly resonates, if it reflects some essential terror within the human animal, then our minds refuse to fix it into a form. The faces of our real terrors shift and warp the closer they come to us: the werewolf becomes an elderly man on our block becomes the local butcher becomes an uncle we remember coming down for the Christmas holidays when we were five. The face of horror freezes but briefly, and as quickly as we jot down its details, it is something else again.

Melanie used to wake me in the middle of the night to tell me there was a man in our bedroom window, or a man on the ceiling.

I had my doubts, but being a good husband I checked the windows and I checked the ceiling and I attempted to reassure. We had been through this enough times that I had plenty of reason to believe she would not be reassured no matter what I said. Still I made the attempt each time, giving her overly reasonable explanations concerning the way the light had been broken up by wind-blown branches outside, or how the ceiling light fixture might be mistaken for a man's head by a person waking suddenly from a restless sleep or an intense dream. Sometimes my careful explanations irritated her enormously. Still mostly asleep, she would wonder aloud why I couldn't see the man on the ceiling. Was I playing games with her? Trying to placate her when I knew the awful truth?

In fact, despite my attempts at reason, I believed in the man on the ceiling. I always had.

As a child I was a persistent liar. I lied slyly, I lied innocently, and I lied enthusiastically. I lied out of confusion and I lied out of a profound disappointment. One of my more elaborate lies took shape during the 1960 presidential election. While the rest of the country was debating the relative merits of Kennedy and Nixon, I was explaining to my friends how I had been half of a pair of Siamese twins, and how my brother had tragically died during the separation.

This was, perhaps, my most heartfelt lie to date, because in telling this tale I found myself grieving over the loss of my brother, my twin. I had created my first believable character, and my character had hurt me.

Later I came to recognize that about that time (I was ten), the self I had been was dying, and that I was slowly becoming the twin who had died and gone off to some other, better fiction.

Many of my lies since then, the ones I have been paid for, have been about such secret, tragic twins and their other lives. The lives we dream about, and only half-remember after the first shock of day.

So how could I, of all people, doubt the existence of the man on the ceiling?

My first husband did not believe in the man on the ceiling.

At least, he said he didn't. He said he never saw him. Never had night terrors. Never saw the molecules moving in the trunks of trees and felt the distances among the pieces of himself.

I think he did, though, and was too afraid to name what he saw. I think he believed that if he didn't name it, it wouldn't be real. And so, I think, the man on the ceiling got him a long time ago.

Back then, it was usually a snake I'd see, crawling across the ceiling, dropping to loop around my bed. I'd wake up and there would still be a snake…huge, vivid, sinuous, utterly mesmerizing. I'd cry out. I'd call for help. After my first husband had grudgingly come in a few times and hadn't been able to reassure me that there was no snake on the ceiling, he just quit coming.

Steve always comes. Usually, he's already there beside me.

One night a man really did climb in my bedroom window. Really did sit on the edge of my bed, really did mutter incoherently and fumble in the bedclothes, really did look surprised and confused when I sat up and screamed. I guess he thought I was someone else. He left, stumbling, by the same second-story window. I chased him across the room, had the tail of his denim jacket in my hands. But I let him go because I couldn't imagine what I'd do next if I caught him.

By the time I went downstairs and told my first husband, there was no sign of the intruder. By the time the police came, there was no evidence, and I certainly could never have identified him. I couldn't even describe him in any useful way: dark, featureless. Muttering nonsense. As confused as I was. Clearly not meaning me any harm, or any good, either. Not meaning me anything. He thought I was someone else. I wasn't afraid of him. He didn't change my life. He wasn't the man on the ceiling.

I don't think anybody then believed that a man had come in my window in the middle of the night and gone away again. Steve would have believed me.

Yes, I would have believed her. I've come to believe in the reality of all of Melanie's characters. And I believe in the man on the ceiling with all my heart.

For one evening this man on the ceiling climbed slowly down out of the darkness and out of the dream of our marriage and took one of our children away. And changed our lives forever.

Awake.

Someone in the room.

Asleep. Dreaming.

Someone in the room.

Someone in the room. Someone by the bed. Reaching to touch me but not touching me yet.

I put out my hand and Steve is beside me, solid, breathing steadily. I press myself to him, not wanting to wake him but needing enough to be close to him that I'm selfishly willing to risk it. I can feel his heartbeat through the blanket and sheet, through both our pajamas and both our flesh, through the waking or the dream. He's very warm. If he were dead, if he were the ghostly figure standing by the bed trying to touch me but not touching me, his body heat wouldn't radiate into me like this, wouldn't comfort me. It comforts me intensely.

Someone calls me. I hear only the voice, the tone of voice, and not the name it uses.

Awake. Painful tingling of nerve endings, heart pumping so wildly it hurts. Our golden cat Cinnabar...who often sleeps on my chest and eases some of the fear away by her purring, her small weight, her small radiant body heat, by the sheer miraculous contact with some other living creature who remains fundamentally alien while we touch so surely...moves away now. Moves first onto the mound of Steve's hip, but he doesn't like her on top of him and in his sleep he makes an irritable stirring motion that tips her off. Cinnabar gives an answering irritable trill and jumps off the bed.

Someone calling me. The door, always cracked so I can hear the kids if they cough or call, opens wider now, yellow wash from the hall light across the new forest-green carpet of our bedroom, which we've remodeled to be like a forest cave just for the two of us, a sanctuary. A figure in the yellow light, small and shadowy, not calling me now.

Neither asleep nor awake. A middle-of-the-night state of consciousness that isn't hypnagogic, either. Meta-wakefulness. Metasleep. Aware now of things that are always there, but in daylight are obscured by thoughts and plans, judgments and impressions, words and worries and obligations and sensations, and at night by dreams.

Someone in the room.

Someone by the bed.

Someone coming to get me. I'm too afraid to open my eyes, and too aroused to go back to sleep.

But we've made it our job, Melanie and I, to open our eyes and see who's there. To find who's there and to name who's there.

In our life together, we seem to seek it out. Our children, when they become our children, already know the man on the ceiling. Maybe all children do, at some primal level, but ours know him consciously, have already faced him down, and teach us how to do that, too.

We go toward the voice by the door, the shape in the room. Not so much to find the vampires and the werewolves who have been seen so many times before…who are safe to find because no one really believes in them anymore anyway…but to find the hidden figures who lurk in our house and other houses like ours: the boy with the head vigorously shaking nonono, the boy who appears and disappears in the midst of a cluttered bedroom, the little dead girl who controls her family with her wishes and lies, the little boy driven by his dad on a hunting trip down into the darkest heart of the city, and the man who hangs suspended from the ceiling waiting for just the right opportunity to climb down like a message from the eternal. To find the demons. To find the angels.

Sometimes we find these figures right in our own home, infiltrating our life together, standing over the beds of our children.

"Mom?"

344

A child. My child. Calling me, "Mom." A name so precious I never get used to it, emblematic of the joy and terror of this impossible relationship every time one of them says it. Which is often.

"Mom? I had a bad dream."

It's Joe. Who came to us a year and a half ago an unruly, intensely imaginative child so terrified of being abandoned again that he's only very recently been willing to say he loves me. He called me "Mom" right away, but he wouldn't say he loved me.

If you love someone, they leave you. But if you don't love someone, they leave you, too. So your choice isn't between loving and losing but only between loving and not loving.

This is the first time Joe has ever come for me in the middle of the night, the first time he's been willing to test our insistence that that's what parents are here for, although I think he has nightmares a lot.

I slide out of bed and pick him up. He's so small. He holds himself upright, won't snuggle against me, and his wide blue eyes are staring off somewhere, not at me. But his hand is on my shoulder and he lets me put him in my lap in the rocking chair, and he tells me about his dream. About a dog that died and came back to life. Joe loves animals. About Dad and me dying. Himself dying. Anthony dying.

Joe, who never knew Anthony, dreams about Anthony dying. Mourns Anthony. This connection seems wonderful to me, and a little frightening.

Joe's man on the ceiling already has a name, for Joe's dream is also about how his birthparents hurt him. Left him. He doesn't say it, maybe he's not old enough to name it, but when I suggest he must have felt then that he was going to die, that they were going to kill him, he nods vigorously, thumb in his mouth. And when I point out that he didn't die, that he's still alive and he can play with the cats and dogs and dig in the mudhole and learn to read chapter books and go to the moon someday, his eyes get very big and he nods vigorously and then he snuggles against my shoulder. I hold my breath for this transcendent moment. Joe falls asleep in my lap.

I am wide awake now, holding my sleeping little boy in my lap and rocking, rocking. Shadows move on the ceiling. The man on the ceiling is there. He's always there. And I understand, in a way I don't fully understand and will have lost most of by morning, that he gave me this moment, too.

I was never afraid of dying, before. But that changed after the man on the ceiling came down. Now I see his shadow imprinted in my skin, like a brand, and I think about dying.

That doesn't mean I'm unhappy, or that the shadow cast by the man on the ceiling is a shadow of depression. I can't stand people without a sense of humor, nor can I tolerate this sort of morbid fascination with the ways and colorings of death that shows itself even among people who say they enjoy my work. I never believed horror fiction was simply about morbid fascinations. I find that attitude stupid and dull.

The man on the ceiling gives my life an edge. He makes me uneasy; he makes me grieve. And yet he also fills me with awe for what is possible. He shames me with his glimpses into the darkness of human cruelty, and he shocks me when I see bits of my own face in his. He encourages a reverence when I contemplate the inevitability of my own death. And he shakes me with anger, pity, and fear.

The man on the ceiling makes it mean that much more when my daughter's fever breaks, when my son smiles sleepily up at me in the morning and sticks out his tongue.

So I wasn't surprised when one night, late, 2 AM or so, after I'd stayed up reading, I began to feel a change in the air of the house, as if something were being added, or something taken away.

Cinnabar uncurled and lifted her head, her snout wrinkling as if to test the air. Then her head turned slowly atop her body, and her

346

yellow eyes became silver as she made a long, motionless stare into the darkness beyond our bedroom door. Poised. Transfixed.

I glanced down at Melanie sleeping beside me. I could see Cinnabar's claws piercing the sheet and yet Melanie did not wake up. I leaned over her then to see if I could convince myself she was breathing. Melanie breathes so shallowly during sleep that half the time I can't tell she's breathing at all. So it isn't unusual to find me poised over her like this during the middle of the night, like some anxious and aging gargoyle, waiting to see the rise and fall of the covers to let me know she is still alive. I don't know if this is normal behavior or not…I've never really discussed it with anyone before. But no matter how often I watch my wife like this, and wait, no matter how often I see that yes, she is breathing, I still find myself considering what I would do, how I would feel, if that miraculous breathing did stop. Every time I worry myself with an imagined routine of failed attempts to revive her, to put the breathing back in, of frantic late night calls to anyone who might listen, begging them to tell me what I should do to put the breathing back in. It would be my fault, of course, because I had been watching. I should have watched her more carefully. I should have known exactly what to do.

During these ruminations I become intensely aware of how ephemeral we are. Sometimes I think we're all little more than a ghost of a memory, our flesh a poor joke.

I also become painfully aware of how, even for me when I'm acting the part of the writer, the right words to express just how much I love Melanie are so hard to come by.

At that point, the man on the ceiling stuck his head through our bedroom door and looked right at me. He turned, looking at Melanie's near-motionless form…and I saw how thin he was, like a silhouette cut from black construction paper. Then he pulled his head back into the darkness and disappeared.

I eased out of bed, trying not to awaken Melanie. Cinnabar raised her back and took a swipe at me. I moved toward the doorway, taking one last look back at the bed. Cinnabar stared at me as if she couldn't believe I was actually doing this, as though I were crazy.

For I intended to follow the man on the ceiling and find out where he was going. I couldn't take him lightly. I already knew some of what he was capable of. So I followed him that night, as I have followed him every night since, in and out of shadow, through dreams and memories of dreams, down the backsteps and up into the attic, past the fitful or peaceful sleep of my children, through daily encounters with death, forgiveness, and love.

Usually he is this shadow I've described, a silhouette clipped out of the dark, a shadow of a shadow. But these are merely the aspects I'm normally willing to face. Sometimes as he glides from darkness into light and into darkness again, as he steps and drifts through the night rooms and corridors of our house, I glimpse his figure from other angles: a mouth suddenly fleshed out and full of teeth, eyes like the devil's eyes like my own father's eyes, a hairy fist with coarse fingers, a jawbone with my own beard attached.

And sometimes his changes are more elaborate: he sprouts needle teeth, razor fingers, or a mouth like a swirling metal funnel.

The man on the ceiling casts shadows of flesh, and sometimes the shadows take on a life of their own.

Many years later, the snake returned. I was very awake.

I'd been offered painkillers and tranquilizers to produce the undead state which often passes for grieving but is not. I refused them. I wanted to be awake. The coils of the snake dropped from the ceiling and rose from the floor…oozing, slithering, until I was entirely encased. The skin molted and molted again into my own skin. The flesh was supple around my own flesh. The color of the world from inside the coils of the snake was a growing, soothing green.

"Safe," hissed the snake all around me. "You are safe."

Everything we're telling you here is true.

348

Each night as I follow the man on the ceiling into the various rooms of my children and watch him as he stands over them, touches them, kisses their cheeks with his black ribbon tongue, I imagine what he must be doing to them, what transformations he might be orchestrating in their dreams.

I imagine him creeping up to my youngest daughter's bed, reaching out his narrow black fingers and like a razor they enter her skull so he can change things there, move things around, plant ideas that might sprout…deadly or healing…in years to come. She is seven years old, and an artist. Already her pictures are thoughtful and detailed and she's not afraid of taking risks: cats shaped like hearts, people with feathers for hair, roses made entirely of concentric arcs. Does the man on the ceiling have anything to do with this?

I imagine him crawling into bed with my youngest son, whispering things into my son's ear, and suddenly my son's sweet character has changed forever.

I imagine him climbing the attic stairs and passing through the door to my teenage daughter's bedroom without making a sound, slipping over her sleeping form so gradually it's as if a car's headlights had passed and the shadows in the room had shifted and now the man from the ceiling is kissing my daughter and infecting her with a yearning she'll never be rid of.

I imagine him flying out of the house altogether, leaving behind a shadow of his shadow who is no less dangerous than he is, flying away from our house to find our troubled oldest son, filling his head with thoughts he won't be able to control, filling his brain with hallucinations he won't have to induce, imprisoning him forever where he is now imprisoned.

I imagine the young man who is not quite our son and is far more than our friend, who lives much of the time in some other reality, who wants so desperately to believe himself alien, chosen, destined to change the world by sheer virtue of the fact that he is so lonely. He hears voices…I wonder if the voices in his head help him ignore his man on the ceiling, or if they are the voices of the man on the ceiling.

Every night since that first night the man on the ceiling climbed down, I have followed him all evening like this: in my dreams, or sitting up in bed, or resting in a chair, or poised in front of a computer screen typing obsessively, waiting for him to reveal himself through my words.

Our teenage daughter has night terrors. I suspect she always has. When she came to us a tiny and terrified seven-year-old, I think the terrors were everywhere, day and night.

Now she's sixteen, and she's still afraid of many things. Her strength, her wisdom beyond her years, is in going toward what frightens her. I watch her do that, and I am amazed. She worries, for instance, about serial killers, and so she's read and re-read everything she could find about Ted Bundy, Jeffrey Daumer, John Wayne Gacy. She's afraid of death, partly because it's seductive, and so she wants to be a mortician or a forensic photographer…get inside death, see what makes a dead body dead, record the evidence. Go as close to the fear as you can. Go as close to the monster. Know it. Claim it. Name it. Take it in.

She's afraid of love, and so she falls in love often and deeply.

Her night terrors now most often take the form of a faceless lady in white who stands by her bed with a knife and intends to kill her, tries to steal her breath the way they used to say cats would do if you let them near the crib. The lady doesn't disappear even when our daughter wakes herself up, sits up in bed and turns on the light.

Our daughter wanted something alive to sleep with. The cats betrayed her, wouldn't be confined to her room. So we got her a dog. Ezra was abandoned, too, or lost and never found, and he's far more worried than she is, which I don't think she thought possible. He sleeps with her. He sleeps under her covers. He would sleep on her pillow, covering her face, if she'd let him, and she would let him if she could breathe. She says the lady hasn't come once since Ezra has been here.

I don't know if Ezra will keep the night terrors away forever. But, if she trusts him, he'll let her know whether the lady is real. That's no small gift.

Our daughter is afraid of many things, and saddened by many things. She accepts pain better than most people, takes in pain. I think that now her challenge, her adventure, is to learn to accept happiness. That's scary.

So maybe the lady at the end of her bed doesn't intend to kill her after all. Maybe she intends to teach her how to take in happiness.

Which is, I guess, a kind of death.

I know that the lady beside my daughter's bed is real, but this is not something I have yet chosen to share with my daughter. I have seen this lady in my own night terrors when I was a teenager, just as I saw the devil in my bedroom one night in the form of a giant goat, six feet tall at the shoulder. I sat up in my bed and watched as the goat's body disappeared slowly, one layer of hair and skin at a time, leaving giant, bloodshot, humanoid eyes, the eyes of the devil, suspended in mid-air where they remained for several minutes while I gasped for a scream that would not come.

I had night terrors for years until I began experimenting with dream control and learned to extend myself directly into a dream where I could rearrange its pieces and have things happen the way I wanted them to happen. Sometimes when I write now it's as if I'm in the midst of this extended night terror and I'm frantically using powers of the imagination I'm not even sure belong to me to arrange the pieces and make everything turn out the way it should, or at least the way I think it was meant to be.

If the man on the ceiling were just another night terror, I should have the necessary tools to stop him in his tracks, or at least to divert him. But I've followed the man on the ceiling night after night. I've seen what he does to my wife and children. And he's already carried one of our children away.

Remember what I said in the beginning. Everything we're telling you here is true.

I follow the man on the ceiling around the attic of our house, my flashlight burning off pieces of his body which grow back as soon as he moves beyond the beam. I chase him down three flights of stairs into our basement where he hides in the laundry. My hands turn into frantic paddles which scatter the clothes and I'm already thinking about how I'm going to explain the mess to Melanie in the morning when he slips like a pool of oil under my feet and out to other corners of the basement where my children keep their toys. I imagine the edge of his cheek in an oversized doll, his amazingly sharp fingers under the hoods of my son's Matchbox cars.

But the man on the ceiling is a story and I know something about stories. One day I will figure out just what this man on the ceiling is "about." He's a character in the dream of our lives and he can be changed or killed.

It always makes me cranky to be asked what a story is "about," or who my characters "are." If I could tell you, I wouldn't have to write them.

Often I write about people I don't understand, ways of being in the world that baffle me. I want to know how people make sense of things, what they say to themselves, how they live. How they name themselves to themselves.

Because life is hard. Even when it's wonderful, even when it's beautiful…which it is a lot of the time…it's hard. Sometimes I don't know how any of us makes it through the day. Or the night.

The world has in it: Children hurt or killed by their parents, who would say they do it out of love. Children whose beloved fathers, uncles, brothers, cousins, mothers love them, too, fall in love with

352

them, say anything we do to each other's bodies is okay because we love each other, but don't tell anybody because then I'll go to jail and then I won't love you anymore.

Perverted love.

The world also has in it: Children whose only chance to grow up is in prison, because they're afraid to trust love on the outside. Children who die, no matter how much you love them.

Impotent love.

And the world also has in it: Werewolves, whose unclaimed rage transforms them into something not human but also not inhuman (modern psychiatry sometimes finds the bestial "alter" in the multiple personality). Vampires, whose unbridled need to experience leads them to suck other people dry and are still not satisfied. Zombies, the chronically insulated, people who will not feel anything because they will not feel pain. Ghosts.

I write in order to understand these things. I write dark fantasy because it helps me see how to live in a world with monsters.

But one day last week, transferring at a crowded and cold downtown bus stop, late as usual, I was searching irritably in my purse for my bus pass, which was not there, and then for no reason and certainly without conscious intent my gaze abruptly lifted and followed the upswept lines of the pearly glass building across the street, up, up, into the Colorado-blue sky, and it was beautiful.

It was transcendently beautiful. An epiphany. A momentary breakthrough into the dimension of the divine.

That's why I write, too. To stay available for breakthroughs into the dimension of the divine. Which happen in this world all the time.

I think I always write about love.

I married Melanie because she uses words like "divine" and "transcendent" in everyday conversation. I love that about her. It scares me, and it embarrasses me sometimes, but still I love that

353

about her. I was a secretive and frightened male, perhaps like most males, when I met her. And now sometimes even I will use a word like "transcendent." I'm still working on "divine."

And sometimes I write about love. Certainly I love all my characters, miserable lot though they may be. (Another writer once asked me why I wrote about "nebbishes." I told him I wanted to write about "the common man.") Sometimes I even love the man on the ceiling, as much as I hate him, because of all the things he enables me to see. Each evening, carrying my flashlight, I follow him through all the dark rooms of my life. He doesn't need a light because he has learned these rooms so well and because he carries his own light; if you'll look at him carefully you'll notice that his grin glows in the night. I follow him because I need to understand him. I follow him because he always has something new to show me.

One night I followed him into a far corner of our attic. Apparently this was where he slept when he wasn't clinging to our ceiling or prowling our children's rooms. He had made himself a nest out of old photos chewed up and their emulsions spat out into a paste to hold together bits of outgrown clothing and the gutted stuffings of our children's discarded dolls and teddy bears. He lay curled up, his great dark sides heaving.

I flashed the light on him. And then I saw his wings

They were patchwork affairs, the separate sections molded out of burnt newspaper, ancient lingerie, metal road signs and fish nets, stitched together with shoelaces and Bubble Yum, glued and veined with tears, soot, and ash. The man on the ceiling turned his obsidian head and blew me a kiss of smoke.

I stood perfectly still with the light in my hand growing dimmer as he drained away its brightness. So the man on the ceiling was in fact an angel, a messenger between our worldly selves and…yes, I'll say it…the divine. And it bothered me that I hadn't recognized his angelic nature before. I should have known, because aren't ghosts nothing more than angels with wings of memory, and vampires angels with wings of blood?

Everything we're trying to tell you here is true.

And there are all kinds of truths to tell. There's the true story about how the man, the angel, on the ceiling killed my mother, and what I did with her body. There's the story about how my teenage daughter fell in love with the man on the ceiling and ran away with him and we didn't see her for weeks. There's the story about how I tried to become the man on the ceiling in order to understand him and ended up terrorizing my own children.

There are so many true stories to tell. So many possibilities.

There are so many stories to tell. I could tell this story:

Melanie smiled at the toddler standing up backwards in the seat in front of her. He wasn't holding onto anything, and his mouth rested dangerously on the metal bar across the back of the seat. His mother couldn't have been much more than seventeen, from what Melanie could see of her pug-nosed, rouged and sparkly-eye-shadowed, elaborately poufed profile; Melanie was hoping it was his big sister until she heard him call her, "Mama."

"Mama," he kept saying. "Mama. Mama." The girl ignored him. His prattle became increasingly louder and more shrill until everyone on the bus was looking at him, except his mother, who had her head turned as far away from him as she could. She was cracking her gum.

The sunset was lovely, peach and purple and gray, made more lovely by the streaks of dirt on the bus windows and by the contrasting bright white dots of headlights and bright red dots of tail lights moving everywhere under it. When they passed slowly over the Valley Highway, Melanie saw that the lights were exquisite, and hardly moving at all.

"Mama! Mama! Mama!" The child swiveled clumsily toward his

mother and reached out both hands for her just as the driver hit the brakes. The little boy toppled sideways and hit his mouth on the metal bar. A small spot of blood appeared on his lower lip. There was a moment of stunned silence from the child; his mother…still staring off away from him, earphones over her ears, still popping her gum rhythmically…obviously hadn't noticed what had happened.

Then he shrieked. At last disturbed, she whirled on him furiously, an epithet halfway out of her child-vamp mouth, but when she saw the blood on her son's face she collapsed into near-hysteria. Although she did hold him and wipe at his face with her long-nailed fingertips, it was clear she didn't know what to do.

Melanie considered handing her a tissue, lecturing her about child safety, even…ridiculously…calling social services. But here was her stop. Fuming, she followed the lady with the shoulder-length white hair down the steps and out into the evening, which was tinted peach and purple and gray from the sunset of however dubious origin and, no less prettily, red and white from the Safeway sign.

The man on the ceiling laughs at me as he remains always just out of the reach of my understanding, floating above me on his layered wings, telling me about how, someday, everyone I love is going to die and how, after I die, no one is going to remember me no matter how much I write, how much I shamelessly reveal, brushing his sharp fingers against the wallpaper and leaving deep gouges in the walls. He rakes back the curtains and shows me the sky: peach and purple and gray like the colors of his eyes when he opens them, like the colors of his mouth, the colors of his tongue when he laughs even more loudly and heads for the open door of one of my children's rooms.

The white-haired woman was always on this bus. Always wore the same ankle-length red coat when it was cold enough to wear

356

any coat at all. Grim-faced and always frowning, but with that crystalline hair falling softly over her shoulders.

They always got off at the same stop, waited at the intersection for the light to change, walked together a block and a half until the lady turned into the Spanish-style stucco apartment building that had once been a church…it still had "Jesus Is the Light of the World" inscribed in an arc over one doorway and a pretty enclosed courtyard overlooked by tall windows shaped as if to hold stained glass. At that point, Melanie's house was still two blocks away, and she always just kept walking. She and the white-haired lady had never exchanged a word. Maybe someday she'd think how to start a conversation. Not tonight.

Tonight, like most nights, she just wanted to be home. Safe and patently loved in the hubbub of her family. Often, disbelieving, she would count to herself the number of discrete living creatures whose lives she shared, and she loved the changing totals: tonight it was Steve, and five kids, four cats, three dogs, even twenty-three plants. Exhausted from work, she could almost always count on being revitalized when she went home.

The man on the ceiling turns and screams at me until I feel my flesh beginning to shred. The man on the ceiling puts his razor-sharp fingers into my joints and twists and I clench my fists and bite the insides of my lips trying not to scream. The man on the ceiling grins and grins and grins. He sticks both hands into my belly and pulls out my organs and offers to tell me how long I have to live.

I tell him I don't want to know, and then he offers to tell me how long Melanie is going to live, how long each of my children is going to live.

The man on the ceiling crawls into my belly through the hole he has made and curls up inside himself to become a cancer resting against my spinal column. I can no longer walk and I fall to the ground.

357

The man on the ceiling rises into my throat and I can no longer speak. The man on the ceiling floats into my skull and I can no longer dream.

The man on the ceiling crawls out of my head, his sharp black heels piercing my tongue as he steps out of my mouth.

The man on the ceiling starts devouring our furniture a piece at a time, beating his great conglomerate wings in orgasmic frenzy, releasing tiny gifts of decay into the air.

How might I explain why supposedly good people could imagine such things? How might I explain how I could feel such passion for my wife and children, or for the simplest acts of living, when such creatures travel in packs through my dreams?

It is because the man on the ceiling is a true story that I find life infinitely interesting. It is because of such dark, transcendent angels in each of our houses that we are able to love. Because we must. Because it is all there is.

Daffodils were blooming around the porch of the little yellow house set down away from the sidewalk. Melanie stopped, amazed. They had not been there yesterday. Their scent lasted all the way to the corner.

One year Steve had given her a five-foot-long, three-foot-high Valentine showing a huge flock of penguins, all of them alike, and out of the crowd two of them with pink hearts above their heads, and the caption: "I'm so glad we found each other." It was, of course, a miracle.

She crossed the street and entered her own block. The sunset was paling now, and the light was silvery down the street. A trick of the light made it look as though the hill on which her house sat was flattened. Melanie smiled and wondered what Matilda McCollum, who'd had the house built in 1898 and had the hill constructed so it would be grander than her sister's otherwise identical house across the way, would say to that. A huge, solid, sprawling, red-brick Victorian rooted in Engelmann ivy so expansive as to be just this side of overgrown, the house was majestic on its hill. Grand. Unshakable. Matilda had been right.

The man on the ceiling opens his mouth and begins eating the wall by the staircase. First he has to taste it. He rests the dark holes that have been drilled into his face for nostrils against the brittle flocked wallpaper and sniffs out decades worth of noise, conversation, and prayers. Then he slips his teeth over the edges and pulls it away from the wall, shoveling the crackling paper into his dark maw with fingers curved into claws. Tiny trains of silverfish drift down the exposed wall before the man on the ceiling devours them as well, then his abrasive tongue scoops out the crumbling plaster from the wooden lath and minutes later he has started on the framing itself.

Powerless to stop him, I watch as he sups on the dream of my life. Suddenly I am sixteen again and this life I have written for myself is all ahead of me, and impossibly out of reach.

Melanie was looking left at the catalpa tree between the sidewalk and the street, worrying as she did every spring that this time it really would never leaf out and she would discover it was dead, had died over the winter and she hadn't known, had in fact always been secretly dead, when she turned right to go up the steps to her house. Stumbled. Almost fell. There were no steps. There was no hill.

She looked up. There was no house.

And she knew there never had been.

There never had been a family. She had never had children.

She had somehow made up: sweet troubled Christopher, Mark who heard voices and saw the molecules dancing in tree trunks and most of the time was glad, Veronica of the magnificent chestnut hair and heart bursting painfully with love, Anthony whose laughter had been like seashells, Joe for whom the world was an endless adventure, Gabriella who knew how to go inside herself and knew to tell you what she was doing there: "I be calm."

She'd made up the golden cat Cinnabar, who would come to purr on her chest and ease the pain away. She'd made up the hoya plant that sent out improbable white flowers off a leafless woody stem too far into the dining room. She'd made up the rainbows on the kitchen walls from the prisms she hung in the south window.

She'd made up Steve.

There had never been love.

There had never been a miracle.

Angels. Our lives are filled with angels.

The man on the ceiling smiles in the midst of the emptiness, his wings beating heavily against the clouds, his teeth the color of the cold I am feeling now. Melanie used to worry so much when I went out late at night for milk, or ice cream for the both of us, that I'd need to call her from a phone booth if I thought I'd be longer than the forty-five minutes it took for her anxiety and her fantasies about all that can happen to people to kick in. Sometimes she fantasized about the police showing up at the door to let her know about the terrible accident I'd had, or sometimes I just didn't come back…I got the milk or the ice cream and I just kept on going.

I can't say that I was always helpful. Sometimes I'd tell her I had to come home because the ice cream would melt if I didn't get it into the freezer right away I'm not sure that was very reassuring.

What I tried not to think about was what if I never could find my way home, what if things weren't as I'd left them. What if everything had changed? One night I got lost along the southern edge of the city after a late night movie and wandered for an hour or so convinced that my worst fantasies had come true.

The man on the ceiling smiles and begins devouring my dream of the sky.

A wise man asks me, when I've told him this story of my vanishing home again, "And then what?"

I glare at him. He's supposed to understand me. "What do you mean?"

"And then what happens? After you discover that your house and your family have disappeared?"

"Not disappeared," I point out irritably. "Have never existed."

"Yes. Have never existed. And then what happens?"

I've never thought of that. The never-having-existed seems final enough, awful enough. I can't think of anything to say, so I don't say anything, hoping he will. But he's wise, and he knows how to use silence. He justs sits there, being calm, until finally I say, "I don't know."

"Maybe it would be interesting to find out," he suggests.

So we try. He eases me into a light trance; I'm eager and highly suggestible, and I trust this man, so my consciousness alters easily. He guides me through the fantasy again and again, using my own words and some of his own. But every time I stop at the point where I come home and there isn't any home. The point where I look up and my life, my love, isn't there. Has never existed.

I don't know what happens next. I can't imagine what happens next. Do I die? Does the man on the ceiling take me into his house? Does he fly away with me into an endless sky? Does he help me create another life, another miracle?

That's why I write. To find out what happens next.

So what happens next? This might happen:

After the man on the ceiling devours my life I imagine it back again: I fill in the walls, the doorways, the empty rooms with colors and furnishings different from, but similar to, the ones I imagine to have been there before. Our lives are full of angels of all kinds. So I call on some of those other angels to get my life back.

I write myself a life, and it is very different from the one I had before, and yet very much the same. I make mistakes different from the ones I made with my children before. I love Melanie the same way I did before. Different wonderful things happen. The same sad, wonderful events recur.

The man on the ceiling just smiles at me and makes of these new imaginings his dessert. So what happens next? In a different kind of story I might take out a machete and chop him into little bits of shadow. Or I might blast him into daylight with a machine gun. I might douse him with lighter fluid and set him on fire.

But I don't write those kinds of stories.

And besides, the man on the ceiling is a necessary angel.

There are so many truths to tell. There are so many different lives I could dream for myself.

What happens next?

There are so many stories to tell. I could tell this story:

The man from the ceiling was waiting for Melanie behind the fence (an ugly, bare, chain link and chicken wire fence, not the black wrought iron fence plaited with rosebushes that she'd made up), where her home had never existed. He beckoned to her. He called her by name, his own special name for her, a name she never got used to no matter how often he said it, which was often. He reached for her, trying to touch her but not quite touching.

She could have turned and run away from him. He wouldn't have chased her down. His arms wouldn't have telescoped long and impossibly jointed to capture her at the end of the block. His teeth wouldn't have pushed themselves out of his mouth in gigantic segmented fangs to cut her off at the knees, to bite her head off. He wouldn't have sucked her blood.

But he'd have kept calling her, using his special name for her. And he'd have scaled her windows, dropped from her roof, crawled across her ceiling again that night, and every night for the rest of her life.

So Melanie went toward him. Held out her arms.

There are so many different dreams. That one was Melanie's. This one is mine:

I sit down at the kitchen table. The man on the ceiling lies on my plate, collapsed and folded up neatly in the center. I slice him into hundreds of oily little pieces which I put into my mouth one morsel at a time. I bite through his patchwork wings. I gnaw on his inky heart. I chew his long, narrow fingers well. I make of him my daily meal of darkness.

There are so many stories to tell.

And all of the stories are true.

We wait for whatever happens next.
    We stay available.
    We name it to make it real.

It was hard for us to write this piece.

For one thing, we write differently. My stories tend more toward magical realism, Steve's more toward surrealism. Realism, in both cases, but we argued over form: "This isn't a story! It doesn't have a plot!"

"What do you want from a plot? Important things happen, and it does move from A to B."

In our fiction, Melanie's monsters usually are ultimately either vanquished or accepted, while at the end of my stories you often find out that the darkness in one form or another lives on and on. There's no escaping it, and I question whether you should try to escape it in the first place.

Since words can only approximate both the monsters and the vanquishment, we wrote each other worried notes in the margins of this story.

"I don't know if we can really use the word 'divine.' "

"If someone looked inside your dreams, would they really see only darkness?"

It was hard for us to write this piece.
"This upsets me," Melanie would say.

Steve would nod. "Maybe we can't do this."
"Oh, we have to." I'd insist. "We've gone too far to stop now. I want to see what happens."
This piece is about writing and horror and fear and about love. We're utterly separate from each other, of course, yet there's a country we share, a rich and wonderful place, a divine place, and we create it by naming all of its parts, all of the angels and all of the demons who live there with us.

What happens next?
There are so many stories to tell.
We could tell another story:

Acknowledgments:

"Prosthesis," *Asimov's* June 1986
"The Sing," *SF International* 1, Jan/Feb 1987
"Resettling", *Postmortem,* ed. Dave Silva & Paul Olson, 1989
"Kite," *Starshore* 2, Fall 1990
"The Tenth Scholar," *The Ultimate Dracula,* ed. Byron Preiss, 1991
"This Icy Region My Heart Encircles," *The Ultimate Frankenstein,*
    ed. Byron Preiss, 1991
"Mask of the Hero," *Chilled To The Bone,* ed. Robert Garcia, 1991
"Beautiful Strangers," as a Roadkill Press chapbook, 1992
"Safe At Home," *Hottest Blood,* eds. Jeff Gelb & Michael Garrett, 1993
"The Marriage," *Love in Vein,* ed. Poppy Brite, 1994
"More Than Should Be Asked," *Scream Factory* 15, Autumn 1994
"Mama," *Sisters of the Night,* eds. Barbara Hambly & Martin Greenberg, 1995
"Nvumbi," *Xanadu* 3, ed. Jane Yolen, 1995
"The Perfect Diamond" *Fantastic Worlds* 1, 1996
"Lost," *Imagination Fully Dilated,* eds. Alan Clark & Elizabeth Engstrom, 1998
"North," *Extremes* 2, Brian Hopkins editor, 2001
"Empty Morning," *The Many Faces of Van Helsing,* ed. Jeanne Cavelos, 2004
"Pit's Edge," *Mondo Zombie,* John Skipp editor, 2006
"The Man on the Ceiling," American Fantasy chapbook, 2000
"In Concert," *Asimov's,* December 2008
"Bees from the Hive" appears here for the first time

IN CONCERT

by Steve Rasnic Tem *&* Melanie Tem
artwork by Howie Michels

The edition consists of three hundred
numbered copies, bound in cloth.

This is copy number

249

[signature]

[signature]

2/11